saoirse's story

THE LOVE CONNECTION SERIES
BOOK 1

A.M. JAXON

contents

The Playlist

Linger: The Cranberries

Beautiful Girl: INXS

Goodbye Earl: The Chicks

Your Latest Trick: Dire Straits

Hurt: Johnny Cash

When Love Comes To Town: U2 and BB King

Here Without You: 3 Doors Down

Welcome to the Jungle: Guns N' Roses

U + Ur Hand: Plnk

Sweet Caroline: Neil Diamond

Are You Gonna Go My Way: Lenny Kravitz

Mr Brightside: The Killers

Yellow: Coldplay

Cruz: Christina Aguilera

Higher Ground: Red Hot Chili Peppers

Stayin' Alive: Bee Gees

Against All Odds: Phil Collins

Empire State of Mind (Part 2): Alicia Keys

Love Is All Around: Joan Jet and The Blackhearts

Spotify QR Code to AM Jaxon: Saoirse's Story Playlist

Saoirse's Story

Book 1 – The Love Connection Series

Copyright © A.M. Jaxon

First published by Hembury Books in 2025

hemburybooks.com.au

ISBN Paperback 9781763727595

ISBN eBook 9781763807709

ISBN Draft2Digital 9798230019176

For Mum
You gave me wings and urged me to fly. Only when you were gone did I realise you'd also kept me grounded by quietly tethering me to your heart.

Anyone can be a word, a sentence or even a chapter in your story.
The worthy ones stay for the whole book.
— A.M. Jaxon

prologue

THERE IS nothing like the sound of a gunshot. Standing only feet away from a firing gun, your body becomes churning liquid and your nerves are a million hot razors trying to explode through your skin. Then there's the ringing, a high-pitched numbing that oscillates through your ears and hammers your skull, lasting far longer than the shot.

In that instant, when the bullet leaves the gun, it can take a life—rarely does it begin one. Although, on a day in January 1997, that's what happened. One woman's life began, and for another, it felt like hers had ended, but it was a beginning of a different kind. These two women were a world apart yet destined to meet, all because of gunshots fired in anger.

* * *

On a Monday morning in January in Perth, Australia, two policemen approached a scarred, dilapidated house. It was a blistering, bitumen-melting day. Ryan Malone and his patrol partner, Todd Chambers, had been called to a domestic disturbance. As Todd eased the patrol car to the kerb, he blew out a slow breath. 'It's the heat. It always sets them off. No money, no food, no aircon, only drugs and booze, all of it worse when the temp hits forty Cs in the shade.'

'Let's hope he's not out of his mind on speed this time. Although, this one usually only goes to town on his missus when he's amped up. Makes you wonder, we bring him in and then she takes him back.' Ryan was already opening his door to push through the curtain of heat that surrounded the car.

Todd slapped his partner's shoulder. 'How about you let me go lead on this one?'

'No chance.'

'I'm on strict orders from Daniella to make sure I get you home in time for Taylor's birthday party.'

Ryan chuckled, his broad smile bending all his handsome linear features. 'Dani got to you, too.' With nothing but love in his voice, he said, 'I should've known. Everyone's invited. You know how Dani loves a good party. She sure can put the fear of God in you when she sets her mind on something. How about we both try to clear this up in time to make the party?'

As Ryan set foot on the verandah, the front door burst open and a shot rang out. At first, because his partner was in front of him, Todd thought his mate had dived onto the dirty floor to evade the bullet. Todd returned fire, and the man ran. That's when he saw the blood. Dropping to his knees, he pushed his hands down on Ryan's chest. He could see Ryan straining for each breath as it gurgled in his throat, causing a pained groan. Todd yelled into his radio, 'Officer down! I need backup, ambos, quick!'

Todd's face was ashen as sweat beaded and then slid down his stubble. 'Hang on, Ryan, for Christ's sake. Don't you go anywhere. Look at me.' Todd couldn't stop the panic surging into his voice. It claimed him as quickly as the blood was spreading through Ryan's uniform. 'Keep your eyes on me!' Todd saw the cold glazing Ryan's eyes. Death seeping in and clutching at his friend.

Shouts came now, backup officers running everywhere.

Todd pressed harder in desperation, but he couldn't stop the blood flooding out. No matter what he did, it began oozing into the verandah's dry wooden floorboards. Todd pushed even harder. The pain triggered Ryan's eyes to flutter open more widely. On a wet wheeze, he slurred, 'Tell Dani, the girls …' He coughed, and with one final blood-filled splatter, one word hung in the air. 'Love.'

Todd shouted, 'Jesus!' He couldn't comprehend the chill that seemed to be taking him over as much as it had Ryan. It was all too much, the heat of the day suddenly overpowered by ice, and then there was the noise. Boots were trampling, charging around him, there was shouting, more shots and screams, and then the noise was crushed by silence.

He lost connection to reality and couldn't understand why. It was eerie. Only he and Ryan seemed to fill space and time. Soon there was nothing. Ryan had run out of heartbeats, and Todd was filled with emptiness. 'Oh God, no!' How, how could he tell Daniella? Taylor was turning three, Hannah was five. They would never really know their father. He screamed, 'Fuck!' as the ambos tried to pull him off his friend.

* * *

On that same Monday morning on the other side of the world, in Ireland, Saoirse Mahoney and her mother, Mary, visited a Donegal bank. The usual stoic quiet of their local branch was devastated by the close and repeated sound of gunfire. Three balaclava-wearing gunmen made themselves known. As one grabbed at Saoirse, she saw hate seething from his charcoal eyes. Trapped by those eyes, she froze. A heartless, malicious smile curled his lips. He fired once more into the air. The gun was so close the heat of the shot seemed to ripple past her ear. A now submissive Saoirse was smacked down to the marble floor. As she shivered on the chilly hardness, she decided that she wanted out, regardless of the proposed peace agreements. She was sick of the violence and tension of the Troubles. When she was old enough, she would pack her bags and fly somewhere warm, peaceful and laid-back.

Late 1999

With a face like thunder, Patrick Mahoney shoved his fingers through his greying hair. 'Saoirse, stop this nonsense.' He stabbed a finger at his daughter. 'You've just finished school. You haven't even turned eighteen. You can't possibly think that we'd let you travel halfway around the world, alone. I thought we'd been through this. You're too young, and you've got no way of supporting yourself. You don't know anyone over there. Enough with this silliness.'

'Are you going to let the girl get a word in edgeways or just talk *at* her?' Mary stepped between the two. 'Unless my daughter's a fool, and I know I didn't raise a fool, she has a plan.' Her blue eyes fell lovingly on Saoirse before they arrowed to the silver-grey of her husband's. 'The more you try to hold her here, the quicker you'll lose her. Anyway, she's only a month off eighteen.'

Saoirse's smooth, milky skin reddened as she released her bottled frustration. 'You can't expect me to stay. Da, please! Don't try to keep me here.' The heat of her anger evaporated the tears she'd been fighting. 'You let Callan and Sean go when they were eighteen.'

'They're men, the world's dangerous enough for them. You don't know what it's like. I see it, tried to send the worst of it to prison. For a girl, it's far too dangerous.' His unyielding prosecutorial glare scoured over Saoirse. It was a stare that had weakened many a toughened criminal.

'Da, I'm no longer your *little* girl.' She stood tall, shedding her little girl soft skin and wistful ways right before his eyes. 'You forget I've already seen some of the worst of it, and I've been part of it. I remember that day in the bank when they took us hostage. I got through that even with the police teargassing us and shooting them. And I've read your trial notes for some of your worst cases. You're not protecting me by wrapping me up in cotton wool. You're only making me soft, too soft to be useful for anything. I want to get out of Donegal, not just to see the world, but to find my place in it.'

Saoirse saw her father blink and take stock. She hoped he saw her, for the first time, as the adult she had become. She knew he was using one of his courtroom tricks when he just let the tense silence linger, allowing it to wrap around her to play with her resolve. Then her hopes dropped like the gavel her dad was used to hearing in the courtroom. 'No. Not now.' His lips formed a hard line. 'You can work for me for a bit longer to gain more skills, then we'll see.'

Her father's stubbornness and mother's strength pumped through Saoirse's veins. 'I've worked at your practice long enough! Da, I think the world of you, but I didn't study as hard as I did, get the grades I did, to end up working full-time for you.' Her eyes were her father's, and she returned his glower with equal resolution. 'I'll go without your blessing.' Her determination ramped up a few notches. 'I have a job lined up and enough money saved to go.'

Mary cut in before her husband said something they would all regret. 'Pat, listen. Saoirse's such a serious soul, far more mature than the boys coming up to their eighteenth birthdays. She deserves as much freedom as you gave them. So she can experience the same injection of self-belief and confidence they did.'

Mary continued, taking a different tack. 'Your daughter is like you, Pat, a quick study. She's learned all she can from you.' She moved closer to him. 'And she's like me in not wanting to settle for second best. It's why I chose you, Patrick Ronan Mahoney.'

Seeing her chance, Saoirse took it. 'Da, you promised if I kept my grades up and worked holidays for you, you'd at least give me a gap year.' Saoirse had learned from the best, her father, how to make an unemotional argument. But she'd also learned how to make an emotional one from someone even better—her mother. Now she used both against the master. 'I've done all you asked of me, Da. You know I'm not some frivolous bimbo. I'm your daughter, my mam's child, and I want to break out like you both did when you were my age.'

'Our daughter has never surrendered to "the calling" to make a home here, like Liam. The girl has restless feet, like Sean and Callan.' The lines ageing Mary Mahoney's face softened. 'She won't be constrained.' Reaching for her husband's cheek, she ran her fingers along his jaw. 'Patrick.' Her touch, with that silky, lilting voice wrapping around his name, had Patrick's temper draining away.

'Mary ... woman, you don't fight fair.'

'No reason to start now.' A smile as easy as her wisdom graced Mary's face. 'Come now, you know as well as I do Saoirse wants to be her own woman, not the local attorney's daughter, nor, for that matter, the headmistress's daughter. To keep her, we must let her go. She's more than ready to face the world.'

Saoirse had been on the receiving end of her brothers' taunts and tricks for years. It had sharpened her mind and strengthened her resolve. She had also looked out for her brothers the same way they'd looked out for her. Then there were the times she'd mother them, which was as much for their preservation as it was for her satisfaction at annoying the hell out of them. Mary winked at Saoirse as she said, 'My girl may be young, but she has a shrewd streak that needs building up.'

On a sigh, Patrick beckoned to Saoirse. 'Come here.' Father and daughter hugged, and he held on for a little longer than usual. 'Alright, then. You'll show me all your plans. If they add up, then yes. And you'll phone home every week and email us every other day.'

Saoirse's sharp silvery-grey eyes warmed, and she dazzled her father with a smile that could light the darkest Irish night. 'Of course.' She let tears of joy run as she gathered her parents in for a long, hard hug. 'Thank you so, so much. I promise I'll be careful. I love you both so much.'

Her mother squeezed her tighter. 'My girl, no matter how far away you are, remember, you're never alone. Whenever you need me, I'll be there as fast as metal wings can take me.'

'On that matter, does it have to be so far away?' Her father pulled back to look into her eyes. 'Why not London like Callan, or Dublin like Sean? Why Brisbane?'

'Because of the weather!' Saoirse said with honesty. Although she also knew it ticked all the boxes she'd opened on the day she was forced to lie down in fear on the bank floor while a gunshot rang out.

This was the whole of Saoirse Mahoney at this time in her life. But, as it is known, the sum of the parts can become larger than the whole. Saoirse still had many pieces of herself to discover. It was time to gather herself and fully explore those parts, to grow and become greater than the whole she was at present. She took her first steps on that journey when she left Donegal to fly to Brisbane, Australia.

one

BECOMING SAOIRSE: BRISBANE
2000

DANIELLA MALONE SAT behind a pile of papers preparing for her latest case. Raven tresses fell over her face, hiding dark eyes that had seen too much sorrow for their thirty-two years. The office was clearing out as people went to disappear-into-the-weekend Friday drinks. Daniella was no longer that woman. The one who liked a good party, and maybe that didn't dismay her as much as it should have. Regardless, she would stand for those who couldn't stand for themselves. There was just enough time to peruse one more page before she headed home to relieve the nanny. Then there was dinner to serve, the girls' baths, and reading a couple of stories to her beautiful, bubbly daughters before they went to bed. Then she'd put the washing on and enjoy a glass of wine with a little more work.

When Ryan's life was taken from Daniella, she seemed to stop, stumble then fall. It took a while to find her balance and stand. When he'd gone, a city had mourned with her. Radio stations had dedicated songs to her, like INXS's 'Beautiful Girl'. People tried to understand her—her plight, her strength. There was no way she could live up to everyone's expectations, least of all her friends'. She wasn't good at playing the grief-stricken widow, the martyr. What

Daniella shared with Ryan was potent and crazy, like a flame to gasoline: untameable and relentless. Then he was gone in the time it took to squeeze a trigger, and she was lost.

Friends had seen her as fearless. She had seen herself as a coward. Eventually, she hadn't been able to face them with their sighs of pity and clichéd words of sympathy. They'd struggled to find some logic to the senseless act, trying to claw back a connection with her. Daniella's life became a sad soapy. Only one person had spoken to her with any realism. Todd, Ryan's partner, had asked, 'So, you sick of all the bull yet?'

She'd nodded. They'd stolen some time watching the ocean sparkle while sharing fish and chips and sinking into the warm sand of Cottesloe Beach. Time had passed, and the sun had baked the beach to an uncomfortable heat. They were about to leave when the rush of a refreshingly cool summer breeze had halted their departure. It had cooled their skin, soothed their minds and given them temporary solace. They'd both known Ryan was with them at that moment, and Daniella had realised they'd shared more than being Ryan's partners.

Within hours of his funeral, she'd packed up her broken heart, an honours law degree and two small daughters, Hannah and Taylor. She couldn't live the police force life any longer, around people who once had laughed with her, but now gave her forlorn looks. Then there were the places that reminded her every day, in every way, of her loss. If she did stay, she'd become a one-dimensional figure in a paper chain. Although in her case, when she finished cutting out her paper people chain, they wouldn't string together. Instead, they'd fall apart, all connections severed, except the one to her daughters.

She had moved them across the Nullarbor to a new east-coast location, close to where her parents had retired. She'd start again. It was necessary, not only for Daniella's salvation and sanity, but also to keep her daughters' future untouched by the sadness of their father's death, yet guided by his light and life.

By the time her daughters were in primary school, she had found she couldn't lead a life built only around them. If their lives were to be well-rounded, their mother needed to show Hannah and Taylor what made life worthwhile. She had to be more than their protector, so she became a protector of women.

She wasn't looking to make sense of Ryan's death. Instead, she found that she wanted to reduce the number of women who died or were harmed at the hands of men. She didn't hate men. She hated the violence that some men thought it was their right to inflict.

'Hey, aren't you coming for a drink?'

Daniella's pen jagged across the page as her reverie was broken by the lilting, sing-song accent of the new Irish legal secretary.

'Oh! I thought I was alone. I don't do after-work drinks. Ask anyone here.'

'I wasn't asking them. I was asking you.'

Daniella took a real look at the fresh-faced woman standing in her office doorway. 'God, how young are you?' With a sigh, she said softly, 'I used to be that shiny and flawless once.'

Then her phone rang, and Daniella's tone turned to all life's dark, flawed realities. 'Yes. Hold on, take a breath. He did what?' Daniella was polished control, and only a tiny furrow on her brow gave anything away. 'Where is he now? Have you called the police?'

From the mobile phone, a woman's high-pitched, panicked babble pierced the quiet of the office. Daniella's calmness settled her caller. 'Stay locked up in there. Yes, I can hear the sirens. I'll call a friend of mine. We'll move you and little Charlie as soon as possible. Yes, tonight.'

The Irish girl's boldness was forgotten as Daniella began gathering her bag and keys. Before hanging up, she said, 'Trust me to organise it tonight. I promise.' Daniella slipped a few files into her briefcase along with the brief she'd been reviewing. Her movements were fluid and calm. She gave nothing away, other than she was finishing up as she usually would at the end of any day.

As the Irish girl watched, Daniella dropped the now-silent phone into her bag and hit speed dial on another. 'Joan, I'm going to be late.

Can you stay with the girls for another hour?' She ran her ringless fingers through her rich, dark locks. 'Appreciate it. Thanks. Tell the girls I love them.'

Stepping out from behind her desk, she nudged past the new girl standing in her doorway. 'Um, sorry. As I said, I never usually make it to Friday night drinks. Thank you for offering. Come see me Monday and we'll do introductions properly.'

Graceful and polished was all Daniella revealed to the outside world, although sometimes melancholy brushed her features. She would soon push it aside like a stray wisp of hair. The Irish woman was left watching the elegant strides of the thirty-something woman as they ate up the carpet on her way to the lifts.

* * *

The rest of the night, Saoirse was treated to after-work drinks Brisbane style. Truth be known, it wasn't too different to after-work drinks Donegal style. While the bar was more modern and the beer much colder, the aim was the same: decompression and fun at the end of the working week.

Saoirse soon discovered that her new colleagues all had one query. How should they say her name? The main difficulty was getting the Australians' harsh nasal twang to bend and soften around the first syllable. It was entertaining for around the first ten minutes. Then almost everyone moved on.

One of the practice's IT geeks was particularly persistent. Saoirse had laughed it off at first. Then she began to get an odd read off him and found he was becoming annoying. He kept asking the same thing. 'Okay, okay, so it's got all the vowels but one, and you say it like Sirrr-sha.' Every little while he'd push his thick, black-rimmed glasses up his long, angular nose and blink.

'Sort of, you have to go a little softer. It's really Sur-sha. Like S-U-R.'

'That's what I said.' His smile was more of a leer.

'Not quite.'

'Maybe I'll just call you S. It's easier.' He licked his lips. 'You're so cute, you know that, S?' He reached out, one hand groping at her breasts, the other gripping her shoulder hard as he tried to clamp his lips on hers.

She went to knee him in the balls like Callan had taught her, but her pencil skirt gave her no room to do what she needed to. In the struggle, she managed to push his sweaty, pudgy body back a little. 'Get off me.' Then her shock was overtaken by anger, and she slapped him, yelling, 'Fuck off!'

A trio of her female colleagues whose names she thought were Kelly, Carla and Linda swarmed around her, banishing the scumbag that was Chad Merritt.

'Don't need any more lessons on how to pronounce that, do you, Chad?'

'You're such a sleaze.'

'Just piss off, sicko.'

His beady, sly eyes didn't leave Saoirse as hate ignited in them. She felt a shiver drive through her, recognising the look from the Irish winter's day when gunfire had rung out.

Carla motioned to a bouncer who was already weaving his way towards them. Before Saoirse could say thank you to her friends, Chad was being perp-walked out of the pub. It didn't matter. Her night was ruined. Kelly, Carla and Linda tried many times to convince her to stay. Saoirse hailed a taxi and escaped home, feeling as small as her rented apartment.

On Monday morning she found a message on her desk asking her to drop by Daniella's office. Daniella, the extra-shot-of-espresso-in-a-tall-latte, was everything Saoirse, the curvy-half-pint-of-Guinness, wanted to be. Saoirse would discover that Daniella's word was iron-clad as she proceeded to introduce herself properly. Then she offered Saoirse an unexpected opportunity.

'Why me?'

'No one has ever asked if I'd like to go to Friday night drinks. Most find me too intimidating. But not you.'

'I could just be the naïve new Irish girl who didn't know any better.'

'Come now.' Daniella was unfazed. 'That statement right there says it all. I know you'd asked about me, yet you still sought me out. That shows a shrewd fearlessness rather than naivety.'

With a slight smile, Daniella whispered, 'I used to be that bold.' Then she sobered to add, 'For some time now, the partners have been after me to take on a legal secretary to help with my workload. How about we try each other out and see if we like the fit? Let's say we give it eight weeks.'

As there was a dazed buzz in Saoirse's ears, Daniella answered for her. 'Good, four weeks it is.'

That sharpened Saoirse's thoughts. 'You do know you said eight weeks then nudged that down to four.'

Daniella smiled in a warm yet challenging way. 'See, that's why I know we're going to work out. You don't chicken out. So, which will it be, four or eight weeks?'

'I'll take twelve.'

'I knew you were brave. Now I see you're determined as well.'

* * *

Three months later, Saoirse was permanently assigned to Daniella. Then she met her boss's daughters, a privilege not many in the office had had. It was the beginning of an enduring friendship.

Saoirse organised Daniella's appointments and court dates, did research and came to act as a sounding board for likely tactics in some cases. She knew about almost every case. She discovered family law was not glamorous, mostly heart-wrenching and often filled with too much hate. Different, but not too dissimilar, from the criminal law her father practised.

Still, there were several of Daniella's clients who Saoirse knew little about. She gleaned bits and pieces about them from over-hearing calls, like the one the first night they'd met. Always urgent, they only ever came through directly to Daniella on her second mobile. Invariably, every call would result in Saoirse having to reshuffle Daniella's appointments and calendar.

Whenever Saoirse asked her boss why these clients were different and warranted the increased secrecy, she found Daniella coated on an extra layer of aloofness, becoming dismissive or evasive.

Outside of work, Saoirse kept her word to her father by staying in touch. Even he had to admit his daughter had chosen wisely, and her parents were genuinely happy for her. They came to look forward to hearing about her latest exploits, whether it was work or play. Reports of the weird native wildlife, particularly the spiders, lizards, sharks and snakes, made her parents' concerns rise again. However, Saoirse put them at ease with reassurances that she was unlikely to run into anything really dangerous until summer rolled around and then only if she ventured out of the city.

One aspect of her life she didn't mention was the growing list of encounters with Chad Merritt. He was a whole different kind of weird native wildlife. He gave a non-apology apology for his attempt to kiss her. Apparently it was all a misunderstanding, where he felt she'd overreacted. Then, as though his apology had smoothed over all the worst of it, he asked her to lunch, telling her he was willing to overlook the whole thing if she'd have lunch with him. She declined.

Carla, Linda and Kelly took her to lunch instead. Unease slithered up her spine when she spied Chad at a corner table. He stared at her all through the meal. The disdain for women in those black-brown eyes made her feel like fire ants were crawling over her skin. She may have been inexperienced, but she knew enough. Her mother hadn't raised a fool.

Yes, she knew Chad only liked the *idea* of a relationship with a woman. The way it looked to outsiders, it gave him normality and a sense of respectability. What he wanted was someone to dominate, to own. She'd seen it on the faces of some boys she'd grown up with. They'd inherited that look, along with the contempt, from their fathers. She was fortunate to have grown up in a home with no heavy drinking and no violence.

A couple of days later, Chad cornered Saoirse in the photocopy room. He shuffled in so close his dirty-sock body odour almost overpowered her. 'You're so cute, you know that?'

'Yes, we've established you think that.'

He disregarded the bite in her words. 'How about we go out to dinner sometime?'

Did Chad think his half-arsed apology was enough, or did he think she was that much of a pushover that she'd immediately fall at his feet? She wrapped her arms around herself to stop him from noticing the tremor. Anxiousness ratcheted through her bones every time he came near her. 'No thanks, Chad. I'm not looking to go out with anyone.'

Before he could make another slime-laced comment, loud, heated voices erupted from the office reception area. Saoirse took the opportunity to slip past him to see what was causing the commotion. A brick wall of a man with a face as rough red as those bricks was wrestling with the building's security guards. He barked, 'Where is she? Where's the bitch taking my wife and kids from me?'

Saoirse knew the face. It belonged to Graham Levitt, a violent man accustomed to getting his way by throwing his considerable bulk around. He'd made several threats to Daniella and the presiding judge in open court. This was the type of man Daniella faced down most days. She never shirked the fight, always maintaining her dignity. Saoirse decided she'd handle Chad the same way.

Levitt was told Daniella was not in the office. That caused him to howl like a rabid dog, 'Come out and face me, you slag. If you're gonna take my kids and turn my Sharon against me, have the guts to face me.' He shoved one of the guards aside and made to enter the offices. 'Hiding behind the judge, are ya? Bitch.' He ranted a chilling threat as the guards pinned him down. 'You think you can take everything in my life away. I'm gonna take everything from you.' Thankfully, the police arrived then.

A detective came to Saoirse after Levitt was removed. 'I understand Ms Malone isn't in the office at the moment. I need an appointment to discuss Levitt. His threats have become more violent. We believe he's determined to harm her.'

The bottom fell out of Saoirse's heart at hearing his words. She dutifully scheduled time for the detective to see Daniella. Having such a disturbance wasn't new to the office, yet the ferocity with which Levitt had delivered his threats had shaken everyone. Chad walked to Saoirse's desk. He hadn't read the room. Pushing up his glasses and blinking, he said, 'A little thing like you wouldn't stand a chance against someone like him. How about I walk you to your car at the end of the day? I know where you park. It can get a little dark in that spot.'

'No. Don't worry about me,' she said firmly. 'I won't need an escort, thanks. When Daniella gets back, we have plenty of work to finish up. We'll be here until late.'

The next morning, Daniella was in court, and as usual, Chad hung around her desk when Saoirse was on her own. 'Hey, sweet cheeks. Lucky security was here yesterday.' Once again, he shuffled too close. 'You know IT security is just as important. Any IT issues you might need me to look at, S?' Her skin was shrinking away from her bones as he leaned and leered. 'How about a good penetration test? I'm told I have magic fingers, the perfect touch.' His reptilian eyes ogled her before he pushed up his glasses and blinked. 'I can make sure your firewall is holding firm. There's nothing like the hold of a firm firewall. I bet you've got a great firewall.'

'No, just stop!'

'How about we go out for lunch today?'

'Please stop asking me out, following me around and generally hassling me. I don't like you in that way.' *Or honest to God, any other way*, she added silently.

His manner turned on a dime, and he gave an icy snarl. 'Well, you better make sure you back up everything properly. You wouldn't want to lose any important files or have sensitive information fall into the wrong hands.'

It felt like she was chewing aluminium foil. 'I'll do that. Bye, Chad.' Controlling a shudder, she walked away to the ladies to escape him.

That lunchtime, she sat at her desk, ducking down behind the cubicle's partition to eat her salad. She tried hard to still her mind by reading a family law paper on child custody cases, hoping no one would see her or bother her. When she jerked at Daniella's gentle nudge, she realised she hadn't quite put Chad aside.

'Hey, sorry, I didn't mean to startle you.' Daniella glanced at what she was reading. 'Oh yes, that's frightening stuff.'

'Lost myself in it.' Saoirse made herself throw off her anxiety by pushing her Guinness-coloured locks away from her eyes to look Daniella in the face.

'Come on, let's get ready for this next hearing. You want to ride shotgun with me this afternoon in court?' Saoirse couldn't contain her eagerness as Daniella said with a smile, 'You've earned it.'

Daniella wasn't smiling when a few minutes later the case file needed for the hearing couldn't be found. When Saoirse went to print a new copy the document had disappeared from their computers. They looked on the company's server, but it had vanished. 'We're screwed. Sorry, Daniella, I swear I saved it ...' Trepidation clutched at Saoirse with sticky fingers. 'I don't know what could have happened to it. It should at least be in our shared folders, and there should be another copy on the server. I don't understand.' But she did, and she desperately hoped there was another explanation. The rising dread started to squeeze her stomach and make her feel sick.

Daniella pursed her lips. 'Maybe we can wing it by pulling something together quickly now. I remember most of it.'

'Hang on, hang on.' Saoirse hurried to the bin full of documents to be shredded. She became frantic as she dug into the depths of the papers, pushing pages aside. Then she cried like she'd found gold,

'It's still here! It has some correction marks and notes over it, but it's better than nothing.'

'It'll do. Great thinking. Now, let's get it tidied up and get going.'

Saoirse shook her head. 'You still want me to come?'

'Of course. When we get back, can you contact IT and see what the hell happened?'

Saoirse couldn't keep her face from blanching. Whether Daniella saw it or not, she gave nothing away. 'Actually, Saoirse, let me do it. Might get more action on sorting it out if I request a please explain.'

* * *

Seeing Daniella in full flight in court was like watching a majestic eagle soar on the edge of the wind. With polished professionalism and charm, she hid that she was on the hunt. Only her onyx eyes shining bright showed her ultimate power. Then with precision timing, she swooped, her sharpened talons unfurling in untroubled elegance as she clutched and skewered her prey.

That night, the calls started. Midnight through to dawn, every hour. Heavy breathing, catcalls and screams of *bitch*. When they went on for a second night, Saoirse confronted Chad privately and politely asked him to stop. He loudly feigned innocence and indignation at being accused of such childish behaviour. Even though Saoirse thought she'd kept the altercation private, it hadn't gone unnoticed.

As promised, Daniella handled the IT problems, which weren't limited to the one file disappearing. Over the last few days her office had been plagued with problems, with Saoirse's computer crashing, a procession of files going missing, or being saved in odd places.

Daniella didn't deal with underlings. She had the IT department manager come down personally to work it all out. Simon unravelled the mess. He'd saved his Mr Nice Guy persona for Daniella and Saoirse. It was clear as he stomped away that his veil of kindness was being eaten away by rage.

'He's going to tear strips off someone,' Daniella observed.

The sun had long set when Saoirse approached her car at the end of the day. As she walked closer, an ever-increasing stench assaulted her nostrils. Although the lighting was dull, she soon discovered what was upsetting her senses. Then her whole body, mind and spirit were overtaken by despair. The word *Bitch* was smeared across her car in dog crap. She stood welded to the spot as the tears came. Daniella found her shaking and sobbing, leaning against a concrete column.

Her boss helped her settle and regroup, allowing Saoirse to see the vandalism for what it was—a small act performed by an even smaller person. Saoirse was grateful for Daniella's generosity and seemingly boundless reserve of strength and energy. The older woman always took time to care for others, even if she might've been facing far more pressing issues herself. It was why Saoirse didn't tell Daniella her suspicions about who'd done it. She'd deal with Chad alone.

Early the following day, they arrived together at a suburban courthouse for a scheduled court appearance. As they walked into the entrance hall, jarring shouts and flustered movement greeted them instead of the usual buzz of regimented order. Daniella's famous polish and composure slipped for the snip of time it took her to utter, 'Nooo. The bastard! Not my girls.'

Plastered around the entrance and waiting rooms were A4 pages with photos of Hannah and Taylor. In warning-red, the heading shouted: *Men, these are the kids of the bitch that's screwing you.* The name of the girls' school was printed beneath their smiling faces.

Court officers and staff were running around, tearing them down. Her shield back in place, those quick black-diamond eyes narrowed, Daniella had her phone in hand, having already spoken to the girls' nanny and the police. She turned to Saoirse. 'I have to stay here and sort this out, and I still have a client to represent. I wouldn't normally ask, but I need you to pick up Hannah and Taylor from school. You can see the address from these goddamn posters. I don't want them to be picked up in a police car. It will scare them and cause too many questions.' She shook her head. 'Joan, their nanny, can't get to the school right now to take them home. The police will wait at the school for you and follow you home. Joan will meet you at the house as soon as she can.' Daniella steadied. 'I know it's not in your job description, but I have no one else I trust.'

'Of course. It's done.'

Daniella placed her hand on Saoirse's shoulder. 'Thank you.' Before dialling another number, she said, 'I'm calling the girls' principal. I'll tell her what's happened, who you are and that you and the police will need to take the girls home.'

'Is this Graham Levitt's doing?'

'Not sure—he prefers to use his fists. But I have a hunch who.'

It was well after lunch when Saoirse returned to the office. She hadn't eaten and wasn't hungry. That didn't change when she saw Simon leaving Daniella's office, followed by the managing partners. With a relieved smile, Daniella took Saoirse's hands and gently squeezed them. 'Just the woman I need.' With evident grace, she said, 'Thank you for this morning. Come, walk with me. We have business to conclude.'

Chad Merritt was standing at the water cooler, giggling with his work cronies. Daniella was, as usual, sophisticated fluidity. Approaching the pudgy, red-haired upstart, she leaned in close to him, and time seemed to slow.

His harsh, angular features were having trouble focusing as Daniella hovered. Not able to control his nervous tick, he pushed his glasses up his crow's beak of a nose. Daniella obliged his habit. Her stylish, hot-pink fingernails rammed his glasses up hard against his forehead. He yelped as three little crescents of blood appeared on his brow. His wide, stunned eyes watered as she whispered something in his ear. He froze. Not so privately, not so politely, Daniella took a vice-like hold on his manhood and twisted. He went red, then white, and then howled. Daniella was gliding away before his greasy body crumpled and hit the floor.

She winked as she strode past Saoirse. 'That should do it. Please join me in my office.'

When Saoirse entered her boss's office, Daniella was cleansing her hands with sanitiser. On her desk were her two mobile phones. She sat and motioned for Saoirse to do the same.

'You know, I don't think anyone would begrudge us an early drink.' She bent, opened the bottom drawer of her desk and brought out two crystal tumblers, followed by a bottle of Lagavulin. As she poured two generous measures, she began, 'I decided, after a violent man shot my husband, that if the law couldn't protect women until it was too late and someone had to die, then I would stand up for them before that happened.'

She pushed Saoirse's scotch across the desk. 'The law and its protection of women living with domestic violence is hamstrung at the very best, and tissue-paper thin at the very worst. Men frequently stomp all over any domestic violence orders. Graham Levitt did that yesterday. His ex-wife is in hospital and he's in custody, facing charges. He didn't have the time or expertise to do what happened at court this morning.'

With a slow sip, Daniella closed her eyes for a moment. When she opened them, her mask slipped, and Saoirse saw the worry. 'Today, my heart and soul nearly died all over again when I became reacquainted with desperate helplessness. All of it caused by the danger that snivelling IT arsehole put my daughters in. I understand the risks that being a family court lawyer poses to me, but my daughters are sacrosanct. That's why I protect their privacy fiercely and don't let too many people know anything about them.'

Daniella took another long sip, visibly allowing the liquid to slide slowly down her throat, the experience appearing to bring solace and melting her tense muscles. She let out a tired sigh. 'I could stop what I do. God knows I'm *not* the only person who has this skill set. But I will not run and hide because of threats made by bullies. I want my daughters to see that I'm more than a mother who works herself to the bone for them, who would do anything for them. I want them to learn through my actions that women have rights. The world might consider them weaker, but women are strong in many ways. And if they feel alone and beaten down, there are people who will support and fight for them. That's why Chad Merritt picked the wrong bitch to mess with.'

'Make that bitches.'

Daniella clinked her glass to Saoirse's. 'Good to hear. Why didn't you tell me he was harassing you?'

'I figured I could handle it. And besides, you have bigger men's balls to rip off and fry. Or is that smaller men?'

Daniella sniffed out a smile. 'I whispered I'd do a very similar thing to Chad if he ever did anything like this again.'

Saoirse took a sip and immediately coughed and turned red.

'First Scotch?'

'Third or so. Still getting used to it.'

'You don't have to get used to anything. If it's not your drink, it's not your drink.'

'Oh, I know. It's just I drink it too quickly, like it's a cider and gulp it down. Like life, I'm learning to savour it. While not my fave drink, I know a good one when I taste it. Like this.' She swirled the amber liquid in the tumbler. 'I don't mind it, and I know I'll be happy to have one from time to time. It's an example of all I'm learning. Like it's good to be more discerning in life. I'll find my drink, just haven't yet, like a lot of other things in my life.'

Daniella smiled. 'Good for you. I've done the same, learned to be more discerning. It's led me to be part of a small but resolute organisation.' She took a breath. 'After today, I know I can trust you. You have a right to know about this other organisation.'

'I gathered something was going on.'

'Of course, you're too astute not to. That said, I hold this other part of my life secret, even from the managing partners and my family. It's the reason I always pushed back against having a personal legal secretary assigned to me. Then you came along, and something about you made me want to give you a try.'

She squeezed Saoirse's hand. 'Years ago, I was approached by a like-minded mother whose daughter was killed by her violent husband, and she introduced me to this network. I do everything by the book. When the book doesn't offer protection, I skate along a very fine line between protection and the laws the book stands for. Before you ask, yes, it's tricky, especially when children and custody issues are on the table.'

'How do you protect them?'

'We call it going underground, total secrecy. We move them around, away from the danger. It's a network of brave women volunteers, all anonymous, and we use coded messages, and no lists of phone numbers.'

'Wow, this is ... I don't know what this is. No word seems to do it justice.' Finally, she managed, 'Amazing, I guess.'

'Mostly, I only provide a shoulder and free legal counsel. I try to find ways within the law to protect women and their children. But at times we must just move them, making them disappear for a while to escape the violent and life-threatening situations they're enduring.'

'Do you have a name for your network?'

'No, not really. It's best not to name it, easier for it not to be found out. In the US, it's been called various versions of the Domestic Violence Underground Railway. It's fashioned on the original mid-nineteenth-century Underground Railway. A clandestine organisation that helped slaves escape to freedom from the South by a network of safe houses and routes where everyone involved was sworn to secrecy.'

As if on cue, her 'underground' phone rang. 'And of course, it goes without saying that each call must be answered.' With that, she picked up the phone. 'Yes.' After a pause, 'Oh God. No matter how many times I hear that it never fails to shock me. What are the chances you can move her safely?'

two

REFLECTIONS IN A REAR-VIEW MIRROR: GABBY'S STORY

The devil doesn't come showing his horns and scaly wings. He comes disguised as everything you've ever wanted.

SERGIO MANCUSO WHISKED Gabby Torres away from her tired, chaotic life to his piece of a peaceful life. A rough, rocky portion of land in Far North Queensland, made worth farming by the channel waters from Tinaroo Dam. Sergio's land was surrounded by the rest of the family's farms, with one border outlined by the thready Chinaman Creek.

Gabby had been travelling the world for five years when she met Sergio in Bali. He was charming in an appealing hometown-boy way. He was on holiday, while she was working. She was writing her final piece for a travel guide publisher on the world's best low-cost destinations. Blogging was just taking off as a viable form of writing, and she was starting to see some returns for her work on her travel blog. It sounded like the perfect life. Yet she was becoming tired of living out of a suitcase. Then there was the stress of meeting multiple deadlines to keep her out of the red.

Her editor, Carol, offered some advice. 'Gabby, this last piece reads a little tired. Maybe you need to take a break, freshen up your outlook on life and your writing.' They turned out to be almost fatal last words.

Gabby first saw Sergio and his older brother, Carlo, while drinking with friends on a frenzied, muggy night out. Coming out of a club, she was surrounded by celebrating locals. One of them had become a little too amorous, which she was handling. Gabby had dealt with worse on her travels. Sergio stalked through the overzealousness and cleared a path for her. 'Hey, let me help. I'll protect you from these sleazes.' *All he needed was a horse and a sword*, she thought at the time. He seemed so gallant.

Lifting one of the happy drunks by the scruff of the neck, he threw the rag doll of a man to the side. 'Get off the lady, will ya.' He shielded Gabby from the rest with his large, slightly spongy body. Later that night, she discovered that under his squishiness, Sergio was a well-built, all-Australian man.

Sergio was attentive, very attentive. It was flattering how he made her his priority. Especially when they were stranded in Bali for weeks because of a volcanic eruption whose dust prevented planes from flying. They spent most of the days and nights of those idyllic weeks together.

His widowed older brother tagged along at times. Carlo was loud-mouthed, rude and coarse. It should have been a warning sign that Sergio's demeanour in Bali was the exception, not the rule. When she looked back now, she realised that even then, Sergio was more than a little heavy-handed.

She hadn't noticed how he manipulated her into doing the things he wanted. He would start a conversation agreeing with what she wanted to do. They would keep talking. Then they'd wind up doing what he'd wanted to do all along. His brother, in one of his many drunken stupors, all but admitted they were wife-shopping. Sergio joked it off. Carlo was an offensive buffoon, so she had no qualms believing Sergio. Gabby swallowed his alluring holiday charm like a hungry fish with eyes only for the bait, not the lethal hook. Before she knew it, she was saying 'I do' on a Balinese beach. It was so romantic.

Once the chase was over and she became his wife, the schism between Holiday-Sergio and Farm-Sergio, the dream and the nightmare, fractured wide open. Gabby wondered how an educated woman, brought up to speak her mind and be independent, had become this person, this woman. The thought only made her slide further into the darkness.

The first time he hit her, he seemed truly stricken and apologised with flowers. She forgave him rather than face the catastrophe her life had become. Her heart died more than a little that day. Gabby convinced herself she was overreacting—it was all her fault he'd hit her—and she bought into the whole of his regret.

'If you'd only do what I tell you to do, I wouldn't get so angry.'

'I'm sorry. I'll try,' she said.

'Don't try, just do it!'

Alas, Sergio's need to control her grew and grew, and as his heart turned to ice-cold stone, every beat of hers came to be filled with fear and pain. Soon she discovered his family wouldn't offer any solace. She found his mother and his sister-in-law Ida, the wife of his younger brother, Guido, kept tabs on her. They watched from their houses, sometimes with binoculars, and relayed any indiscretion to Sergio. Then Sergio would chide and deride Gabby if she strayed from what his mother, Francesca, thought was appropriate behaviour. 'All you have to do is keep the house clean, do the washing, feed the chooks and cook for me,' he shouted. 'How hard can it be?'

Harder than Francesca, she thought. Gabby and Sergio's house was a hovel. A ramshackle weatherboard/fibro house held together by peeling paint, mould and ageing wood. The other homes on the property were brick/fibro and in relatively good condition. At least they kept the dust, vermin and weather out.

Sergio smacked his palm on the table to return Gabby's attention to him. 'Just keep this place clean, and in return, I've given you a roof over your head. No more roaming around the world like some media whore, looking for the next story.' He'd never understood what she did as a writer.

Now he was tomorrow's husband. If she asked him for anything, he'd say, 'We'll be able to afford that next month, or maybe in three months. Anyway, you shouldn't need it. If it's good enough for my mama to live with, it's good enough for you.' The only things that materialised were her hopelessness and his temper.

Then Sergio began to pull her hair to make her look at him or follow him. Once, she resisted and he pushed her into a wall. The force was so brutal her body cracked the fibro where she hit it. It was too late to heed these warnings. She was in too far. The bleakness and desperation of her situation began destroying her spirit, eroding her very essence.

'Please, Sergio, we need a new washing machine. This one is leaking all the time and doesn't finish the wash properly. Can't we use the money my mother gave us as a wedding present? It won't cost much, and it'll help me out.'

'Nuh. Don't worry your silly head about that money. It's gone into things for the farm. All gone.'

'A washing machine is a thing for the farm.'

As she walked out of the laundry to hang the washing on the line, he tripped her. She fell onto the ground, made muddy by the machine's leaking water pump and hoses. The clean clothes she'd just finished washing ended up covered in mud. Sergio thought it was hilarious, sneering and kicking more mud in her face while she struggled to stand up. It was the last time she recalled arguing with him without fear and hesitation following each word. Now she was like an obedient dog, tail between its legs, skittishly trailing behind its tyrannical master.

Then the family decided Gabby didn't need to travel to the small town nearby to do her grocery shopping. Sergio's mother would buy in bulk and give them what they needed to survive. It would save money. Gabby was now totally isolated. She found it harder and harder to keep a sense of herself and not get lost in the despair and hollowness that consumed her.

He'd taken her mobile phone after a couple of months of marriage. When she asked for it back, he said he'd lost it. 'Anyway, the coverage is shit out here. You're not going to get much of a signal to use it. The telephone in the house will have to do.' She didn't have the energy or the will to demand her phone back.

Before her marriage, she'd speak to her mum each week, but now it was difficult. The landline phone was old and the connection dodgy. Each time she dialled the number, there were always several clicks and buzzing before she could hear her mum's voice. Now she called less often. It caused too much pain for both mother and daughter. Gabby was becoming more and more ashamed of her life and couldn't find the energy to answer her mother's questions. 'Gabby, what's really happening? You're not happy. I can hear it in your voice. Come home. If you can't afford it, I'll send you the money.' It had been three months since she'd spoken to her mum.

The afternoon after that call, Sergio came home, vibrating with anger. 'What gives you the right to go crying to your mother? I give you a home, food, clothes.' He back-handed her off her feet. 'Don't you dare disrespect me in front of my family by telling your bitch of a mother anything about us, about how we live.'

'What are you talking about?' With tears blurring her sight, she gingerly pressed shaking fingers over her pulsing cheek.

'Don't you fucking lie to me. I hear things.'

'What, how?' She was hurt and angry that he would sneak around to eavesdrop on her phone calls yet, with her heart plummeting through her stomach, she was not surprised. 'That's private. You shouldn't be listening in on phone calls. You bastard, that's so wrong.'

'What did you say?' He moved his hand back. 'Go on. Say that again.'

She cowered away. The vileness in Sergio's eyes froze her. She'd never seen anything like it, never believed that she could inspire such hate in another person. At that moment in her life, she unconsciously began questioning everything about herself, her judgement, self-worth and wisdom. How could she have thought she loved this man so much that she married him?

He back-handed her anyway, giving her a shiner. 'You stupid bitch.'

'Can't you see this is so wrong? I can't do this anymore. I want out.'

Laughing now, he pulled her up by her limp, brown hair. 'You're out when hell freezes over, because you're mine. I own you. You don't have money, can't go anywhere without us knowing. We know people everywhere. You leave, we'll find you. I'll bring you back and tie you to the bed. Now get me my dinner. See if you can do that right.'

Later that night, they were woken by an engine revving and then raised voices. Sergio dressed. When Gabby went to do the same, he grabbed her throat and squeezed. 'Stay here if you know what's good for ya.' He shuffled out. Then she heard the gun safe open and shut.

Gabby waited for the outside door to slam and then dressed. With the moonlight to guide her, she snuck out the front door. They'd see her if she went out the back door. The cool night air was a soundless, refreshing swirl around her body as she ran down the side of the house. The light and noise came from the small shed almost hidden by bush at the far end of the property. The shed was the only one on the farm with a door. She'd never seen inside as it was always locked. Now the door was open. Her heart ramped up and drummed against her ribs.

The dirt in front of the shed was bathed in pale light, interrupted by the violent movement of elongated shadows. The pure night silence was polluted by harsh voices that echoed off the dark sky. Her shoes whispered across the dry grass as she made her way to the long grass at the back of the shed. She climbed up the stack of rough-cut fence posts, her fingers punctured by the splintered edges of the wood. The skin of her fingertips and palms felt like pieces of fabric being held together by rough wooden pins. The pain didn't stop her. She didn't make a sound, although it felt like her heart was pummelling her chest with the noise of a freight train running down a track. Balancing on top of one of the triangular-cut logs, she peered through the space between the corrugated iron wall and roof.

Before her eyes registered, her nostrils understood what was being unloaded from a small, covered truck. Marijuana. She'd had a full life before she fell for a brooding, built Italian. Large plastic bags filled with dried green leaves and others full to overflowing with trimmed buds were being unloaded and piled onto a wooden pallet. This was what the family actually farmed and why they were so secretive and preferred their farm's isolation. It was why her in-laws were watching the new wife with ruthless discipline. She guessed it would continue until they deemed she was trustworthy, and that seemed far from possible.

The loading had stopped as the three men started yelling and shoving each other. Besides Sergio, his brother, Guido, was also one of the yelling, gesticulating men. The other, a shorter, thickset man, was unknown. He was dressed in camouflage fatigues not as threadbare as the brothers' khaki work clothes. Behind Guido and the new guy, Sergio moved back and forth like a bear in a too-small cage. At one point, Gabby glimpsed a bulge at Sergio's back under the tail of his shirt.

The meagre living the family made from farming fruit and vegetables was a front. She gathered from the argument that the unknown guy wanted a larger share as he took more risks by living at the property where the crop was growing. From what he said, Gabby worked out he was living up in the ranges behind Sergio's family's farm. It seemed the hills were alive with the sound of pot growing.

As she squinted through the slit, she realised she was not alone. Something brushed her leg and she froze. Adrenaline spiked, rendering her whole body a jangling mass of short-circuiting nerves. Had Carlo come up behind her? She looked down frantically to see several shadows zigzagging across the lattice of the stack of fence posts. Then one shadow split off to run up a long piece of four-by-two, which leaned against the wall. Rats. Big ones.

The adventurous climber—a rat that looked like it could eat a full-grown Chihuahua and chase its owner—walked towards her along one of the shed's beams. God, she hoped the ones below didn't try to be as adventurous and climb up her leg, or worse still, up the inside of her trackpants. As she shuddered, one skimmed past her ankle. She kicked at it, nearly toppling off the angular tip of the log. Now she had two situations to keep an eye on—all involved rats.

The two brothers began circling Camo-man. He spat at their feet. Sergio flicked up the back of his shirt to whip the pistol out from his waistband. She assumed it was his beloved Beretta M9. He'd bragged to her about Italian ingenuity and the beauty of his gun. It was on one of the nights he'd intimidated and forced himself on her. Most times it was less painful than his fists and rage.

Camo-man backed off. Chihuahua-rat waddled forward faster along the wooden beam. One eye was scarred over, blending with the other missing chunks of fur from its scar-ridden face.

Speaking of scar-ridden repulsion, Guido threw three wads of golden-coloured bills at the guy. Fifty-dollar notes, lots of them. There had to be at least twenty or more in each stack, held together by an elastic band. As Camo-man bent to pick them up, Sergio shoved the pistol into the top of the guy's head, pinning him in a kneeling position, Mafia execution style. Gabby's heart was now ballooning out of her chest. A nip at her ankle and the balloon exploded, causing blood to pump and thump in overdrive around her head. Gasping, she ducked down and kicked out. The toe of her old sneaker hit the corrugated iron wall with a dull thud.

Nippy-rat squeaked as she connected with it. It sailed through the air, a piece of Gabby's skin between its teeth. The sound startled Chihuahua-rat, which jumped to fly off the beam, trying to escape by landing on a stack of wooden pallets, making more noise. A shot rang out. Nippy-rat had saved Gabby's life as a bullet ripped through the iron above her head, close enough that she was deafened in that ear by the clang of metal piercing metal. She scurried down the fence posts like the scattering rodents and ran.

Expecting another shot and with not enough oxygen filling her screaming lungs, she crossed the open ground on shaky, pumping legs as she rushed towards the house. The truck flew out of the shed, and for a harrowing moment she was caught in its headlights. She froze. Camo-man sped by her. Their eyes locked, fear anchored in both. They were the unlikely beneficiaries of rodent curiosity. The brothers' shouting scared her survival instinct into action and started her moving.

Guido yelled, 'Why the fuck would you shoot at a fucking rat, you dumb shit.' They were rolling down the door.

Sergio yelled back, 'I heard a noise. I thought someone was there. How was I to know it was a fat turd of a rat.' They were walking now.

To elude the brothers, she had to sprint down the other side of the house to the front door, further than the brothers had to travel. She slid in through the front door as they were coming in the back through the laundry.

Sergio slapped Guido's back with a chuckle. 'Sure made that motherfucker nearly shit his pants. He'll be careful before he asks for a bigger cut again.'

She was caught in the hallway, only just making it past the bedroom door, as Guido rounded the corner. He licked his lips as snake-like eyes slithered up her body, making her skin feel like slime. 'Hey, Sergio, your missus is outta bed.'

Sergio rounded the corner. Her hands sang with pain as she pushed them into her pockets and took a few steps back. 'I-I heard a shot. Ah, I got dressed. I was coming to make sure no one was hurt.' She was shaking and white. 'I was worried.' She looked convincing, even if she was shaking for an entirely different reason.

He hesitated, then spoke with a calmer voice. 'We don't need your help. Go back to bed. I'll deal with you later.'

'Can I go to the bathroom?' She knew he'd like her submission in front of Guido.

'Just get out of my sight.'

She went into the bathroom, washed her hands and then tried to pull out some of the bigger splinters. Their sting was keeping her from cracking open and losing it. She found some tweezers but was trembling too much to use them. She used the toilet, flushed, washed again and left for the bedroom, telling herself to hang on to the person she was, not the submissive drone he was forcing her to become.

Sergio and Guido sat down and drank the red wine they bought in two-litre glass flagons, and drank a lot of it they did. She had a torch in the bedroom and dared switch it on to attend to her hands as she settled, telling herself, *Deep breath in, deep breath out.* Gabby didn't hear Guido leave. When a sickly sense skulked through her, she glanced up to see Sergio standing in the doorway.

He staggered into the bedroom. 'What the fuck are you doing?'

'I ...' Her mind went blank.

He grabbed her fingers and squeezed. The pain crystallised her thoughts. 'I was moving firewood for the stove today, and got some splinters.' It was almost the truth. The woodfired stove in the kitchen was from the thirties. The woodpile was under a lean-to shed at the back of the house. She often got splinters from moving chunks of wood to the kitchen.

He was too drunk to care, pushing her down. She lay very still, almost daring not to breathe. He crowed as he fell on top of her. 'You need to respect me more. Not be like a board when I fuck you. You know, I have a shitload of money in the safe. You ain't getting any of it, ain't going anywhere until you show me some respect.'

He smelled of sweat, alcohol, dirt and marijuana. He wrenched Gabby's face around to shove his red-wine-soured mouth over hers. He tore off her T-shirt and tried to get himself harder by rubbing up against her. With desperate need and frantic thrusts, more sweat came, then grunting, then nothing. He was as soft as a rotting piece of old rope left out in the rain. Gabby was frozen. He'd lost his energy and rolled off her. It wasn't the first time he'd forced himself on her.

It was the first time he'd been too drunk to finish. She tried not to throw up before she got to the toilet.

The following morning, she had his breakfast ready for him on the table: strong coffee and sardines on toast. He snarled, 'Funny how the firebox has no wood in it.' Her insides quaking, she stepped away, expecting a slap. None came as his cruel eyes flicked to her hands. The glare was vile and cold. Point made, he finished his breakfast and left. Now he didn't even have to abuse her physically. The mere thought of it imprisoned her. Once she saw he was well and truly gone, Gabby sank into a chair and cried.

* * *

Gabby had found some solace by emailing her widowed mother on the couple's computer. She usually sent and then deleted all records of the emails. Until one afternoon, when Sergio surprised her. He smashed up the desktop in a rage driven by alcohol and sustained by a heightened level of vitriol.

Gabby felt the smack explode on the side of her head. Turning, she shouted as pain bit into her world and white splotches blurred her sight. 'No, stop!' Too late, she couldn't see but felt the punch to her face. Crippling blows thundered into her stomach. Pain slashed and tore as further hits sent warping black-and-white stars firing to deaden her sight, and acid nausea rose.

Everything paled when more terrifying misery erupted as he twisted her arm up behind her back. The excruciating agony from the blows peeled away as the crude crack of bone shearing away from bone caused an explosion of new pain that slammed into and ruled her being. Her world descended into an unbearable hell. The slap of her body hitting the hallway floor was the last thing she heard before he was on her. Claws that were once fingers grabbed at her breasts, fangs that were once teeth bit down on her throat, snarls that were once words shredded her psyche, as the animal that was once a man forced himself on her.

The fight Gabby thought she possessed had been stolen. Fear petrified her. Those fangs bit her breast, claws ripped her legs, shoved them open and tore her underwear. He grabbed at the most private, treasured part of her, which should only ever be a woman's to give, not a man's to take. Her body, mind and spirit didn't so much surrender as short-circuit into blackness.

When he finished, she managed to drag her crushed and brutalised body to the second bedroom. A figure that once was Gabriella Torres curled up on the small, rag-covered mattress lying on the floor. Moonlight laid itself gently over her. No matter how tranquil the house was now, it couldn't soothe the savagery of the pain beating through her body or hide the brutality of the blood oozing from her. As she passed out, she heard the beast lock the door behind her.

The echoing agony that woke her the following morning didn't wane. Instead, its pulsing intensified. Her arm screamed when she tried to put weight on it. Her skin was slick with the sweat of nauseating fever, and she realised she was lying in a tepid pool of blood. With stale acid and bloody metallic bile coating her tongue, she knew something was gravely wrong. Defeated, she lay back down and hoped to die, like her spirit had done hours before.

The lock squeaked, and the door thudded open. 'Get your useless arse up and make me breakfast.' When she didn't move, he got down face-to-face and yelled, 'Did you hear me, you lazy bitch? Get up.' He yanked her up by her lank hair to slap her face. She heard a sound like cloth ripping, and new hurt jagged through her as her hair was wrenched from her scalp. She didn't care. She was now drowning in a sickening, surging ocean, filled with the heat of fever and howling pain. Sergio saw the fresh blood oozing down her legs, between her thighs. Repulsed by it, he threw her down. Gabby curled up once more. Darkness smothered her, and she surrendered.

* * *

With her unresponsiveness, Sergio realised something was wrong. He didn't call a doctor. He called his mother, Francesca. The diminutive woman was a piece of toughened steel that made nails look like boiled noodles. When she couldn't even rouse Gabby, Francesca knew enough to realise that whatever was claiming her daughter-in-law was beyond her self-taught nursing skills. There was just too much blood. The young woman needed to go to the community clinic.

Francesca asked Sergio to bend down to her. Gnarled arthritic fingers snatched at his ear and dragged him out of the room. She swore in Italian and then punched him in the face, blackening his eye. Later, Gabby would find out it wasn't because her son had beaten his wife. It was because he'd injured her so severely, she needed a doctor's care. The family didn't like any community involvement in their affairs.

Francesca told the medical staff that Gabby's injuries were from her falling off one of the harvesters. Only one nurse understood what was going on and tried to help. Sally was told to mind her own business. The clinic's and town's only doctor, Dr Alf Orsetti, was an old man and a distant relation of the Mancusos. He didn't want any trouble.

Then he studied the X-ray of Gabby's arm. The telltale spiral fracture had him start a fresh page in her patient notes. He wanted to be accurate in his documentation. The nature of her injury wasn't caused by falling off a harvester, it could only be from a deliberate twisting of the arm. He became even more horrified with what one final test revealed.

* * *

After four days in the hospital, Sally sat down at Gabby's bedside to deliver even more tragic news. Although Gabby tried to hide it, her bones seemed to rattle from fresh sobs when she heard she had been in the first trimester of pregnancy. The suffering, fear and shaking that engulfed her were powerful, like a gale snuffing out the weak flame that was her hope. She couldn't comprehend how life could form in such a crucible of hatred and hardship. It made her think of a green seedling pushing through the blackened, scorched earth to grow after a bushfire. She'd thought her missed periods were because of the stress of forced, rough sex and her violent living circumstances.

Sally took her hand. 'I can help you. You could press charges. Get away from him, them.'

With her throat closing over, she cried, 'I can't lay any charges. The town's policeman is Frank Mancuso, Sergio's uncle. I'm surrounded by his family.' She sobbed. 'My mother-in-law and sister-in-law's houses overlook my home. I can't move without them knowing.'

Sally pushed a piece of paper into her hand. 'Here's my number. Call any time.'

'I don't have a phone. He took it from me. If I use the house phone, he could overhear me. It's happened before.'

'Don't you give up, okay? There must be something. Let me check with the women's shelter in Mareeba.'

Now Gabby was shaking, her eyes darting around. 'Please don't. They'll hurt you. They're dangerous men. He has guns.'

'Look, you'll have to come back here in a week for us to follow up on your wound management and to fill the repeats of your prescriptions. I'll see if we can't get you some help by then.'

Sally hugged her, saying, 'I can see the fight in your eyes. Your body is battered, but your spirit isn't. Don't let him defeat you.'

Gabby swallowed her tears. 'You're right.' There and then, she promised herself she'd resist turning into the woman her husband was trying to pummel her into being.

The family forbade her from returning to the clinic. There would be no follow-up exam and no refilling of her prescription.

* * *

Weeks later, a police car arrived at Francesca's house. Gabby saw the small town's highest-ranking police officer, Sargent Frank Mancuso, was visiting his relatives. Whatever he said, it forced Sergio to yield a little. Sergio's new wife had to be seen around town, mainly to stop tongues wagging and a possible visit by a government social worker. Murmurs of serious problems with the family and Gabby's welfare had begun to reach higher authorities in Mareeba. The family didn't want anyone from the government sniffing around.

When Gabby's arm was healed enough for her to drive, she would be allowed to go into town once a week to do some grocery shopping and pay bills. The family had only just begun to use banks. They all shared one bank account with a skinny balance. It was to appear normal. They didn't want to attract the tax office's attention.

The family still hid most of their money around the property, buried in tin boxes. Gabby knew this was how they operated but had no idea where they stashed any of the tins. They wouldn't give her cash because she could steal and hoard it.

Even if Gabby had to be seen in town doing everyday things like shopping, the family would still control her. The night before, Sergio would write a cheque for an amount for groceries and some farming bills, leaving her with no extra money for herself. She had a tight timeline so she wouldn't waste time making silly gossip with other women. Because according to Sergio, that was all women did when they got together. They gossiped and disrespected their husbands who slaved away on the farms to give them a good life.

At times, Francesca and Ida, the favourite daughter-in-law, accompanied Gabby into town. The two women sat in the back seat of the car and spoke Italian. They hardly even acknowledged Gabby was present. Little did they know that her time as a travel writer had taught her enough of the language to understand what they were saying. Gabby never gave them a hint of her knowledge and just drove them around in her own Godfather version of *Driving Miss Daisy*.

On one such trip, the riddle of how Sergio heard her phone

conversation was solved when Francesca bragged to Ida how she listened in on Gabby's phone calls. The landline set-up was an old 'party-line' type, which the family never allowed the phone company to modernise. Francesca could lift the receiver and hear every word of Gabby's conversation. The answering machine rigged up to Francesca's phone would record all of Gabby's conversations, even if Francesca wasn't home, so she could eavesdrop later. Gabby thought she couldn't hate her life anymore. Now, as she bit back tears, she couldn't understand how her life had become so foreign to her.

She discovered an unexpected speck of light on her dark horizon. One of the tellers in the bank was about Gabby's age. Trina had noticed Gabby's bruises, which she tried to hide with the abused wife's uniform of makeup, dark sunglasses and long sleeves. This day, Trina smiled. 'It's Gabby, right?'

Gabby gave her an uneasy nod.

'I went to school with Sergio,' Trina told her in a hushed voice. 'We dated for a bit before he bared his real teeth. I know what his family's like. Carlo's wife died in childbirth because they wouldn't let her go to the hospital.'

Gabby hung her head to glance at Francesca, who was hovering at the bank's door, not trusting anyone. 'I don't know what you're talking about.'

Trina bowed her head, causing her blonde hair to curtain the side of her face. Francesca wouldn't see her mouth move. 'I'm Sally's partner. You can trust us. Before we were together, we both knew men like Sergio.'

'I can't do this,' she said, as the burning in her throat choked off the air. 'Not now.'

'Stay strong. You have support.' With the money, Trina slid a piece of white paper to Gabby, who gave a tight smile and hurriedly shuffled everything into her purse. Now she understood why Francesca had allowed her to go to the town's health clinic. The family couldn't afford two dead wives.

Because the stitches to repair her internal wounds still oozed some blood, Sergio found her unappealing. Leaving her alone, he vented his frustrations by yelling at her to cook and clean the house. To say she was relieved was an understatement.

Weeks passed. Gabby cleaned the house as ordered. Scrubbing her dried blood off the second bedroom's floor, she found the water run-off didn't pool. Instead, it drained away between a join in the linoleum. When she lifted the lino and pulled up a piece of wood, she found a safe in the floor. It wasn't a figment of a drunk man's imagination.

Sergio was spraying young mango seedlings with insecticide, so he'd be out of her way for hours. Playing around with the safe's dial, it didn't surprise her that the combination was his date of birth, day, month and year—the same as the gun safe. Sergio wasn't a rocket scientist.

The drug business was doing well. Seeing the size of the wads of cash, Gabby estimated that there was over one hundred thousand dollars in the safe. She was careful to put everything back the way she found it.

A woman grows with the greatness of each task.

Gabby read and re-read Trina's note. It rekindled her hope. The flame and light it shone within her began to grow. The three women began formulating a plan to get her out. Over the following weeks, she and Trina passed notes back and forth at the bank. Gabby made sure to always return home on time to prepare Sergio's lunch. Until one fateful day when Francesca hadn't been with her, she was delayed.

She hadn't noticed him in the grocery store until he came in close, reaching across her to grab a bottle of olive oil. His other hand seized her elbow. 'Next time, you should invite me in for a drink.' He smelled of smoke and sickly sour sweat. 'A pretty young thing like you doesn't want to go too many places on your own.'

She yanked her arm out of his grip.

'I mean it. With what you know.'

Her heart was ballooning out of her chest again.

Camo-man gave her a look, not like Sergio's. Not like a lion about to feed. It was more like a hyena feeding on scraps left by the lion. 'I'm not going to hurt you. But they can. I'm sure you know. I wanted to let you know your secret is safe with me. But that'll only continue if you give me something.' Now those scavenger features looked like they were eyeing a prized piece of discarded flesh. 'A man has needs that a woman like you could ease.' He snaked a finger down her arm, smacking his lips together. 'You understand what I want?'

After she swallowed down bile, she said, 'Yes.'

He sniggered. 'Here's my number. When you're next in town without the mother-in-law in tow, you let me know and we'll hook up. The back of the truck is cosy enough. You know the car park behind the shopping centre, it's nice and quiet. Don't leave it too long. Otherwise, they might find out.'

She took Camo-man's number and nodded.

Almost a week later, Francesca visited to say she wouldn't be accompanying Gabby to town the following day because she was helping Ida bottle olives. Gabby waited until she saw Francesca return to her own home and then phoned Sally. 'Hi, I'm in town tomorrow around nine. Will you be able to supply me with antibiotic lozenges, lotion, gauze and ointment?'

'Yes. I'll have everything you need organised.'

She wrote a list for the next day's shopping and showed it to Sergio at lunch. As usual, he crossed off a few things that he thought were unnecessary. In an unusually good mood, he increased the total when he wrote the cheque. 'Since you've been so well-behaved, I'll give you a few extra dollars to get yourself something special.'

She barely stopped herself from rolling her eyes. 'Thank you.'

He stroked her hair and then grabbed her ponytail, tugging it almost playfully this time as he smirked. 'You should make sure to freshen up down there.' He scratched his balls. 'Tomorrow night could be your lucky night.'

Now she barely stopped herself from dry retching.

He took a phone call, and Gabby gathered that Camo-man would be in town and making a delivery the following night.

After Sergio went outside, she watched him meet Guido as they rolled up the drug-shed door. She needed to access the safe, and she needed to do it now. It was risky. Sergio could come back at any time, and it would be incredibly dangerous if he went to the safe that evening to grab money to pay Camo-man.

It had to be done, no matter that every nerve in her body was jangling like bells on a galloping horse. She needed money for her plans to come to fruition. Bracing herself, she walked to the second bedroom, keeping an eye on the shed, before she dropped to the floor. She began taking four fifty-dollar notes from each of the stacks in the safe, which contained forty notes bound together by an elastic band. She hoped he wouldn't notice the stacks were short if they all looked the same height.

About halfway through, her whole body jerked and her hands shuddered as the back door banged. The bills from the stack she was working with splattered out over the floor. Her heart took a few tremendous hard, rapid beats. She raked the notes back into the hole the safe was in and dragged the mattress over the top of it to dash out, closing the bedroom door. She was shaking, with no way of stopping it. She fully expected to see Sergio and Guido in the kitchen, wanting her to wait on them. Nothing. She went through to the laundry and found the screen door open and banging against the doorframe in the afternoon breeze. With streams of sweat slinking down her back, she brought her breathing under control and shut the laundry door. Gabby eyed the shed. The door was still up. She hurried to the second bedroom and picked up speed in shorting the money stacks. She then steadied, ensuring everything was back in place before shutting the safe and replacing the wood and lino.

She'd taken ten thousand dollars of Sergio's money. She felt it was only fair. It was the amount she'd brought into the marriage yet had never seen a cent of it. So, she was returning the favour, but only for the money he'd stolen. She could never recover the countless other valuable things he'd ripped away from her.

She hid some of the notes by taking a razor blade to her sanitary pads and slipping them inside. Most notes she hid by replacing the entire pad altogether with the bulk of the fifties folded to about the pad's size. She repackaged these in the outer wrapping, making them look like a standard pad. She knew it was safe because there was no way Sergio would go near her feminine products.

Two hours later, Guido came in with Sergio to have an afternoon drink and a smoke. She did as she was trained and put out a plate of olives, cheese, salami, bread and oil. Then she made herself scarce as directed.

Smiling to herself, she folded the morning's washing and put it away. After that, she gathered up some of her clothes and underwear and threw them in a black trash bag along with three full packs of sanitary pads.

While grabbing the rubbish bag from the bin in the kitchen, Sergio slapped her arse. He winked at his brother. 'Knows what to do now. Getting back on the bike soon, too.'

Her teeth crawled as she smiled. The sickness in her stomach levelled out as she walked through the carport to the rubbish bin. She deposited a bag in it.

The next morning she was more jittery than the fleas on Guido's mangy dog as she tidied up the kitchen. She relaxed a little when it came to nine a.m. and Francesca hadn't shown up to surprise Gabby with her company on her trip to town. Instead, she watched her mother-in-law walk the short distance to Ida's house further down the road. Gabby had until lunchtime as usual.

Before sliding into the car, she called Camo-man on the landline and told him he was on. She'd meet him in the car park at the back of the shopping centre at eleven-thirty. She told him not to be late as this was the only time she was allowed out of Sergio's sight. His eagerness about what he intended to do to her was evident as she listened to his schoolboy boasting about his sexual prowess. It made her feel like a layer of crawling grime coated her skin.

With no regrets, she raised a middle finger at the house and drove off, trying not to speed along the dirt road that wound its way through the farm. Everything had to appear normal. Once she turned onto the main road, leaving the farm behind, she gunned the engine and sped towards town.

Driving into the deserted car park, she picked a spot at the far end. She grabbed the rubbish bag with her things in it and locked the car with the keys inside. Wrapped around them was a note for Sergio. It would take him some time to open the vehicle to find the note.

He'd go for Camo-man first and spend time on him. He was more of a threat, given his job and knowledge. He had also inflicted a more insulting betrayal by making advances towards Gabby. He'd want to make sure he brought Camo-man to heel to keep him silent. Plus, the Mancuso brothers would believe she would be easier to track, given their opinion of women. That would bite them.

On the note wrapped around the keys, Gabby had written that she was leaving Sergio. She would contact him from a safe place through a lawyer about a divorce. He would give her one because she didn't want anything from him except her freedom. If he argued or tried to make it difficult, she would go to the police about his drug operation. She signed off the note—*Hell just froze over.*

Once her car door slammed shut, she took a shaky breath. Only then did she notice a vehicle mostly obscured from the car park by bush, the person inside watching, waiting. Gabby ran to the fence at the edge of the parking area, then into the shade and cover provided by those trees and bushes.

By the time the car's engine started, with Sally's help, Gabby had changed into different clothes, a blonde wig and dark sunglasses. She had confirmed with Sally and her network that the plan could go ahead, even knowing Francesca would hear the call. The confirmation was from the drug list order and the first letters of each item. Antibiotic lozenges, lotion, gauze and ointment—Sally knew that Gabby was *ALL GO*.

No one saw anything out of the ordinary as the young nurse from the clinic drove her partner, Trina, who had the day off work, towards Mareeba. There wasn't anything different about hearing loud music blasting from the car as the two sped up and away from the small town's sixty-kilometre speed limit zone. What was different if they cared to listen closely was the song thumping out happened to be The Chicks' 'Goodbye Earl.' Not the usual music the two young women listened to.

In the car, Gabby felt the stress blow off her shoulders. They'd cleared the town limits without drawing any attention. All too soon, they were singing-shouting their own words to the song, 'Serg's time to cry!' A still young but much wiser Gabby couldn't hide the outrageous smile and euphoric relief that flooded her. It only intensified with every mile that passed, because the town and beyond that, Sergio's farm, her prison, shrunk in the rear-view mirror.

As they eased into a parking spot at the back of a women's shelter, Sally gave Gabby a large brown envelope. 'Here, you'll need this for your divorce lawyer. It's the medical records of your injuries. You'll be pleasantly surprised that Dr Orsetti signed off on them. Turns out he has ethics, after all. "Harvester accident, my arse," he said when he saw the X-ray of your arm. I think while he was disturbed by the whole incident, it was that Sergio had caused you to lose your baby that incensed him the most.' The two women hugged. Gabby would never forget the kindness, inspiration and care that Sally and Trina had shown her.

While at the shelter the women gave her a quick makeover. Her mousy-brown hair was dyed to a rich copper red. Then her long strands were styled into a sleek bob. They gave Gabby an emerald-green shift dress and a stylish pair of matching heels from their second-hand charity clothing store. An entirely different outfit from the rags she'd been wearing around town. They even gave her some basic make-up and a backpack for her few personal belongings. A black garbage bag would draw too much attention. They didn't know if Sergio's threat about the family 'having people everywhere' was real or not. She left them with a donation of five hundred dollars. All this was done in under two hours, before noon. The deadline before hell broke loose on the farm.

From the shelter, one of the women drove Gabby to Cairns, where she flew to Brisbane. When the plane was wheels up, she took a cleansing breath as a free woman. She was forever glad she wouldn't witness Sergio finding her note in the car. She didn't feel sorry for any of them. They'd filled her with fear and hadn't shown her anything but hate. It was time they lived in her world, even if only for a bit.

* * *

The only thing that stays the same is change.

In Brisbane, Gabby stayed at a safe house where she spoke on the phone for the first time to her saviour, a lawyer whom she knew only as Five. They never met. The inspirational Five explained that it was to keep them both safe. They spoke on the phone, and different people delivered documents for Gabby to sign.

Even with proof of Sergio's brutality, Gabby was dismayed to find that Queensland law required her to wait a year for her divorce to come through. She had to hide while trying to live. It would have been devasting if not for Five.

She did call her mum, and they arranged to meet, but only after agreeing to take a roundabout way to meet up. They took buses and trains in different directions before they finally met in a small café in a town south of Brisbane. They spent a beautiful day getting reacquainted. They ate, cried and talked their way around picturesque

Mount Tamborine. Most of all, there were smiles, lots of broad, relieved smiles.

With her mum by her side, Gabby found a part of her real self began to ignite and fire her soul. The strength that had been in exile returned to rise to the surface. She jettisoned some of enslaved Gabby and the piece of second-rate jewellery that represented that imprisonment. When her wedding ring sank into the murky water and slid without resisting down a roadside drain, it succinctly symbolised everything. Ownership, filthy degradation and helplessness all washed away. She would never want for marriage again. It held no sentiments of love or security for her.

Of course, Gabby was lighter for her emancipation. Her face showed it, didn't it? She certainly smiled a little more. Yet, she hadn't regained any of the weight she'd lost while living with Sergio. She couldn't regain a healthy weight when there was still the stress of hiding from him. Unfortunately, she still carried the psychological heaviness of being married to him.

With support from her lawyer and a therapist, Gabby learned to cope with the chilling reality that Sergio could walk through whichever door she was cowering behind and kill her. He—or whoever he enlisted—would do it like they were swatting a fly, especially if it stopped her from talking about the family's real business. Nonetheless, she grew bolder each day, finding the nightmares and panic attacks lessening.

Her brittle bravery lasted until one cold afternoon when she sat at a small street-side coffee shop in Brisbane. She stretched out, enjoying the surprise of the sun arriving on a wintery day. She took off her oversized sunglasses and closed her eyes. Without realising it, she relaxed for those few minutes, the gentle sun warming her face.

Later she'd chastise herself. It wasn't relaxing. It was complacency. Because it wasn't only in that split second that she'd failed to hide. It was a mistake that had taken months for her to slip into. Her hair had returned to its natural colour, and she wasn't wearing dowdy clothes or a hat as a disguise. She'd stepped out as free

Gabby, leaving the fearful one behind. All it took was for a Mediterranean-looking guy to ask, 'It's Gabby, isn't it?' and her face plummeted like her stomach, which had fallen into a pool of churning nerves.

'No,' she said. 'I-I don't know who that is.'

He leaned over her. 'Sure you do. You're Sergio Mancuso's missus.'

'Who? I don't know who that is. Should I know you?'

'No, but you will. I've been looking for you.' He gave a cocky, greasy smile of a man who saw women as commodities, a way to scratch an itch or earn his next meal ticket.

She made her jelly legs stand and walk, trying to think as he kept dogging her. 'Come on. It's you. I know it is.' With a growing chill tracking up her backbone, she saw a slow-moving black van pull to the kerb ahead of her. Then he grabbed for her.

She pushed him away, heading back into the coffee shop, but he latched on to her. She felt her jacket rip away as she ran and shouted, 'Help, help me, this guy's trying to hurt me. Help!'

People started noticing, standing to leave their quiet cups of coffee, running to her while yelling at the guy to move away. A woman with a mobile phone screamed, 'I've called the police!' The bulky guy jumped into the van, which sped off.

The police arrived. Gabby called Five and didn't go back to her apartment. She left Brisbane that night.

Five helped Gabby stay alive for the next ten months by moving her every two or three months. It stopped Sergio or his extended family, his informants or whatever rats he had unearthed, from finding her. For those months, it was like Sergio was torturing her all over again. It grew a new kind of courage within her.

The day finally came when her divorce was finalised. She met Five in person for the first time and discovered why she was called Five. It was because she was the fifth lawyer to join the secret organisation. Gabby learned that Sergio was to be imprisoned for assault. His punishment was four years. It was not for what he did to Gabby, because she wouldn't testify against him. It was for what he had done to Camo-man. The pressure on her eased a little.

Camo-man was more valuable to the police. In exchange for his protection, Gabby learned he was negotiating with the police about testifying against Sergio and his family over their drug operation. Nonetheless, it would take years to bring them to justice. Gabby didn't want any part of the negotiations. She just wanted to escape all of it.

Death threats were made to both Camo-man and Gabby's lives. He immediately went into hiding, prompting Gabby's no-nonsense lawyer to recommend she change her name from Gabby Mancuso to Ella Saunders. It was an adaption of her grandmother's maiden name and a version of her first name. Five also suggested Gabby move from Queensland to reduce the likelihood of being harassed.

Ella began to plan for a future, one where she was her own woman. A woman who knew her worth and strength and this time around would keep her dreams alive. She reconnected with Carol, her old editor, who still published travel guides and a worldwide syndicated e-travel magazine. She was more than happy to take content from Gabby, now Ella. It was a start. No rear-view mirror views for Gabby any longer. Everything Ella needed was in front of her.

three

IN THE YEARS since Chad Merritt's actions saw him ceremoniously fired, Saoirse's fortitude grew as she watched and learned from Daniella. She believed she was becoming more adept at handling whatever the future held. This confidence saw her ignore Daniella's advice to enrol in a self-defence course. After all, Chad was only one sour grape out of a large, sweet bunch. He was not going to spoil Australia for her.

Since that fateful morning when she'd collected Daniella's daughters from school, Saoirse had become an official member of the small Malone family and an unofficial surrogate aunt to Daniella's two dear girls. Hannah was coming up to her twelfth birthday and Taylor her tenth. The girls were clever and determined, sweeping Saoirse up in their fun and mischievousness whenever she was around them.

They shared Daniella's lovely latte-coloured skin, dark hair and those powerful, sparkly black-diamond eyes. In the last three years, Saoirse had learned more than she realised about raising young girls —a skill she'd need to rely on sooner rather than later in her life.

* * *

The Australian way of life came easy to Saoirse as she travelled around its wonderous, wide-open spaces whenever she could. While snorkelling and scuba diving the Great Barrier Reef, she based herself at a Cairns backpackers. She realised that she'd become a little more comfortable surrounded by the weird Australian fauna while living in the tropics.

The green frogs weren't so bad, even when they appeared in her toilet bowl. But she drew the line at the horrible cane toads. She'd almost become used to spiders, although the large huntsmen still gave her the creeps. She discovered a huge one camped out in the corner of the laundry when she was searching for some lost under-wear. Her skin shivered over itself when the furry brown spider, the size of her hand, casually shuffled closer on its long, spindly legs. That's when she decided she was trespassing on its territory and the underwear was lost to a washing mix-up or pilfering that sometimes happened when travelling.

In the north, she saw her first saltwater crocodile, a huge 'salty' called Chucky. Saoirse was grateful he lived behind the thick wire of a massive cage. All these encounters she relayed to her parents. She didn't mention the snakes, which Queensland had its fair share of, both dangerous and harmless. She would've been happy to live out her time in Australia without any firsthand snake experiences. That changed one fateful night at the backpacker hostel.

In the room she shared with four others, a large king brown, one of the country's deadliest snakes, was found under her bed. It freaked out all the women. The manager of the hostel reassured them it was a one-off occurrence. He was at a loss as to how the snake could have got into the room. Harmless carpet snakes or pythons were known to come into houses but not generally king browns.

When Saoirse found her much-loved Cranberries T-shirt covered in kitchen grease in the laundry, nerves flickered edgily around her belly like the evil-looking king brown's forked tongue. She decided that when she returned from her tour of the Atherton Tablelands, she'd hang the expense and find a reasonably priced hotel room.

She hadn't set out to meet anyone. Then a guide on the Tableland's tour offered to take her four-wheel driving. Apparently, it was the only way to see more of Tropical Far North Queensland, so she jumped at the opportunity.

Damian Costa, Damo to his friends, had a stocky frame and tough, gnarly skin, like rough-cut ironbark. His brown hair matted around large, rum-coloured eyes sitting back in a heavy-set face. While not classically handsome, he had many more worthwhile qualities. Top of Saoirse's list was that he was very respectful of women, with eyes that made her feel safe.

They visited stunning waterfalls, majestic curtain fig trees and deep, cool natural swimming holes. At one pool the locals called Fairy Dell, Damo encouraged her to climb up a high rock face. Once there, he handed her a rope, and with a scream of scared delight, she swung out over the pool, Tarzan-like, to plunge into its emerald depths. It was the essence of freedom.

As she broke through the surface of the pristine water to take a cleansing breath, Saoirse looked upwards at where the rope was attached. She wondered who had been brave or stupid enough to tie it to the soaring tree's branches, which arched over the pool like the buttresses of some impressive Gothic cathedral. The foliage they supported formed the thick, jade-coloured rainforest canopy.

She climbed the rocks once more, sucking in a breath of pure, perfumed rainforest air. She held it until her lungs hummed. This time when she swung out she released her breath in a glorious shout. 'I'm free!'

Damo laughed when she resurfaced. 'It fits. Of course, my lovely Irish warrioress should be free. Isn't that the Celtic meaning of your name, freedom?'

Saoirse's smile was so effortless it spilled across her face, like the water flowing off her body as she emerged from the pool. Their eyes met, hers mischievous, his intrigued. 'My. So charming and well-read.' She heard his sharp inhalation as she rose on her toes to kiss his throat and nip his earlobe, equally surprised by her boldness.

Driving further north to the Daintree, they had no particular plans. She lost track of time and gave in to the beauty of the wilderness. She often didn't know where he was taking her. There was no alarm. He had this quality that had her trusting him. Each time they went down a local bush track or narrow trail, it would lead to a rare or untouched natural treasure.

Travelling day after day with the top down meant the sun kissed her hair, leaving amber highlights streaked through her dark locks. Saoirse felt like she was in heaven as the sun gifted her skin a healthy, golden-honey glow. Everything was so bright and vivid. She hadn't even realised that the sky could be such a clear, bright blue.

She'd felt it brewing for days. The swirling, intensifying emotions needed release, as sure as the circling storm that had been threatening all day was Mother Nature's way of finding relief. Damo's dependable eyes locked on hers. She wanted to lose herself in the bottomless depths of them like she had in the beauty of their tropical odyssey. Her eyes shimmered silver like the lightning. This time there was no mischievous nip to an earlobe. This time, her lips covered his, all velvet rough. The charge that filled the air surrounding them was driven by a different storm from the one stirring the rainforest.

This storm would not be soothed by the dance of lips and tongues or by the frantic sweep of hands over skin and muscle. They both knew it was a holiday fling, but that didn't make it any less exquisite.

With the scent of coming rain haunting the rainforest and encircling their tent, Damo caressed her clothes from her willing body to lay her bare. Saoirse trailed her lips over his chest as she unbuttoned his shirt and pushed his jeans aside. He watched her every move with reverence as she captured him in her hands. He groaned his thanks as she stroked him to harden. Wants became needs. Lust curled around them and opened them to each other.

Saoirse knew she possessed him the moment he drove slowly into her and held himself there. With bodies fused, their heartbeats blurred and then combined to drum out a rhythm in time with the tumbling rain. As the storm deepened, the thunder, lightning and rain came harder, as did the sound of flesh smacking together. Intense need cradled, crushed and then consumed. Their rainforest haven bore witness to the splendour of the couple's lust, his desire, and her joy. Amid a booming crash of thunder, they screamed their climax.

Forevermore, thunder, lightning, mugginess and the smell of rain would arouse Saoirse. Other than the memory of the great sex, maybe it was because the dark clouds and unsettled skies reminded her of the dark spaces within her that she enjoyed reaching with ecstasy-filled deeds.

Meandering down the coast, they remerged into civilisation when they stayed overnight at a Kuranda backpackers. The Cairns backpackers operator owned both places and wanted to make it up to Saoirse for the snake incident, so let them stay the night for free. In the morning, they headed out. Halfway down the Kuranda range, the old four-wheel-drive coughed to a standstill in a cloud of choking grey smoke. A car trailing close behind them sped past, even though their vehicle was clearly in trouble. 'Must be a tourist,' Damo said. 'A local would have stopped.'

Damo proved himself a man for all seasons. Nothing rattled him. Through a process of elimination, he worked out the fuel line was blocked. 'That's odd, bugger if it doesn't look like sand in the fuel. No worries, I'll call a mate to help us.' Saoirse would be safely delivered back to Cairns in plenty of time to catch her flight to Brisbane.

Before she slid from the car at the airport, he combed his fingers through her hair, looking deep into her silver-grey eyes. His soft yet rugged lips found hers. She was still tingling from the beautiful goodbye kiss miles after he'd left her. They parted as good friends, her first and only holiday fling.

* * *

Over the years, Daniella and her daughters had become Saoirse's solid base. Because of them, every time Saoirse returned from her adventures it became easier to slip back into Brisbane life and work. The mother of two showed Saoirse what life could offer a girl from a small town in Ireland as she ran towards the woman she wanted to become.

Nonetheless, Brisbane wasn't the place Saoirse would call home or find love. Without Daniella's support, Saoirse may have given up on love altogether. The older woman kept her believing. Still, each time the men left, Saoirse toughened up a little more. After four years, she hadn't found a love to call hers. Daniella suggested it might be time for Saoirse to cast her eyes towards the next peak on her journey. It was the only way she would become the fully realised Saoirse Mahoney.

As if on cue, an email came from Sean, the youngest of her older brothers. He needed her help with his new business. Then he called, pestering her like he always had. 'Come on. You're there. And I'll be coming over soon. I need you.'

'Really? You're clutching at straws, Sean. I know nothing about pubs and renovations.'

'You know how to organise things, manage people and make sure things get done. Well, that's what Daniella tells me.'

'You've spoken to Daniella? She said nothing to me.'

'She suggested you might need a new challenge. I needed to find out what you were like at your job. I already know you're a good younger sister, if a little too motherly. Daniella said she'd be sad to lose you but that it was time.'

'Oh, I see.' Silence crackled through the air.

'I'll offer you more money and a new adventure.'

Maybe Daniella was right. Perhaps she did need to focus on a new peak to keep climbing towards that more worldly woman. And it seemed inevitable that this was her destiny. 'You couldn't think of anything more original than managing and franchising Irish pubs even if you have an innovative computerised darts system as the main attraction?'

There was a smiling pride in his voice. 'The McDonald's of Irish darts pubs. Do you want authenticity with that? Well, we've got it. What more could you want?' With a tone more serious than pleading, he said, 'I need to have someone on the ground to get the ball rolling. From what Ma tells me, you've learned quite a deal about Australia. Please say yes?'

'I don't think you realise how big Australia is. It's not like Ireland. Sydney isn't somewhere I can train to each day from Brisbane.'

'I can pay for your relocation, anything you need.'

Saoirse and Daniella had been through a lot in their four years together. Daniella's eyes swam with tears as she embraced a now twenty-two-year-old Saoirse. 'When we meet again, and we will, we'll both have found love.'

'Promise.' Tears tumbled down Saoirse's cheeks.

'That's a promise on both.' Daniella hugged Saoirse as she sagged into her. The now-blossoming Irish woman set off to Sydney, a city still buzzing four years after hosting the Olympics.

* * *

Sydney 2004

In the years Saoirse had been in Australia, Sean's life had been sent to hell. Now he was crawling out from under the weight of monetary and relationship debts.

At first, the siblings shared a small apartment in the Sydney suburb of Randwick. It was close to where Saoirse had set up an office for Xanthe's Plan Incorporated, Sean's company. There was much to be done in the early days. Sean's overseas business success funded expanding his empire into Australia. He and Saoirse set about organising renovations and the electronic refurbishing required to fit the darts systems, and then there were the franchise agreements for the pubs they'd bought.

Used to their close family ties, the Mahoney siblings found that they'd pulled and stretched those connections in different ways in their time apart. Each had changed enough to find working and existing in family-home-like conditions once more, not conducive to smooth living. Needing their own space saw Sean move to a swish newly renovated apartment over one of his pubs.

There wasn't much time for socialising as they both worked long hours to launch the business and then had to keep it running efficiently. After some months, many worksites were underway around the city. Sean's time was being spread too thin. 'I need you to oversee some of the renovations while I fly back to head office in London.'

'What? No! Backroom girl, remember, seeing the right paperwork is signed to keep it all running and paying the bills on time. I can't go on site. I don't know the first thing—'

'I need to make these few meetings to press the flesh face to face. I'm relying on you to keep things running. I've got a guy to help you out, but I trust you more. Family. Saoirse, you can't beat it. And besides, you're a natural.'

She believed him on the first sentiment, but not the second, which led her to study up. Even though she was armed with facts and all sorts of figures, the architect's plans began blurring together in her mind. However, she set out with a rudimentary understanding of the work required.

On the first day, Saoirse found herself already late, especially if she intended to complete her day's appointments and report back to Sean via video conference at the end of the day. She rushed through the construction chaos at the first site. The clip-clop of her heels on the bare concrete was drowned out by laughter, the hammering of wood, cursing, the whine of a bandsaw and then the harsh clunk and clatter of wood falling to the floor. All the while, the odours of renovation filled the air. The earthy smell of sawdust and the dank tartness of freshly poured concrete hit her.

She hurried down a hallway, looking for the project manager, the one Sean had said was her go-to guy. She rounded a corner and ran into a brick wall in the shape of a hunk of a guy. Saoirse scrambled, limbs flailing as she tried not to fall over her heels onto her arse. The air froze in her chest as she felt his big mitts skim across her belly and cage her waist. 'Hold on. What's your hurry,' boomed a voice like a roll of thunder.

Bowing her head, Saoirse spoke to his feet. 'Sorry, I didn't mean to, um ... ah ...' Swallowing hard, she raised herself up, trying to recapture her pride, which, unlike her, had fallen on its butt. 'I'm looking for Will Sewell,' she blurted as she slapped his hands away to straighten her trim grey dress.

'You've found him.' His eyes were travelling up her body like vapour from a kettle, hot and steamy. 'Besides wearing silly shoes around a worksite, who might you be?'

Whipping her head up to glare at him, she said, 'Why don't you watch where you're going? Anyway, my shoes are fine, thank you very much.'

'Sure they are.' He pushed his hard hat up from his forehead, his blue eyes laughing down at her. 'Been round a lot of worksites, have you?'

She tapped one of her black stilettos on the concrete floor like a frantic typist. 'No, but I'm not working here, am I? I'm visiting to check on things.' Her jaw set and her spine stiffened.

He hitched up his tool belt over one of his narrow hips. 'Irish, fiery manner, long dark-brown hair and silver-grey eyes—you must be the big boss's little sister. He said you'd be coming around to oversee the work.' One of his large hands came to rest on a claw hammer hanging off his belt. He stretched out his other arm and leaned it up on the doorjamb. Intentionally or not, he was blocking Saoirse's way.

She gritted her teeth, finding his whole manner annoying. 'Yes, that would be me. *The little sister*. Now I'm on a bit of a tight sched-ule, so can you take me to the fireplace first?'

'Hold your horses, would ya? You need a hard hat to be in here. There are guys still up in the ceiling, fixing the roof. You need to go back out front to Vince, the big-arse Italian who's tiling the front entry. He'll fix you up.'

'You're kidding.'

His eyes were on another slow trek up her body. 'No, I don't kid about stuff that could put a good-looking woman such as yourself in danger.' Shaking his head slowly from side to side, he added, 'Plus, if a building inspector comes through from the council, he could shut us down if he sees you parading around without all the equipment. Although, you do have rather nice equipment all of your own.'

'I beg your pardon!'

'You heard me. Now run along, little sister, and get a hat from Vince. I'll wait right here for you.'

Raising her voice and her body, she got in his face. 'Listen, sonny Jim, that's enough of your male chauvinistic bullshite.'

Shrugging his shoulders then holding up his hands, he said, 'Just telling it like it is.'

She felt confused. She wanted to be angry, but her temper cooled as he started making sense.

'I figure we can stand here arguing over silly things while your tight schedule gets tighter, or you can go get the hard hat, and we can start to go over the plans for the fireplace in the front bar.' He chuckled. 'And my name's Will, not sonny Jim.'

Trying not to seem like a petulant child, Saoirse turned and stomped down the hall to find Vince. Feeling the heat of Will's eyes scorching her body's every move as she swayed away had her regain some control. After grabbing a hard hat, she met up with Mr Smartarse and they managed to sort out what was needed for the fireplace and front bar fittings.

With the sun setting, Saoirse rushed to open the office just before the video conference with Sean. She'd been running all day, but as she reached the door, she saw red mist—and not from the red of the sunset. She demanded, 'What are you doing here?'

'Hello to you, too, little sister. Sean asked me to sit in on the call. So don't get your knickers in a twist.'

Saoirse fought not to gnash her teeth, fuming at what she saw as Sean's lack of faith, and felt even more peeved that he'd chosen to show it through inviting this knuckle-dragging Neanderthal to join them. Mmm, so much for *you're a natural, sis.* She gave Will a tight smile as she opened the office door. He took a chair as she set up.

During the conference, her ire cooled as Sean explained that Will was there to relay specific information on one of the pub's foundations that needed strengthening. They finished up with Sean pleased with the pairs' work. Everything was on track.

Silence was their best friend as Saoirse locked up, although Will waited for her. 'How are you getting home?'

On guard, she replied, 'I don't have far to go, and my car's just ...' Her words stalled as she saw her car had a flat back tyre. 'Shite, how the hell?'

'Looks like you need a hand.'

'I'm quite capable of changing a tyre, thanks.'

'Look, how about you and I get something straight? I'll apologise for being a bit of a dick this morning, if you apologise for being one as well, with the whole, *I'm too busy and important for a hard hat.*'

'I never said ...' It was then she saw a sincere smile spread across his face. 'Alright, yes. Sorry, okay.'

'Accepted. I'm sorry too. Now, I'm sure you can change a flat, but I'm here. What kind of bastard would I be if I didn't help you out?'

'That would be nice, thanks.' She moved to the hatchback's boot to get the spare. 'What the fuck!'

At hearing her, Will took a better look at her car. Even in the dull light, he saw it. 'Jesus, someone's done a number on your car.'

They both walked around to see she had three slashed tyres. When Will hunkered down to run his finger along the jagged rubber, she noticed how long-limbed and toned he was.

Later she'd reminisce about how when he stood, a perfect vee formed from his broad shoulders to where his navy blue work shirt tucked into the narrow waist of his dusty jeans, which he filled out equally as well. For now, she was struggling to get a hold on what had happened.

'Do you have insurance?'

'Yes.'

'Okay, but you'll need to get a tow truck to move it.'

'You'd be right.'

'How about I call a friend of mine? He's a mechanic with his own garage and he's got a truck. He can winch your car onto his truck and take it to his garage tonight, lock it up, keep it safe. I'll get you home from there. Tomorrow he can sort you with a new set of tyres at mates' rates.' His lips curled. 'You'll be back busting my balls on site before you know it.'

Saoirse gave him a small smile and dropped her head, only to feel his surprisingly gentle fingers take her chin and lift it so she'd look at him. 'It'll be okay. It's just some arsehole-good-for-nothing who has nothing better to do. You're safe. It's only time lost.'

A broader smile graced her lips as she laced her fingers through his, moving his hand cautiously away from her chin. 'You're right. It's just ...' She steadied. 'Um, yep, time and money, that's all it is.' She couldn't burden him with the feelings that tore through her. The same ones that had plagued her when her car was smeared with dog crap in Brisbane.

When she resurfaced from her troubled thoughts, he was speaking. 'How about before I take you home, we have a schooner to settle the nerves, and I bet you haven't eaten all day.'

How did he know that?

'Everything is better after a chicken parmie and chips. I just happen to know a great pub not that far from my friend's garage. It serves really good ones.'

She nodded yes, even though she had no idea what the hell a schooner and a chicken parmie were. He tugged her towards what she assumed was his work ute, and before she could think better of it, they were laughing over a cold glass of beer while scoffing down the best chicken parmie she'd ever tasted—local jargon she hadn't picked up in Brisbane.

The next day she collected her car with its fresh tyres from Mick, Will's mechanic friend. She felt on top of things again, complimenting herself on her recovery and silently thanking God for Will being there.

As work continued over the days, she started enjoying visiting the sites as the guys came to know and respect her. Late Friday afternoon of the second week, her final stop was the pub having the most done to it. The one where Will was spending the majority of his time.

'Hi, little sister. It's a bit late for you. Most of the guys have gone for the day.' With a dry chuckle in his voice, he said, 'Is there something you need to break my balls over?'

She found herself smiling before she turned to face him. 'Not yet, but I haven't started looking.'

Will had a toothy grin plastered over his face as he walked towards her, hands behind his back.

She pointed. 'You know, every time my brothers walked towards me hiding something behind their back with a smarmy, goofy look like that, it usually meant a frog, pond scum, or God knows what was going to get flung at me.'

He moved his arms forward and she braced, then burst out laughing. He held a pink hard hat with her name on it in red and a border of black stiletto shoes painted around its edge. 'You can take it with you from site to site. No need to borrow Vince's anymore.'

She could feel her cheeks heating and had to look at his feet as she took the hat. 'Thanks.'

He tilted her face up to his. The callouses on his fingers sent a tingle over her skin as they wrapped around her chin. 'My pleasure. You do that a lot.'

'What?'

'Go all shy and look at your feet.' Leaning in, he whispered close to her ear, 'But your secret's safe with me.'

Her lungs filled with the smell of sawdust and his spicy cologne.

'Huh.' Her mind seemed to short-circuit. It often crashed around Will Sewell. He was the first male she could not think straight around, which was why she looked at his feet as she tried to reboot.

She regained control. 'Oh, with three older brothers, I didn't have a chance to be shy around guys.' Looking around, she saw they were alone and reached up with her free hand to drive her fingers through his hair. Wrapping them around his neck, Saoirse tugged, then crushed his lips to hers, commanding his submission. She murmured, 'Just to prove you wrong.' She tapped her hand on his unyielding chest as she began to push him away. 'Not shy.'

He wanted more and pulled her against him. Wrapped in another hard-rugged kiss, the glowing attraction that had been steadily growing stronger exploded into a starburst of blinding white light as they touched and tantalised each other. Then, a loud bang had them jerking apart. They stared at each other, dazzled, like deer caught in a powerful light, chests heaving. Trying to settle, she said, 'I guess my newly minted hard hat has passed its first test.'

On weakened legs, she scrambled to pick up the hat off the floor. Will struggled to suck in enough air to clear his throat. 'Um, I guess you should come and look at the front bar. The new ironbark bar top is in.'

When they'd finished going through everything, it was dark outside. 'How about a schooner and a chicken parmie?'

'Are you trying to sound like an Aussie, little sis?'

'Yes, did I pass the test?'

'No.' Her face fell, and he laughed. 'It's Friday night, little sis, it's fish-and-chips night, but you got the schooner right.'

While enjoying their meal, Saoirse tried to stave off the intense emotions sparking and zinging between them. She told him about her family and Brisbane. Will spoke about his dream of owning his own renovation company, something he said he'd never told anyone about. Sharing dreams and histories had them lean in a little closer, eyes lingering a little longer and voices pitching a little lower. The light-hearted flirting became heavier than she cared to acknowledge.

The night was coming to a crossroads, and she needed to catch her breath. 'Why do you call me little sister? You do know my name's Saoirse, right?'

'Yes, but you've never introduced yourself properly to me. Not even that first day when you were all little Miss Huffy-puffy. Out of you two Mahoneys, Sean's the only one who told me your name.'

'Oh.'

'You don't like the nickname?'

'It makes me feel like you think you're one of my brothers.' His longing look made her belly clench. She became overwhelmed with need, giving her words a smoky lilt. 'I think we'd both prefer that not to be the case.'

Her tone had his eyes heat as she offered him her hand. 'Will Sewell, I'm Saoirse Mahoney, pleased to meet you.'

He drained his glass, and with a reckless smile, said, 'Saoirse Mahoney, I'm *very* pleased to meet you. I'm even more pleased we cleared that up.' He took her hand and shook it. Instead of letting her move away, he pulled her to him smoothly and took her lips, then murmured, 'Your place?'

A hot, burst of blinding light ignited the dark places in Saoirse where she wanted him to take her. 'Yes.'

He followed her in his ute to her place. They met at the door to find it unlocked and a light on inside. 'Did you leave—?'

'No! Of course not.' Her spine gripped like a bandsaw was cutting up it.

Will pushed her behind him and walked through the door, body coiled, ready for whatever. When they reached the living area, they heard the pitter-patter of her shower. The light from the second bedroom spilled out down the hallway. As they edged closer, the shower stopped. After a few heartbeats, Sean walked out, towel around his waist. He jumped almost as much as they did. 'Shit, you gave me a fright.' Then he frowned. 'What the hell, Saoirse?'

'Sean! I thought you weren't due until next week?'

'I was, but things finished earlier, so I moved my flight up.' He looked between Will and Saoirse. 'What are you two doing here?'

She glared back at him. 'I live here!' Sean's eyes drifted to Will as she added, 'And Will, um ... he was just seeing me home.'

'Yeah, man, your sister's car tyres were slashed a couple of weeks back. I was making sure she got home safe and sound.' Saoirse was relieved that Will had thought quickly on his feet and was convincing enough to have Sean settle down.

'Oh, thanks.' Her brother shook his head. 'Hang on, what happened to your car?'

'It doesn't matter. It was just some idiot.'

'Seems my work here is done. I'll see both of you next week.'

Awkwardness filled the room, so she offered, 'Stay for a coffee.'

'Yeah, it's the least I can do to thank you for looking after my little sister.'

'Ah, I really should go, leave you two to catch up.'

With three purposeful strides, Will was out the door. Saoirse ran after him, catching him as he was unlocking his ute. 'Hey, don't run off. Sean's got a key. I guess he felt like some company and didn't want to go to his place. I'm all he's got here.'

'It's alright. I don't mind.'

'But what if I mind and want to thank you some more?' She surprised herself when she stretched up on tiptoes to place her lips over his, kissing him into a place where she felt him struggling to breathe.

'I'll take that thank you and raise it.' His hands rode her curves to her arse, pushing her into him, his mouth ravishing hers. When they broke apart, she was still humming.

Will rasped, 'Would you like to do something on Sunday?'

'Maybe, I'll let you know.'

He just smiled, having none of her hard-to-get act. 'I'll see you then. Shall we say lunch? I'll pick you up from here, midday.' Then he took her in his arms and gave her another smoking-hot kiss.

When she floated back into her apartment, Sean was dressed and had his feet on her coffee table, watching TV. 'Things seemed to have moved on quite a deal since I've been away.'

'Yeah, most of the renovations and refits are on track.'

'Aha.' Nodding then pinning her with hard eyes, he said, 'Come off the grass. We both know I wasn't talking work.'

'About that, um, me and Will.'

'He's one of the best project managers and tradesmen we have. I can't have you screw that up by screwing him.'

'Steady on, who said anything about screwing him? We went out to dinner ...'

'If you haven't screwed him yet, you're going to, and that could mess with my plans.'

She snapped, 'I'm not you! I don't screw someone and then fuck up their life.'

Like a too-sharp razor blade, Saoirse's cutting words caused Sean to wince. 'Point taken. Yeah, I stuffed up with Xanthe and lost the love of my life and nearly everything else. I just don't want to see you get hurt like that.'

She felt her stomach lurch. 'Sorry, Sean, that was below the belt. I guess you struck a nerve.'

'Seems we both did. But I'm going to try to find Xanthe while I'm here in Sydney. You being here, managing everything so well, gives me time to do that. I'm planning on working hard to get her back.'

'Do you even know if she's in the city?'

'No, but her parents are, so I'll use some of the Mahoney charm to see if I can find out where she vanished to. Then I want to make every day about working my way back to her.'

'I don't know about getting her back. You stuffed her around big time and broke her heart. Not to mention breaking yours as well.'

'Don't worry about my heart.' His face softened. 'I think yours is in more danger.'

'I'm a big girl.'

'That you are, but you'll always be my little sister. That means I'm allowed to look out for you, always.' He stood, and with a jet-lagged sigh, hugged her.

She felt him sag in. *There's nothing like family*, she thought. 'Glad you're back.'

* * *

By Sunday, Sean had moved to his place. Saoirse awoke in the morning as unsettled as the weather. She tried to restrain her sultry urges, but then she opened her door to Will's knock and desire hurricaned around them. There he stood, all freshly shaven, messy blonde hair, black T-shirt hugging him like skin. As her tongue stuck to the roof of her mouth, her eyes tracked further south to where his jeans were slung just right on his svelte hips.

He simply smiled, blue eyes igniting silvery-grey. Unable to resist, he reached out and took a strand of her dark hair, running it over his fingers. The rising tension of yearning stalled her breath in anticipation. Lightning seared across the grey sky and broke her. They never made it to lunch.

Attraction was usurped by burning need. The sensuality that caressed and urged was like floating on a bluesy saxophone's sexy, sophisticated vibes. Long velvet notes were filled with just the right amount of smoke to draw out and captivate unhurried foreplay. Their music glided and curled with every laid-back touch, rousing sinful desires, entrapping their hearts and firing their souls.

As they wove their way to her bed, he slipped her out of her jeans and shirt. She grasped his T-shirt, and in the flick of an eye, whipped it off. He bent and dragged his tongue over her silken skin to find a nipple, bringing it to a caramel peak as her heartbeat stuttered under his lips. Her breath caught and her insides melted when he sucked her nipple into his mouth. She rubbed her palm along his zipper, feeling him grow harder. When she freed him and pushed his boxers away, his cock bobbed forth like it was paying homage to her.

They fell naked on her bed, enjoying the feel of each other's heated skin. The unrestrainable cravings rose and whipped around them. Saoirse's lips skated over his perfectly butter-smooth skin. He rumbled, 'Jeez, Saoirse, how I've wanted you from that first day.' Her mouth took his before any more words formed. His tongue slid over hers, taking the kiss deeper and deeper, her need stronger and stronger.

Saoirse gripped Will's sandy mop, holding him to her, and when her breast fell from his mouth with a silken pop, she let him move lower to stroke her wetness with his tongue. When he sucked her nib, goosebumps bloomed across her skin while a husky moan left her lips. With her fingers bunching the sheet, her hips automatically arched into him, and she lost herself to lust.

Saoirse may have been revisiting stormy sex initially, but all before was forgotten as she was dazzled by Will's scent, taste, and commanding ways. Reality melted away as he circled a finger into her. When her eyes glazed over, he rolled two fingers into her. Chasing the raw pleasure of the electric throb, Saoirse ground herself into his palm, harder. His loving ways were destroying her. Her whimpers of need and the scent of her sexed-up body, driven to the point of breaking, had Will an enthusiastic prisoner to carnal pleasure.

Finally, he rolled a condom on and pushed into her hot, tight slickness, and every desire intensified. When she coiled around him, surge after surge of charged erotica lay within her grasp. All she had to do was chase, capture and feast.

The hot summer downpour continued to mirror their assault on each other. Their skin misted with sweat, and each lightning strike gave it a silver sheen. They were like two molten veins of silver, flowing, twisting and blending into each other. Violence and beauty melding together in perfect harmony. His body rock hard, manual labour having honed every muscle and sinew. Her body lithe, blossoming femininity refining every wondrous delight. He, with all his gentle strength and she, with all her strong gentleness.

They moved and kissed recklessly. He consumed her cries of ecstasy, releasing his own as they feasted and plundered, closer and closer, higher and higher, faster and faster. Reaching out, Saoirse clutched and finally captured that exquisite erogenous high. They detonated, finishing with an explosive climax that left them spent. The storms within and without had passed.

'My God, Saoirse, you are fucking amazing,' he panted. 'Never been taken like that.'

She couldn't speak, only nod.

He stayed until early evening after they'd found another thunderous high.

The following stormy Monday morning had a buzzing Saoirse arriving early at the office to meet Sean. When he said he still wanted her to visit the worksites, her sigh was both excited and relieved. She would have legitimate reasons to see Will while Sean spent his time overseeing a newly opened pub.

The thundery weather set in for the week and swept into the next. Will and Saoirse spent days looking over the sites, standing too close to each other, enjoying the zing of secret touches and kisses, which led to unabated stormy sex in her bed.

She understood why he never stayed overnight. His place was closer to all the sites, making it easier for him to arrive in time for the very early morning starts. 'Besides, if I wake up next to you, I'll want to have my wicked way with you, and then we'll both be late, and I don't want Sean angry at you because of me. You undo me, Saoirse. You really do.'

The non-frivolous Saoirse agreed with his practical thoughts. He'd admitted sheepishly that his place was very much a single man's dump. He shared it with a smelly flatmate called George Papasomething. Not to mention she preferred sex in her bed or on her table or floor or couch, as sometimes lust and need meant they didn't make it to the bedroom. The current arrangement suited everyone fine, until Sean dropped by unexpectedly on a humid Thursday evening.

Looking at Will and Sean's reactions to each other, Saoirse sensed the weather wasn't the only thing making the room feel sticky. Will moved towards the door as Sean thumped down a six-pack of Crown beers, which looked a little worse for wear. Three containers of what smelled like Indian takeaway were then tossed onto Saoirse's table next to the beer. Angry eyes swept the couple and landed on Saoirse. 'I need to speak to you—alone.'

'It's okay, Sean. I was just leaving.' Will hesitated, looking at Saoirse.

Uncharacteristically, Sean snapped, 'For God's sake, man, I know you've been tapping my sister. I have bigger things to discuss with her. Just kiss her and push off.'

'Sean! That's enough. Just because you're in a shite mood, don't take it out on us.' Saoirse punched Sean's shoulder and scorched him with a look that made both men quake with more than a little trepidation.

Walking Will to his ute, she decided he couldn't leave thinking she was mad with him. Giving him a scorching look of a different kind, she planted a kiss on him, aimed at leaving Will with no choice but to have not-so-sweet, spicy dreams. When Will returned the heat of the kiss, she knew she'd achieved her goal and spun on her heel to stalk back into her apartment to sort out Sean.

The first mouthfuls of curry could have been tasteless for all the enjoyment the two shared. Eyeing him, she sat back and took a swig of beer. 'Well, out with it, then. What's crawled up your arse? If it's about Will and me, I don't want to hear it. Nothing is being missed, all the site builds and renovations are on track, actually better than on track. The office is running, wages and bills are up to date. So just shut the feck up.'

'I've found Xanthe. She's here in Sydney.'

If his goal was to shock her into silence, he'd achieved it—and more. 'I ran into her by chance last Wednesday. It didn't go well. I visited her parents tonight. That didn't go much better.' He ran his hands through his hair before slumping.

'What's happened?'

'She was broken, and not just by me. It was bad. Her parents filled me in.' He took a deep breath before straightening up. 'I'm going to make things better. Make amends and get her back. To do that, I need you to stay focused. I need you to run things for a bit longer while I start another, slightly different renovation.'

She stood, wrapped him up in a warm hug and gave him the solace he needed. She'd always have a bottomless reserve of whatever was necessary for her family, as they'd have for her.

They worked hard over the next three months. It was rewarding seeing Sean's vision coming to fruition. Overwhelming happiness began anchoring within Saoirse. She found herself frequently twisted around Will beneath tangled sheets. Here, they shared whispers about their dreams, which had her believing in him, and Will saying, 'With you beside me, I actually believe my dreams can come true.'

Sean's three months were far more arduous as he worked his way back to Xanthe. Saoirse saw him brightening as if Xanthe held the light he needed to see them both through the darkness.

With Sean's projects close to completion, Saoirse wondered if her time in Sydney was coming to an end. Was Sydney the city where she could set down roots? Was Will Sewell the man to do that with because he was someone to call hers? At times she felt it. Then her serious soul swamped her into nagging doubt. The latter would churn her stomach each time he left her.

Needing answers to quell her doubts, she asked him one evening, 'Why don't you stay tonight? Most of the sites won't need visiting until later tomorrow.'

'Saoirse.' He blew out a deep breath while shoving on his jeans. 'We've been through this.' He rushed to tug on his shirt. 'I just can't, okay.'

'Sean's chill about us. None of the guys know anything. Why not stay?'

'Because I said no!' The bitter edge to his words was something she'd never known in him before. 'Enough with the nagging. Just listen, damn it. No.'

She moved to him, rolling her fingers over his tense shoulders, but he jerked out of her reach, leaving her feeling cold and vulnerable. At hearing a car alarm, he snatched at the blind, forcing the slats to squash together in an unforgiving V. 'Shit!' His movement was so violent that when he pulled back his hand, the slats didn't quite return to a horizontal line. 'What the hell.' He bolted out the door, Saoirse wrapping her bathrobe around her naked body to follow.

The ute's alarm was screeching, jangling and slicing their nerves. It was as if it was alive and screaming in pain because a huge rock had shattered its windscreen.

Will pushed the fob on his keys and the alarm cut. In the shadows of the streetlights, Saoirse wrapped her arms around him to rest her head on his chest. He welcomed her, holding her close. She mumbled, 'Why?' The one question that needed so many different answers from Will.

He ran his hand across her back and pulled her tighter to him. 'No idea.' His voice soft now, he asked, 'Is your car okay?'

Saoirse looked towards where it was parked in front of Will's. 'Its alarm's not going off.' He released her so she could move to the black hatchback. Then she added, 'Not that that means much. It didn't when the tyres were slashed.' She moved closer as something caught her eye.

Tucked under her car's windscreen wiper was an A4 envelope. Those swirling questions found answers printed in large, grainy black-and-white photos. Two were of her and Will embracing and kissing in the street outside her apartment. There were two others. One of Will outside a house waving goodbye to a woman in a bathrobe. Similar to how Saoirse was dressed right now. The last photo was of him kissing the woman. Of all the daggers that were plunging through Saoirse's heart, the one with the sharpest blade was the one that carried a scrawled handwritten note. It screamed in large red capital letters: *HE'S MARRIED, WHORE.*

Saoirse turned and looked at Will, who was watching her. She saw the moment his eyes understood. In that instant, she knew Sydney wouldn't be where she put down roots.

four

SOUL GAZING: SEAN'S STORY

IT WAS A SCHIZOPHRENIC WEDNESDAY. There had been rain and hail, followed by sunny patches. Then it turned bleak once more, and of course, she'd been trapped in a relentless downpour. Slick, icy veins of water meandered down Xanthe Kazan's soggy legs. Her totally impractical-for-work Manolos were ruined. A small ripple of pride stemmed the grinding of her jaw. Truthfully, being able to walk around in them meant more to her than what they'd cost.

For salvation rather than entertainment, she ducked into one of the supposedly authentic Irish Darts pubs that had sprung up all around the city. She usually avoided the stereotypical sameness of such places. Her appraisal of the bar improved as she found it had a raging fire and was unique and cosy despite itself. She flung her large, sopping-wet trench coat onto a rack near a welcoming lounge chair. Defeated, she sank into the chair's soft leather depths, only to spy her sodden shoes again. Her grinding jaw released a decidedly unglamorous, 'Oh, *fuckity* fuck, fuck!'

After a moment's shock, a figure leaned forward from behind the wingback of a lounge chair. A gravelly voice chuckled. 'I thought I recognised that fuckity, fuck, fuck.'

His Irish brogue hadn't lessened with time. Father Time hadn't hit the Irishman nearly hard enough with his stick, club, or whatever it was the old guy used to ring in the years. Infuriatingly, Sean seemed even more handsome. His ebony curls were hotter with a sprinkling of grey. His square jaw and salt-and-pepper stubble wrinkled in all the right places when he smiled, softening his dark-grey eyes. Then there was the curve of his lips—those lips, which, much to Xanthe's exasperation, she quickly remembered. They'd felt like cool satin against her hot skin. She tried to catch herself and not lose her mind in the depths of his striking features. Her hands fiddled with the chair's armrests before gripping them, knuckles white.

Memories flicked through her mind like a speed reader looking at an old photo album. So many memories, mostly good, except for ... And then it was there, the unassailable wall. Her hands fisted. What to do? Should she slap his face, walk out, or rage at him? What?

She blew out a growling breath and cocked her head. 'Oh. It's you. What's the appropriate greeting for a duplicitous fuck?'

His smile shrank as his hands picked at non-existent fluff on his jeans. 'I see you're still firmly gripping your anger.' Then with sad, heartfelt hoarseness, he added, 'I never had a chance to explain.'

She hissed, 'I didn't need it.' He'd never said what he meant, and Xanthe had come to think he never meant what he said. 'I got the message loud and clear.' They'd had—well, she didn't know what to call it. It had been intense, something more, but the painful memories that hollowed out her chest told her it had been just a fling. Sean Mahoney was her grand Irish fling. Once, Xanthe had loved him too much. Now she'd never love that much ever again. She'd come home a shadow and shrunk into a shell of her former self, only for circumstance to break more than her heart.

Xanthe wanted to understand how she'd missed seeing the arsehole he had turned out to be. She stopped the curt shaking of her head, trying not to stir up the sediments of memories that would only cloud the clear mind she needed to deal with him.

She would not entertain any hope for them. She ran her hands quickly back and forth over her thighs like she could feel the violence of the pins in her bones. Not that she needed reminding of the hard work endured over five long years of pain and rehabilitation to crawl back to square one. These raw, bitter thoughts suffocated any feelings for him.

She didn't cringe when she saw his eyes travel slowly up her body and fill with something more potent than admiration. She took pride in knowing her curves were still in all the right places because of her hard work. After all, she'd overcome the heart, bone and nerve pain he'd caused to recover them.

Guys looking from afar may have thought she was a damsel in distress. She was anything but. She'd always been such a fearless, trusting free spirit who was as vibrant as she was generous. He'd taken all that from her and filled her with suspicion, calculation, anger and hurt.

The beginning of the end had sunk its teeth into her when he'd betrayed her. She hadn't waited to hear another word from him. Fleeing in the dead of night, Xanthe's heart had become as dead as that Irish night. And there it was, the wall that stood between them. He'd laid the firm and broad foundations and she'd taken it from there to build the impressive, impervious structure that now protected her heart, her life.

* * *

Sean watched her intently, deciding he needed to be closer to make sure he wasn't dreaming. He swivelled across from his chair to sit on an ottoman at her feet. When he'd first heard the expletive-filled voice, his world had held its breath. When he'd laid eyes on Xanthe after all this time, his heart had started thumping so hard it felt like it could crack his ribs. He still found her simply breathtaking. Her sodden hair tumbled chaotically around her shoulders, not too different from when he'd first caught sight of her in Ireland. He remembered her so clearly that he knew her face had paled from its healthy olive glow to strained, white porcelain. He saw that her lips weren't as vibrant as the striking red he'd fallen for years before. And the vitality in her green eyes was dampened.

Reaching out, he interlaced his fingers with hers like he'd never left. A sudden crack from the fire sent a smattering of scorching embers spewing forth. Sean saw the moment his tender touch had Xanthe double down and she bit back. Her tongue spat forth a scorching rasp, 'How's the wife?'

'Dead.'

An awkward silence crashed over them like a raging sea's wave. As Sean was about to be sucked under with the wave grabbing at him, Xanthe pulled her hand from his grasp. 'How can I believe you?' Her eyes skirted to his fingers. He wasn't wearing a wedding ring. He hadn't back then, either.

'Want to see the death certificate?'

'Actually, I don't care.'

'Let me explain.'

'I. Don't. Care.'

'She'd left me. I swear. I didn't think she was coming back.'

She wiped her fingers over bluish lips and shivered. 'I believed in you and your company when no one else would. I gave you my considerable savings, and most of my parents' life savings, as starting capital. I thought we shared something. I really did.' She released a harsh chuckle. 'Turned out the only thing you wanted to share was *my* money. No, wait, you didn't want to share it, did you? I was just a mark, some woman with money that you'd decided to charm the pants off to get at the dollars.'

'Just stop, will you! You weren't the mark, I was. I went through hell, and you were caught in the crossfire, collateral damage. For that, I will always be sorr—'

'Yes. That's it. That's what I was, damaged. You'll never know the half of it.' The edge to her voice was a vicious scythe to his heart.

'I have your and your parents' money, plus the interest and profits. The dream came true. It's still growing.' He wouldn't let her go and reached for her hands again. 'I've changed the company's name—'

'I can't do this.' Her thoughts were overwhelmed by the pain radiating through her heart while the physical pain speared down her legs. The first pain she'd worked at ridding herself of forever. After all, only a tiny, vulnerable piece of her heart remained, and it was protected behind the thick, tall wall they'd built. 'You have no idea.'

It had been six years, six months and six days since they'd laid eyes on each other. In that time, he had no way of knowing that Xanthe had found real pain, unlike any other. 'Huh, you think you went through hell, well baby, I lived there.' Wrenching her hand away, she ground out between clamped teeth, 'Keep the money. I don't care to have any dealings with you ever again.'

* * *

Xanthe almost believed what she said as she stomped to the door. She wouldn't run. It was still pelting down, and she'd left her coat. But she didn't care, didn't look back. She hailed a taxi and sped home. Once there, Xanthe found respite in the familiar and safe walls of her home, every bit as impenetrable as the one surrounding her broken heart and shattered dreams.

She began to suffocate her sorrows in Johnnie Walker Blue, another luxury she'd enjoyed since the accident. She listened to Johnny Cash's 'Hurt', trying to erase the hurt and the stain Sean had left on her life. Then the anger came, always the anger, and holding its hand, hate. Since Ireland, they were her old familiar friends.

Filled with the perfect gravel, Johnny's voice lamented. Her evening turned darker and darker as the other Johnnie slid down her throat, the vapours clutching her soul. The smoothness of perfectly aged Scotch swept away the nasty taste of her tears, but not her memories. She callously swallowed some pills to ease the pain of everything as she sought solace, once again, in her other friends, alcohol and drugs.

She tossed and turned the whole night and took more pills as flashes of her last night in Ireland came back to gnash at her. The hurt overwhelmed the defences of her wall and the reinforcements of booze and pills. It invaded her heart as Gina's sharp words twisted with Sean's.

'I've transferred the money. It's finally happening. We're going to be in business together.' She was so naïvely bubbly, her eyes so bright, her lips so satiny red.

There was hesitation in his eyes, but she didn't heed it. 'Wow! X, thank you from the bottom of my heart. Sean Mahoney Incorporated is almost on its way. Give me a couple of days.'

His voice sounded different, not quite right, so she asked, 'Why a couple of days?'

'I have to tidy up a few loose ends, that's all, I promise. Then we can start putting the money to work. How about we meet up at the pub tonight to celebrate?'

A trickle of alarm prickled down her spine. *Why not now?* Something was off. No, Sean wouldn't betray her. He loved her. He wouldn't cheat her out of her money, would he?

Gina Mahoney kept her flame-red hair untamed, like a charging lion. Her large, haughty eyes were as hard as the emeralds they resembled. Xanthe had always remembered those eyes because they drove through her like bullets and were just as damaging. Her face was splattered with a harsh smattering of freckles. Fine barbed-wire lines jagged around the Irish woman's wide, painted mouth. Those harsh lines deepened as she sized up Xanthe while taking a long drag on a glowing, ash-tipped cigarette.

She blasted out a stream of smoke directly into Xanthe's face. 'So, you're the woman who thinks she can have my Sean.'

'Oh, I've definitely *had* him.' She stood to her full height, one lioness facing off against another. 'It's a free world. He's a free man.'

'You're as stupid as you look.' Xanthe's stomach flipped when those barbed-wire-ringed lips curled into a sick, predatory leer. 'You stupid bitch, he's not free in any sense of the word.' Gina pushed her adorned left ring finger into Xanthe's face. 'Mine.'

Xanthe tried not to fall into the hole that was opening up at her feet. Gina then flipped up her middle finger in triumph, saying, 'You were the easiest of marks and you've paid twice.'

Somehow, she knew it was true. The trickle of alarm became a tsunami that swamped her. Not waiting for Sean to join them, Xanthe left the pub but not before she poured her Guinness over a stunned Gina. The only thing she hadn't understood was what Gina meant by paying twice. Within twenty-four hours, Xanthe did. With no word from Sean and no access to her money, the answer was easy. He'd chosen Gina, and Xanthe's investment—her heart, her money —both stolen.

The bank told her the account was frozen due to criminal activity. He called, but she didn't answer. What was there to say? She'd all but collapsed into her economy seat, barely staving off the brutal devastation and abject humiliation. Once the plane was in the air, she broke. It felt like she cried every tear created during the twenty-two-hour flight home—a flight of escape and self-preservation for a condemned woman.

* * *

The regular morning pain snarling around her legs woke Xanthe, bringing her back to her present reality. Sydney was her home now. She'd taken refuge in the city and rebuilt her life. Even though it was an anaemic existence, Xanthe was alive. With her head and legs suffering from the gnashing of biting pain, she managed to sit. It was five a.m. and her sheets were a twisted mess, like her mind. Further sleep was unlikely, so she staggered to the bathroom, the need for drugs consuming her. This was what he'd reduced her to.

A day later, between muggy, broody showers, Xanthe rode the lift from the forty-first floor to search for lunch. As the aluminium doors slid open, her thoughts, as usual, were focused on the grumbling pain in her knotted back muscles. But those thoughts dissolved because there he was again, unexpected and unwanted. Somehow, he seemed to fill the colossal foyer of her office building, making it so she couldn't slip by him.

Sean's index finger curled around a wire coat hanger from which a plastic-covered dry-cleaned coat flowed over his shoulder, gleaming in the downlights. His eyes were filled with a similar gleam as they met hers. She caught the look and tried not to think that his captivating eyes were eye-fucking her. She reordered her thoughts. His fucking eyes were not captivating, then she sniped, 'There's a name for you, which do you like to go by? Sick stalker or desperate degenerate?'

His shoulders rose on a long breath before a tight smile slid across his lips. 'You left it with me.' There was a crinkling swish as he offered her the jacket.

'How did you find me?'

'Business card in the pocket. Xanthe Kazan, CEO.' She wanted to add, *high-functioning, drug-dependent CEO. All thanks to you.* It was her dirty little secret.

Her teeth were grinding again. It was becoming a habit around Sean. 'Get out of my sight. My company owns this building.' Motioning to her left with her head, she said, 'See the guy over there? He's a personal friend and head of security. I don't want to have him hurt you. I might enjoy it too much. But one nod and Jack will do it for me. Take a hint.'

'Got it. Just give me lunch to explain. If you don't feel anything after that, I'm out of your life for good. Promise.'

'Don't make promises. I know you never keep them.' Something pulled at her, however. She couldn't make it stop. Maybe curiosity, but that killed cats, and she wouldn't be destroyed by him again. Then she heard herself agree to coffee, like some stranger in a mist.

* * *

He wasn't surprised she'd agreed—not to lunch, but at least to hear him out. She'd never been afraid of anything, so why did she look so beaten? As they sat down, he saw her teeth grinding had faded, like he imagined her expectations of the meeting changing her mind. He ordered her coffee, a double-shot espresso. 'It's good to see some things don't change.'

'It's about the only thing that hasn't.' She didn't take her eyes from him. He noted the frigid green stare, fearless and full of more anger than hate. He also noted with more than a tinge of sadness the haunted shadows smeared under her eyes.

'As I said, make it quick, or I'm out of here.'

He blew out a sharp breath. 'I met Gina in Dublin, where I'd just graduated in business management. We got married too young. I saw her as full of daring, sparkling fun, while unbeknown to me, she saw me as her latest ticket to money. I had a degree and was the youngest son of a successful lawyer, after all. We settled in Dublin. Straight after the wedding, she started spending more money than we had. My ma never took to her, but tolerated her because I thought I loved her. My sister hated her and never hid it.'

'I always liked Saoirse.'

'Gina would stay out all night. Then I wouldn't see her for days. I wanted a divorce. My ma was with me on it, and naturally, so were my brothers and Saoirse. My da was not for it at all. We're Catholic, and so was her family. He put his foot down. I went back to Dublin to try again. Within weeks, she was back to her old tricks. This time she hooked up with a guy with better connections than mine. She cleaned me out and went off with him to the US.'

Sean was a desperate man, fighting a past that ended with Xanthe leaving. He wanted to start a future with her coming back. 'I went home with my tail between my legs. My father apologised unreservedly for making me take Gina back. Da and Ma made sure I recovered, supported me in every way. When I met you that rainy afternoon, I hadn't seen Gina in a year. I hadn't bothered with a divorce because I couldn't afford one, and no one knew where she'd gotten to, which part of the US. She didn't tell anyone.'

Running his hand over his face, he continued. 'Getting a divorce hadn't worried me. I never planned on getting involved with another woman, ever. I just kept drifting along, managing pubs and restaurants to pay off the debts she'd run up in my name. When I met you, my life reignited, as well as becoming too complicated for words. You were like a warm, brilliant summer sun leading me out of the cold darkness her pale candlelight had led me into.' He slid his hand over hers, interlacing his fingers to open her clenched fist. Even though he wedged open her hand, he knew by its coldness that the wall was still there.

'Sure, sure. It doesn't explain why you didn't come clean before you got your hands on my money.' Xanthe bowed her head. He sensed the bitter anger surging within her as she muttered, 'The way she gunned for me. It was clear I was just another bit that you'd had on the side.' She pulled her hand away, rubbing it on a forehead that looked far too full of pain. 'I hadn't come down in the latest shower, Irish or not. You're gonna have to do a hell of a lot better than that weak-arse explanation.'

He gripped her other hand tighter. 'Xanthe, please!' His eyes punched into her, changing to a deeper gun-metal grey as he implored her to stay a little longer. 'I promise you. From the first day I met you, I fell in love with you. The very next day, I started the divorce process.'

'Why not tell me? I'm pretty sure I'm not an unreasonable person. Well, I wasn't then anyway.'

'I didn't tell you, hoping I could get the divorce sorted and never need to have you be touched by the mess of my life before you walked into it.' He took in a shuddering breath. It was like he was breathing in grains of sand. 'When my lawyer tracked her down about the divorce, she was on her way back to Dublin. Unfortunately, she'd found out I was coming into money. She didn't know it was your money and thought she could pick up with me again because her welcome with the Irish–US meal ticket was wearing thin.' His brow fixed into tight wrinkles. 'I met her at the lawyer's, but she refused to sign the divorce papers. Then that night I was supposed to meet you at the pub to celebrate, she got there first. Told you that vicious pack of lies, and you stormed off. When I got to the pub, she was waiting for me, somewhat coated in Guinness, but there. Before I could go after you, Gina and I were arrested and taken in for questioning.' He could see Xanthe was remembering the pain as if he was personally delivering fresh blows to her as she sat at the table. That sight cost him. He hadn't wanted to hurt her, ever. 'I didn't choose her over you. There was never a choice. It was always you. You weren't the mark, I was. Even before she walked down the aisle to me, she played me.'

A hint of a malevolent smile curved his lips. 'Seems she met her match, though. The Irish–US whale she bagged was into some dodgy shit. Interpol was after him. That's why she'd left him. Because they wanted him, and as she was associated with him, they wanted her, too. They froze his accounts, and as she'd fled back to me and I'd just come into a large sum of money, they froze my—our—accounts also.' He motioned between the two of them. 'I had no money until they could verify that she, or more importantly, her sugar daddy, hadn't funded our new venture. I wasn't allowed to leave the country to chase after you because of the suspicions on me due to Gina. You wouldn't take my calls. Then the number went dead. Your parents wouldn't speak to me. It was like you dropped off the earth.'

'You lost their money as well. Even though I was the one who convinced them to invest with you, they stood by me, gave me a place to live when I came home penniless.'

He scrubbed his free hand through his hair. 'It was the government. It was bureaucratic. It took ages for them to clear me.'

She murmured, 'I worked three jobs for a while before I could make it back into property development. My dad had to take on extra work. You could've at least had the decency to give their money back. That would have meant something, especially to me.'

'I didn't have it then.' He tugged her hand so she would look at him. 'It took me some time to get our company back on track. These Irish pubs you see popping up around Sydney, they're ours,' he told her proudly. 'We're a chain, baby. Worldwide. I can finally return your investment and that of your parents' with interest and a sizeable profit.'

She shook her head.

'Ever since you left, I've set about working my way back to you.' He took her other hand. His lips sighed against the taut skin covering the too-bony hand as he kissed it. 'I never loved her.' Sean's voice husked over with emotion. 'But you ... I'll never stop loving you.'

He thought he saw a flicker of warmth in her cold, unblinking eyes, then it evaporated. 'I ... I can't do this.' Her voice cracked over the words, 'Us ... not again.'

'I didn't plan it like this. I figured I'd call on your parents and dog them until I wore them down, and then they'd tell me where you were. I had no idea whether you'd be in this wide, brown country of yours or somewhere else in the world. And then of all the places, you dropped into my world, all fuckity fuck. It's got to mean something.' A hopeful smile graced his face.

'What! Are you fucking serious? Of all the Guinness joints, in all the towns, in all the world, I walked into yours?' Her anger was shredding her as she seethed. 'That's a tired old line from a much simpler, charming time. I'm not simple and hardly charmed, but I am tired. You can't expect me to drop everything just because you told me a sad story.' She could only snatch one hand away.

'X, please.' It was a pained whisper. He held on to her other hand like it was a lifeline. He'd been looking for her for so long, and even if she'd found him, he wasn't letting go.

'I don't do the relationship thing anymore.' Her face fell to a mask of stone, except for the pain in her eyes. 'I'm done with the whole coupledom, happy-ever-after shit. I'm never going to have that. So, what do you want? A quick fuck? One last fuck for an old fling's sake.'

She was far more callous than he remembered, although given how they'd parted, she had every reason to be. 'I need you. That's all I want. I'm not going anywhere. I'll make sure we work this time.'

'How? How can I believe you?'

'X, please.'

'Stop with the *X please*! Nothing about seeing you again pleases me.'

'Listen to me!' His voice shuddered with desperation. 'About the money—'

'I. Don't. Care.'

She seized her overcoat, and in a whoosh of dry-cleaning plastic, left him sitting alone with two cups of cold coffee. It was as if she was only ever going to be his for as long as pure snowfall lasted in the spring sun.

* * *

Sean was working from home. He had an office in the two-bedroom apartment that sat above the pub Xanthe had stumbled in to on that fateful rainy day. He stretched his stiff neck out and away from his computer with its spreadsheets. Rolling his shoulders, he noticed the light was fading from dusk to night. It had been four days since Xanthe had walked out on him, again.

In that time, he'd visited her parents. They were angry too, but eventually they spoke to him, and he finally convinced them to accept his money. When he all but begged, they filled in the blank spaces about Xanthe's life after she'd left Ireland. The knowledge shocked him and left him wondering, was it even possible for him to persuade her heart to come back to him?

For days, his head had been pounding like it was being hit by a hundred hammers. He made his way to the kitchen for some ibuprofen. Before he had a chance to do anything, there was a soft knock at his door. When he opened it, his heart had an abrupt, beatless moment.

'I needed to thank you for visiting Mum and Dad and returning their money, plus the sizable return on their investment. It meant a lot to them and me.' Xanthe flicked at her hair. 'It was one of my biggest regrets, losing their money.' When her eyes swept up to his, they were like pools of the richest green ocean water, yet too large for her drawn face. 'So, thank you.'

'Come in.'

'I'm not staying. I only wanted to say thank you to your face. That's done, I'll go.'

He stepped across the threshold and tried to take her hand. 'Don't go. There are other things to be said.'

She stepped back from him. Not a skittish house cat, more like a powerful lioness defending against danger. 'You know about the accident.'

He rasped, 'Why didn't you tell me?'

She straightened, her eyes going hard. 'I thought you were with *her* and had stolen all *my* money. Why would I have thought you'd help me?'

His voice had all but rusted over. 'God, Xanthe.' He stepped towards her again.

This time she met him, toe to toe. 'Six years ago, I was lying in a hospital bed, barely able to move anything except my little finger. That's when I vowed never again to give my heart to any man so cheaply.'

Everything he'd ever felt for her rose up and made his chest ache. He had to be much smarter. 'I wouldn't expect any less from you.' She'd constantly tested him. It was that spirit more than anything that reminded him why he'd fight for her—always. 'If you won't take your money back, then at least come in and spend a little time to see what your investment has given rise to.' He swept his arm back to the open door. 'Come in and look over the plans, the books.'

He saw it in her eyes first, then it spread across her face—the lure generated by the artistry of business. She stepped into the hall, turning in a circle as she looked at the beautifully restored Art Deco cornice and ceiling, the classic paint colours and polished wooden floors. Her eyebrows rose in amazement. 'Sean, this is lovely. You do good work.'

'It's mainly due to the guys who work for me. Go through to the office. It's past the lounge.' As she walked in front of him, he noticed the limp. She hid it well. He hadn't noticed it the last two times she'd stomped away from him. This new knowledge made his stomach feel like it was on a spin cycle.

* * *

An hour later, she was sitting in his chair behind his desk, engrossed and energised. 'Your business plan is brilliant, and it's working very well.'

'It's mainly your plan and with some hard work, I got it rolling. It's all been worth it.' The lightness of his voice and his smile revealed he'd relaxed back into a familiar role with her. She didn't like that. It was too quick, too easy.

'X, you need to get it into your head. It's not my business. It's ours. Xanthe's Plan Incorporated.'

'You changed the company name and named it after me?'

'Of course, it was always your plan driving it.' He smiled again. The joy creased his sparkling eyes.

The smile, more than the words, sobered her, and she stood. 'I've stayed long enough.' Her back and legs, as always, were stiff from sitting for any length of time. She hid the associated spasm and nerve pain, which gnawed at her right butt, by skipping a little as she stretched out to grab her umbrella. The weather was still fickle, like her thoughts about this man.

'How much does it still affect you?'

Realising it was pointless to try to hide it, she said, 'Well, I can walk, so yay me.'

Her bitterness only incensed him. 'Damn it, Xanthe, how bad is the pain?'

'Why do you care?'

'Because I still love you. I want to ma—' She hadn't seen him for a long time, but she knew enough to know he changed what he was going to say. 'Manage the business with you. Give you half.'

She couldn't afford to give his sentimental words any value. He'd lost all currency with her long ago. Knowing how to hurt him and burst his bubble, she slapped back at his shame. 'Remind me, how did your wife die?'

He didn't flinch. 'Gina died in a skiing accident in France three years ago. It was an odd accident. There was a rumour that this time she'd stolen from the wrong guy, and he had her killed to stop him from losing any more. The other rumour had her becoming a liability because she screwed around on the wrong guy with another wrong guy. It seems the first wrong guy had her killed to stop her talking to the second wrong guy and give away any, let's say, trade secrets.'

'I can't say I'm surprised.'

'Now I've told you everything. It's time for you to tell me some things. The accident, Xanthe, what happened?'

'My parents told you. I owe you nothing else.'

'From your lips, Xanthe, what happened?' There was no place for joy or a smile on his face as his eyes glistened with tears. 'Did it get so bad that you tried to ...' He swallowed. 'Did you try to take your life?'

If he had wanted to anger and hurt her, again, he succeeded. 'Stop! You haven't earned that right.' If any tears threatened, she swallowed them back with anger. 'Not that, not yet, not ever.'

His voice filled with sorrow. 'Christ, Xanthe. If I could take it all back, go back in time, I would. If I could take the pain and damage away and let it be me, I would. You must know that. Deep down, you must know I still love you.'

His words shocked her, and she tried not to let them soften her resolve. Her temper spiked as she tried to bristle. 'I'm not that woman anymore. The one easily tricked.' Her heart wasn't in the fight, and he sensed it. Before she could step away, his arms came around her, gentle but authoritative.

Her gaze fluttered from his sad eyes to his mouth. She'd always been drawn to his mouth, and now it was so overpoweringly close. *Just once more*, she thought. Her desires escaped, the need to drink in his woody scent, to feel, to plunder, unstoppable. There was no grace at first, only an explosion of taste, yearning, and could it be truth? It might have been the tension that railed between them, but something snapped, unleashing a torrent of longing. The pure nakedness of it, the beauty of it, consumed her.

His grip slackened with the surprise of it. Xanthe continued her assault, pouring six-and-a-half years of frustration and anger into the kiss. And when unexpected tenderness flooded back in, there was love.

Climbing sensation ruled, and the kiss intensified. With her hands roaming over his chest, she felt his heart thundering in time with hers.

His hands skimmed and then squeezed her butt cheek. Pain spiked. Everything collapsed faster than if he'd swatted a house of cards. She jerked back. Yes, there was frustration and anger and by her reckoning, worst of all, there was still love. As it always seemed with Sean and her, discovering love would end in inescapable pain. 'No. This can't happen. I won't go back, Sean.'

'Then don't. Take a step forward with me.'

Her fingers ran over her swollen lips as she struggled to bring her floundering heart under control. Confusion reigned, joy rose within her because he held her once again, and simultaneously there was rage—that he dared do such a thing. Now, in what had become the norm in her life, most of the fury was reserved for herself. It was anger at being weak, allowing him to lay hands on her, mortified that she'd started it. Reverting to her one core hurt, she said, 'Your dreams may have come true. Good for you!' She was snarling now. 'But mine, of owning a club and restaurant, they're destroyed.'

She took one last look at him. This time she did run. Her face was burning and every part of her body more alive and tingling than it had been, except since the last time she'd kissed him.

* * *

He was left drained while yearning, burning for her. He couldn't think, destroyed by his hope—the feel, the taste and the scent of the woman who was both his resolve and his kryptonite. Every time he closed his eyes, Sean saw her, the perfect vibrant gift she'd been. Then a nightmarish fog would swamp and haunt him. It was full of the suffering she wouldn't show him and the pain her parents openly carried. The agony they begrudgingly had shared with him. The night was long and each hour, he relived the hurt he'd heard in her mother's words and the pain he'd seen in her father's eyes.

'It happened about six months after she'd come home from Ireland,' Dareia said. 'Took another six months to get her back to some sort of functioning after the car accident. Then when it looked like she might lose the use of her legs, and the pain was too much, she lost her way there for a bit. It triggered a ... You see, she tried to ...' Tears rolled down the older woman's face.

Dareia gathered herself. 'She made it to rehab. She was doing so well —close to being able to use a wheelchair. Then an infection hit, and we almost lost her for the third time.' Rubbing at her temple, Dareia said, 'But she's strong, our girl, and she came back yet again. This time, she came back changed. There was a renewed strength and resilience about her, but also there was this coldness.'

Phillip added proudly, 'She's like reinforced concrete now. Hard as.' With a tinge of helplessness, he said, 'Doesn't feel anything anymore.'

Dareia sighed. 'Yes, and she's not happy, not how she used to be. She tries to hide it from me.' Her eyes flattened. 'A mother knows. Any thought of weakness and she comes out swinging—everything overwhelmed by anger. She won't forgive herself for what happened.' Focusing her eyes lovingly back on Phillip, she said, 'She's worked hard to get back on her feet in every part of her life. Xanthe surprised her doctors to walk again. She *applied the same determination to her career. Now she's earning good money, really good money.*

'It's the wreckage you left, Sean. I'm hoping the real Xanthe will come back to us one day. She's lost her carefree spirit and vitality. You took most of that. The accident claimed the rest.'

'Thing is,' Phillip barked, 'she wouldn't have been driving home so late in that shitload of rain if she hadn't met you. That bastard, idiot drunk driver would've missed her.' Phillip nailed Sean with a stony glare. 'She wouldn't have been working herself to the bone with three jobs. But she needed the money to survive from what you took. No matter what we said, she wanted to pay us back, too.'

Before the sun deemed to grace the day, Sean woke from his latest nightmare. Covered in sweat and a blanket of heavy sorrow, his torment had left him with one chance, and he'd take it. He'd use her own words to get her back and lessen the pain of her reality.

* * *

He dogged her for a month. At first, it was only questions about Sydney property. He called her, surprised she took the call. 'X, I've been reading about your company and its developments.' He heard her angry groan but continued. 'Are there any new high-rises where a pub serving food could locate and gain a licence if city zoning allowed?'

'Possibly. Are you thinking of basing it around a pub located on the ground floor, along with coffee shops and pharmacies?'

'Yes, can we get together and discuss?'

'I know what you're doing.'

'Can't shoot a man for wanting to mix business with bits of pleasure.'

'I could easily set your so-called pleasure bits on fire. And no, that's not a double entendre,' she said. 'I find the property development potential interests me.'

Letting Sean buy her lunch followed. They talked about business, and he kept away from taboo subjects. Then there were a few more lunches and one dinner. The wall wasn't weakening. It was more like a door within it was opening. Eventually, a weekend lunch led to spending an unplanned, fantastic Saturday afternoon together at the football. All was wonderful until the end of the game.

Because the plan had changed, Xanthe had unexpectedly spent over two hours sitting, with little time to stand. She didn't have any medication with her. She couldn't hide the limp or pain. Her skin pale and her brow beaded in sweat, she stumbled down some stairs. He caught her, only to be pushed off as she fumed, 'Get off me. I can walk it off. I'm not an invalid.'

He hated feeling helpless around her, and she told him she despised him for being so helpful. Silence was their friend in the taxi to her apartment. It had followed another heated confrontation about whether or not Xanthe needed him to accompany her home. 'You're not my friggin' carer!' she'd shouted.

With her hands visibly shaking, she hissed as she opened her door, 'Just go, Sean. Please. I don't need you. I'm quite used to dealing with this on my own.'

'Like hell you will.' With the door open, he couldn't stand the struggle any longer and swept her up off her feet, carrying her into her apartment.

He suspected the pain stopped her resisting. He back-heeled the door closed. 'Where's your bedroom? And believe me, there's nothing on my mind except getting you to stop this nonsense and letting me help you get rid of the pain.'

'You can just piss off! Leave me here and go.'

His anger rose to match hers. 'Not on my watch. One of these days, Xanthe, you'll stop being so angry. Not only at me, but mostly at yourself. Then maybe you'll forgive yourself for something that wasn't your fault.'

Her mouth dropped open.

'Now, what medication do you take when it's like this? And where the fuck is it?'

'I suppose telling you two or more fingers of Johnnie Walker and an oxy is the answer won't stop you?'

'Not unless you're Janis Joplin, no.'

'I think you'll find Janis liked Southern Comfort.'

'Christ, X, shut up and tell me.'

'Morphine and diazepam tabs in the bathroom. Washed down with ...'

He glared at her, which she met with a sad mumble, 'Water's fine, thanks.'

He placed her gently on the massive bed, removing her shoes. With his temper still simmering, he didn't ask for permission to rummage through her wardrobe to grab trackpants and a T-shirt. He looked up at her, and for the first time since the unveiling of her agony, she couldn't hide it. He saw beyond the pain and anger. There was fear consuming her. Not from him. He knew she wasn't troubled by him. It was fear from the pain, and that destroyed him. His throat suddenly tight, his temper doused, he managed, 'I'll go get the tablets. Do you need me to help you out of your jeans?'

When she didn't answer he said, 'Do you need help? Don't lie, I'll know.'

She gave in and almost whispered, 'It would be better if you helped.'

'Tablets first.'

'Yes, Nurse Ratched.'

When he started undressing her, it was the first time he'd seen her scars. He skimmed his fingers over the jagging and spider-webbing on her thighs and pelvis. It simply crushed him. 'Oh God, Xanthe. If I could only take it all back, I would. I love you so much. I want to marry you.'

'Not the time, Sean. Too tired, too sore, I might say yes, and it won't mean anything because I'm on drugs where I shouldn't be operating heavy machinery.'

'Stop that, don't make light of it. It's been foremost on my mind since you left me.'

'Don't say it now. It's pity-talking and machismo to save the damsel. Put it away.' Xanthe was drifting as he pulled her close, her back to his front.

As he revelled in the heady scent of her closeness, Sean wished he'd timed it better, hadn't rushed it. The proposal wasn't reflex pity at seeing her wounds. It ran to the core of him and his loving of her. Nonetheless, he didn't stay disappointed for long. There was no quick flash of anger or an outright rejection. She'd given him hope.

* * *

Xanthe had the best sleep she'd had in months. She woke first to find she had minimal pain. She swallowed the tablets he'd left on the bedside table and took stock of what had happened the day before.

The nerve pain that had racked her legs was like a thousand hot wires, burning their way to both heels. Lodging there meant piercing agony whipped through her with every step. Then it had ricocheted back up her legs and spine, sending her muscles into spasms. It was the worst agony she'd experienced in a long, long time.

Then a realisation hit. Sean should have been a constant reminder of her shame, the hurt, the pain. But there was a moment the day before when she'd simply let go, relaxed and forgot. She never forgot. Managing her pain was her life. It angered her, and then it didn't. Sean had stopped her from being fixated on the bad in her life.

Then he'd nailed the leading cause of her imprisonment to the front of her mind as if he'd tacked a sign to her forehead. Being angry at herself had become a habit, with self-forgiveness never on her radar. Could she stand down her anger—her best defender and welcome jailer—to forgive herself and let her skittish heart and life come out from behind the wall?

Of course, there was a sheer mind melt when he'd said he wanted to marry her. It had opened something in her. He'd stripped away her defences and made her once again believe that even she deserved to be happy. All the psychotherapy she'd endured hadn't achieved what he had with one sentence of understanding. Was part of the wall weakening?

With her mind and heart slowly shuffling through the exciting possibilities, she looked down at him. His long black lashes covered peaceful eyes. His strong, smooth features were calm. Features that had always ensnared her. He was shirtless, with only boxers covering the skin of a man she couldn't banish. Forgetting herself, she ran her fingertips up his arm, snuggling down to stroke along his back in a long, languid caress. With a feather-light touch she trailed her fingers around his angular jaw, fuzzed with unshaven growth. In that liberated moment, she didn't keep her distance. In kissing his forehead, the wall began to crumble.

With eyes still closed, he murmured, 'I take it Nurse Ratched did a good job?' He'd been lying very still.

'Passable, yes.'

When his dark-grey eyes trapped her as they sleepily opened, her heart somersaulted. She took his lips, curious to see if they could repeat the electric jolt of life which drove through her from their last kiss. She was wrong. It wasn't repeated. It was surpassed. Sweet heat and the pulse of thrilling feelings grabbed, held and overpowered her, yet again. Then the heat intensified and shook her.

His voice was smooth as molasses as he pulled back. 'I don't want to hurt you, but ...'

'I have my pain control managed, not like yesterday. Sean, I'm not made of glass.'

'That I know, but still ...'

She pushed him down and rolled on top of him, tossing off her T-shirt. Trying not to rush, she brought his hands to have them cup her breasts, relishing the feel of him, the glorious tone of his muscles against her. She saw his eyes widen a little as his hands glided over her smooth skin to catch on the rough contrast of her scars. Ashamed, she tried to push his hands away.

'Don't. X, let me touch you, all of you. They are a part of you and all of you holds my heart. Nothing about you disappoints, you only ever captivate me.' He continued to push her trackpants off as she sank into feelings she hadn't entertained for so long.

His eyes were rolled up under heavy lids when she left him to peel off his boxers. When she came back to him, she teased his lips before stealing his groans of adoration with her next kiss. Sweeping her hands over his belly and lower, she found him growing harder with each nip of her teeth on his throat and brush of her hands over him.

She felt the tension in him as he fought his desires so he could be gentle with her. Having none of it, she reared up and framed his face with her hands. Omnipotent, her green eyes smouldering, she commanded, 'Don't you dare hold back. I forgot yesterday, okay? I forgot the pain, forgot to worry. I was so at ease because of you. That's such an amazing realisation.' She bent to take his lips and mouthed against them, 'Yes, the result was a disaster. The point is, I haven't experienced that freedom since the accident. Pain management is a learning process. I never thought I would say this, but I must learn how to fit it and you into my life. That's a first. Self-recrimination, pain and anger have ruled my world for so long. You make it go away.' She sat back, catching his stunned look. 'I've already taken some tablets, so let go and give me what I want because I know it's what you want, too.'

Xanthe still straddled him when Sean rose to kiss along her tapered neck before his mouth toyed tenderly with hers. There were long, unhurried strokes of his tongue on hers. His touch was gentle, slow and silken as he coveted her body once more, and the heat returned. She merely let go and fell like molten, liquid gold, pouring out of a cup in an ever-thickening ribbon—hot and beguiling.

He rolled over her, and she welcomed the weight of him. He continued to tantalise her with his searing touch and the magic taste of his mouth as he kissed her. The feel of his fingers, lips and tongue as they roamed over her released and claimed her. She was hyper-responsive to his expert ministrations and surrendered to the heat and unbridled longing when his fingers found her willing and wet. Her first orgasm struck in a frantic rush of brutal desire. It broke her as much as it made her feel alive again.

Before she recovered, he shattered her mind with pure sensation as he plunged into her rippling core. With eyes locked, she catapulted towards rapture. She gripped his shoulders, kissing along his jaw, twisting her fingers in his hair, barely matching his restraint. At first, his thrusts were tentative and long. When she took him higher, and he was surer of her climb, they rocketed into each other tenderly yet with the desperate need to chase a more demanding rhythm.

She had him losing his control, his finesse. With a rolling soft-gravel growl he said, 'We're in this together, always.'

A precious passionate love swarmed and wrapped exquisitely around them. The molten heat of it drove so deep it began fusing their broken hearts back together into the one love they had shared before. She mouthed his name, then shouted, 'Yes, always together.'

He thickened further and quickened his pace, driving hard and fast into her. Vivid colours were exploding behind her eyes.

She trailed her nails along his muscular back and he responded with a flurry of final thrusts. Her core clasped his manhood harder and harder, his size driving her wilder and wilder, their combined need, greater and greater until she detonated into a thousand shooting sparks, taking him with her. With nothing left, she drifted back to earth with the ashes of her sanity.

He'd attacked the wall, invaded her disdain, destroyed her misguided, angry defences and conquered her reluctance to trust— all to free her. She sighed with a velvet huskiness. 'You need to hear this.'

'Did I hurt you? Oh God, I'm so sorry I lost myself to you.'

'Just stop.' She slid her hand up onto his chest to rest above his heart. 'I'm not feeling anything except glorious heaviness after amazing ecstasy.' She was so overwhelmed. She didn't realise tears were tumbling down her cheeks as her other hand tugged his chin so he'd stop worrying and look at her. 'They told me everything would be different after the accident. They told me I could never feel like I had before, if at all, during sex. No one proved that wrong.' Her breath caught. 'This'—she moved her fist from his heart to hers—'you proved everything wrong. I only needed you to make the difference.'

* * *

While it took months, Xanthe eased back into a relationship with Sean. It was like she was dipping her toe into a steaming hot bath, knowing the urge to submerge her whole body into the almost unbearable warmth would eventually overpower her. Initially, she didn't want to get burned, so she took her time before sliding right in to welcome the heat. With that comfort came the gradual re-emergence of her bold, carefree spirit. It melted her bitter anger and condemnation of Sean, but mostly herself.

The tragedy in her life, which she hadn't overcome with self-recrimination and anger, wasn't Sean's fault. Some of it was caused by a man who thought he could have too many drinks and still drive. Gina, a greedy, spiteful woman, triggered most of it. She didn't have a clue about what she wanted or the treasure she had. Unlike Xanthe, who now knew the prize she had and exactly who she wanted.

Then, after many nights together, they shared an intimate dinner at an exclusive restaurant. Hushed words gave way to smoky laughs, and they enjoyed the beauty of a lit-up Opera House, sitting at the end of Circular Quay, paying homage to the gleaming Sydney Harbour Bridge. After all her time back in Sydney, it was only now, with Sean beside her, that Xanthe noticed how truly beautiful the everyday things in her life were. As they walked through The Rocks and rounded a corner, another fantastic sight caught her eye.

She had seen trendy bars and clubs pop up in the place she'd come to call home. This bar/club was a new treasure, yet she'd seen it before—in her dreams. Materialising in front of her was a stylish and sophisticated nightspot with an elegant neon sign, 'Xanthe's Dream'. Her heart became whole, filling the hole in her chest in a few excited beats.

Sean blew out a breath. 'It's yours, bought and established with the money you wouldn't accept from me. I had your parents' blessing. You can manage it the way you want, change everything or nothing. Or we can manage it together. Whatever you want, but every part of it is yours.'

'You're nuts!' she squealed.

'Takes one to know one.' He smiled with relief.

When she kissed him, Xanthe felt his contagious excitement and let him lead the way.

'Come and look it over.' He guided her through the queue, which curled around the corner. As they entered the chic bar, soft, smooth vibes flooded the air of the restaurant area. The cool, funky lighting had her relaxing and wanting to be held by him. They sipped wine in the lounge bar, where they spoke in shameless, sensual whispers. Then Sean moved her through to the club. Bone-rattling, hot beats had their bodies moving in perfect sexual symmetry, shimmering against each other. Hope and faith rekindled.

When they stepped into the darkened space off the dance floor, Xanthe decided it was time. It had to be the perfect place—he deserved no less. 'Where's the engine room?' She sent him a searing, mischievous smile, then moaned, 'You know, where the balls hang out.'

He nearly lost his balance before saying, 'I take it you mean the office.'

In the spacious office, they found a bottle of Dom Pérignon reclining in an elegant silver ice bucket sitting on a large modern desk. She had to admit he'd chosen what she would have, right down to the feature pieces of quirky décor and vinyl-only music in the lounge bar.

She locked the door before locking her lips on his. He puffed, 'I take it you like what you see.'

'Yes, all of it.' She kissed him again, dragging her satin lips over his throat, whispering, 'This place, yes, but having you back in my life, most of all.' Torturing him, she brought her body against his, anchoring him hard between her thighs. In contrast, her lips were soft at the corner of his mouth. 'Why don't we open the Dom and make a toast to you, us and to making dreams come true.'

Sitting on a leather lounge, they touched glasses, enjoying the velvetiness of having each other close. Sean told her hoarsely, 'When you came back into my life all fuckity, fuck, fuck, it had been six years, six months—'

'And six days.'

He nodded. 'Since you'd left. I thought about it later.' He smirked. 'Six, six, six.'

'The devil's number.' She laughed, taking a long sip.

His eyes lasered hers, his voice never wavering. 'Yes, but it brought you, my angel, back into my life. Releasing us both from hell.' As he gazed into her soul, Xanthe realised this was where she belonged, in the orbit of Sean's arms.

'Took me a little longer to notice I had the power to walk out of my hell.'

'You're here now and that's all that matters to me. I've always loved you, Xanthe.'

At that moment, she understood. When she stripped away everything life had thrown at them, the flame of their love had survived. She'd catch that flame because it remained defiant, the weapon to obliterate the wall between them. It had only ever been their love. 'I love you, Sean, so, so much.' Her eyes glistened vibrantly and truth flooded her. Her dreams, her life wouldn't be the way they were before the accident. Everything would be better. It was simple, her words firm. 'Marry me?'

five

BECOMING SAOIRSE: LONDON 2005

SAOIRSE HADN'T SCREAMED. She hadn't hit Will. She'd walked towards him, holding up the note and the final photo of him kissing his wife. He'd seen them clearly, almost as much as the hurt that had been all but crushing her. The other photos had fallen to the pavement, blown away by a cold wind. He may have said something like, 'Saoirse. It's only you I want to be with.' She couldn't be sure, because with her heart shattering, she wasn't able to hear anything more from such a beautiful liar. She knew she walked back into her apartment, locked the door and then her heart. He'd knocked, then shouted he was so, so sorry. Then he'd phoned, but Saoirse was long gone when it came to Will Sewell.

The next time she opened her door it was to Sean. She'd expected him to be bouncing. She'd desperately wanted some good news. For his sake, she'd hoped Xanthe had understood Sean's unreserved love for her, especially once she saw the new restaurant and nightclub named in her honour. Unfortunately, Sean was anything but happy, and Saoirse's stomach had twisted in knots. 'Please don't say anything about Will. I don't think I can bear it.'

Sean had taken her shaking frame in his arms and held her. She'd found herself latching on. Then he'd choked out, 'Forget that prick. It's Callan. Lara's dead.'

'What! How?' She'd sobbed into Sean's chest as the siblings held each other tighter.

Later over a whisky, he'd explained, 'Dad called earlier. Callan's a mess.'

'He's just lost his wife. He'd be devasted. What about Jessica?'

'Mum's flown to London to help with her. Lara's family are already there.' He took a sip and hissed out after he swallowed. 'Lara had some kind of attack. Give me a minute ... Ah, an aneurysm, it burst. We need to fly to London.' Eventually, Sean had said with a tearful smile, 'Xanthe has asked me to marry her. I've said yes.' There was a silver lining, albeit thin.

* * *

They flew to London as soon as they could find a flight. On the plane, Saoirse cried alone deep into the night as a heavy melancholy engulfed her. Even knowing there'd been more than a hundred days of lies and flying thousands and thousands of miles, she still couldn't stop him from invading her dreams. She was drowning in terrible hurt, hers, Callan's, and the anguish of his twelve-month-old daughter.

Why hadn't she seen it in Will? Why hadn't she asked the question? She knew he couldn't wear a ring. Most tradies didn't. They were using machinery, working with tools that could snag rings and cause fingers to be broken, cut and lost. Was Will such a good actor, or was she still that naïve, small-town Irish girl who'd learned nothing, progressed nowhere?

'I didn't know either. If I had, I would've knocked his block off. As it was I nearly did,' Sean told her.

The bitterness within boiled over, giving a caustic edge to her words. 'My tyres, his windscreen ... the photos. Were they all her, his wife?'

'I didn't ask, sounds likely.' Sean rested a hand on her shoulder. 'How can I help share some of the load?'

'Sean, please. I'm okay. There are more important things we need to attend to.'

'Saoirse, you don't always have to be a strong and serious second mother to us boys. We're older than you. You know that, right?'

'I was a bloody fool, so gullible. No wonder Will found it so easy to lie to you about the real reason he was at my apartment that night.' He cocked his head, she explained, 'The night when you returned early from London. He'd had a lot of practice at it, hadn't he? I should have picked up on the lies, given what I've seen, what I know.'

'If you mean the family's experience with my ex-wife, that she should have taught us all something, I think you're looking for the wrong lesson. If anything ...' He rubbed Saoirse's arm so she'd look at him. 'Gina taught us that you don't have to be an innocent to accept a lie. I mean, look at me. She hooked me. I definitely wasn't naïve. Sometimes we thirst to believe, and other times the lie is so well crafted Houdini couldn't escape it.' He took her hand. 'If it's any consolation, he told me to say sorry. That he could believe in his dreams coming true with you. With her, he can't.'

She pulled her hand away. 'Don't.' There was nothing left inside her for Will.

* * *

Callan was distraught. At first, there was the torture of watching his little daughter's confused fretting and inability for anyone to settle her. Her crying crumbled his already broken heart. She would crawl from bedroom to bedroom looking for her mother, sobbing when her search failed. Jessie took her first steps looking for her mother. Steps Lara would never see, and that tore something deep inside him. Then later there was the devastating realisation that Jessica was forgetting her mother, and that shattered him even more.

The family rallied, and Mary Mahoney decided she would stay. Lara's family were also willing to help take turns being there for Jessica. After another two weeks, everyone could see that it was only a band aid solution to what required a full-blown surgical intervention if they were going to lessen Callan and Jessica's pain. Saoirse stepped up. There was nothing for her back in Sydney. Sean and Xanthe could run things and manage the expansion of their businesses.

She would stay with Callan and Jessica and help them get back on their feet, because family was everything. Everyone felt relieved, particularly Saoirse. She had a new project to numb her feelings and give her time to collect her thoughts before moving forward.

After the funeral, the family congregated at Callan's house in Stratford, East London for the wake. The slender ray of sunshine they enjoyed was that Xanthe joined them.

* * *

The months peeled away slowly, like the wound Will had inflicted on Saoirse was shedding its scab as she healed. Still, Saoirse found herself lying in bed one morning pretending she could sleep. She tried to believe closing her eyes a little longer would stop her body from feeling so heavy it could fall through concrete like it was smoke. When the tiredness wouldn't seep away, she rose and attended to Jessica. Saoirse's mood lightened as she listened to Jessica's excited, bright babble while she dressed her niece to go shopping.

On their way home, as they exited the train station with the crowd streaming past and around them, an older woman in front of Saoirse stumbled and fell. At that moment, she let go of Jessica's pram to help the lady and took the time to steady her.

When she turned back, Jessica and the pushchair had disappeared. Esme, the lady she'd helped, stayed with her as they searched and called out for Jessica. Saoirse couldn't breathe, let alone think. Her mind surged with terrible scenarios as she frantically searched the crowded station. She wasn't prepared for the dread and fear that kicked up and stormed her.

Esme went for help while Saoirse stalked frantically around the station and its car park. It took five agonising, exasperated minutes, which felt far longer, for Saoirse to realise Jessica had disappeared. All the while, she felt like a vicious, powerful fist was tightening around her heart, squeezing harder and harder, then pounding her stomach. It was the panic and the not knowing seizing her.

Esme returned with a British Rail employee in tow. Saoirse was verging on hysterical as a fresh-faced man with a barely post-pubescent voice snapped into action. He spoke into his two-way, alerting the driver of the train that had just departed. Soon more staff arrived. Someone put in a call to the police.

A policewoman began asking Saoirse questions. Between the tears and the shakes, she felt stupid. It only got worse as she found herself struggling to remember what she'd dressed Jessica in that morning. Couldn't they just let her catch her breath? If she could only quieten her mind to have time to think. 'It was the pink tights and red polka-dot jacket with a blue T-shirt underneath. No, hang on, it was the red polka-dot tights and blue jacket with a pink T-shirt.'

The police officer who said to call her Maddie spoke calmly and deliberately as she sat next to Saoirse. She had caring eyes and a body that looked like it could lift the weight of the world with ease. Maddie's reassuring hands took Saoirse's as she said, 'Take a breath. Good. Now try going back to this morning when you were dressing Jessica when it was peaceful.'

'She was so chatty and happy.'

'That's good. What did you dress her in, Saoirse?'

'The pink tights, red polka-dot jacket with a blue T-shirt underneath, pink joggers.'

'Great. Now, I see you have Jessica's bag still with you. Does she have a favourite toy with her?'

Somewhere in the middle of it all, she called Callan. He was rightly fearful and didn't hold his temper. 'Saoirse, for Christ's sake! How could you?'

Her throat was tight and dry from crying. 'I know, I've totally failed. Let you and Jessie down.'

'How long did you leave her?'

'Seconds, I swear.' More tears came now as she told him what happened. 'I let go of the buggy for only a second. I swear Jessie was right there!' Wiping at the tears, she added, 'There were just so many people passing by. No one offered to help Esme, and when I looked around, Jessica was …' She swallowed a sob as her voice crumbled. 'Gone.'

'I'm leaving home now. I'll be at the station in ten.'

Esme held Saoirse as sobs racked her body. 'I'm terribly sorry, Saoirse. You were the only one kind enough to stop and help. I can't believe people these days. That someone would take advantage of my misfortune and your kindness.'

Saoirse blew her nose using a tissue from Jessica's backpack, which she'd clung to for dear life. She started to pull herself together. Her mind finally began to break away from the fear and panic.

Then there was a soft tap on her shoulder. She swung around and saw the sweetest sight she'd ever seen: a smiling Maddie with an equally as smiley Jessica sitting in her buggy. Maddie placed a gentle hand on Jessica's head. 'Here's our little traveller.' Saoirse swept Jessica up in a tight hug, tears bursting forth once more. Maddie's smooth brown face creased into a broader smile as Saoirse brought the policewoman into a tight hug.

'How, where?'

'She was at the far end of the car park off to the left of the station, sitting there humming to herself. You wouldn't have seen her from the station's entrance or from where you looked when you ran out to find her. She was behind cars and a low brick wall.'

Saoirse held Jessica tight, not daring to let her go, even when her angst started to ebb. 'I'm so thankful.' Happiness flooded over her shame.

Maddie's smile faded as she asked, 'Is everything as it should be with Jessica?'

'Yes, yes.' Saoirse now had a good look at her niece. She was as Saoirse had last seen her, clothes in place, her arm wrapped around her favourite toy, Lamby.

'I'm so grateful. Maddie, how can I thank you? I don't know how I could have been so stupid.'

'You weren't.'

Saoirse focused on Maddie's furrowed brow and saw the flash of concern in the policewoman's eyes. 'What aren't you telling me?'

'We found a note with her. It's a little strange.'

Saoirse's head began to spin again with the fear that had lulled. 'What did the note say? Oh God. Is it a threat to Jessie's life?' At her loud, panicked words, Jessica began to fuss.

'Just hold your horses,' said Maddie.

Saoirse placed Jessica back in her pushchair and swung the backpack off her shoulder. Diving into it, she retrieved a sippy cup for Jessica. The little girl gladly accepted it and smiled again as she took a sip.

Saoirse looked to Maddie. 'Why strange? What does it say?'

Maddie read the note that was in a clear plastic evidence bag. 'It says: *Pay attention to me. You need to keep a firmer hold of your niece.*'

They spent the rest of the day with the police, answering questions. Saoirse and Callan racked their brains, trying to think of anyone who may have wanted to cause them heartache. Then when the CCTV footage showed a guy close to where Jess was found, the atmosphere eased and then became heavy again with new questions.

Maddie said, 'That's Howie, real name Howard McNamara. He's a harmless serial pest that lives close by with his family. Usually, his brother looks out for him. Kidnapping's not something he would do, and I don't think he can write. I mean, not with the sophistication of the note. First off, using those words and spelling them correctly. He's not all there.'

Saoirse's head was thumping like a jackhammer digging its way to hell. 'I don't remember seeing him on the train or platform.'

Esme shook her head. 'I know Howard. I didn't see him on the platform today, either. He would have helped me if he was anywhere near us. He is, as Maddie says, harmless, there's no mean in him, especially to take a little girl. Well, he just wouldn't.'

While wiping crumbs off Jessica's face from a biscuit she'd devoured, Saoirse asked, 'I've never seen him before. How would he know Jessica is my niece and not my child?'

Maddie, who'd been taking notes, met Saoirse's eyes. 'First things first, we'll talk to Howie, see what he says. I'll hang on to the note. Could be something has happened at other stations and we haven't heard about it. Let me make enquiries.'

'Do you think this could be some serial sicko?' Callan asked.

'I don't know. The use of "niece" and "pay attention to me" sounds personal. But more likely, it'll be a random oddball who's seen you around and gleaned that Jessica is your niece from overheard conversations and took advantage today.'

Maddie passed Saoirse a business card. 'Call me on this number if something comes to you that may help. I promise we'll keep looking. For now, we haven't got much to go on. I'll go through the CCTV footage again and get in touch with other stations. I think it's time you all went home and got some rest.' She tweaked Jessie's nose, who was proudly wearing Maddie's police cap. 'You must be exhausted, my little lady, although you've been very well-behaved.' She turned to Saoirse. 'You've done all you can. I don't want this to spook you. I know it will, but keep doing what you're doing. You should be able to have a child in a pushchair and help an old lady and not have this happen. It's now on me to make sure you're safe in the future and find out what happened today.'

Once home, they found solace in routine as they organised Jessica's bath and dinner. Saoirse was very thankful that Jessie was unharmed and that she remained blithely unaware of any problem.

Callan cleared his throat. 'I apologise, Saoirse. I shouldn't have snapped at you. It was wrong of me. I ... I mean, Jessie and I are very much indebted to you for your love and care of us.'

Saoirse embraced him as she sniffed away a tear. 'Totally understandable.' Even though they'd said the words, the atmosphere between them remained a little bumpy for a couple of weeks before they settled.

While Saoirse was shaken, life went on. She tried to push the strange incident behind her. Because it was never entirely out of her mind, she remained ever vigilant around Jessica while growing a harsher, tougher hide because of it.

When Sean heard about the incident from his mother, he called Daniella. When she rang to offer a shoulder, Saoirse felt some heaviness lift. Daniella shared her stories of motherhood's dilemmas, triumphs, fears and stuff-ups, assuring Saoirse that all mothers, even aunty/surrogate mothers, had the same ups and downs. As usual, the bottomless care of her world-wise friend eased Saoirse's angry embarrassment.

Daniella's work eventually drifted into the conversation. Saoirse was glad of the distraction. It was then she heard the cold fatigue tinge her former boss's voice. Without giving any names away, Daniella voiced concern for a client's safety. She had an abusive ex-husband whose criminal connections made it easier for him to terrorise and hunt his ex-wife these past years. 'It's one of the toughest cases I've had. We've been extra careful with her protection. It's been very complicated as the police are now interested in her to help them prosecute the ex-husband over drug trafficking. We've had to tread a fine line as this bastard could have dirty cops in his pocket.'

Saoirse wondered how many years a woman's strength could persist with such ever-present fear walking as her shadow.

six

STRANGE COMPANY: ELLA'S STORY

AS ELLA SAUNDERS, Gabby began to feel a warm sun penetrating the shadow she had lived in for years, and she began to grow in strength. She shed some of the baggage she carried because of her previous life by embracing the excitement of setting out on a working holiday to the Middle East. She'd decided to immerse herself in ancient history to free herself from her ancient history. It was also a place where Sergio or any of his rats were unlikely to find her.

As she moved through passport control at Melbourne international airport, the officer she handed her passport to shot her rapid and repeated razor-sharp looks. This frayed her composure, sending a shudder quaking through her. Taking a breath, she tried to stop thinking every man who looked at her more than twice was working for Sergio. It almost worked until he asked, 'You look familiar. Have you changed your name?' His eyes cut to her travel agent's name tag on her backpack.

The shudder now multiplied and invaded her whole body and mind as vulnerability and confusion stormed her. The officer had the power to stop her from travelling. Was it a real question required by his actual boss, or was Sergio his boss? With her stomach doing a triple twist, she said, 'No.' Grabbing back her passport, she moved through his station. Ella made herself walk, although she wanted to drive her legs into a run.

He had everything: her name, address and which travel agent she'd booked her trip through. Was he a bona fide government official? Would she be apprehended at any moment for lying to a government official? Ella folded into a chair, bringing her head down between her knees. She barely brought the panic attack under control. It ebbed when no one came for her. *It will be okay*, she told herself. She felt a little more in control. The address on her passport was legitimate, one offered by the network of women her lawyer, whom Ella still only knew as Five, had introduced her to. If it was Sergio, the address would lead him in circles.

Nonetheless, could the information he had lead him to her? Surely the Middle East was too far away for Sergio to get to her. She couldn't think. Her mind and heart didn't step down from alert until the plane was in the air.

* * *

As Ella flew towards her destination, the man she was flying towards tried to restrain his frustrated worries. Times were tough. Thanks to an uncaring, alarmist Western media, tourists were afraid to visit Egypt. It meant money for exploration and the restoration of ancient artefacts couldn't be found. Danyal's job at the Museum of Egyptian Antiquities had dried up faster than water in the burning Egyptian sands in July. His anger had grown because he had to become a lowly guide, fighting for scraps with every other common guide in Cairo. It didn't matter that he had a doctorate in Ancient Egyptian and Greek civilisations.

The lack of money was at the root of his problems. He would do whatever he could to earn it, because he had to provide for his family. The woman he was picking up had paid extra for a solo tour, but he still needed more money. He hoped she wasn't a tiresome, overweight Westerner who'd ask arcane questions and treat him like her personal butler. Yet he wouldn't hold his breath.

Then in the last hours before she'd arrived, a nondescript Australian company emailed him, offering a bonus. They wanted Danyal to pass them information about the Western woman he was to guide around his country. Innocuous facts like where she really lived when she returned to Australia, who employed her and whether she was involved with anyone. If he agreed and the information was useful, he'd receive his money at the end of her tour. He was mulling over what to do as he headed to the airport. His priority had to be keeping his family fed, and for that, he couldn't be too picky about how he did it.

* * *

Landing in Cairo, a smiling Ella was met at the airport by her guide. She noticed his brusqueness as he led her to his car. It didn't dampen her mood because she was too over-the-moon happy at fulfilling her childhood dream of visiting the Pyramids and the Sphinx. She greeted the slightly chubby man with a respectful salutation in Egyptian. He flashed her a forced smile then scratched his thinning head of hair when she told him to leave her bag. She'd carry it to his car. As Ella sat in the back seat, she saw her guide's tiger eyes study her from time to time in his rear-view mirror. His glare set her teeth on edge.

Regardless, the next day she couldn't keep the smile from her face as she walked around Giza, listening intently to Danyal's histories of each pyramid and the Sphinx while taking copious notes. He appeared indifferent until halfway through the site tour. 'You surprise me because you ask thoughtful questions, unlike most of my previous clients. I have to ask, why do you take so many notes?'

Her answer was guarded to begin with. 'I write a travel blog that has a respectable number of subscribers.'

He all but rolled his eyes. It incensed Ella, and she snapped, 'If I can write about more interesting facts than a person could get from Google or Wikipedia, it may allow me to put a different slant on this experience. What I write could be picked up by Lonely Planet.'

'Is that true?' His lack of trust was evident to Ella. It was on par with her faith in him.

'Yes. If you're different from the average guide, which your website said you were, I can give you free publicity.' His eyebrows knotted as her temper pushed aside her caution. 'Pull out your phone and open Google.'

Scepticism slapped his face as he gave her his phone.

After persevering, she showed him an article she'd written on a Lonely Planet site. He stood back and rubbed his chin. 'I better give you my best, then.'

Her anxiety didn't settle as her misgivings about him grew. Had she just opened herself up to someone who'd help Sergio? She knew that her lawyer was still handling threats from the Mancuso family, demanding the right to know where Gabriella Mancuso was so Sergio could face his accuser. That fear gripped her like the night grabs the sun, full of unstoppable inevitability. She tried to tell herself to stop jumping at shadows. Cairo was a long way from Australia.

It became harder to believe Danyal was different when she felt his golden predator eyes rasping over her as they walked to his car. No, she wouldn't let her holiday be spoiled. She'd try to overcome her mistrust of men and get to know her guide. In any case, she was so tired of always being on guard.

* * *

After a week in Cairo seeing all the close surrounding sites, she and Danyal were more at ease with each other. She'd even met his family. His wife, Reem, had invited her to dinner one night, where she met the couple's four children and Reem's sister. Ella found herself relaxing around Danyal as she fully immersed herself in Egyptian culture.

For the next part of her tour, they had to head out of Cairo. Since they had become easier with each other, Danyal asked her for a favour. He explained that he needed money and had the chance to take an additional booking for the next leg of the tour. Even if he refunded some of Ella's money because it wouldn't be a solo tour, he would earn more overall.

Ella was enjoying herself so much she forgot to be suspicious. 'Danyal, don't worry. If we get on with the person and the tour goes well, keep all the money.'

A woolly mammoth of a man joined them for the road journey to Luxor. He was abrupt and smelled like he hadn't washed in days. She was immediately dismayed that she hadn't said no. She would have paid Danyal twice to stop the powerlessness that stormed her body like a sickness.

It wasn't only because he was a man, and mistrust of men had become her default position. It was that he never met her eyes and most of the time his long fringe covered what she thought were shifty, dark eyes. Worse was that his sweaty smell and dust-covered khaki shorts and shirt had her teetering on the edge of panic, reminding her of Sergio. Her old fears pounced, feasting on her mistrust. She wondered if somehow Danyal had contacted the Mancusos. Had they found out where she was and sent this guy? Was she jumping at shadows again? It seemed no matter how much Ella tried to flourish, Gabby still lingered.

After the journey from Cairo, they were to check in to their floating hotel, the Sonesta St. George. It was a Nile cruise boat known for its sweet-smelling, air-conditioned luxury, with very Downton Abbey-like décor and additional touches of replica Egyptian artefacts, complete with gold trim.

Danyal spoke to his new client before they left the car to begin their five-day, four-night cruise from Luxor up the Nile to Aswan. His voice was full of humour laced with something else. 'Sir, Ella and I have been together for a week now. I have come to think of her as a sister. You, I don't know.' It was apparent to Ella that Danyal's jovial banter was a thin mask hiding his seriousness, which his eyes reinforced. 'Until you prove differently, I shall keep an eye on you like I would my next-door neighbour. We could be friends, but I'll watch you for many different reasons. Most importantly, so you aren't enticed into upsetting my hen house.'

Ella watched Danyal and the man chuckle. Danyal's golden eyes were ice as they remained trained on the newcomer, the warning clear. Scruffy man's smile evaporated as he trudged off to board the riverboat. Ella walked with her guide while his big-cat eyes warmed. 'I've noticed how you are a little jumpy around men. I promise to keep you safe.'

Her hackles flared, then she looked into his eyes and saw kindness. 'Thank you. I'm getting better, though.'

'Yes, you are, day by day.'

'I feel I should explain.'

'You don't need to. I know a thing or two. I've seen the same unease in my wife's sister. A man who was going to be her husband beat her. That's why she lives with us now.' He moved Ella forward to lead the way up the gangway as he said, 'You and I will keep an eye on our dirty, scruffy companion who disrespects my homeland by showing up to visit its treasures looking like a street thief.'

She found herself grinning at him. There and then, the journey towards absolute trust between Ella and Danyal took significant steps forward.

The tourists had cabins on the top deck, while Danyal's was on the lower. Later that night, as Ella made her way to the restaurant, a woody-smelling, clean-shaven man started following her. It unnerved her. Shadows of Brisbane had her ready to fight. Steadily, she made her way to her table. When she was closer and saw Danyal walking towards her, eyeing the man over her shoulder, she turned. Not looking at the man's face, she jabbed the heel of her hand into his soft solar plexus, pushing him back. 'I'm not looking for company, okay, pal? This table is reserved for me, my guide and a smelly, dirty, scruffy man.'

Sucking in air from the blow, he coughed. 'I'd be the smelly, dirty, scruffy man. But you can call me Liam.'

She looked up and met his dark-silver-grey eyes. Showing fewer ruffles than her cotton blouse, Ella turned to mutter, 'It's an improvement. Danyal will be more impressed than me.'

* * *

The following day, after visiting Karnak, they cruised up the river. Ella, Danyal and Liam found themselves on the upper deck by the pool, watching the expanse of the banks of the Nile sweep slowly past. There was the heat, which she loved, but add to it the look of the old lean-tos, the greenery of banana and mango trees, and she was in trouble. Within the time it took her body to be racked with a violent shudder, she was back on the farm. Heart thundering, she recoiled and made an odd sound that drew Liam and Danyal's attention. They watched her smile die as she ran.

* * *

The boat continued to plough up the river while Liam and Danyal looked at each other. They knew they'd entered a troubling situation, but neither had a clue how to find an exit.

The older man nodded at the younger. 'It'd be better if you went to her cabin. For me to be seen, it could cause trouble.'

'She may not be in her cabin.'

'Liam.' Danyal put a hand on Liam's shoulder. 'I hear they say your God goes with you into the lion's den.' He made a shooing motion with his hands. 'Let us both go and look for her.'

* * *

They found her on the lower deck, in one of the lounge bars, wedged into an oversized plush lounge near a window. Liam didn't speak as he sat beside her. Danyal wandered off, but kept an eye on his two clients as they talked.

Ella had thrown off the flashback and calmed the panic. Her breathing back under control, she eyed Liam with suspicion. Gripping a can of cola, she hid the remaining slight tremor by taking a long sip. It helped her stall. Then she realised he was doing the same thing by taking a deep breath.

'I needed to grab a cool drink. It seems hotter today.' She found her fingers were denting the can.

'Yes, it's been hot.'

Danyal had told them that the morning was cooler than usual. The lie was transparent yet valuable, as the awkwardness between them trickled away. She saw Liam struggle for words, before casting his eyes down. Ella discovered that his habit of not making eye contact was because of shyness, not dishonesty. She recognised it because she was the same.

'The breeze's come up. It's pleasant now,' he managed. 'Let's go, Danyal has more to tell us.' Before she could feel shaky or wary, he gently took her by the hand. 'I've got you. It'll be alright.' A male taking her hand after an attack, even half of one, should have plunged her back to panic, yet his manner comforted her. They walked back to the top deck, where Danyal joined them.

Liam was correct. The breeze was refreshing. She found that once he moved past his shyness, he had an easy going, caring nature. Was this Holiday-Liam or Real-Liam? How could she know? She'd been tricked before.

Ella's bad memories were washed away temporarily by the fresh smiles of people waving at the boat as it passed lazily along the river. There were donkey-drawn carts and shrill screams of joy as children splashed and played by the riverbank. The simplicity of happiness echoed across the Nile, sweeping away the shadows of anxiety that had jumped at her. These rural people had a precious life. Ella took stock. She had to move beyond panic and mistrust and find a way to move forward as a stronger woman.

* * *

While watching his two clients, Danyal made his daily call to Reem. It had been hard for her to discover anything specific about the company wanting to pay Danyal extra money. The company's name, Smith Trading, was too common. 'I don't think we should take money from this company. What if they have something to do with the man that has caused Ella to be so fearful? You know how long it took to rid my sister of that low-life who hurt her. He hounded her with things like this.'

Danyal scratched his balding head. 'Yes, I agree.'

'Are you worried about the street thief being a rat? Do you think they sent him to spy on her because you haven't got back to this company? Sounds like he's the type of man who'd take money for something like this.'

'He's cleaned up his act, but which is the disguise? The street rat or the clean, softly spoken man? I can't be sure yet.'

It grew hotter over the next couple of days as they visited many more beautiful sites and interesting tombs. Liam found a quiet moment to speak to Danyal without Ella overhearing. 'She is soft and sharp, all at once. It makes her unpredictable and about as good a travel companion as an unwelcome visitor in an already crowded house. Do you know much about her? Where is she from in Australia, and what's bothering her?'

Danyal muttered, 'It's not for me to tell you those things. It is for Ella.'

* * *

They spent the next afternoon listening to Danyal's cultured tones as he walked them around the Kom Ombo Temple. When night descended, Liam and Ella stood on the pool deck, overlooking the riverbank markets. In the distance, the Kom Ombo ruins stood magnificent, bathed in golden light against a darkening sky.

Ella knew she'd been walking around a twisted mass of conflicting emotions, one minute calm and upbeat, the next anxious and low. She tried to smooth out the swings. It was the dark memories that were upsetting and the hardest for her to hide. She hadn't realised she was acting like a woman struggling to keep her secrets.

The heat of the day had gone. The magic of the night captured them, as the perfume of flowering jasmine sweetened the air rippling off the Nile. 'Can you answer a question for me?' Liam asked her.

'It depends.' Her nerves rose to claw at her happy mood.

'You're brave enough to come to Egypt on your own. Yet you seem to jump at any small shadow. Why is that? It makes you strange company.'

She slammed her hands on her hips to growl, 'Is this how you do it? The caring, sweet talk, with your cute Irish easiness. Is that the way you think you'll win me over, maybe even get into my knickers?'

'Good to know you think I have a cute Irish accent.'

She didn't correct him as she crossed her arms defiantly.

'I was only asking, thinking it might help to talk about it.'

'Is it bullshit or shite where you come from?'

'Right, then. I'll tell you a little about me, shall I?' His eyes trapped her with their calmness. 'Finding out a little about each other might make the rest of our time together easier and not spoil a great holiday experience for both of us.' He took a breath. 'I'm from Donegal in Ireland. I work as a petroleum engineer in the North Sea, fly-in-fly-out. While home is always home, sometimes when the North Sea world turns the same grey as Ireland, I like to see a different world's colours.

'I usually travel alone, no organised tours, no guide. For Cairo, I decided not to use a guide, and I ended up living rough. Which meant I hadn't had a proper shower in days before I first met you. I must have looked a sight, and I know I was abrupt as I was tired and in a mood because of my stupidity. Danyal's tours had a good rating, and he had space for me, so here I am. Plus, it's Egypt. I'd be stupid not to have a guide outside of Cairo. I didn't want to miss out on, well, anything.

'My ma always says, "troubles shared are troubles halved". I only asked about you because I thought you might want someone to talk to about whatever has you so nervous. I could help and protect you—'

'Let me stop you there.' She raised a finger when his words cut too close to the bone of Sergio's words. She wouldn't fall for them again, and more anger rose at having fallen for them the first time. 'If you want to know, I'll give you some important facts so you won't miss out on—how did you put it—anything.'

She loaded up two shotgun cartridges, one frustration, the other anger, and let him have both barrels. 'At twenty-three, I was travelling the world, making a living as a writer. At that time, I was tired of living out of a suitcase. I fell for this guy I thought was great.' Her anger was now pulsing off her and she forgot to hide who she was. 'It turned out that I only imagined his goodness and overlooked his cruelty. Holiday romances do that. I thought I could change him, smooth out the coarseness. Then I thought it was me.' Her voice cut the night air with a bitter edge. 'Sounds stupid, I know. But I thought I was the reason he was angry all the time and why he hit me.'

'Jesus. I understand.'

'No. No, you don't. I thought my husband was all I deserved. It took many kind women to show me I deserved much more. Now, I deserve time to become my own friend again, first and foremost.'

'Yes, of course.'

She didn't care that she'd sprayed her secrets around indiscriminately. Because she began to understand her old spirit was re-emerging. In a contemptuous tone she hadn't released in Egypt, she asked, 'What do you see in me?' She whipped her hair off her face. 'Is it some single woman to have as a holiday conquest? Or is it a sad damsel in distress that needs rescuing? Or worse still, because we've shared our pasts, and even though we've only known each other for days, do you think it's love?'

'Hey, I was only asking the question.' He held up his hands. 'My sister has told me many times that I know nothing about reading women. But I don't need Dr Phil to tell me that your little explosion is a defence mechanism to push everyone away from what is still a painful, unhealed wound.'

'You don't know anything. Which means I'm not looking for a holiday hook-up.'

He put down his hands. 'I'm not hitting on you. I was concerned, that's all. You need to recognise that not all guys are bastards.'

'You sound like you're trying to convince yourself.'

'No. I'm trying to help you.' He laid a hand on her shoulder, looking like he was struggling to tame a wounded lion. 'If you want to get back to your real self, then you need to start by letting the bastard who hurt you go. That comes with starting to trust the world again.' At his following words, her mind stopped spinning. 'We are all the authors of our own life story, Ella.'

He eased his hand away to lean back against the railing, then lifted his head to the night sky. 'How about we go back to where we were before? Before I asked that stupid question about you being scared. Let's just watch the moon and start a new chapter.'

She shook her head. 'Just like that.'

'Yep, just like that.'

'Okay.' Her voice drifted. 'You are ...'

'Infuriating.' He shrugged. 'Yeah, my sister tells me that all the time. I don't mean to be.'

'Well, you are,' she snapped, then tilted her head. 'How many sisters do you have?'

'Just the one, but she's enough, because between her, my cousins and my mother, I've learned to let them talk it out and strip it back to the simple things in life. Other than trying to keep everyone calm.'

His easy manner had Ella only half settling. 'Alright then, the moon and the simple things it is.'

Even as they enjoyed watching the night-time Nile float by together, her guard came up, smothering her emerging spirit. Could those stray words set her new life on fire? But even if they did, she didn't think she'd rise from those ashes.

* * *

All too soon they sailed into Aswan, where they said goodbye to their luxurious floating hotel. The three checked in to the Old Cataract Hotel, a fantastic piece of Victorian-era opulence. It was like they'd slipped back in time to the stylish world of *Death on the Nile*, where Egyptian and French architecture collided with colonial luxury. There were striped Byzantine arches, mahogany carved fireplaces and Victorian-era furniture. The ambience it created had Liam and Ella feeling like they could walk into any lounge and catch Winston Churchill puffing on a cigar while sharing a brandy with Agatha Christie. Ella lost herself in the nostalgia and romance of a hotel built over a century ago when times were simpler and grander.

They rested overnight before flying to Abu Simbel, where they spent the next day walking around one of the most impressive sights in the world, modern or ancient. The heat waves shimmering off the desert sands made the four giant statues of the pharaoh Ramesses look like they were squirming while sitting on their thrones. As the day wore on, the Great and Small Temples' sandstone changed from brownish to golden.

Ella's concerns about Liam lessened each day, no matter how hard she tried to stop them from slipping away. Nothing seemed to ruffle him. Even what they'd christened her 'Kom Ombo outburst' hadn't concerned him. If anything, it smoothed out the bumps in their relationship. She never heard him raise his voice, not even at street peddlers. One thought wouldn't be banished, though. *Holidays*, she remembered, *make men seem reasonable, lovable even.*

Although she was yet to conquer this belief, Ella found herself relaxing more around Liam. She enjoyed his quiet gentleness and how now and then, when something caught his eye, he'd point it out and guide her by resting his hand on the small of her back. After the first couple of times, Ella didn't shy away from the first skerrick of tender male physical contact in many years. Eventually, she felt better about herself because she could enjoy it and not feel distrustful or submissive. Ella appreciated the ripple of the electric vibe his caring touch gave her. Maybe if she was a different woman, had a different history, she'd break out of her frail skin and take it further.

They sat down at a café for a late-afternoon refreshment, still buzzing from the wonderous sight they'd experienced. It was exhilarating, not only the sight, but for Ella, the realisation she wasn't just an older, wiser version of Gabriella. She was simply liberated and closer to becoming a full-rounded Ella. She smiled for the first time in years. That was, she smiled with her heart and soul tied to it.

She saw Liam catch the long curl of her lips, and his gaze intensified when it met hers. They could only stare at each other. It wasn't the first time Ella noticed his face was sincerely kind. He made her want to continue to unearth the real woman she was becoming. She wasn't ashamed when she locked eyes with his—or that she'd been noticing the more subtle things about him. His eyes were a unique colour when the sun caught them at a particular angle, and he was smiling. They shimmered and appeared bewitchingly more silver than grey.

That night after dinner, they stood together on a balcony to share a brandy and watched the curtain of a starry Aswan night fall. The Nile flowed silent and strong in the dark, the ripples of its surface glistening in the moonlight. The candle at their table burned low. Caught up in the moment, Liam yielded to what the scenery demanded. Moving to Ella, he touched his lips to hers. A velvet explosion of passion gripped Ella. The dull brown eyes she had brought to Cairo were no more. They gave way to a stunning amber, where the candlelight captured hints of gold.

Ella could have quickly become overwhelmed by the waves of need flowing between Liam and her. Instead of diving in, she held the thrilling feelings in check, and she could see him doing the same. She was too cautious about letting it break the delicate connection they were building. Yet the moment was as meaningful as it was beautiful.

The candle's flame tried to resist a strong gust of wind sweeping off the Nile, but it succumbed. 'Sorry,' Liam said. 'I hope that wasn't … I forgot myself.'

She smiled, and her voice thickened when she said, 'Don't regret it. I don't.' She took his face in her hands. 'I want to believe that what's pulsing through me is real. Only, Liam, I can't trust myself. I made such a terrible mistake before. I just can't. Not yet.' Her lips touched his but barely, and she trembled. Without any more words, she left him to share the last of his brandy with the fickle night-time wind.

After landing back in Cairo, they said happy goodbyes to Danyal, assuring him they'd given his tour the reviews he deserved. Ella left him with a copy of her piece for a Lonely Planet Egypt travel book. Once he read it, he embraced her, something he rarely did.

Unbeknown to Ella, Danyal and his wife never accepted the bonus money. They saw it as betraying a beautiful woman fighting to rekindle her inner strength and who was generous in using her talent to help promote their business. Danyal was an honourable man who would not support his family via deceit. They never uncovered much about the strange company other than that it operated from a remote Australian town called Mareeba.

Liam and Ella made their way from the domestic to the international airport. When they'd cleared customs, Liam caught up with her. 'Would you like to grab a coffee before you fly?'

'Sure.'

Once their coffee arrived, he slid a velvet pouch across the table. 'This is for you.'

She reached into her pocket, pulling out a similar velvet pouch. 'Seems we both shopped at the boat's jewellery store.'

He nodded. 'You may not have thought of buying one of these for yourself. I hope it's okay.'

'Funny, I thought the same of you.' Their eyes locked as they enjoyed the feelings bouncing between them, which lured Ella to move her chair closer to pick up her present as he grasped his. Then they grinned at each other like giggly children.

Her fingers ran over the smooth and rough parts of the slim rectangular golden cartouche. Her name's letters were engraved into it in hieroglyphics and displayed like the pharaohs' ancient cartouches. 'Great minds think alike.'

'And fools seldom differ.' He held the elegant silver cartouche keychain in his hand, admiring the four hieroglyphic symbols that spelled his name.

'Yet we're not fools, are we?' Finally, for an instant, the real Ella emerged, leaning over like she had all the time in the world as her lips teased and lingered on his.

His face reddened. 'Thanks ah, Ella … for the gift.' He paused before he smiled. 'And the kiss.'

She sat back, stunned for a beat, as the feel of the kiss rocked her more than it should have. 'Yes, um, thanks, Liam. I'll treasure both.'

'Listen, Ella. I'm not a smooth or quick operator.' He pushed his dark locks back into place, neat, as he usually wore them, apart from the first time he'd met her. 'My sister tells me I have no moves of any kind when it comes to the opposite sex. My brothers tell me a glacier could outmanoeuvre me. After this trip, this is nothing new to you.

What everyone fails to understand is I haven't been interested.' His tone became husky. 'That was until several days ago.'

She felt her heart give a stuttered thump.

'I guess I'm trying to say...' He rubbed his suddenly sweaty palms on his jeans. 'We don't always make the right choices in our life. Don't let one bad choice stop you from having the ability to keep making better choices. Don't be scared of me.'

'I'm not.' She folded her hand over the cartouche. 'And I have made new choices. I've chosen not to have men in my life for a while.'

'Let me try this. You can trust me. It can get lonely travelling solo. I have holidays twice a year so, would you be willing to ...'

'Yes.' The realisation that she wasn't afraid to see him again wasn't as big as her understanding that she trusted this man. 'I enjoyed travelling with you. But you'll have to fit in with me about destinations and times as I must go where my editor or my blog sponsors need me to go.' She smiled, feeling warmth rise within her. 'It'll be good for me to change it up occasionally and write from the perspective of a couple travelling.'

'Fine with me. So, when the dates line up ...' he shrugged his shoulders '... we meet up. No big deal other than ...'

'We'll be travel companions.'

He nodded. 'Sounds like the perfect plan.'

'I'm off to Petra now. Maybe we can plan to meet up when I'm hiking the Grand Canyon. I know that's one of the next places on my sponsor's itinerary.'

'Easily done.' He looked up at the monitors. She saw the sorrow on his face mirrored what she was feeling. 'I need to go.' He stood and pulled on his backpack. When she came around the table and reached for him, she saw his ease as he embraced her. 'Take care, Ella.'

'See you soon and travel safe.' Unlike his calmness, it had taken a significant effort for her to put one foot after the other to reach for him and then hug him. She released the breath that had stalled in her lungs as she found she enjoyed having his arms around her. With her defences down, it was his lips that moved to capture hers. This time they both took the kiss deeper.

Magic! A euphoric charge drove through her, and she was more confident in the rush's power than she was from their Aswan kiss. He looked like he floated away to his gate. She dissolved into her chair, watching him disappear. Then she realised the lightness about her was hope. Hope that she had a shot at a future she'd dreamed of before being forced into a dark, violent detour. Now she was walking back to the light.

seven

BECOMING SAOIRSE: LONDON 2006

EVENTUALLY, Saoirse saw Callan take steps towards a new life without Lara walking beside him. He went back to work and sold the house that reminded him too much of his lovely wife. He and Saoirse bought another in the same neighbourhood, closer to the park.

When he started confiding in Saoirse, she hoped he was finally healing. 'When I'm kept busy with Jessie or at the pharmacy, I feel almost normal. Like the hole in my chest and life is manageable.' She understood what he meant.

He blew out a long, tired breath. 'But it's the long hours of stillness and quiet when the heartache storms back, and no matter what I do, I can't fight it.'

She took his hand in hers. 'I know what you mean. It's worst on weekends.'

'For me, it's on my days off. When I have to confront the unending silence and think about whether it's even possible for me to build a new life when my solid ground has been blown away.'

'Yeah. But we'll get there.' She released his hand to rub his shoulder. 'But Jessie comes first and that's a pretty good place to start.'

'Yes, yes, it is.'

Over the year, all the Mahoney family visited to help and keep an eye on Callan and Jessica while making sure Saoirse had time to be a single twenty-something. One morning while Liam was visiting, Saoirse stumbled out of her room to find him sitting on the stairs with his laptop on his knees. In the few glimpses she caught as she walked towards him, she saw photos of the Grand Canyon. He'd settled on one photo. She saw his shoulders rise and fall in a sigh. The picture he lingered over featured the smiling face of a bright, brown-eyed woman.

Saoirse's voice was still sleepy as she scratched out, 'Liam, you dark horse'.

Liam jolted around. 'Saoirse, must you creep up on a man?'

'I wasn't creeping.' As her bum hit the carpet on the stair, she slid her arm around his shoulders and leaned in. 'What's your lovely lady's name, and why haven't you said anything?'

'It's Ella, but she's not mine, and that's why.'

'Liam, have you told her how you feel?'

'Not in so many words.' He shrugged her arm off his shoulders. 'And before you tell me that I move with the speed of a tortoise around women, it's a mutual agreement.'

'I see. How long have you been together?'

'We met up when I was in Egypt.'

'That's a year ago, and you haven't said anything, not even a hint to us?'

'She's had it pretty rough, and now she's been badly hurt, again.'

His silver-grey eyes were like Saoirse's. When they clouded, she softened her tone. 'What's happened to her?'

'Abusive nutter of an ex-husband. He caught up with her last week after she returned home from our holiday to Cinque Terra. He nearly killed her.'

'What! Liam, that's terrible. Why don't you go to her?'

'She doesn't want me to. She doesn't want me to see her in such a state.'

'Where's home for her?'

'She lives in Melbourne. Well, it's her home at the moment. She doesn't go home a lot, probably much less after this. She's a travel journalist, has a blog, publishes articles in some travel e-magazines and contributes to travel books for Lonely Planet.'

'She sounds pretty amazing.'

His emotion broke through his usual easiness. 'More than that, Ella's pretty *and* amazing.' The pride in his voice pushed away the desperate sadness in his eyes.

'How come we know nothing of her. You and her?'

'We found that we enjoy each other's company when we travel. Since Egypt, every time I've been on holiday, it's been with Ella. The Grand Canyon, and most recently Northern Italy.'

'Oh, Liam.' She wrapped her arms around him and felt him shudder.

'Last month, the shithead ex was not long out on parole. He'd spent three years in jail for beating up a guy in the town where they used to live. During their divorce, he made threats against Ella. Even after three years, she still wasn't safe. The scumbag was waiting for her.'

Saoirse blurted out, 'How did he know where to find her if she moved and was hardly home?'

'Not sure, something to do with the drug business network he has set up. Lots of people kept an eye out for her for the right amount of money. She only found out recently he had people in passport control in Australia.'

'That's terrible.'

'Yes, he's a fucking bastard. He broke his parole to cross state lines to get to Ella. He wanted to fucking kill her.' Liam was the most softly spoken and well-mannered of the Mahoney children. Given his conversation was harsh and littered with curse words, it left Saoirse in no doubt about the desperation her big brother felt.

He snarled, 'Now he's also facing a shitload of drug charges, including cultivating, distribution and dealing. In fact, his whole family are facing charges. It turns out the guy he beat to within an inch of his life the first time around was in the business as well.

He'd been dancing with the police for years about giving up details. He spilt his guts to them when the ex-husband was released. He didn't want to wind up dead by the thug's hands. The informer got a reduced sentence.' Liam hissed, 'With all the ex-husband's crimes, he should get about twenty years in prison. Thank Christ.'

He ran his fingers through his coal-coloured mane and then pulled at his fringe. 'Says something about how society treats women when he's going to get more years inside for the drug stuff than for stalking and nearly killing his ex-wife.'

Saoirse felt his anger and noticed once more that her usually unflappable brother did indeed have a fire about him.

'She's broken again. She's second-guessing herself. Even regretting going to Italy. She thinks that's how he found out where she was. He's Italian, still has family there. But they're from Southern Italy, which is why we headed north. She thinks they somehow tracked her through passport control.' He fisted his hands. 'It took her so long to believe she could be happy, and he's taken it all away, yet again.'

'Liam, you can't wait. You've got to go to her. Make her understand she deserves happiness. Everyone does.' She caught herself and thought, *I should take my own advice.*

He nodded. Saoirse could see her silent, stoic brother settle on a plan. Although he wasn't the fastest when it came to women, when he set his mind to something, it happened. She nudged him. 'You might be like a tortoise, but they do say slow and steady wins the race.' That brought a sad smile to both their faces.

Taking her own advice meant Saoirse had to stop drifting. Jessie and Callan couldn't be her whole world. She found her answer in an ad in the weekend newspaper.

* * *

Saoirse began an undergraduate finance degree at the London School of Economics and Political Science, better known as LSE. Callan agreed to support her while she continued to help him and Jessica.

At LSE, she met Dr Julie Casna. Her friends called her Jules. She was bold yet lovable, brash but amiable. Jules was older and a post-doctorate, lecturing undergrad students to give back while working for a top firm in the Square Mile, London's finance and business district. The blonde, blue-eyed tornado of sass and style took hold of Saoirse and spun her around, setting her on a new course.

In the months before they met officially, Jules observed Saoirse, who stood out in an economics class she guest-lectured. The student was bright yet rudderless. Something about that interested Jules. They'd spoken at various staff–student functions, which Jules and Saoirse had agreed were about as exciting as ironing handkerchiefs.

The friendship had grown by the time Dr Jules Casna slipped with a lithe glide onto the one remaining barstool at the bustling coffee counter. It was a rainy afternoon, and many others had scurried into the crowded university café to escape the determined drizzle. While tucking in her soggy elbow, she reached for her order and bumped Saoirse, who was squeezed in next to her. 'Hiya, Saoirse.'

Saoirse blew out a frazzled puff to move her damp bangs. 'Hi,' she said, before taking a good look at who'd addressed her. Then her spine straightened. 'Oh hello, Dr Casna.'

'I enjoyed your arguments in your latest essay. They were bold and well thought out.'

'Um. Thank you.'

'You're a little older than the fresh-from-school types. You've learned well from your experiences. Not everyone does. It's a good quality to have.'

'Thanks … again.'

They were acquainted well enough for Jules's usual frankness to cut through any further small talk. 'It left me wondering why you're not so bold in real life.'

'How do you know I'm not?'

'Because you act and look like you've got the weight of the world on your shoulders?' Jules recognised the gloominess that sometimes engulfed Saoirse from observing her sister Sabine. It was what had drawn her to the young student.

Saoirse's silver-grey eyes fired as she answered, 'Because for now, I do.'

Jules saw the fire. 'There's that boldness.' She'd seen a similar spirited flash often in her sister's eyes. 'It would help if you practised using that boldness more often. Start having some fun with it, and then the rest will come more easily.' If she couldn't save Sabine from duty and the pressures of family responsibility, maybe Jules could help this young woman. 'If there's no time to unwind, your obligations will jaundice your work and eventually your life. This'll sound clichéd.' Jules tilted her head with a teasing smile. 'It's more like a sarcastic joke, especially coming from me, but you need a work–life balance.'

Jules saw the gloominess return to cloud the fire and almost overwhelm it.

'Yeah, well, my work is here. I do balance it with my life, which is there.' The young woman's words saddened. 'There, at present, is being a mother to my young niece. Making sure my widowed brother gets up in the morning, keeps breathing, and enjoys his daughter without putting too much pressure on her to fill the hole his wife left.'

Jules's sister, Sabine, had done something similar for her when their mother passed away. Although, at the time, Jules was ten and Sabine was sixteen. Sabine had no choice but to follow duty and family responsibility. By doing so, she gave Jules freedom.

Saoirse continued, 'Your next question will be, what about the rest of the family or something like that. It falls to me. I don't mind because my brother's helping me pay for uni. It's a family thing.'

Jules drove her velvet steamroller on. 'That's only part of it.' Jules had been a shoulder for Sabine to use when the responsibilities of duty wore her down. She sensed Saoirse needed someone to share some of her sadness and frustrations. 'I understand more than you know. Who hurt you?'

'No one!' Saoirse growled. 'Well, no one that deserves any time wallowing over.' Her shoulders rose, but she held the sigh, meeting Jules's challenge.

Jules pursed her perfect red lips. 'Okay.' Then she rested her chin on her fist, looking Saoirse dead in her eyes. 'Losing a first love, no matter what the circumstances, is always hard. But we'll open that vault of intrigue later.'

'You're very forthright.' Saoirse edged away.

'Yes, that's me. Why waste time on the preamble when we'll end up here anyway?' Combing perfectly manicured nails through her golden tresses, Jules said, 'If you need any help with uni, just ask.' Her lush red lips widened into a caring smile. 'Now, before you ask why, it's because I can see a smart woman who is learning and thinks she needs to be uncaring to stop life from piling its crap all over her. You don't need to be a bitch all the time. Quite frankly, who has the energy to sustain that? You need to know when to bite and when to kiss. A woman can own both roles.'

Jules moved her upturned hands up and down like scales. 'I call it the jump-rope philosophy. You have to know which side to jump to when needed. I can help with that balance, too.'

'Uh-nah, I can't ask you to ... Look, you're very presumptuous.'

'No, no. Don't answer now.' The steamroller kept rolling on. 'Think about it. I'll be in touch.' She slipped a card into Saoirse's hand before squeezing it and then chuckled. 'And just in case it crossed your mind, I'm not hitting on you. But you need to know when to use sugar or spice, kiss or bite.'

eight

JULIUS CAESAR: VENI, VIDI, VICI:
JULES'S STORY

VENI, *VIDI, VICI* —over the years, it came close to being Jules's catchcry. She loved it fast, uncomplicated and intense. She'd personalised Julius Caesar's words to suit her world, just as she'd tailored every other facet of her life. The Roman general said: *I came, I saw, I conquered.* Jules Casna smiled to herself. She definitely agreed with Julius when she was in work mode. When it came to her play mode, she put her unique stamp on his words. At play, she was all about the *vidi, vici, veni*: I saw, I conquered, I came.

Jules Casna slipped seamlessly between her two Julius Caesars, some would say shamefully. To those who thought her shameful, she would say life was simply a game. Games were played for pleasure. Consequently, work and play were all about pleasure to Jules, and there was no shame in that. She wore her Play-Jules leather as impeccably as her Work-Jules silk.

Work-Jules Caesar-Casna was a thirty-something forensic accountant and finance analyst. She was never to be called *just* an accountant, although to the uninitiated, her day job may have seemed dull. Unbeknown to them, it was filled with excitement. There was the constant challenge of chasing down the clues and anomalies that numbers gave up. Jules relished pitting her mind

137

against those big fat pigs who were greedy feeders at the stock market trough. Those gluttonous few who wanted more than was legitimately offered.

She worked for one of the top three international forensic accounting firms, bringing down many a fat, dangerous pig. Because of the danger, life was never dull. Each time she cracked open the books of a selfish financial swine, it was reported as a team effort. Jules's name was kept out of it.

On the other side of the coin, Play-Jules Caesar-Casna was a thirty-something, red-blooded woman who loved sex and enjoyed making love as much as fucking. Why shouldn't she? In this age of sexual freedom and self-expression, Jules embodied a woman's right to be as hungry for forbidden desires and as superficial regarding the results as men were.

She wasn't a slut. Although society may have judged her as one, Jules didn't care. She was a discerning hunter, gatherer and discarder of men, not open to any man, any time. Her tastes were more boutique. Jules was always in control. That was her point of differ-ence: she didn't succumb easily to her primal needs. She wouldn't scratch her itch with any nilly-sized willy.

A woman who looked like Jules could study her prey carefully, hunt for quality and have it in sufficient quantity. She entered into no emotional contracts or connections. The consenting adults joined her party for two or three on occasion, fully aware of the rules and expectations. She took what she needed for her satisfac-tion. Jules shed society's norms and restrictions like she lost her shadow when she walked away from her sunny, everyday life to slip into her dark, sensual one. Here the use of her name was optional too.

Further complicating any pigeonholing of Jules was her upbring-ing, guided totally by her mother. Audrey Casna had instilled in her daughters a sense of duty to give back. It was why Dr Jules Casna gave back by lecturing as a post-doctorate at LSE and why she chose the work she did.

* * *

Work-Jules Caesar-Casna

Another day dawned, and Jules peeled away the thrill of her night-time hunting outfit to slip into the excitement of her daytime-conquering attire. She balanced the two lifestyles as easily as she balanced on her designer heels. They were one of many items that suited both her realities.

Today was all about *I came, I saw, I conquered*, and was more special than most. A unique lunch awaited. It was a day where she was giving back, and so she brought the full Work-Jules Caesar-Casna to the fore.

Napoleon Beaumont sat at a front and centre table, as Jules had wanted. She knew he liked having the best spot at the best restaurant. With this in mind, she'd called in a favour and reserved the perfect lunchtime table at La Tamise. He stood as she made her way to her seat. As usual, he was dressed in the best Savile Row had to offer. His bespoke navy suit brought out the blue of his eyes as he gave her a smile as tailored as his outfit. Jules, stunning as usual in her silver-grey power suit, obliged him by painting on an equally designer smile. It was how it was between them.

Napoleon was a short, squat man with a cue-ball head that shone majestically. Jules always saw her father as a caricature of a caricature. Rich Uncle Pennybags from Monopoly came to mind. All her dad needed was the top hat and monocle.

As he stepped forward, Jules did as scripted. Gushing, she bent and gave him a soft hug with an air kiss on each cheek. She heard his deep inhalation and hum as her father slid his hands down her arms. 'You always smell so good, my little honey.' She tried not to recoil when he slid one hand past her open jacket, over the red silk of her blouse to pat her outer thigh. 'My friends still get a kick out of me telling them my littlest honey has a job as a number cruncher in the Square Mile. It just tickles them when I try to tell them that you're there because of your smarts, not just your beauty and those fine, long legs you inherited from your mother.' He tweaked his finely waxed silver moustache with a flourish. The light caught the large diamond in his signet ring. 'I always thought you'd go into something more exciting than being a finance geek. Although I hear you're a whiz of an accountant, making all those high-profile books balance.'

'You're too kind, Father.' Jules smiled dutifully at him.

'It's high time you spread that expertise around and helped your old man out.'

He'd always been a small man. Jules and her sister had inherited their mother's beauty, smarts and stature. Every day, Jules thanked her mother for many things. Beauty and long legs weren't high on the list. When it came to traits her mother had gifted her daughters, fortitude and intelligence were at the top. Jules rubbed her hands together. 'Now let's get down to it, shall we?'

Holding his smile as they sat, Napoleon said, 'Of course.'

'I've delivered what you asked. I looked over your accounts and tidied them up.' She held up a thumb drive. 'This software program's been written specifically for you. I need your laptop to complete the install. The algorithm driving the software will automatically sort any future trades into the right accounts.' Jules slid the thumb drive onto the pristine linen tablecloth. 'Did you bring your laptop as I asked?'

He pulled his laptop from his briefcase and gave her a wink. 'Leave it to a woman to clean things up the best. It's what I need.' It seemed impossible, but as Napoleon's smile widened, it became genuine, and his over-confidence blossomed. 'That's my little honey. I knew you'd still help out the old man. All would be forgiven and all that. In for a penny, in for a pound.'

'Yes, as you always say, Father.' Jules took his laptop plugged in the thumb drive, and installed her software onto it.

Napoleon didn't know much about computers and was happy to let his daughter weave her magic. He sat back, steepling his thick fingers while he waited. As he peered over at the screen, Jules saw how he enjoyed the sight of his high-flying daughter doing work for him for free. He still thought she was 'just an accountant'—a fact she was willing to overlook to have this interaction with him.

She narrowed her eyes to watch her father more carefully. 'I've managed to strengthen the maze around your shell company, distancing it from your public buys and sells.'

'Hey now.' His eyes rolled as he patted her hand. 'I don't know what you're talking about.'

Resuming tapping away, she said, 'Father, you came to me, remember? Looking over your books, the numbers didn't add up. So I did a bit of digging, looking at your trades, the stock exchange records and company registries. Remember, I'm good at what I do. It didn't take me long to hack your security. Then I didn't have to dig too far to find the other company, the dates, the buys and sells you've made as your shell company. Oh, and I found the money, of course.'

He cleared his throat. 'I see. I'm not stupid, love. I did have an associate's top man put in protection. I was told it would stand up to most attacks, especially from any government number-crunchers who might look my way. But because I discovered it wouldn't stand up against someone with your particular expertise, I called you.'

Jules met his gaze. 'Well, you need more protection. Because I also found the emails showing you had dealings with some of the directors of Sentcor and Agazzi Industries. It seems your recent success is due to something other than good management.'

She spoke through a tightened jaw. 'Napoleon, it's insider trading.' She leaned in closer to hear him, wondering if she could catch it for herself, the tone her mother, Audrey, had heard too many times. Then again, Audrey hadn't fallen for it too often, either.

'Don't worry your pretty little head about things like that. Of course I have it all under control.' And there it was, the condescending, self-serving tone and arrogant smirk. Jules said a silent thank you to her mother.

'Come on, Father, you can tell me.'

Adjusting his Piaget watch, he crooned, 'It's just idle chat between friends. Who does it hurt, only some slob who thinks he knows what he's doing, playing the stock market while driving a taxi. A fool and his money, Jules.'

It was pointless to mention that he had a solid gold track record as a fool who readily parted with his money. Arching a finely styled eyebrow, Jules retorted, 'Father, you've just admitted you were forewarned that Sentcor and Agazzi Industries were not going to have their drugs approved by the Medicines and Healthcare Products Regulatory Agency. That you sold your stock before the company's share price tanked, making over five million pounds in profit.' She finished up with his laptop and removed the thumb drive.

Using the tone she now recognised as signalling a lie, he purred, 'Darling, it's fine. You know I would never do something underhand.' With a twist of the thick signet ring on his fat pinky, he continued. 'Anyway, you've fixed it. So anything else will be sorted too.'

She didn't want to stop him talking because he rarely spoke to her so openly. When she was growing up, Napoleon Beaumont had made it clear that Jules wasn't worth his time. She was the second child—and a girl at that.

'Father, if you give me specifics, I can fix your accounts more expertly. So how many?' She needed to give him a chance to explain as she shuffled closer once more.

'Oh, only a few, three or four here and there. But those weren't directly with Ari. It'll be alright.'

'You mean ... you're admitting you're in bed with Ari Hajib?' She stopped short of saying that after he left her mother, he'd always chosen dubious bedfellows. 'Oh well, I guess it's, as you always say, in for a penny, in for a pound.'

'Well said, girly. It was Ari Hajib's man who put in the first round of security you cracked. Now, with you on my side, I'll show those amateurs at the Financial Services Authority. Your work should make my little problems with the FSA all go away. Imagine that! They thought I wouldn't know they were looking at me. Why, it's almost insolent of them, thinking that a man like Napoleon Beaumont would need that Indian piece of work to make money.'

'Ari has his rotten fingers in many pies. The FSA is closing in on him, and people are worried.'

'But I've just had my books fixed by one of the best in the game. Let's celebrate, shall we?' Instantly, he clicked his fingers at the closest waiter. 'Be a good fellow there and bring my little honey here and me a bottle of Bollinger.'

Jules had no doubt she'd be picking up the bill. Her father always looked a million pounds, but had only pennies to his name. Her mother had paid the price in all the ways only a woman could. That said, Audrey always shielded Jules and her sister from the fallout.

'Little early to be celebrating, don't you think? You never know, the FSA might get lucky.'

'Never too early to celebrate, my little honey. I knew you'd eventually come through for me and help me like Sabine does. Her Jonathon also helps me occasionally. He's very astute at what he does. Your sister did well, nabbing him.'

In reality, Jonathon had been fortunate to 'nab' Sabine. Both he and Napolean had punched above their weight when it came to their wives. Napoleon twirled his moustache again. 'Your mother was lucky to snatch me up, you know. Of course, Audrey was good for me at times.'

'Mother certainly looked out for you as best she could.' Jules gave her father another painted-on smile while her feelings towards him iced. Sabine tolerated her father far more than Jules did. Jonathon helped him because, like Sabine, he was a duty-bound saint. By helping Napoleon out of a jam this time, Jules had a chance to rid Sabine and Jonathon of the bothersome Napoleon Beaumont and help restore her mother's reputation.

When Jules refocused on her father, he was still talking. 'All water under the bridge. However, she was such a stunning woman, your mother. So smart, too. Alas, my Audrey had a fickle mind, and that family of hers lured her back to them. They never liked me. I was too reckless for them.' Jules held her tongue as he prattled on. 'It was what attracted her to me, you know—my devil-may-care ways.' Then he winked. 'Best not to dwell. Let's have lunch, and I'll tell you more about the deals I have on the go. Maybe I can bring you in on some. You don't need to be a boring accountant all your life.'

It amused her that he still thought she was that little girl who would smile more adoringly and stand straighter because he was giving her praise, no matter how tired and clichéd it was.

Napoleon Beaumont had always been a compulsive skite, especially to those people he thought he could swindle. She would enjoy him telling her everything he had on the go. After the waiter poured the champagne, Jules picked up her glass. 'Let's make a toast to fixing your accounts and exciting new ventures.'

Today, it didn't matter that he was calling her 'little honey'. She knew he called all his girls that. It saved him saying the wrong name when he couldn't quite remember who he had on his arm, or on the other end of the phone, after he'd popped a blue pill and was looking to hook up. Of course, Jules's mum had always known about his little honeys, even when she was forced into the marriage.

His motto should have been *In for a pound, chasing a penny*. He'd gambled away his esteemed family's wealth and then part of her mother's inheritance. Jules's paternal grandfather, Sir Harold Casna, protected the rest of Audrey's money from the silver-spoon-sucking Napoleon. In the process, he preserved most of Audrey's dignity. His granddaughters greatly admired him. After the divorce, Harold understood their need to rid themselves of the detested Beaumont name and helped them take their mother's surname.

Audrey Casna shook off her shame and her broken heart to throw herself into charity work and finally enjoy life on her terms. She and her long-time friend, Sarah Carlson, started a highly successful worldwide charity. Audrey taught her girls well. At the heart of Audrey's lessons was that they should become educated, independent women who wouldn't rely on marriage. For Sabine, that changed when Audrey was caught in the crossfire between rival tribes in a war-torn African country. Her girls found it unbelievably tragic that their amazing mother, whose heart grew back stronger, ultimately died of a broken heart when a bullet pierced it.

It had struck a very frayed raw nerve when Napoleon had said Audrey had a fickle mind. Jules's mother never had anything remotely resembling a fickle mind. Audrey was wilful and spirited. Jules had been called the same things many times by the privileged drones she'd grown up alongside. Audrey preferred to call it strategic confidence. Mindful of this history, Jules used her strategic confidence and tolerated Napoleon Beaumont. Him entertaining her over lunch would be worth it.

Once Jules left the restaurant, she walked to a nondescript building where she met an equally bland but stern-looking man in a nylon suit and tie. He led her to a row of beige doors, choosing the one at the end of the hallway. The stale air slapped at her as she entered. A group of serious-looking men and women didn't pay much attention to her as they sat studying banks of monitors. Others poured over reams and reams of printouts that flowed over tables like erratic waterfalls.

The room was bordering on stifling as the computers and the sheer number of people nudged the temperature up. Jules took off her jacket. Only then was the slim bulge at her back noticeable under her red silk blouse.

She shook the hand of the lanky John Ellingham, chief investigator on the FSA's insider trading taskforce. His pasty face was as crinkled as his suit, which looked like he'd been wearing it for twenty-four hours straight. He closed the door. 'Jules, please tell me you got something. I need good news even more than a fresh shirt.'

This was Jules's giving-back time, freelancing for the FSA, the government's stock market watchdog. 'Better than good.' She reached under her blouse, pushing it up to peel off the small recording device at her back and wire wedged between her ample breasts. She handed him the device and wire microphone. 'This has him admitting to all his dealings. And over lobster, he gave me the names of all his partners in crime. There are more involved than Ari Hajib.' She showed him the thumb drive. 'This has all his files and spreadsheets from his legitimate company and his shell company. I had a very clever friend of mine devise a program for Napoleon's accounts. I uploaded it from this USB, so it is inside his firewall and will beat his security. It will allow you to trace any future trades he makes, even those on behalf of his shell company that makes all the dodgy insider trading deals.'

Wagging the thumb drive around in the air, she said, 'As good old Dad so nicely put it, I fixed his accounts. His laptop is yours, all his emails and trading accounts, you'll have every keystroke he makes and be able to track every trade, legit or not.'

John gave her a genuine toothy smile. 'I could kiss you. Thank you so, so much.'

As ever, Jules was strategically confident. She turned her face and offered her cheek. 'Here's the thumb drive, and here's my cheek. I'll take that kiss now.'

His pale cheeks that had spent too many hours under fluorescent lights flooded with colour as he gave Jules a quick peck. With the information she had collected, she undoubtedly came, saw and most definitely, conquered.

* * *

Play-Jules Caesar-Casna

It had been a long week in which her father's calls were constant, and her discounting of them unyielding. Finally, after months of further investigations and still more time to get their ducks in a row, the FSA moved. They'd kept her name out of it, so she continued to work and play as usual.

It wasn't revenge so much as destiny. It was always going to end with some dramatic tragedy for Napoleon Beaumont. He probably never envisaged it would be at the hands of one of his little honeys, especially one so close. He would spend four years in jail. Discredited, he would no longer demean her mother's reputation.

It was time to unwind. Jules slipped with ease into her seductive nightlife. Her Play-Jules Caesar-Casna persona flexed and was released to hunt for *vidi, vici, veni*.

The bar, although small, had a seductive ambience. The elegant décor was dimly lit in all the right places, and even darker in all the better places. Jules had chosen her vantage point carefully. She saw him from across the bar as he entered. Tall, ebony and stunning. Mmm! Jules watched and waited.

* * *

Tomas had been to the Nail Hard Bar before. He wasn't sure why he was back. It was a meat market. Tonight was Halloween, and he wasn't looking for a trick or a treat. He just wanted to drink and drown the stress. Jack, Tomas's friend, had convinced him to tag along as his wingman. As if Jack needed one. Jack would fuck anything. Not Tomas. He didn't like attracting the wrong type, Jack's type: the skanks. Tomas was a connoisseur. He wanted something that didn't smell of desperation, cheap perfume and nasty. It didn't matter anyway. Tonight, he wasn't in the mood.

A half-hour later, he'd been polite to Jack's hook-up's bimbo friend. He'd blown enough smoke up her arse that she wouldn't notice he'd blown her off. Having just extricated himself from her, he settled his bill. He had every intention of leaving until a Talisker, neat, appeared in front of him.

'Didn't order that.'

The bored bartender gave a fleeting smile before saying, 'Lady over there did.'

Tomas followed the tilt of the barman's head. His midnight eyes locked on to the clear, haunting blue ones that belonged to a well-put-together blonde. His interest was piqued as he raised his free scotch to her, expecting her to move towards him. She didn't.

Instead, she flashed him a predatory smile and turned her full attention, for the first time, to the guy next to her. He was chewing her ear off. She was not paying attention to anything he said, other than as an excuse not to meet Tomas's gaze.

Tomas drained his drink and moved over to lean on the bar next to her. She ignored him. He ordered another scotch, neat, and a Grey Goose vodka on the rocks. As she received the drink and the barman's message, she turned her back on Mr Mundane Grey Businessman and faced Tomas.

Without as much as a thank you, but with a honey-smooth voice, she asked, 'And what do you do?'

'I'm in construction. And you?'

'Really?' A single, perfect eyebrow arched as she dryly said, 'I took you for more of a Square Mile guy.'

'Now, why would you say that when I was trying so hard not to come across as a tosser?'

'Talisker, neat.' Her eyes hooded as she scoffed, 'If you were in construction, I'm thinking a pint of anything with hops and yeast.'

'Ah, I might like a change.'

'I'll save you wasting any more of my time. If you're in construction, then I'm just a humble fitness instructor.'

His eyebrows rose. This one was interesting, confident. 'Let me return the favour.' He stood back, openly tracking his eyes up her body. 'Not a fitness instructor, although your body would say yes. The rest of the ensemble would say corporate, investment banker, high end of town. Work hard, party harder.'

'Damn, you picked me.' Her tone scraped along his ego. 'But then again, I wasn't pretending that hard. Wasn't screening my hook-ups.' Before he could object, she added, 'Why did you feel the need? I'm pretty sure I didn't have that desperate, blonde-and-nasty look about me. Certainly not like the sorry piece of arse you just got rid of.'

'You didn't screen just now because you had already screened me. I spotted you a little while ago ... watching.' His lips lingered over the word. *This one was smart and sassy*, he thought. 'Maybe I was setting you a test like you set me. Maybe I wanted to see if you passed.' He met her gaze fully. 'You'd already chosen.' He rolled his tongue back and forth against clenched teeth, something he only did when he wasn't sure of the numbers behind his trades, which was happening more lately. Although he wouldn't have a job next week. His firm was being suspended from trading by the FSA because of his fraudulent dickhead boss's boss. He deserved to have some fun. His jaw unlocked. 'I'm just catching up.'

She nodded. 'Oh, a clever one. You could prove far more challenging than I was expecting to come out to play. Especially on desperate, any-excuse-to-party theme nights like Halloween.'

He took another swig of his scotch, his eyes roaming slowly over her face. 'Not many women get the chase, but you, you seem to have made an art of it.'

'Why should I make it easy? Too much of that going around.' She motioned her head over her shoulder to Mr Try-hard-in-a-designer-suit.

His eyes fired as he said, 'I guess there's no pretence as to what this is, then?'

She purred. 'You're so much more than a wingman.'

'Uh-huh. Now you're just blowing smoke up my arse.' He was impressed despite himself. 'But you already knew that. Testing me again.' He raised his chin to her, but his eyes didn't move off hers. 'Did I pass?'

'Yes, and by now, you should be ushering me out of here to grab a taxi to go to your place.'

'Oh, didn't I tell you?' he quipped with a slanted smile, 'I don't do that until I at least know the woman's name.'

'Jules, and you are?'

'Tomas. Pleased to meet you.' He paused. 'You haven't finished your drink. Drink up. Then we'll grab a taxi.'

Her eyes singed his ego. 'Don't need to. You've finished yours, and I didn't pay for this one. So ...' She nudged the glass the barman's way, and with an untameable smile said, 'I'm good to go.'

He wasn't going to argue. The flame stirring at the base of his spine made him move to follow her out. All the way, he enjoyed the sway of her arse. The cut of her black silken dress showed off every movement of her elegant legs and wondrous body. She carried herself with sophisticated confidence: very Hollywood, silver-screen chic. Very much steel with curves.

* * *

Jules needed that steel when her back hit the wall of what she assumed was his apartment's living room. He kissed like Ogun and looked like Michael B. Jordan. Suddenly, she didn't care that he lived at a fine Chelsea address. They were all over each other, chasing a frenetic jungle lust.

She sensed Tomas was mesmerised as she moved her hands up under his shirt and tweaked his nipples. He pulled back and shook his head. 'I see you like to play.'

'Have you just worked that out? What've you got?'

'Sure you can handle it?'

Jules moved her hand down to run it against his bulging zipper. 'You're not quite ready yet, but I reckon I can take you and give you a ride like never before.'

'Stop talking, and we'll see.' His lips were back on her and slid down her neck. He hitched her leg up over his hip. She wrapped it around him as her back hit the wall again. Jules levered up to wrap both legs around his lithe hips, her arms around his broad shoulders. She walked her lips up his throat and sank her teeth in.

He only needed one powerful arm to hold her to his muscular torso. With her open to him, his free hand travelled quickly up and along her leg. He trailed his fingers over her skin to the prize he was seeking. He moved her G-string aside and sighed, 'Not quite ready, either.'

She moaned huskily, 'Impressed.' Her lips trailed over his bulging shoulder muscles. 'You have potential. Most don't take the time to consider a woman's ...' she dissolved, 'needss,' as his finger entered her. She was lost to lust as he began to move his hand slowly and sensually while still holding her to him. She breathed in his heady, spicy scent. He was everywhere: in her lungs, on her lips, around her body and rolling through her hot folds.

Jules ran her teeth over his designer stubble before biting down on his shoulder. It spurred him on. His lips slid over hers to swallow the huskiness right off her throaty moan. He held her tighter as she moaned into another kiss, which resonated through his chest. His lips worked down her throat, tasting her exoticness, feeling her desperate panting, making his hand pump harder, needs and urges blurring into irresistible desire. He watched her eyes bliss out as she detonated, coating his fingers in heat. When Jules slid back from the high, her mind was stripped bare and her body breathless. She puffed, 'I'd like to come many times tonight, and I hazard a guess that you're a man who delivers.'

His smile said I'm-going-fuck-you-but-good as he threw her over his shoulder and slapped her butt cheek. With smouldering hoarseness, he said, 'Then let's stop feeling each other up.'

As Tomas marched them across the apartment to the bedroom, he growled, 'I like that you know what you want and aren't afraid of what that means.' He set her down near the bed, running his hands down her silken curves before they began to strip each other in a frenzy of fingers, teeth and hands. Material yielded and buttons flew.

She stooped to kiss his throbbing crown before pushing him back onto the bed. Her eyes were on the hunt as she stalked up the bed before taking him in her mouth. Initially only halfway, then a little further, preparing herself for the challenge of his length.

Twirling her tongue over the throbbing veins of his cock forced a grunt. 'You're killing me.'

She pulled up along his length, her cheeks hollowing. The pressure enveloping his cock was divine. She let him slip from her mouth. 'That's the point. A ride like no other.'

'For the love of God. Don't stop.' He didn't have long to wait as he watched in awe when she took him to his hilt. She felt omnipotent as her tongue worked his shaft. He groaned, 'I thought you'd be all about your needs. So many are. However, this—how you're working me—it's about my pleasure as much as yours.' He was her captive, and she knew it as he became even harder.

He was close. She had a better plan.

His eyes widened when she pulled off him. Desperation laced his words. 'Hey, come back.'

She flicked her hair aside. 'I want something from you.' She slid her body alongside him, her head still hovering over his shaft.

He understood what she wanted. 'Yesss. My pleasure.'

He grabbed her legs, spreading them so he could bury his tongue in her hot centre. She went back to pleasuring him, and he began returning the favour. Tantalising her by wagging his tongue just barely over her clit, urging her to lower herself to his lips. She dipped closer to his mouth. His fluttering became incessant as an erotic warmth began to unfurl through her core. When he drew her clit between his lips, Jules pushed her tongue into the slit of his proud velvet crown. Then she took him deep. Her satin heat took him to the edge. Sucking and nibbling, he fed on her relentlessly. It wasn't long before she burst into a million pieces and Tomas followed. Their release shot them far over the edge, leaving them to fall into satiation before rolling onto their backs, looking upwards, gasping for breath.

Jules noticed for the first time that she was lying on a luxurious four-poster bed. Four ornate metal beams connected the four intricately carved heavy wooden pillars. She caught her breath. 'Impressive bed.'

'We'll sample all it can do later.'

Tomas moved to tilt his hips down against hers while leaning in to kiss her. His smooth, charcoal-coloured skin was wrapped drum-tight around his toned body. There was no mistaking the satisfaction in her eyes as she watched his muscles bunch and move.

'Let's have a drink.' He jumped off the bed and left the room. She was slightly confused as he'd left her churning, ready to consume him.

He returned, carrying two crystal shot glasses and a frosted bottle of Belvedere. Jules had a few tricks of her own that would add some further spice to their enjoyment. 'Not so fast. I'm not that easy. Vodka is for earlier in the evening. Now requires a far finer spirit. Got any cognac, preferably Martell Extra Old?'

'The woman has style.'

Returning, he poured her a measure of Martell XO and one for himself, handing her an elegant balloon glass. 'A toast to finding a fucking equal.'

Jules smiled with as her eyes traversed his naked form. 'Oh, how I'm going to enjoy us again tonight.'

They touched glasses and sipped, enjoying the heavenly descent of the fine, smooth cognac as it momentarily soothed the beast rising within.

'It's good to find a connoisseur,' she murmured. 'Glad you like to share.'

'You're worth it.'

'Even if I do this?' She took his balloon in her hand, took a long swig, and pushed a quizzical Tomas back onto the bed. She set both glasses down on the bedside table. He let her kiss her way up his torso to drag her tongue over his throat. Once at his lips, she didn't kiss him but nipped the bottom one before pulling back to take another sip. Returning to Tomas this time, she kissed him properly. She heard his breath catch as the warm liquid entered his mouth from her lips.

She pulled back when he groaned, 'You, your scent and cognac vapours. Fuck, I'm never going to be able to drink cognac again and not think of you.'

That brought her eyes to his with a smile—predator to prey.

Then her lips danced over his skin once more. This time, she took the cool cognac to his torso and allowed it to trickle down to his navel. Her tongue swiftly followed, licking over the undulations of his contracting abs to catch the liquid, sucking it in and awakening his skin. He rolled them so she ended up under him. He took a balloon from where she'd left them.

In one swift movement, he took a sip and swooped down on her, returning the treat, kissing her and depositing the amber liquid into her mouth. It both tingled and burned as she swallowed. He was above her, dribbling Martell XO over her chest. She giggled because his tongue tickled as it flicked across her breasts, suckling the cognac from the valley between them, chasing the spreading tawny liquid.

The amber liquid slid tantalisingly down her body. Tomas savoured it, sucking more cognac off her magnificent flesh. When she leaned up a little, his lips and tongue had to work quickly to catch the spirit just above the waxed apex of her thighs. After lavishing his tongue over her, Tomas rose. Then, with the look of a noble knight but with a smile like a devil, he slapped her thigh.

She whipped her head up and saw a surprisingly tender look of veneration flow over Tomas's face as he started to caress her reddening thigh. His handsome features were a treat in themselves, yet his loving ways were sublime. Especially when he kissed his way up her thigh to soothe the sting with his tongue and lips. It eased, but his attention ignited her desires further. Then his tongue slid over her wet, hot slit, and she lost her mind. Emotions stirred and commanded the beast of their combined lusts to awaken, stretch and hunt.

Then his dusty voice seemed to make everything come to a standstill. 'How lucky was it that you bought me that scotch?'

'Luck had nothing to do with it. I observed and chose you.' She smiled wickedly. 'The chase, remember?'

'Then I'd say we both have good taste.' Tomas reached over and took a condom from the bedside drawer. He looked as though he could barely contain himself as he rolled it on before pushing her down.

Jules kept her eyes firmly on his. Wrapping her arms around his neck, she pulled him to her to take his mouth in hers, relishing his feel. He nipped her tongue, pulled back, and with a velvety voice said, 'I want to taste you again.' His touch was as silken as his voice as he set about sliding his finger into her hot core. He tortured her over and over before rolling his fingers over her breasts, around her nipples and down the middle of her chest. She was climbing again. He followed the slickness left behind with his tongue, and she could almost feel heaven.

He sucked one of her full and ripe breasts into his mouth, then drew out the nipple with his lips and tongue. When it stood erect, he nipped it gently with his teeth. Jules quivered as she flung her head back, letting the erotic burn quicken her blood and soak her.

'You have an amazing body. Your breasts are divine.' She arched and bucked under him. The beast pounced and he succumbed to the moment by plunging into her. She gasped at his beautiful, big roughness. She hungrily rippled around him as he slipped into her warm depths. Giving her no time to recover, a ricocheting withdrawal and thrust impaled her once more, rooting himself deep.

Tomas's guttural cry rumbled into Jules as electricity radiated through her. He thrust harder and rougher. His fingers groped at her thighs for leverage, leaving bruises as erotic sensations overwhelmed and fed.

As he rocketed into her, he nipped along her jaw, only to soothe it with his lips before kissing her. This time she clung on to kiss him deeply, his tongue meeting hers. She wrapped her fingers into his hair so she could hang on and keep kissing him. She loved his taste and the new depths he found within, a different sensual spot.

Tomas then moved back to her breasts so he could take them and graze his teeth over them as he pleased. He drove further shards of pleasure into her as he banged her in short and sharp thrusts and sucked on her breasts. Her nails raked over his skin. He groaned against her nipple, 'God, you're so good, so tight.' He slipped his hand down her body to where they'd joined. He let his fingers roam and work her clit. The result had her rocket higher and the beast within roar.

'It's all so fucking good ...' It had been some time since she'd been taken with such perfect savagery.

He spoke dirty words to her through gritted teeth. Jules moaned something feral as the animal they had created freed itself to fly and touch the face of the sun, such was the heat and brightness of their freedom in climax. The animal's appetite was only sated when she detonated, and he thrust one final time to pump the last of his desire into her.

As they came down, he hung onto her, whispering, 'You are so filthy gorgeous. I want to fuck you again and again.' With one long exhalation, he puffed, 'What a ride.'

'I deliver on my promises.'

'That you do. A ride like no other.' Still joined, his cock was treated to the zing of her retreating electricity. 'Beautiful,' Tomas murmured as he collapsed onto her. They lay almost fused to each other, both boneless.

Eventually, he rolled off her to dispose of the condom. Jules found some bones and was about to sit up as he returned. She thought she saw some hesitation and then he surprised her. Men rarely did. He crisply brought her close to him, her back to his front. Then she surprised herself by wanting to stay where she was. *Just for a little longer,* she thought, then fell into a sated sleep.

* * *

When he'd returned, the tangled beauty twisted around his sheets was making slow moves to leave. She smiled at him like she knew all his moves. Then it was automatic: he brought her to him, his front, her back, all silky heated skin. Her essence, her scent of flowers and honey, saturated his senses. All he needed, for now, was within his arms. *Yeah*, he'd made the right move.

He didn't usually sleep with the women he brought home. Yet this one, she had something he couldn't quite put his finger on. The feel of her creamy-smooth skin and the sight of her toned body spread over his bed wasn't too different. But her golden hair wild around her beautiful face was sublime. She was fearless in attitude and easily walked all her talk. It had turned into a far more treat-filled night than he'd expected. She was the panacea for his stress and far more than rock 'n' roll between the sheets, vanilla sex and a shower.

Her laughter was like relaxation therapy for his mind. Any lingering stress from his precarious work situation flowed off him as quickly as the cognac had rolled over her body, especially when her giggling made it move faster. He loved the way her skin bloomed under his touch and how her scent of flowers and honey was made exquisite by the addition of cognac.

Unusually for him, and he suspected for her, they'd sleep together before either of them could decide their next move. He fell asleep with a smile on his face.

* * *

The blind shut out most of the morning light's intensity, only slithers of sunlight sneakily peeking into the bedroom from its edges. It had been a long time since Jules had slept with a conquest. Sex was one thing, but sleeping with a guy and facing him the next morning was not her regular MO. She rose, gathered her clothes and headed for the bathroom while Tomas slumbered.

In the bathroom, carelessly thrown on the vanity, she saw his security ID key card. The sight snatched her breath. *Damn!* He worked for Ari Hajib. What were the odds? The upcoming court case against his boss's boss relied heavily on her evidence. This knowledge added an extra layer of irresistible danger to the hook-up.

With the investment house shutting down, Tomas wouldn't be working for Ari much longer. She noted his position within the company. He was unlikely to face charges. He didn't need to know she was the one who'd brought his employer undone, did he? He was only a one-nighter, after all. Then her strategic confidence stumbled. Did this have to be it? She did enjoy him not being her typical ride.

On her return, he was sitting up in bed, the sheet bunched around his waist. 'Given our night, you put yourself together well. Leaving so soon?'

Jules narrowed her eyes. 'Of course, I wasn't expecting hearts and flowers. It was good ...' She refocused to settle into her standard MO, 'A good distraction.' She sighed as she met his deliciously sinful smile. 'And now I must go.'

'Friday night, for round two.'

'Mmm?' The scales in her mind swung up and down, the negative and the positive. She liked his confidence. So many men these days were emasculated, confused by mixed signals and expectations. Tomas was an unusually talented and adventurous lover. Yet she didn't need the complications, and this guy had 'big complication' written all over him in capital letters. Although he could be worth a second dance. Who would it hurt? They were consenting adults after all.

'We still have so much more to explore.' His tongue slid over his devilish lips. 'I have a feeling a woman like you may like to sample some of the hardware this bed allows me to use.'

'Why don't we start now, then?' Jules coated another layer of sexy over her beauty with a husky morning laugh. 'I so hate to let things go to waste.' There was no hiding her gaze, sliding over his body to land on the growing bulge in the sheet at his crotch.

The animal attraction between them began to stir, stretching to raise its head in the peaceful morning light.

His gaze flitted from her to an elegantly carved, large mahogany cabinet sitting along one wall of his bedroom. Jules glided to the wooden cabinet. Upon opening it, a delighted shiver captured her.

The outside world would have to wait a little longer as the beast began to growl, baring its teeth. Jules's jump-rope philosophy came to the fore. With her feet still firmly planted on Play-Jules's side, she pulled out a piece of hardware that had chains rattling against each other, connected to strips of leather. Jules had indeed found herself a sex-fiend equal. The excitement vibrated through her.

Naked, Tomas moved like a panther to her, sleek with danger. He took the sex swing and attached it to the frame of the bed with minimal fuss. Once finished, he chuckled, running his finger down the silk of her cleavage. 'It's not such a shame that I get to peel you out of this magnificent dress again.'

'Don't be too quick there.' She grabbed the swing and shook it. The chains jangled, causing Tomas's darkening eyes to follow hers from him to the swing. A slow smile traversed her full lips. 'More efficient if you just climb on up.'

'You want me to …'

'Yes.' Leaning over and stroking him, she pouted. 'Do you need convincing?' She didn't have to ask twice.

He was naked, strapped to his sex swing, standing to attention with arms cuffed above his head, while she was fully clothed. Jules's lesson had begun. She took out her lipstick. Being a woman who didn't need a mirror, she applied a perfect fresh layer, leaving her lips wrapped in dewy red nectar. He strained against his restraints, telling her he needed to taste her. Jules obliged, parting his legs so she could lean in closer. She kissed him, knowing she already possessed him. Her tongue danced with his while her elegant fingers stroked his hardening manhood.

When they came up for air, she pushed him away from her and moved to kiss his nipples, leaving silken lipstick lips around them. Tomas groaned, and the weave of his magnificent abs bunched as she kissed his nipples once again.

The calmness of her eyes belied the heated emotions arching between them as the animal gnashed its teeth. Jules's control was flawless, while Tomas was steadily unravelling before her.

Now the chase was well and truly on. She was hunting him and steadily overwhelming him. By now, she knew her perfume filled his lungs, her lipstick marked his skin, her taste lingered on his lips, and her tongue began to caress a lazy path down his body to his cock. Dragging her nails along his sides caused him to jerk into the warm velvet of her mouth. She held him captive. Her audacious sexual prowess had him a willing prisoner.

Jules took his length and began working him, in total command of the act of topping such a fine specimen. Her core began rumbling as a soft blush fanned over her cheeks. With a half growl, half hum she nuzzled the thick nest of curls from where the root of him emerged. The vibrations had him moaning in response. Then she did her signature move—a twist, grazing and twirl of her tongue and lips, and he was groaning at the entrancing painful pleasure of it.

All too soon, she pulled off him, and Tomas opened his eyes to find her smiling at him with sultry blue eyes. Dominating him had her glowing, yet she turned to go.

An unashamed craving tainted his words. 'Are you just going to leave me like this? Hanging, so to speak.' He pulled on his bonds to the point of pain. Almost howling out his desperation, he pleaded, 'Jules, there's got to be more?' It was the first time either of them had uttered the other's name.

Considering Tomas's wild eyes, Jules decided there wasn't much of a downside for either of them if she took pity on him. Enjoying her omnipotence at having his fate in the palm of her hand, she decided to use it. Locking her smoky-blue orbs on his lusting ebony, she wrapped her fingers around his throbbing length and worked him. Her voice dripped with sensuality as she said, 'Yes, we have so much more to explore.'

He rolled his head back, his senses succumbing to the untamed, divine ecstasy coursing through his body. He exploded over the tight weave of his tensed abs. 'Yesss, yes.' When he came back to the now, a predatory smile claimed his lips. 'Now it's your turn.'

She uncuffed one of his hands and skipped away before he could touch her. Alas, Jules had graduated with honours in the chase. Apart from a slight flush to her cheeks and her fuller lips, she looked unaffected, pristine. Jules was sublime, sophisticated class. Tomas was frayed and spent.

'I'll be at Nail Hard Friday night.' He was still trying to free his other hand so he could catch up with her. 'If you're there at nine, great, if not, *c'est la vie.*'

His eyes hungrily tracked her as she strode across the room. Then she flicked him an intoxicating stare. 'Don't be late. You know I may choose another.' Then like smoke, she slipped through the door and let it close behind her.

nine

SAOIRSE'S third and final autumn as an LSE undergrad rolled on, with her knowledge of Jules and her jump-rope philosophy growing stronger. She'd learned many varied skills, not necessarily meant for the business of finance, but definitely for the business of fun. More importantly, Saoirse saw Jules as less than a study in the type of woman Saoirse searched for in herself and more of a true friend.

Saoirse had cut her hair to a sleek, sophisticated, bob framing her face in shiny black. It suited her high cheekbones, which had emerged from the puppy fat of her late teens.

Her mothering of Jessica became more natural as she grew into the role. Callan and Saoirse had settled into life as an odd couple. She, the messy young aunt-cum-mum-cum-uni-student. He the dour-father-cum-fastidious-pharmacist, where there was a place for everything, and everything in its place. His persona carried a bitter edge. He still couldn't reconcile living in a world without Lara.

Trying to lighten his outlook, Jessica and Saoirse added a rescue dog to their family. The part-Jack Russell and part-West Highland Terrier was a lovable, feisty bundle of wiggles, licks and giggles. She was a small mutt with a cute face and tawny coat splattered with white spots. Jessie named her Waffle, because that's what the dog reminded her of, and there was no changing her mind.

Meanwhile, Saoirse worked hard to make the top three in her class. However, when it came to men, mishaps and odd happenings seemed to follow her personal life, no matter how careful she was. As always, she learned well from her experiences. To those looking from the outside, she seemed a well-rounded, confident woman. However, on the inside, her heart and outlook on life were becoming skittish and defensive.

After three years, it seemed Saoirse was also destined to graduate top of the class in women who chose the bad guy. Something always happened, causing the journey to terminate at Splitsville. There were typical excuses, like she spent too much time dealing with her niece, managing her brother, or buried in study rather than her relationship. But it was the atypical excuses that caused Saoirse the most heartache. One partner accused her of calling him and hanging up before speaking. It had happened all through the night and early morning before an important exam. The sleep-deprived guy broke it off, not accepting her innocence.

Another accused her of trying to disguise her voice to call his widowed mother late at night, telling her to stop monopolising her son's time and cut the apron strings. Saoirse had no idea what he was talking about. Not believing her, he left.

On more than one occasion, the departing male told Saoirse her standards were too high. No man could meet them, and was destined to fail. Mere males had no choice but to give up and leave. Enter the barrel-chested, dark and brooding Tyson McNamara.

The morning they met, he'd sat next to her on the train. 'I've lived in the area since I was a boy,' he said. 'I've noticed you strutting around the neighbourhood with your niece.'

'I don't strut.' *A little harsh*, she thought.

But then he gave her a heart-melting smile. 'Imagine my surprise to see you at the same LSE lectures as me.'

She became closer to him than most by overlooking what she told herself were his quirky rough edges.

Not long after the beginning of their journey together, his rough edges started to jab more frequently, causing minor scrapes. The middle part of their trek became dotted with abrasive arguments as those rough edges became coarser, more resistant to polishing. Being rubbed the wrong way far too often saw the thicker skin of Saoirse's lowered standards start to thin. As a result, their relationship journey ended in a surprising squeak, rather than the expected explosion of Tyson's scathing anger.

Nonetheless, any lingering friendship was eroded completely when his rough edges fell away to reveal a corrosive, toxic core filled with hate. He said that Saoirse couldn't take that he'd broken up with her and was harassing him with abusive, spiteful emails and texts.

The exclamation mark to the total destruction of any civility between them came one Saturday morning. He arrived at her door, fuming, anger blighting his face. 'You just couldn't leave me alone, could you.' Loathing filled his dark-brown eyes as he spat, 'You vindictive bitch. Did you fucking do it? Well, did you?'

'Tyson, I have no idea what you're talking about. Please don't use that language. You know very well Jessica is upstairs.' Her stomach lurched with fearful dismay.

Scrubbing his hands over a peach-skin face, he almost bayed in anguish. 'You sent me another email. I opened it because it looked like it was from the course supervisor.' He slammed a fist into his palm. 'It was a virus. It wiped all my work for this latest major assignment. All my course work is gone too.' He stepped towards her. 'Fuck you and your *I have no idea what you're talking about* bullshit. Months of work. Gone. Fuck you.'

She watched, half in shock, half in alarm, but totally immobilised as his hands jerked around violently. Before she could summon the good sense to move, Callan pushed in front of her, blocking the backhand. 'Stop right there.'

Callan carried his phone in his other hand. 'Tyson, get away from my sister. Unless you calm down, I'm calling the police.' Being far angrier at life than most, Callan didn't take bullshit from anyone these days. He stepped onto the testosterone-soaked ground radiating around the younger man. Tyson blinked at his hand as if it had acted of its own accord. His bullying posture immediately deflated as his voice broke. 'She fucked up my work, man.'

Saoirse stepped past Callan, and although her words rattled like loose change, she managed, 'I didn't do this. I swear, Tyson. You can have all of my stuff, my research, my references, my notes, everything.'

Against a smaller foe, his vitriol returned. 'Fuck you. You better watch out, Saoirse. Your day is coming. I'll get you. I'll make sure of it.' He stomped to his car and sped out of their drive with tyres screeching and stones spitting up like tracer bullets. Barely restraining his anger, Callan turned to move past her, but Saoirse grabbed hold, wrapping around him, searching for support.

Callan pushed her off. 'Saoirse, you've got to stop bringing home arseholes.' The part of Callan that used to give her solace without question was frozen. Any warmth in his heart had perished when Lara died. Saoirse ran to her room and tried to find a skerrick of redemption to rebuild her shattered self-worth.

* * *

The semester moved on, and Saoirse completed the assignment Tyson had accused her of sabotaging. She submitted it online days before its due date. Later that week she met Jules to celebrate finishing the significant piece of work and coming up to three years of friendship.

Their plans to dine at the hottest restaurant in London took a dive. The reservation Saoirse had made months in advance—which was required if you wanted dinner at La Tamise—had been cancelled. The snooty maître d' seemed a little too smug when he told them Saoirse had incurred a one-hundred-pound late-cancellation fee, and the table had been given away.

'You concocted this story about late cancellation so you could give the table to Bono or Robbie, didn't you?'

'I assure you, Dr Casna, no.' Saoirse thought she saw his nose actually turn up.

'Don't deny it. You can move someone else around. You've done that for me before.'

'We may have before, but that was for lunch. This, however, is dinner. I simply can't.'

'It doesn't matter.' Jules took Saoirse's arm and began to walk out. 'We don't need this place to enjoy our night.'

While they were walking out, Jules's phone pinged. She read the text from Dr Jordon Howe, Saoirse's course coordinator, and texted back, *Yes*. It was her last frown of the night. They did find a place to eat and, of course, party as the night demanded.

The next morning, Saoirse rose late to notice she'd also received a text from Dr Jordon Howe. She was required to attend a meeting in his office later that day. It was unusual but not unheard of. She texted back, *Yes, I'll be there*.

* * *

As the door closed on a fastidiously tidy office, the similarly presented Dr Howe pointed to two brown chairs in front of his desk. 'Please sit.' The course coordinator's handsome face stretched tight with concern as he took a deep breath, before sitting at his desk.

Jules strode in. 'I was called,' she said, catching Saoirse with a wink and a smile. 'I came.'

'What's going on?' Saoirse sat up straighter. 'Why's Dr Casna here?'

After asking Jules to be seated, Jordon began, 'I asked you here, because we've had a series of unsavoury occurrences. And I require you, Ms Mahoney, to answer some questions to clarify your involvement. The department and faculty have questions.'

Saoirse's heart immediately kicked into her throat. Before she could say anything about not being responsible for Tyson's computer problems, Jordon continued, 'Also, it's unlike you to miss submitting a major assignment.'

'Even for me, it's a little early to submit the one given to us three days ago. It's due two weeks from now. I want to say—'

'No. It's the one from last month, that was due last week.'

'I submitted that with days to spare. I've got the submission-received email here.' She grabbed her laptop from her bag and struggled to open it. Trepidation rumbled through her like thunder dominating a storm. The more she scrolled her inbox, the louder the thunder sounded.

'She's allowed to be late once in her life.' Jules sniffed. 'Why summon me?'

'There's more.'

Closing her laptop, Saoirse clenched her fists on top of it. 'Like what?'

'Some department personnel have received some very unsavoury emails. They look like they were sent by you, Ms Mahoney.'

'What? No! I wouldn't do such a thing.' She didn't notice she was squeezing her fists with such force her nails started to cut her palms. 'I've also had troubles like this. It's not me.' Saoirse was drowning in angst and didn't notice the bite of pain her nails were causing.

Jordon adjusted his gold-rimmed glasses to let everyone take a breath. 'Before we could investigate, another flurry of sickening emails arrived, this time to the school's head and higher-level faculty staff. These emails had more vile accusations and comments made about the faculty and students. Again, they seemed to be sent by Ms Mahoney.'

'This is bogus, Jordon,' Jules exclaimed.

Jordon, although a muscular native of Barbados, winced like she'd slapped him. 'We would've treated them as nuisance spam, except the new emails made specific threats to some of the staff and their families. Some of the faculty had their computers debilitated by a virus. Again, it looked like Ms Mahoney sent it. Then your assignment, a major piece of work, wasn't submitted.'

A bead of sweat began a meandering run down his temple. 'Then we received an email from an unknown account saying that Ms Mahoney was on the verge of a psychotic break, that you were dangerous. It appears you'd threatened this person, who was too scared to tell us their identity, fearing reprisals. In fact, anyone around you needed to be careful as you could snap at any time.'

All Saoirse could think of was Tyson McNamara. Her head started to pound, and her chest tightened with each breath.

Jordon gave a sympathetic sigh. 'I've asked Dr Casna to join us so you'd have an advocate, a friend to support you as I informed you about these incidents and that we've begun investigating you and them. However, we feel we have a duty of care to the school and the faculty and must suspend you, Ms Mahoney, at this time, pending the investigation's results.'

Saoirse wheezed out the words between shallow breaths, 'What? This is crazy. You can't,' as her world started to collapse.

Jules rose like an elegant, scorching flame. Jordon outmuscled her two to one, but as she swept around his desk, he looked like an ant about to be engulfed by an all-consuming fire. 'You could've at least told me what you were planning. I would have addressed your concerns. You've ambushed Saoirse. Of course, she has nothing to do with any of this. I vouch for her unreservedly. She's not having any sort of break, psychotic or otherwise.'

He snapped back, 'Exactly, Jules.'

She fired him a ball-shrinking stare that had his shoulders hunching.

'Um, Julie, Dr Casna.' Jordon cleared his throat. 'We agree with your initial assessment. However, Ms Mahoney's laptop needs to be taken to Hilton Oh in tech services to resolve this matter properly and thoroughly.' He dabbed a handkerchief over his vast forehead. 'I need to take custody of your laptop immediately. It is evidence. Hence the need for the surprise nature of this meeting. I couldn't give Ms Mahoney a chance to delete anything from her laptop.'

Jules had walked back around to stand in front of Saoirse, like a mother hen moving to protect one of her chicks. 'This is outrageous! You won't take her laptop. She'll walk it to Hilton while you and I accompany her.' She took her hands from her hips and crossed her arms. 'Why suspend her? Surely do your investigation and then see where the cards fall before suspending her.'

'It's what policy and procedure call for.'

'Well, you know where you can shove your policy and procedures.'

It was the beginning of Saoirse's nightmare, or maybe it was only a continuation of her torture. It seemed one more poisoned dart had been thrown at her by an unknown hunter, and until now, she was his unsuspecting prey. Time was running out. Eventually, enough darts would stick and bring her down.

* * *

Dr Howe decided they should take the stairs to the basement area where tech services lived. The stairs went further and further downwards for what seemed like an eternity. Saoirse was alone with the echoing clack of footsteps bouncing off the harsh concrete of the stairwell. The light became dimmer, the air more recycled and cloistered.

Finally, they came to a small room where a wooden counter halted their entry to a weakly lit larger room. The part of the space seen from the doorway was crammed full of discarded computer hardware, while several monitors were whirring away, their screens scrolling through outputs of code, layer upon layer. Jordon rang the old-fashioned metal bell.

The ping sliced through all the clatter in Saoirse's head. Then Jules shouted, 'Come on out, Hilton. The bell's a little low-tech for you. You would've seen us coming before we hit the last flight of stairs. We would have triggered some sort of sophisticated sensor that would've set off an equally clever surveillance system that you have running down here.'

A voice with an extremely proper British accent rang out, 'Dr Jules Casna, I believe. To what do I owe such a pleasure?'

From behind the mission-brown partition stepped a butterball of a man whose head was as devoid of hair as a Sphinx cat. He wore old red Converse sneakers, khakis and a black T-shirt with 'The Codefather' printed on it in white. He had a smooth face with a light dusting of wrinkles set in the permeance of happiness. His eyes looked like they were forever telling a joke.

He pushed up part of the counter, tilting it back to allow him to step forward into Jules's open arms. 'Mmm, you always smell so good, sweetheart. Makes me almost want to leave my computer dust behind.' He bobbed his head. 'Not much of a competition. I love my computers too much.' He didn't chuckle. It was more like the sound a hiccupping hooting owl would make. 'Who, who, whoo.' An even more indelible smile set on his face. 'Hey, hey, did you get my algorithms and did they help with crunching those numbers for that client?'

Jules bowed her head. 'Yes, thank you, I'm in awe as always. They were exactly what I needed. Did you get paid for them?'

'Yes, yes,' he dismissed with a wave of his hands. 'The money's not important, honey. Helping catch those greedy egomaniacs is.'

Jules turned to Saoirse. 'Hilton, this is a very dear friend of mine who needs your help. Saoirse Mahoney, meet Dr Hilton Oh.'

'Most happy to meet you. Any friend of Jules's is a friend of mine.' Peering around the two women, he said, 'Oh, Jordon, you're here, too, of course.'

Jordon nodded. 'Hilton, Ms Mahoney has run into some trouble, and we need to ascertain if it's a mishap with her or something more sinister.'

While Hilton may have had smiling eyes, they were shrewd.

Before Jordon had said a word, Saoirse had felt his intriguing caramel eyes lancing through her like they weren't only seeing her innermost thoughts, but her innermost demons too.

As if reading Saoirse's mind he said, 'Yes, yes, I see all.'

She stiffened, setting her shoulders back to say, 'I have nothing to hide.'

'Of course, of course. I saw some of the emails sent earlier to the school. Terrible emails.' His eyes and smile warmed. 'I should elaborate. The computer sees all. You see, coding and programming have no emotion. Therefore they cannot lie. Even code aimed to cause distress in human life, once uncovered, has no disguise or pretence to the analyst's eye.' Tapping a stick-thin finger to his temple, he added, 'Studying those first emails and the code behind them, I wanted to meet the woman at the centre of them.'

Strung tighter than a violin string, Saoirse snapped, 'You can't think I wrote them. I don't even know half the faculty members, let alone have time to send emails about them. And I don't know how to do anything with computers other than using them for my work. I certainly have no idea how to infect them with a virus or even make a virus. If that's what you do.'

Hilton's gaze hardened for the first time as he glared at her course coordinator. 'Jordon, you shouldn't have got that cheap-as-chips IT operator to look over the initial breaches and fiddle with your department's cybersecurity. I've worked hard to fix the breaches and to make the school safe. I can tell you that Ms Mahoney is unlikely to be the initiator of the attacks on the department and staff. I'll confirm on inspection of her laptop, but I don't believe she should be suspended.'

'I've just told Ms Mahoney she's to be suspended. How did you—'

'I know you, Jordon, better than you know me. You should've come to me first before doing what you normally do. You know, make decisions based on emotions. When I looked at the breaches, the coding told me all. Plus, you told me. Jordon, you're clearly stressed, and Dr Casna wouldn't be here if it were a normal IT issue.' He continued with a slight bow. 'Plus, Ms Mahoney clutches her laptop like it's both a shield and a lifeline. So please'—he beckoned to Saoirse—'let me take it and start revealing its truths.'

'Don't you mean secrets?' Jordon said.

'No. No.' Hilton's eyes were as sharp as his voice. 'You never listen. Code has no emotion. Thus, no secrets, no lies.' He softened his demeanour. 'Please, Ms Mahoney and Jules.' He motioned for both women to move into his inner sanctum. 'Jordon, you can go.'

Once the sound of Jordon's footsteps died on the stairs, Hilton's lined face formed its usual happy features. 'Ms Mahoney, friend of Jules, let me have your laptop.' Then he gestured for Saoirse and Jules to sit on wheeled office chairs near him. 'What can you tell me, lovely?'

Saoirse went to answer, then realised he was talking to her laptop. After she gave him her password, he started running the computer and typed stuff into it. Immediately its monitor broke into a cascade of code, running up the screen. Hilton scanned the screen with his quick eagle eyes.

Saoirse's mind quietened, allowing her to think. Was this Tyson? She'd seen his type before. Graham Levitt came to mind, the vengeful wife-basher back in Brisbane, all bluster and physical intimidation. It wasn't the first time she'd thought Tyson had the potential for violence towards women. Saoirse had seen it before Callan had stopped him. She'd seen it slither just below his skin before it would surface with a vicious flash in his eyes, harsh words or a violent fist clench. It was why she'd broken it off. It was he who couldn't understand that she could leave him. Could he have the patience to play the game she found herself unwittingly playing?

Hilton's fingers flew over the keyboard in a flurry of keystrokes. He frowned and then, 'Ah-ha.' He tapped out a few more keystrokes. 'Tell me, Ms Mahoney, have you been on any dating sites recently?'

'Let's get this straight, Hilton. If you're going to ask that, please call Ms Mahoney Saoirse.' Jules nodded at Saoirse.

'Please do.' Saoirse took a deep breath. 'I guess as with my laptop, I can't hide anything from you, so yes. I was curious. Make that desperate, stupidly so. Anyway, I went on one.' She frowned. 'Um, didn't do much with it.'

He studied the screen. 'Was the site 4Eva-Love?'

'Yes.'

'Did you engage with anyone?'

'Not really.'

'What does that mean? I need you to be precise.'

'Okay, okay. One guy.'

'Continue.' Now Hilton rolled his fingers around on his mouse.

'We direct-messaged each other through the site. I got a bad feeling like he wasn't who he said he was. His profile picture seemed fake. The more questions I asked, the more his profile seemed fake as well. I stopped messaging him and quit the site. I went on the site after Tyson, about ...'

'Four months ago.'

'Yes.'

'What was this false guy's name?'

'So, he was false.' She groaned. 'I can't remember. It was one of those things I moved on from.'

'Think, please.'

Closing her eyes, Saoirse flicked through her memories. 'Mitch, um, Trader.'

'Yes, that would be it. Mitch Trader.'

'Why, has he done something?'

'First things first. Have any other strange things happened in the last months, maybe more.'

'Like what?'

'Similar things to your assignment submission going missing?' Hilton kept working on her laptop, scrolling through code.

Jules was more than interested now. 'How did you know that, Hilton? Even Jordon didn't say anything to you about an assignment going missing.'

'It's here on your laptop. I want to confirm a few other things. Saoirse, think.'

'If you already can read it there, why do I need to tell you?'

'Proof you're not who this person is trying to make you out as.'

'Shite.' She blew out a deep breath. 'Okay.' A headache lurked, drilling away at her temples. She told him about the various 'boyfriend killer' incidents and her latest issue with Tyson McNamara. 'Then there was the problem when I was with Jules.' Saoirse looked at her friend.

'Oh yes, La Tamise.' Jules told him the story.

Hilton pursed his lips. 'A booking made online months in advance, deposit paid, deposit lost.'

'Yes. Not really a hundred I could spare, but what are you going to do?'

'Okay, what else?'

Closing her eyes, she reached back into her mind. 'I was fined for a library book not being returned. It seemed just a simple mistake at the time. I hadn't even taken it out. I managed to salvage that because I could prove I was visiting a GP with my niece, Jessica, when it was taken out.' She took a shaky breath. 'The library backed down.'

'What was the book in question?'

'I told you I didn't take it out.'

'I know, love.' He reached out and laid a gentle hand on hers. 'I'm verifying what I'm seeing.'

She murmured, 'Arrh, let me think. It was something like *The Dark Psychology of a Psychotic Break*. Not my field of study.' She huffed. 'But given what I'm accused of, it seems someone was laying a path of breadcrumbs to lead people to think I'm an awful person and a psycho.'

Jules wrapped an arm around Saoirse's shaking shoulders. 'We know you could never be that person.'

Hilton nodded. 'Most assuredly. Let me dig a bit more, and I'll find out who did this to you. So, anything else?'

'There have been some bizarre and embarrassing purchases I didn't make that were delivered to my home.' She rolled her eyes. 'My brother found my young niece playing with a butt plug she'd ripped out of its wrapping from the mail. It looked like I'd purchased it. He was not impressed. Each time things like this happened, I cancelled the credit card used. All these things occurred sporadically over months. I didn't connect the dots. I thought it was all part of life in a new age of online ordering and relationships.' Her shoulders rose as she took a deep breath. 'Until now, when you've forced me to lay it all out.'

'Saoirse, you're a victim of a hacker who has serially attacked you. He has infected your laptop with a virus that then loaded a Trojan horse program on your laptop. It's not that sophisticated. Someone like me can easily uncover it. Nonetheless, it's troublesome enough that it wasn't detected by your antivirus software or the crap program and firewall Jordon's IT contractor set in place for the school. It was introduced when you were on the site communicating with this Mitch Trader. He then also attacked the school and faculty. He, as you rightly detected, was a false person.'

Hilton rubbed his hand over his bald head, all the way to the back of his neck. 'Odd, isn't it, that with all the names he could choose for a false name, he'd choose Mitch Trader?'

'Like it's a moniker for some kind of finance guy,' Jules offered. 'Does it sound like Tyson?'

'Could be.' Saoirse was stoic, while internally, Callan's words haunted her.

'Anyway, whoever it was, he infected your laptop with this virus. It installed a keylogger that tracked every keystroke you made. Especially your web searches and email.' Hilton pointed at another screen. 'He's behind the emails that were sent to the school and faculty staff. If those emails are anything to go by, he has a lot of anger. They were meant to point at you so that you'd be kicked out of the course. Luckily, your good work and reputation have meant the school considered it unusual. It's good the department brought you into my orbit.'

He tapped at the keyboard once more. 'Don't you worry, I can fix this and provide undeniable proof to the department that you have indeed been hacked. All this nonsense will go away. You'll need to change all your bank details and credit cards once more. I'll set up security around them, which can alert me to anything unusual. Your bank will have done this, but I'm better.'

'The bigger issue is who is doing this?' Saoirse held her head in her hands. 'Why?' The ache in her head was now a full-grown elephant thundering around her mind.

'We're meant to think this Mitch Trader did it. But as I said, he's a made-up name. After that, the real person has covered their tracks extremely well.' Hilton frowned, before shaking his head. 'Mmm.'

'What?' said Jules.

'It's almost like he wanted us, and in turn, Saoirse, to find out she'd been hacked, that he could get to you. Yet after that, he's hidden his tracks very well.'

He rolled his hand over his head again. 'He wants you to know he's watching you, doesn't want you to know who he is, not yet anyway. He wants to let you know he can get to you.'

Jules erupted, 'That's a bastard move. *He*, whoever *he* is, is a fucking coward. That's what *he* is. If he had balls, he'd face you. Then if you didn't, I'd kick them up his throat.'

'Ouch! Remind me never to get on your wrong side, Jules, my sweet.' Hilton patted Saoirse's hand. 'No need to worry. I can shut him out from your laptop and most of your life. I'll resubmit your assignment, but I'll need your laptop for the rest of today and most of tomorrow.'

'That's doable. How much will it cost?'

He rubbed his chin before smiling at Saoirse. 'How about you drop by tomorrow, closing time with Jules, and you can buy me a drink and dinner for fixing this.'

'Definitely.'

That night, sleep eluded her, like her hacker. Saoirse twitched and turned until the restlessness had her rise at dawn, deciding she couldn't settle until everything with her laptop— and life—was resolved. She needed to make sure that she was back on track, although her reputation had taken a hit. She made lists and began to work through them so the part of her life her laptop ruled over, which was significant, was back in order, or would be once Hilton performed his magic.

After leaving Hilton the day before, she again cancelled her credit cards and changed her bank account details. Saoirse needed this guy to be stopped, so she visited her local police station. They were as useful as a porcelain hammer, telling her they could only act if she had her pest's name or if he'd committed a crime like physically assaulting her.

The bored constable suggested that computer issues were still not really police issues, but technology issues. They had no expertise in cybercrime at a local level. She saw him become more attentive when she said the hack had occurred from a dating site. He flashed her a cheesy smile, advising her the only crime committed was that a woman who looked like Saoirse had to go on a dating site. Then he made a clumsy attempt at asking her out for a drink to discuss it further.

Fucking men, she thought. Which meant the early morning found her working through every aspect of her life. She came to the soul-destroying realisation she was being hunted, most possibly by Tyson McNamara, but she had no proof to confront him with.

Saoirse worked until she heard Jessie stirring in her bedroom. Family was the one constant in her life, and that was as uplifting as it was grounding.

* * *

When she sat across the table from Hilton Oh the following evening, her world seemed to brighten. He was sparkling company. Jules had been caught up at work in the Square Mile and sent her apologies. Saoirse was more than happy to let him entertain her. She was intrigued by this odd-looking but so totally content-with-himself man. 'Hilton, that's an odd name for a South Korean.'

'Ah, now that's a story, darling.' With a wicked smile and a wag of his finger, he held court. 'Nearly forty years ago, my parents immigrated from South Korea. My mother was heavily pregnant with me. When they arrived at Heathrow, they took a bus from the airport. They were so happy to finally be in this country that my dad decided to celebrate. He looked around for inspiration from their first experience in England.'

Hilton's smile began to grow and cheekiness beamed from his face. 'My father proclaimed there and then, to my mother, that the baby would be a boy. As he said that, they passed a very fine hotel. My father says to my mother, "And we shall call that boy Hilton." You see, Hilton, that's me.' Now hooting like an excited owl once more, he said, 'True story, Saoirse darling, true story.' He tapped her shoulder. 'Lucky for me, it wasn't a Best Western!' Hilton's laughter was infectious, and her worries were shaken loose with each chuckle.

'You're gorgeous,' he said. 'Why hasn't some strapping young man been Rhett to your Scarlett and swept you off your feet?'

With the best Southern drawl she could muster, she said, 'Why, Mr Oh, we've only just met.' She dropped the accent to shake her head. 'You should know, there's no Rhett for me. My laptop would have yielded my pitifulness.'

'Shhh, you're no such thing. Eventually, I'll get this guy out of your life. I'll keep trying to find out his real identity.' Hilton reached for her hand. 'I do know the Tyson guy who went all *The Shining*, 'Here's Johnny!' on you. He wasn't worthy, darling. It was good you kicked his sorry balls to the kerb.'

Talking to Hilton was emancipating. 'I don't think I'm destined ever to have real love. At this stage, I'd take having someone who'd stick for a while and not bail at the first speed bump in the road.'

'I hear you there. Sooo, share, who was the guy who broke your heart and has you so scared to love?'

She jerked her hand back. 'How—do I look like such a sad sop?'

'No.' His eyes still smiled as he held up his hand before tapping a finger to his temple. 'Not to the normal man. But my superpower – as well as reading code, my love – is reading people. It would seem I have hit on something with you.'

Before she could stop herself, she said, 'A married man.'

'Me too!'

It was cathartic for Saoirse to let it out. To talk to someone who'd walked the same track as she had. 'How are you so easy about it?'

'Oh, honey, I'm *soo* not easy!'

Saoirse's face dropped. 'Hilton, I didn't mean ...'

He gave a hiccupped series of hoots again. 'Seriously, it was a joke. Loosen up, Saoirse. Because I'm not at ease with it. At least I wasn't. I was devasted.' He took a sip of wine. 'It was ages before I met this other great guy, and things turned around. Then he became afraid of what was happening between us and pulled back.' Clutching at this heart, playful now, he fluttered one hand over the other. 'In this case, it *was* him, not me. He told me this many painful times.'

'Bastard!' she growled semi-seriously.

'Yes and no. He kept coming around, and we'd get back on the horse again, so to speak. Then he'd pull back again. Eventually, I told him he needed to get his house in order. When he did, then he could come round and see me. He's a big man from Barbados, looks like a young Danny Glover. He needs time.'

Her eyes shot wide. 'You mean, you and Jordon?'

'Yes. I find it equally as amazing.'

'Hilton, you know I didn't mean it like that.'

'I know, lovely. Just pulling your chain, again.' He squeezed her hand. 'Let me tell you a story because I think it may help you.'

'Please, I'm all ears.'

'At first, with my Barbadian dream, I wasn't as strong as you with

Tyson. I should've kicked his handsome arse to the kerb. With this big, muscular Barbadian interested, I felt like I was the ugly stepsister, but I'd gotten the prince. I mean, look at me. I'm a man with the body of Buddha and a mind like C-3PO. Guys aren't exactly throwing themselves at me. I felt so unworthy that I did everything he wanted. To make sure he stayed, I devalued myself.

'He left anyway. I was broken-hearted. Then he came back, got my hopes up again. I acted the same way once more, desperate to keep him. He left again anyway.' Hilton took another sip of wine. 'That's when he got that cheap-arse company to do the department's e-security. It was a major rejection. Which ultimately blew up in his face. I've had to pick up the pieces and sort out everything IT in the department.'

This time Saoirse squeezed his hand. 'I'm sorry, Hilton.'

'That's when I decided I needed to value myself above everything, especially love. Because love should be a partnership, have balance. It doesn't mean the two parts are equal all the time. To reach that balance, each goes up and down. It changes with who takes and who gives, and that's love, highs and lows, but in the end, you come together, which is beautiful.'

A slow smile crept up to his eyes. 'When he came back last time, I said no. He needed to sort his all-so-loco coconut self out.' Hilton rolled his eyes. 'He's so straitlaced and uptight, white on the inside. You know, he won't ride in elevators, totally paranoid about getting trapped in them.'

Hilton sighed. 'Anyway, when I say out, I mean out. He needs to stay out of my life until he sorts his life out. I don't need him to come out to the world, but he needs to come out, at least to himself. Until he can do that, I can wait.' Now a wicked smile claimed him. 'Who knows, there may be another gorgeous hunk just around the corner, waiting for yours truly.'

'I'm telling you now, Hilton Oh, the next gorgeous hunk that's around the corner is mine!' They laughed deep belly laughs, which shook loose some of the chains restricting Saoirse's hope. Their laughter didn't stop until Saoirse made it home late that night, where she slept like a baby. Her laptop and future were safer, with a fantastic new friend made.

* * *

As winter warmed to spring, Saoirse, Jules and Hilton caught up at least once a week for more than a little Saturday night fever, grinding the night away at whatever club was the place to shout Pink's latest angst-ridden anthem about leaving the guy at the bar with his drink and his dick in his hand.

They were irresponsible about their night-time drinking, and more than responsible for their morning dehydration and hangovers. Alas, no gorgeous males were sighted for long enough to be worthy of Hilton and Saoirse's company while they rehydrated with water, ibuprofen and coffee. Nonetheless, the enigmatic Tomas, with eyes only for Jules, started to make more frequent appearances.

Saoirse and Hilton were sure there were no sparks between Jules and Tomas because to describe what they were seeing as sparks was too small and dull. The friends were overwhelmed by watching the searing, white-hot lightning arcing between their friend and her new lover. All the while, Jules and Tomas continued to dance around their explosive electricity, trying to avoid the shock of what it meant.

The highlight was celebrating Hilton's fortieth birthday. It was riotous and, for want of a better word, a sophisticated pub crawl. Jules's sister, Sabine, joined them. If Jules was a blonde, blue-eyed tornado of sass and style, Sabine was a blonde, blue-eyed summer breeze of dignity and duty. Softer, but no less sharp.

Saoirse spoke over the *doof-doof* sounds of celebration and mayhem, trying to make sure Sabine wasn't feeling left out. 'How do you know Hilton?'

'I work for a charity, and Hilton provides his IT services free of charge. He's such a sweetie. Jules hooked me up with him, of course.

Underneath that party girl, there is a caring, loyal, smart heart. I don't need to tell you that, though.'

There was a lull in the music, which heightened the human buzz. 'Yes, she's been very kind to me. Then we party, of course. It's like the two must go hand in hand.'

'I'm the duty-bound one of the family, reserved and proper at all times.'

'I know what that's like.' Saoirse nodded. 'Being duty-bound. I'm the youngest of four children, with three older brothers. I always felt like I had to clean up after them when they drove Mum to distraction, you know, to help her out. That led to looking out for them even though I was the younger one.'

'I'm the older one, so like you, only in reverse. Although I only ever had to keep Jules in line.'

'I imagine that would've been more work than keeping three older brothers on track.'

Turning her head back to the bar, Sabine said, 'You know it.' Pride flooded her eyes as she watched her sexy, beautiful sister. 'I rest my case.'

Jules had thrown her arms around Hilton, kissing his shiny head before loudly shouting the whole bar a drink in Hilton's honour. Tomas's besotted ebony eyes tracked her every move. When she let go of Hilton, he nabbed her around the waist before dipping her, tango style, in a dazzling move that ended in her planting a sizzling kiss onto his lips. The Nail Hard Bar began pumping all over again.

'Oh my, that's a surprise.' Sabine clutched a hand to her chest when she saw the look Jules shot Tomas. 'She's never given that much away before. I wonder if he knows she's as wrapped up in him as he is in her.'

Saoirse took a sip of champagne. 'Maybe. Either way, they haven't worked out what to do with it. Although for us mere mortals, it's like watching a thermonuclear meltdown. All that heat and energy with nowhere to go unless they tame it together.'

'It's going to be spectacular when they do.' Sabine's carefree smile showed a deep love for Jules and lifted the melancholy that seemed to live in her eyes.

* * *

Although the bar was small, because of the partying, the dull lighting and pumping music, no one noticed the guy drinking by himself in a dark alcove at the back of the room. He sat in the shadows, nursing the same beer for almost an hour. He kept his head down and eyes up, carefully scanning the bar. He may have gone unnoticed, but he had a clear view of Saoirse and every move she made.

He left when Saoirse and her friends were noisily organising where to go after the bar closed. With his face hidden, he bustled past Saoirse as she and her laughing friends were in a scrum trying to get out the door. Cold, spindly fingers gripped her arm as he bumped her forward into the giggling bald geek. He got tremendous satisfaction from seeing her smile turn into a worried frown before the blonde Square Mile slut swept her into a waiting taxi.

He relished her feel and scent. His first physical contact in some time had him half-hard. He would wait. The time was not right—yet.

ten

A STILETTO TO THE HEART: SABINE'S STORY

SABINE CASNA HAD BEGUN WALKING A PREDETERMINED, well-paved road of good intentions ever since her mother died. That's when she was forced to traverse down the aisle to Jonathon. While it wasn't her road, and it didn't lead to hell, it did lead to less than. No heaven in this marriage, but heaven enough.

Coming from many generations of money, Jonathon's family had no particular aptitude for anything except nepotism. Sabine's family were old money too, and they liked Jonathon Wordsworth's old money. Out of all her suitors, and there were many, he was one of five on her grandmother's shortlist.

Sabine had tried to stay true to the defiant words she'd overheard her mother, Audrey, shout six years earlier, as she left for what came to be her final trip to Africa. Audrey was arguing with her mother, Virginia, who had hissed, 'Sabine is nearing an age where she must find a suitable mate.'

Audrey remonstrated, 'Mother, she's not some thoroughbred broodmare. Sabine—and Jules, for that matter—will choose who they fall in love with and who they marry, if they even choose to marry. Your match for me was catastrophic. The only good to come from it was my two beautiful girls. They will have a better life than I did, because I stood up to your outdated ways and divorced that bastard.'

Virginia sneered, 'Do not use that tone or language with me.'

Audrey radiated power like a lightning bolt as she scolded her mother. 'My daughters will not be pressured into becoming a cardboard cut-out of every other woman that's carried whatever old-money name you deem suitable for them.'

* * *

Lady Virginia Casna was the self-appointed custodian of the Casna family legacy and reputation. If she was to bear the responsibility of duty and title, there was no room for frivolity or ease in her life. She became a cold-hearted woman best described, in the kindest light, as set in her ways.

Napoleon Beaumont was from a family with title and prestige but no honour. He was thrust upon Audrey because their union was an excellent match for both families. Almost immediately, he squandered money and Audrey's love. The loss of the money didn't matter to Audrey, but the gambling with her love did.

After the first affair, Audrey was forced by her mother and Napoleon's parents to take him back. Audrey's father was out of the country and couldn't dissuade Virginia from sending their daughter back to her cheating husband. 'It's what women of her station must do,' Virginia had said to Sir Harold when he'd phoned. 'Don't be so quick to lay all the blame at Napoleon's feet. Audrey must become accustomed to her husband discreetly taking a mistress from time to time.'

After another affair, where Napoleon embezzled more money and fathered an illegitimate child, Sir Harold Casna boomed, 'Enough!' He was a statuesque man who never raised his voice at his wife. Because he had, Virginia seemed to shrink when he said, 'I have sat by and let my lovely daughter be traded like nothing more than prize livestock down at some saleyard. I will not see that rake hurt my wonderful, strong-willed daughter any longer. Divorce is no shame compared to the cost to Audrey by staying with him.'

He bent his tall frame to encircle his arms around Audrey and her little girls. He offered an easy, unwavering strength as he announced, 'Welcome, my lovely girls. You will stay with us. For as long as you like.' His eyes glistened as he searched Audrey's face. 'I will not see the light pass from your eyes because of this abomination of a marriage.'

The family went through the ignominy of divorce. In high-society circles, even in late 1970s England, it wasn't the done thing. For goodness sake! They were still coming to terms with the scandal of Princess Margaret divorcing.

When Audrey was shot dead in Africa, and Sir Harold passed not long after, Virginia stepped in as a surrogate mother and father to Sabine and Jules. That's when many of Audrey and Sabine's wishes were bent or diverted. But Sabine fought for three significant concessions. First, she would not marry until she finished a university degree of her choosing and worked for at least a year. Second, while not allowed to choose for love, Sabine would be allowed to choose the next best thing—a kind, honourable heart. She chose Jonathon Wordsworth. He wasn't like her father and much more like her maternal grandfather. For that, she was thankful.

The third and final request Sabine was granted was that if she accomplished the first two of Virginia's demands, Jules would be set free to have a life as Audrey had wished. A freedom Jules would be forever grateful to her sister for, and why she would do anything for Sabine.

While Sabine endured six years of Virginia's heavy hand, she didn't go meekly. On the contrary, the fighting spirit Audrey was so proud of was never far from the surface.

Virginia snapped at Sabine in her toxic tone, 'Do not sneer at me, young lady. I will not have you becoming one of those graceless ladies, like your mother and younger sister.'

'My mother and sister have a style and grace that far exceeds any of the women you think I should aspire to be like.'

'Like your mother, your sister is wild and uncouth.'

'Both prove it takes courage, love and vitality to find true purpose in life.'

'You know as well as I do you can't entertain such fantasies. For the sake of this family, your future as the eldest child will be different. Duty, Sabine, it's what keeps life ordered.'

Ever so slightly, Sabine's shoulders slumped, moving away from the posture driven into her by the finest finishing school.

With cold fingers, Virginia grabbed her granddaughter's chin and shook it. 'Stop that. It doesn't behove a woman hoping to carry herself as the lady of Wordsworth Manor.' Virginia pursed her lips. 'You need to maintain refinement and composure if you are to be a woman worthy of the station that is your destiny. Jonathon is an excellent catch for a woman like you.'

'What do you mean, Grandmother?' Sabine asked, not fully accomplishing an unruffled manner. *'For a woman like me?'*

'There are many reasons. Quite simply, you are a child of divorce.' Virginia licked her now sneering lips. 'Not to mention the poor choices and embarrassing escapades of your unscrupulous father. Deplorable.' Her porcelain cheeks rose and almost wrinkled into a smile. 'Yet you, my girl, have done exceedingly well to catch the eye of the Wordsworth heir. It's more than you could hope for.'

It was duty on the part of both the young betrotheds. Although for Jonathon, it was genuine. He told Sabine he'd found love and everything he'd hoped for in her. For Sabine, it wasn't true love, but true enough. More than most women who travelled in her level of society, Sabine knew that happiness didn't necessarily follow a title and money. Jonathon offered security and his brand of staid happiness. She found escape from her father's crimes and her grandmother's tyranny.

* * *

The couple seemed happy. The love they shared was reliable, like a friendship. Not much of a spark or raging passion, but passion and spark enough. As the years rolled by, Sabine did everything required of her. No one could fault her attention to detail and sacrifice to the duty of old money and title. She'd provided the Wordsworth name with a male heir and a reproducing mare-spare.

Then, to Sabine, sex became another duty to perform. One of her friends had once joked, 'It's just one more chore, and I'm sooo happy when *all* my "chores" are done.' Sabine laughed at first. Now she fully understood. When did sex become scary?

After two children, maybe it was her fault they didn't have fantastic, heavenly sex. Perhaps, her hardware didn't grip as tight as it used to, or was she loveless and frigid like her grandmother? Every time it was over, a sad frustration and an edgy discontent swamped Sabine. Was it her desire not to have a less-than life that gnawed at her resolve?

Then Jonathon's words, weighed down with expectation, would pierce the darkness. 'I love you. You make me very happy. Do I make you happy?'

'Yes, of course, darling.'

Jonathon would kiss her lovingly. 'Thank you. It means more than you know.' Yes, she'd be happy for the security and his kindness. It was less than she wanted, but more than her mother had.

* * *

Station dictated the firstborn son was named after Jonathan, as were all the Wordsworth heirs who'd gone before—he was the sixth. A girl, a second child, didn't rate as much to old money. Yet, she was loved dearly by Sabine and Jonathon, and they christened her Audrey after Sabine's brave mother. To Sabine, the name was perfect. Audrey meant 'noble strength'.

Both children had boarded at exclusive schools from an early age.

Sabine hated that they were away from her, but Jonathon's family's tradition dictated that this was the children's path.

Feeling empty and desperately lonely, she started working for a not-for-profit that helped addicted street kids. The charity was the Carlson Foundation, which her mother started with her great friend, Sarah Carlson. It had grown into a worldwide humanitarian fund.

Finally, she put her commerce degree to proper use and felt worthwhile. At the charity's community outreach program's office, there was a counsellor who worked with the worst of the troubled kids. This counsellor was unusual, able to match caring, practical talk with a no-nonsense, tough walk.

As much as Chris would frustrate Sabine, she couldn't stay away. It came to the point where she'd seek Chris out just to rise to the challenge of a stimulating conversation. She began cherishing their lunch-room discussions.

Sabine couldn't understand what was happening. There was nothing that should have attracted her. The Australian was far too bolshie. Sabine's type was not long, slender limbs tending towards rangy. Yet the muscular tone and how those muscles moved when Chris strode towards her had Sabine trying not to stare. Even when she didn't, knots tightened in her stomach and heat ignited in places where heat shouldn't have been when Chris was close.

Chris's hard body seemed to go hand in hand with the counsellor's arguing, which reminded Sabine of a whip. At times, Chris's argumentative style would be smooth but rigid, like the handle of a whip. At other times, the Australian's challenging questioning would be all fluid, like the length of the whip itself. Then, like the whip's popper, it could snap with the power to command attention, although in Chris's case, not necessarily to hurt, which took Sabine a little longer to understand.

They soon settled into regular lunchtime chats. Then came the one discussion that shattered Sabine's polished, duty-bound composure. In an instant, she had a full-on, shouting-banshee moment in her head. Because of Virginia's training, Sabine's stress and anger came out as a refined growl. 'Do you have to? I mean, really. Why would you say that? Jonathon's not like that. He doesn't scheme to be mute to avoid an argument.'

'It's what happens, isn't it?'

'It does not.' A whisper left her lips. Its coldness was far more threatening than the previous growl. 'You need to stop. Just stop.'

'You're giving your power to him. It's another routine you've fallen into.'

Sabine took a deliberate deep breath. 'It's not like that.'

'I bet before you were married, before you became just another chattel acquired in a marriage that was more a business merger—'

'How dare you!' The colour rising in Sabine's cheeks was the only hint of her inner turmoil.

'Okay. Either way, you were the higher achiever. Better at school and, I bet, university. It's because of your sex, your firstborn status, you had no choice but to become imprisoned to an old-fashioned ideal of duty.'

'You Australians may think family heritage and duty are stupid, but it's my life. It's. My. Life.' Sabine's rare cold fury continued. 'It's the life I was born into. Yes, duty has moulded me, but it's not all I know. Other elements were thrust upon me, which meant the freedoms I might have had weren't available.'

Her ice-blue eyes burned Chris. Her usual decorum took on a razor-sharp coldness. 'It's not Jonathon's fault. He's quiet and doesn't like conflict. We work with it. I may've been a higher achiever, but due to my father's gambling, which lost his and my mother's money, I am where I am today.

'My mother's humanitarian work was her way of giving back for having a second chance at building an honourable life. Audrey Casna showed her sense of duty was not to herself, her title, her money, or to overcome the shame he brought. It was to show the world and her daughters that there are better ways to use your money and standing in society. She began giving back to the less fortunate and started to wipe out the hurt he caused her and us in the process. It was her call to the duty you scoff at that was next level. It's the reason you have a job and why this charity exists. Her unfortunate death changed where my life was heading. I couldn't let my father's treachery overshadow her beauty or her achievements. It fell to me to correct all the wrongs and shield my sister. At least Jules could be free to live the life she wanted.'

Chris's face fell as shocked green eyes widened. 'Your mother's Audrey Casna!'

'Yes. You don't know me. Money is as much a corroding curse as it is a liberating luxury.'

'I'm sorry. You're right. Audrey is a legend.'

'Sometimes in life, to save others, you have to forgo personal needs and wants. And, like it or not, your life is changed. It depends on who you ask if it's better or worse.' She stood with a come-on-try-to-take-me posture. 'Just as your Australian life of freedom and thumbing your nose at authority honed and shaped your life. There's no best way for everyone.'

'You don't know me either, or what I've been through.'

'Well then, we've both perceived the other as a stereotypical cliché.'

'Point taken.' Chris smiled sincerely. 'I apologise. It was wrong. Honestly, I never thought you were a superficial, entitled woman.'

'Then what was the point of the comment about Jonathon owning me, not allowing me to know my own mind except as a duty-bound robot?'

'I'm not sure I said that, but it drew out the real you. You made a good argument and defended yourself. It was also refreshing to see the real Sabine finally surface and use all that fire and passion you bury deep down under that polished veneer.'

Chris's unexpected words took Sabine's hurt and anger, wringing them out, leaving only a trickle of frustration as she quipped, 'And here's me thinking you just enjoy riling me for sport.' Sitting down, she huffed, 'You're pushy and annoying. And for some reason, I keep coming back for more. Like I want you to draw that passion out.' She cocked her head. 'Maybe it's to let the fight my mother loved about me get a chance to be exercised again.'

Chris walked around the table to gently pat Sabine's shoulder. 'You're welcome.'

It made Sabine's mind drift to Jules.

Her sister was a woman who raised a middle finger to tradition, forgoing its security and its shackles. Women like Jules took on whatever presented itself with flair. These women laughed loudly, got drunk and danced with an uninhibited essence, long forgotten to Sabine. Most of all, this new generation didn't just love. They fucked unashamedly whenever the need took them. They merely lived their lives, making their own rules.

Sabine didn't dance much, never swore, never got drunk, never laughed raucously and certainly never fucked unashamedly or took part in any kind of fuck. The type of woman Sabine had become made love discreetly. It wasn't the done thing for a lady with the Wordsworth name and responsibilities to do anything but. While Jonathon and Sabine had fallen into their designated roles, Jules was free to try on as many roles as there were letters in the word 'undesignated'. When done, she'd start all over again.

From afar, it seemed the only similarity that Jules and Sabine shared was a love of shoes. Stilettos always had attitude. When these ladies wore them, they gave the shoes life. Nonetheless, to a hurried, superficial world, it was all too easy to see the sisters as totally different. If an observer took the time to burrow deeper, they'd find that where it counted, there were many similarities at the heart of the sisters' existence. Moreover, an unbreakable bond existed, created when two little girls united to join their brave mother on the battleground of a doomed marriage, and then to survive an autocratic grandmother.

Now Sabine struggled to hold on to a fading dream that she wasn't as old as her younger sister made her feel, or the shell of a woman Chris had described. 'Anyway, what's your story? Why do you seemingly want to break me down?'

'I don't want to break you down. I'm waking you up. With your children old enough to almost be off your hands, dare to be all you deserve to be, not less than you want.'

* * *

The red carpet, ball gowns and black ties rolled out for the charity's £500-a-plate fundraiser. Sabine used her network, rediscovering her considerable charm and persuasiveness, to have many influential and wealthy acquaintances do the right thing. She realised that she had a knack for the sale—persuading people to follow their social conscience. She wielded upper-class guilt like the Pied Piper's music.

Jonathon couldn't make the occasion. He'd been unable to shake a nasty flu and terrible cough that had lingered for weeks. Sabine was once more left alone for the evening.

'My God, look at you! I feel outgunned.' Chris took Sabine by surprise with a gentle hug and kiss on the cheek. 'You're stunning.'

Sabine's body quivered from the warm tingle the Australian set free. To Sabine's dismay, she realised she automatically smoothed it away as duty demanded.

She'd also followed the dictates of her station and experience, setting the standard of elegance necessary for the night. She was wrapped in a black sequined dress, so well-fitted it could kill simply by the attention it commanded. And her make-up was immaculate, as were her shoes and jewellery. The outfit showcased her fabulous body and curves. It wasn't anything new to Sabine, although the dress she'd chosen was a little racier than she'd have worn when on Jonathan's arm.

Chris continued, 'Even though you've made it clear I rile and annoy you, I hope we can call a truce tonight. I'm told you should compliment a lady on her shoes. In this case, Sabine, there is no pretence. Those are fabulous.' Chris handed her a flute from a passing server's tray. 'My God, how high are they?'

Sabine set about quickly greeting and smooching the guests,

making them all feel welcome and special, ensuring that they bid big on the auctioned items and their qualms about paying handsomely for partaking in the night were small.

She sat at the high table, charming all the charity's dignitaries and patrons. Chris was seated next to her because they had both come without a plus one. They laughed and talked the night away. The champagne flowed freely, and Sabine found herself invigorated and full of more joy than she'd experienced in a long time.

With her work done, the night progressed to dancing. She and Chris enjoyed the unfolding evening. Sabine finally let herself experience a night guided by her own needs. She drank a little too much, laughed a little too loudly and danced a little too closely. The success of the night gave her confidence, and champagne enhanced its shine.

The night culminated in the charity's workers holding each other around the shoulders, performing a can-can in a circle screaming The Killers' 'Mr Brightside'. Most unlike the usual MO of the reserved and refined Sabine Wordsworth. When the music stopped, they were suitably hoarse and falling over each other with happiness.

Chris caught Sabine as she almost toppled over on her stilettos. 'While I love your killer heels, let's limit the killer part to their height, shall we.' Sabine's heart also stumbled at the Australian's rare, gorgeous, goofy smile.

They made their way back to the table as the night had aged and given way to the infancy of a new day. Sabine pulled out her phone to call her driver. That was until Chris grabbed her hand. 'Let me drive you home. I've only had a couple of glasses of champagne, and it'd be my pleasure. This night wouldn't have been half as successful without you.'

Sabine could think of no excuses. They left the event together with only a few high-society stragglers noticing.

To Sabine's amazement, Chris led her to the only Subaru WRX in the car park. 'Is this yours?'

Chris's sharpness cut the air. 'Yes. It may not be an Aston Martin, but I'll have you know, it's pretty quick off the mark.'

'No, no,' Sabine said, reaching out and squeezing Chris's elbow, 'it's brilliant. I used to have one and loved it. A little older than this one, though.' She pulled Chris around to face her. 'Despite what you might think, I'm not a snob.'

'I never said that.'

'You didn't have to. Yes, my husband has money, and my grandparents have money, but my mother urged us to go to uni. She wanted us to get a degree to support ourselves if needed. I did commerce, Jules, my younger sister, finance and computing. We wouldn't be reliant on a man if something went wrong, as was the case with my mother. While at uni, I worked and bought a second-hand WRX with my own money. I used to drive it to work after I graduated and kept it right up until I got married.'

She smirked. 'My grandfather taught me to drive in his old, much-loved manual Land Rover.'

The Australian's head dropped. 'I'm sorry, I shouldn't have jumped to conclusions. It was stupid of me.'

Sabine chuckled at having caught Chris in a double-take. 'Apology accepted. Now, are you going to drive it, or do I have to show you how?'

Chris gunned the engine, and they sped off.

'Oh yes, this is how a car like this should be driven.' Sabine couldn't hide her delight.

'I imagine you drive like there's no tomorrow, especially behind the wheel of that Aston Martin. You and Jonathon must love it.'

'Jonathon, no. He bought the Aston for me. He drives like he does everything else in life, very carefully.'

'Uh-oh.'

'No, no, don't get me wrong. I adore Jonathon. He's just not too adventurous. Let me put it this way, if we chose songs to drive to, he'd be Neil Diamond's 'Sweet Caroline', and I'd be more Lenny Kravitz's 'Are You Gonna Go My Way'. But despite it all, he's my anchor, my bedrock, and that's enough.'

'It's an odd way to put it, Sabine.'

'Can you stop analysing every damn thing I say for just one minute!'

'You're right. How about I pull over, and let's see what the master, or is that the mistress, can do.'

Chris's adventurous nature released something profound and exciting in Sabine. 'Thought you'd never ask.'

Laughing and singing Human League's 'Don't You Want Me', they soon pulled into Sabine's considerably expansive driveway that led to her considerably expansive mansion. 'Chris, that was so, so good. It took me back.' She was giddy, smiling like an idiot. Her euphoria died when she looked at her front door—a door that led to her alleged safe haven yet simultaneously her prison. On a heavy sigh, she whispered, 'Way back.'

As Chris's long, toned arm reached across Sabine to open her door, it brushed a shot of electricity through her. Close now, the Australian's moss-green eyes flitted to Sabine's dewy, red lips. Sabine saw Chris's yearning to taste overwhelm the need to hide. The forthright Australian gently grasped Sabine's satiny chin.

The counsellor's touch called to Sabine. A sigh whispered from willing lips as she closed her eyes. Chris's lips skimmed and then claimed Sabine's. It was tender, and held more promise and confusing sexual tension than had stirred her in twenty years. Sabine's reticence weakened. She slipped, teetered on the edge and then floated into a long, beautiful fall. The lips that held her were giving and sensual, igniting her very core. Had a kiss ever evoked such blissful turmoil in her? Sabine welcomed it, falling further into the heated depths of the kiss.

Her familiar voice of propriety began to call, *This can't be.* Not for a woman in her position. Then came the warning scream, *This is wrong!* The cold hand of Sabine's duty jerked her out of the wonderous warm fall.

Sabine pushed away. 'No! I can't.' She cleared her throat, sat up taller. 'Thank you ...' With her mind spinning on frantic wheels, she thought, *What am I thanking Chris for? Is it for reawakening my passion*

—yearnings I'd dismissed years ago? As if drunk on the intoxicating vapours of Chris's taste, she rasped as she bowed her head, 'Um ... thanks for the lift home. I'm sorry.'

'I'm not.' Then, with a defiant chin jut, Chris snapped, 'You shouldn't be either.'

'I ... I ... Chris, you can't think ... I have to go.' She escaped the close, dazzling heat of the car for her home—a cold, lonely cavern where her existence was in shadow. Once inside, she was as empty as the luxury mansion she cohabited with an absent husband and family.

* * *

A troubled Sabine fell into her deserted bed, which in minutes caught fire as she relived the flames of desire Chris had lit. Rolling and restless, she thanked Jonathon for his thoughtfulness. His consideration, not wanting to interrupt her sleep with his coughing, meant he slept in another bedroom and wouldn't witness her self-flagellation. He was indeed her rock, and she loved that about him.

Yet Chris's scent and taste seemed to cling to her. She stumbled to her bathroom, determined to gain control. A shower had no hope of drowning the power struggle between bouts of heated pleasure and waves of icy shame. She tried to settle, but now it felt like a gloved hand had a death grip on her heart while its partner pounded on her head. The tug of war between her heart and her head threatened to rip her refined decorum apart. Now she whipped back and forth between understanding her need for Jonathon's honourable ties to banal duty and Chris's exciting companionship on a dishonourable path. Then there was the soul-destroying thought: was it a choice between being like her grandmother or like her father?

Each night after the first, she couldn't settle. Each day she worried, couldn't face food, and withdrew into herself. Finally, irritation conquered her brooding because the decision should've been easy. Yet the kiss had awakened a truth and vitality in Sabine.

She kept her distance from Chris and had lunch away from the office. However, she couldn't hide forever, and within the confines of a management meeting, it was inevitable that they had to face each other. Chris caught Sabine by the shoulder when the room cleared for a break and they moved into the busy corridor. 'Hello, stranger.'

Sabine blushed, then bristled. She could only nod, her sandy locks thankfully falling over her anxious eyes.

A plea left the Australian's lips. 'We need to talk.'

Sabine hadn't been happy without Chris's friendship. Nonetheless, that's all it could be. Sabine mumbled, 'Yes … Really need to.'

Chris pulled Sabine into an empty side office. 'Sabine, what's going on? I thought we shared something. I know you felt it, too. Why have you been avoiding me? Don't be scared. Please.'

'Chris … we have to forget about anything other than friendship. The kiss has to be just that, *a* kiss, singular, a mistake.'

'It wasn't.' Exhaling sharply, Chris pushed a not-so-steady hand through unruly copper hair. 'I know it was a shock to both of us. I never realised how much I was attracted to you.'

Frustration mixed with anger stormed Sabine's words. 'You of all people should know I can't throw my family into the middle of a scandal on one kiss. I'd be just like my father, a punchline. You can't ask me to jeopardise—'

'I'm not! You're getting *way* ahead of yourself.'

'Am I?'

There was a long silence, before Chris said, 'Um, all I want to do is talk, to work out—'

'There's nothing to work out. It's simple, I drank a little too much and did something I shouldn't, let my guard—'

'You let yourself be free. Are you afraid to be happy, or …' Chris's words were a cold burn. 'Is it that I haven't got money?'

'How could you say that? I've never treated you with anything but respect.' Sabine felt the hurt and fear rise. 'This is what happens when I break the rules of duty.' She finally pulled some of her self-discipline back into place. 'Either way, I can't act on any of it, not if you think I only care about money. You don't know me at all.' She strode away from a mortified Chris.

* * *

That night, Sabine went straight from work to meet Jonathon at their favourite restaurant for their usual weekly date night. Her mind was a metronomic mess as she walked into the restaurant, swinging between guilt and trepidation. Jonathon was already seated. He rose before giving Sabine a full, deep kiss, catching her breath with his. He held the tight hug a little longer. Now she was filled with suspicious surprise. She could always read him, but tonight her senses were off.

They ordered, and soon Jonathon was talking. She was used to him dominating their conversations, talking about his work. Then an unusual look settled in his eyes, causing Sabine to take notice, catching up to his words. Something was wrong. While it seemed like he was remorseful, like he needed her more than usual, it also felt like he was leaving her.

Then an odd kind of sad relief washed over her, because he wasn't leaving her. No wait, Sabine shook her head as the words sank in. He was leaving her, but not because of the kiss. It was because of something far more sinister than another person disrupting their married life. It was cancer.

Her world stood still and then came crashing down. Their love for each other wasn't vibrantly painted in all the brightest colours. Their love was more a watercolour filled with pastels. Even though it was subtle, the picture was beautiful. The thought of losing even these colours struck Sabine and shook her to her very soul. They didn't finish the meal, they went home and held each other, and she cried.

The next day she walked into Chris's office, determined to sort out the unsettling way they'd left things. Chris, as ever, understood. 'Everything I admire about you, your bottomless compassion and your unerring loyalty, is why you have no choice but to be there for Jonathon.'

'Thank you. That means a lot.'

'Call me if you need anything, a friend to talk to, a shoulder to cry on. That's all it will be. You have my word.'

Sabine's mass of conflicting emotions smashed together like Humpty Dumpty falling from the wall. She couldn't piece anything back together as she said, 'Chris, I ... you'll be the first person I call if I need a shoulder. I promise.'

Sabine saw Chris's forehead crease and knew the Australian had seen through her charade, catching her out in a dutiful promise. Sabine wouldn't call. Not because she didn't want Chris's shoulder. She wouldn't use anyone's shoulder.

* * *

For almost two years, Jonathon's cancer took a toll on both of them. However, Sabine's energy and love kept them going. At times, she even surprised herself with her capacity to keep pushing through, not only for Jonathon, but also for their family. Jonathon believed he owed an extra six months of life to Sabine's tireless nursing. It took until he was in the last stages of his disease before she reluctantly agreed to have a live-in nurse come to help her care for him.

At the insistence of her family and the nurse, Sabine took some respite. She could only be coaxed into taking a weekend break at the Savoy, where she would be pampered at the hotel's prestigious spa.

The two sisters made a loose dinner arrangement for one of Sabine's free evenings. However, if she preferred room service, a good book shared only with a glass of wine, Jules would be happy with whatever Sabine decided.

She enjoyed the first day of her break, and as the afternoon wound down, she sought out the surrounds of a sophisticated bar to enjoy her freedom a little longer.

She didn't need to actively share in the happy buzz of the people in the bar. She didn't have the energy to expend to be included. She only wanted to observe the interactions and enjoy the energy flowing over her, much like she would enjoy the warmth of a beautiful fire while she sat at its edge on a cold day.

She found the perfect spot to settle and escape. A small table lit by a dull candle next to a large window. She sat in quiet warmth and watched the world go by, loving the vitality of the humming bar. As she took a sip of her pinot gris, warm hands nudged her shoulders with a whisper at her ear, 'Hello, stranger.'

Her head shot back, causing the contents of her wineglass to slap at its edge as a familiar green gaze captured her eyes. 'Chris!' Spontaneous joy was ignited by the affection of an enchanting smile and overwhelmed any sadness.

Chris ordered a red as they chatted the dusk away. Sabine let herself drift away as the friends reconnected.

The sun had long gone when they finished up a shared meal of spices and conversation. The feelings pulsing through Sabine hadn't weakened with time. Finally, Chris broached the subject they'd avoided, and spice of a different kind heated their conversation. 'Sabine, we can't choose who we fall for.'

'You don't know what you're asking me to choose.'

'Maybe I do. I've made many sacrifices. Some have cost me. Others have shown me great rewards. Sabine, it's been two years. The feelings are as strong as ever.'

'It could break me. I don't think I'm strong enough. Yet it's so tempting.' Sabine looked down at her hands where the dull light winked from her wedding and engagement rings. 'I'm not cold-hearted. I can feel what's fired up between us.'

'Believe me. You are one of the strongest warm-hearted women I've ever known. It seems like fate has brought us back to each other for a reason.'

'You believe in fate?'

'Tonight, yes I do. I was literally just walking by. Something made me look up. I saw you through the window, looking so sad and alone. If this time is all we have, then we owe it to ourselves to share it together. To find answers. But one word from you and I will leave forever. Do you want me to go?'

'Jonathon is dying.'

'That's three words, and you still didn't answer the question.'

'Every part of me is saying it feels so right, seeing you again—there's a freedom that you give me. Feelings are swirling around me, grabbing at every part of me, my mind and heart. All from just the mere sight of you.'

'With everything we've been through, this amazing pull between us has to be real.' Huskiness roughened Chris's usually golden-smooth voice. 'Sometimes, the bigger the risk, the better the reward.'

'But ...' Sabine's chest ached as she looked at her hands once more, only for warm, slender fingers to slip over hers and break the spell of her wedding band. There was a dangerous wave bearing down on them. Rhyme, reason and rational thought were in peril. Trusted fingers tingled across Sabine's skin as a murmur left her dewy lips. 'It's so far out of my reality—'

Chris's marvellous mouth travelled over Sabine's throat, desire touching her in places she'd never dared to explore, yet somehow were always known to her. The wave of a never-experienced intense passion crashed over her. In its wake, conscience and duty's grip on Sabine were lost. She sank willingly into the surging desire, all her guilt swamped by yearnings for more than she had. She had no comprehension of the power of the pull unleashed until Chis seemed to hum, 'You can't deny it. We have a chance at something special, even after all this time.'

'Chrisss.' By lingering on that one word, the rest that followed drifted from her lips with more smoke and heat than she'd intended. 'If this is all we have, my hotel's not far.'

Once they were in Sabine's suite, they faced each other. There was no hesitation, only care. 'Sabine, God, how I've wanted you.' Chris's elegant fingers skimmed up her arms, sending sparks flying.

Sabine no longer planned, evaluated or considered. 'I've spent too many years overthinking every move in my life. Tonight, let's just do.'

The Australian's arms held Sabine as those heated lips skated over her skin once more. Chris moaned against Sabine's silkiness, 'You pull me in, twist me up and smooth me out.'

Sabine swayed back on a sigh to hold Chris's face in her hands, slowing it down to savour the reawakening of forgotten sensations as she lost herself in those jungle-green eyes. 'When you touch me, I feel so vital and whole.'

Exquisite, long-repressed sensations began to blow through Sabine, stirring and tantalising her desires, a prelude to the coming rapture. Loving fingers left Sabine's skin to slip her blouse from her. It was like it had wings to fly off her torso all of its own accord. Chris's hand travelled with a feather-like touch over Sabine's shoulders to rest above her heart. 'There's an ache here that can't be denied. It undoes me to see you hurting. Steel runs through every part of you. Pain is never allowed to show itself. I see it now, and all I want to do is banish it and bring happiness to the beautiful mix of loving grace that is you.'

'Your words destroy me.' Running her fingers through Chris's thick locks, she sank into a kiss, tasting and taking. Sabine's heartbeat kicked up. It was like the earth rumbling under the force of a not-too-distant tremor. Those first vibrations began rolling through both, commanding attention and releasing power. It had been so long since any energy had flowed into Sabine. For two years, she'd been giving every ounce of herself selflessly to Jonathon.

After shedding her bra, the rest of their clothes were tugged, pulled and thrown aside until flesh was felt on flesh and touch claimed the moment. Talented fingers came back to stroke Sabine's skin. Her breasts became heavy as those supple fingers moved to her nipples. On a sharp, pleasure-filled inhalation, she murmured, 'It's never been like this. It can't be wrong.'

The surge of attraction was as deep as it was taboo. Chris's breath disappeared to whisper, 'You're married, have kids, but I can't stop.'

In tune with her unlikely lover, it was Sabine's turn to reassure. 'Don't think, not now.'

Her words saw the pulses surrounding them strengthen. All the sexual tension that had built between them began to break free, unleashing an exquisite sensual crush that broke them away from their solitary less-than realities to bring them together in a world they shared this night. This seismic shift had Sabine gladly falling into the invigorating change. She welcomed the ground underfoot, shaking from all the overwhelming sensations rumbling through her.

Chris's fingers hummed over Sabine's thighs. She felt herself clench as that touch skated higher. Another silky shudder saw goosebumps cascade over her skin. Then those fingers dipped deep to find her hot and slick and hungry for more. With the first taste of burning release, love exploded, jolting her heart and marking her soul.

Chris's mouth was everywhere, uncontrollably grazing, nipping, kissing, sucking. Sabine was rocked by shivers and charged by shudders as she began to climb. It was fast and quickened the blood as the next temblor began rolling through her. Then she was lost to the wildness. Sighs and moans paid homage to the intense passion unfurling between them as the latest violent quiver became a resonant quake, and it crashed around them.

Sabine gladly fell into Chris's potent, loving ways. All those feelings that had eluded her with Jonathon crowded and excited her. Finally, she found the earth-shattering ecstasy she'd been searching for all these years.

Those sensuous fingers entered her again, slowly, causing a craving as new as it was intense. It rolled and boomed through her until she was overcome by an unstoppable force of nature. Attuned to Sabine's every need, Chris replaced smooth fingers with the silk of lips and tongue that caressed and drew Sabine up higher and higher to the next shockwave. Then she found herself sighing into the next erotic upheaval that whipped and swept her away.

No longer vulnerable or hesitant, Sabine's lips and teeth found Chris's skin, with her mouth roaming over that long, lean torso to kiss, taste and nip at its tone. A slave to the ecstasy, she reached for Chris and drew the Australian's arousal higher.

Chris welcomed Sabine's attention as searing need and want collided, showering the couple with overwhelming pleasure-filled energy. They were both spiralling free, out of control. Desire ruled and claimed them, to ride its power, to tame it, and once spent, to fall into bliss. Sabine moaned out a benediction of release as they fell into the calm of happy satiation.

As she rode the retreating high of being discovered and no longer hidden, she rested in Chris's arms. She didn't sink into the ebb's low and try to worry. Instead, she drifted into an untroubled, satiated sleep.

* * *

When Sabine awoke the following morning, her peaceful mind perished as reality immediately hit. What she shared with Chris was what she'd been searching for in her life. Yet their connection could not withstand the harsh light of morning, which spotlighted her duty and guilt. These two monsters had sharp teeth, tearing Sabine's heart apart. What would Jonathon say? What would the kids say? Did it matter what her peers said? This was the hangover from the intoxicating high of their forbidden love. Frightening guilt covered her like a feverish sickly sweat.

Now a new tug of war played out. Sabine wanted—maybe needed—Christine, and the energy and love that she gave freely. Simultaneously, Jonathon needed Sabine to give him all her energy and love to sustain him. She couldn't entertain the first because she had to submit to the second, yet again. Be the good wife, the patient woman, the duty-bound spouse. Would Chris be able to understand?

* * *

Christine awoke with a start, sensing Sabine's turmoil. Immediately, she took Sabine's hand in hers, forcing her to focus on her green-eyed gaze. 'It'll be okay. I know what you're feeling.'

'Christine, what have I done? I've hurt everyone. You, because I can't stay. Jonathon and the kids, because I didn't stay. He'll never understand, and my children will be ...' Sabine brushed at tears sliding down her cheeks.

'You'd be surprised how much kids understand, even before their parents do.' Chris was surprised at how much her heart was breaking.

'You can't know that.'

Chris had expected regrets, but not like this. Sabine looked so stricken. 'Try to hold on to what was the beauty of last night,' Chris said. 'That amazing feeling was your freedom.'

'There's no freedom now. All of that is gone, lost. Like a dream.'

'We have a connection, something powerful.'

'Yes, I'm not stupid. I feel the connection. You've proven to me I'm not frigid like my grandmother. I have my mother's capacity for love. That fills me with such joy, to know I've found overwhelming passion with you. Yet that knowledge is also soul-destroying, because it's a passion I can't have.' Sabine stabbed her finger into the mattress. 'Last night was the dream. This now, this is reality, my reality. He's dying. I was wrong to think I could balance your loving and beauty with my duty to him. Now I've hurt you and him.'

'Sabine ...' Chris's voice was like distant thunder. It rolled through the silence growing between them, commanding attention. 'Yes, he's dying, and it's horrible, but don't let this die too. Don't hurt yourself more than anyone else.'

'You have to trust me. Give me time,' Sabine reasoned.

'Why does it feel like you're running away?' Chris's eyes searched Sabine's for answers, anything tangible.

'I'm not thinking straight. I'm off balance. Please, the last thing I want is to argue with you.' Sabine sniffed. 'You're too good at it, and I'm not at my best.'

The attempt at humour was a circuit breaker. Chris sighed. 'I don't want to lose you now that I've just found you.'

'Then give me time.' Sabine's velvet tone hung in the air. Words and air were the only things between them, yet the words were like a wall because they resulted from the overwhelming, solid reality standing between the women.

Chris sucked in a shuddering, fading breath. 'This is too hard. You're right. He's dying. It's wrong of me to want ...' Her mind cried, *you, any part of you.* She understood the pressures of the level of society Sabine moved in and the duty she was bound by, much more than Sabine would ever suspect. Chris knew that while the lack of acceptance of such a love in Sabine's world was devastating, it was deceiving Jonathon that hurt more than anything. 'I can't be the person who stops you truly sharing and treasuring the time you and Jonathon have left.'

'I don't want to hurt him, but I don't want to hurt you, either. This is tearing me apart.' Heavy tears glistened down Sabine's cheeks as she tenderly reached to smooth Chris's new tears away.

Chris cupped Sabine's tear-soaked cheek and sucked in a deep, wet breath. 'As ever, my timing is bad.' She willed her voice to stay even, not break like her heart. 'I'm selfish. There's just too much going on in your life, too much pressure on you for me to ask such a thing. I, of all people, should've known better.'

Sabine blurted out, 'You're not selfish. I am.'

'No.' Unable to form any more words, Chris shook her head as she squeezed Sabine's hands. Lifting her willowy frame from the bed, Sabine carried herself with the understated grace that a Swiss finishing school had drilled into her. Chris grabbed her clothes and walked to the bathroom. 'I apologise for pushing you. It was too soon.'

Chris showered, the heat of the water not warming her as she cried. Had she pushed too hard, wanted—no, needed—too much, too soon? She dressed and looked at herself in the mirror, a cold, hard stare. Her father's eyes stared back at her, tear-stained-green and bloodshot. It was the last look she'd seen in his eyes. A glare full of confused hurt, burning with disappointment. It was back when he shut the family home's door in her face.

Deep down, she knew Sabine had always been a long shot. Christine had been a long shot once. When her family had ripped themselves away from her, it had almost broken her. She'd persisted. It had taken longer than she thought, and at times she'd suffered. But even her baby steps became more robust and, eventually, she'd flourished like she believed she would.

She and her beautiful mother had reconciled, short but sweet. Her dad, who she adored, hadn't spoken to her since that fateful day. It had been five years ago when she'd told them. Her father had shouted back. 'You're confused. You're not one of those women. You're just not gay! Christine, you're beautiful, successful.' Then his anger came when she made it clear she was resolute. 'Don't throw your life away on cheap infatuation. Money just doesn't grow on trees. You won't get any more from me.'

She walked away from her privileged family, high-powered job and life to follow the dream of a happy, more fulfilling life. She'd lived off her savings, scraped and scrimped until she eventually found the work she loved and carved out the life she wanted. Reinvigorated, Chris had even returned to law. She'd worked on some pro bono cases for the foundation and rediscovered her love of it. She was considering a return to some paid work. Her old firm was eager to have her, even if part-time.

Now, all her brilliant successes seemed to dull at having to leave Sabine. As Chris was about to walk out of the hotel room, Sabine reached for her hand. Fighting back the tears, she said, 'I'm so sorry. You're the first person who has ever evoked such strong passions in me. Oh God. I have nothing else to lose, so I'll say it. Chris, you fill me with such hope for real love. That's what you've brought to me, at one of the lowest points of my life. But I need this, this time.'

'I felt it, too. So, I will wait and hope.' Yes, she could wait, leave the door open for another long shot to walk through. Even a long shot still had a shot.

Chris stepped forward and took Sabine's silken lips with hers one last time. It was selfish, yet Sabine's mouth met hers and deep electricity pulsed between them. Finally, Christine fought against every emotion and pulled back. 'When you find your balance, I'll be waiting.'

Sabine nodded, tears streaming down her cheeks. She choked out, 'Thank you,' and she shut the door on happiness once more.

Sabine went straight to Jonathon's room when she returned home and hardly left it in the months that followed. Together they finalised his affairs. Jonathon left her everything, and they made generous provisions for their children—how he loved Sabine and his children, his finest accomplishments.

On a crisp morning, young Audrey found her mother alone in her father's study, tears tracking down hollowed cheeks. Sabine was looking out the study's window, not seeing the world outside the room. Audrey wrapped her capable arms around Sabine, resting her head on her mother's shoulder, which for so long had carried so much weight. They shared one of the most important of love's connections, that of a beautiful mother–daughter bond.

'Mum, you've given everything to Dad, Jonathon and me.' She hugged Sabine tighter. 'You've always kept all the worst of the Wordsworth family pressures away from us, letting us find our paths to success, and still kept the Wordsworths on our side. That's no mean feat. You're amazing.' As she pulled back and swiped at her own tears, she turned Sabine to face her. 'All we ever want is for you to be happy. Now you must follow your dreams, your passions. We'll support you.' Then she looked Sabine dead in her eyes. 'No matter what they are or who they're with.'

When the final hour came, Jonathon was made comfortable by his doctor. Sabine was sitting by his side with young Jonathon and Audrey. The teenagers said their goodbyes and left their mother and father, sensing they needed to be alone. At least Audrey did, and pulled her brother along with her.

Jonathon's words scratched out. 'Sabine, you chose me. You could've had anyone.' His breathing came in pained wheezes. 'You're my electric charge ... of wonder. I needed you more than you ... me.'

'Jonathon, I adored you every day. You're the only man I've ever loved.'

'I know.' Tired eyes searched hers, showing understanding.

With a thud of her heart, her mind exploded. 'You knew! How?'

'Didn't fully. You just confirmed.' Shock and embarrassment rose with a blush that flooded her neck and face. Jonathon grasped her hand. 'I know you love me.' Another rattling breath carried his words. 'And always gave me the best ... you could.' He swallowed while she was stunned into silence. 'It meant what you gave me ... did for me, more ... special. God, I love you.'

Sabine nodded, silencing a sob. Jonathon kissed her hand, beckoning to her. She did as she had always done, bent to him.

Summoning all his breath, he said, 'Be true to yourself now. Find your electric charge of wonder.' Crumbling into tears, she tenderly placed her lips to his and they shared one last painfully exquisite kiss. And in that moment the world stopped and surrounded them in a love that wasn't painted in the pastels of just enough, but a vibrant more than.

Sabine held him, yet no matter how tight she clung to him, he slipped from her, leaving only a shell. Even before the nurse came in and urged Sabine to let Jonathon go, she knew his soul had departed, drifting away on a warm, loving breeze.

After months of sorting out her life, Sabine's first step back into the world of society was a lunch for bitter women of 'old money'. While that wasn't its official title, it could have been. She wanted to see if she should hang on to this world. She soon had her answer. The conversation at her table turned to how *hard* these women's lives were, dealing with the pool boy or having to oversee the laundering of their children's clothes so they didn't scratch poor little Harrison's neck. She'd heard it all before. Yet this time she was struck with a renewed awareness and felt positively sick at their superficiality and uselessness.

Just as she was about to leave, one of the women, whose name was Lavinia and who liked to pronounce it Lavinierrr, began to gossip a little too loudly. 'I can't believe that such a well-respected law firm would take someone like her back. It's a travesty.' Lavinia crowed, 'You did some charity work with her, didn't you?'

'Sorry, who are you speaking of?'

'Christine Larrimar, of *the* Larrimars.'

'Who?' Sabine tuned into the conversation more keenly.

Lavinia tossed out a malicious smirk as she dabbed a crisp linen napkin over her artificially plump lips. 'She's the girl that gave it all away. She went to all the finest schools and a top finishing school. Her family owns half of all the prime real estate around Canary Wharf, and her father owns most of Australia. However, he's an English citizen now, typical Antipodean. Apparently, she was this successful lawyer in Sydney and then London, but gave it all away to work with street kids at a charity. Sooo, Sabine, a little bird told me you were quite close to Christine when you volunteered at the Carlson Foundation?'

Bunny, another Botoxed Barbie, interjected, 'Sabine did more than volunteer. She worked there for *nothing*, to run all their accounts, didn't you?'

Resisting the urge to explain volunteering, Sabine answered, 'Um, yes, something like that. Although I met a Christine Tate.'

Trying not to give too much information to the eager-to-hunt society piranhas, she asked, 'That's not who you're talking about, is it?'

'Oh yes, lovey.' Bunny's lips curled. 'Haven't you been listening? She goes by her mother's maiden name. She has some silly notion that the Larrimar name is toxic for what she wants to achieve. Heavens. Just imagine. It must be all that time she spent in Australia.'

'Yes, I did meet her. She's a remarkable woman. The charity is lucky to have her. What have you heard?' Sabine was sorry she'd asked, as a feeding frenzy on the woman she felt so deeply about was unleashed. It was appalling, like they were biting off chunks of Sabine's flesh as they stripped Christine apart between sips of imported champagne and inbred sniggers.

There was one homophobic story after another, each more sordid than the last. The entitled women didn't realise it, but they were getting their rocks off talking about the very thing they were saying disgusted them. Lavinia, the queen piranha, put her final bite of disapproval on Christine with a terse, 'Her father has disowned her. It's so shameful. Oh yes, definitely bats for the other team, wears comfortable shoes and all that. Isn't it so, Sabine?'

Sabine's chest ached as she sighed, 'She's a beautiful woman.' Then with a jut of her chin Chris would have been proud of, she said, 'I happen to know she's worth more than all of you sitting at this table put together, and I'm not talking money. I'm talking about what counts in life—integrity, grace and consideration for others. She's one reason the charity is so successful. I don't expect you to understand. She's strong and courageous, daring to strike out on her own. Her life will amount to something wonderful. She has true purpose, whereas your lives are just all cardboard cut-outs of every other woman that's been before you.'

Sabine rose to her full height, staring each down. 'And might I add, you're all pretty pathetic copies of those women who previously bore your surnames.' She turned to go. 'Yes, in answer to your question. Yes, but I did more than just meet Christine. I happen to love her. I mean really L-O-V-E her.' She pushed her hair back. 'Plus, she definitely wears far more stunning stilettos than any of your sad excuses for style. Chew on that. Choke for all I care.'

As she strode away, she could almost hear their plastic surgery and Botox failing as the luncheon ladies tried to raise their eyebrows and furrow their foreheads. The strain almost cracked their brows, which usually looked like large, flat-screen TVs where no transmission was possible.

Sabine walked away knowing she wasn't anything like her grandmother—and was most assuredly nothing like her father. She was far closer to being like her mother. Better than that, she was the woman Audrey had dreamed she'd be. She was Sabine.

* * *

A week later, Sabine accepted an invitation to the foundation's annual gala ball. When she entered the mood-lit ballroom, Christine stood chatting to a significant donor. Chris didn't know Sabine was attending until she turned towards the room's entrance. As the DJ began to play Coldplay's 'Yellow', it became Sabine's anthem. She cut a dazzling swathe through the crowd like elegant, golden scissors slicing through black silk. The golden gown she wore was fitted and cut low at the back, with a split that commanded attention to her legs. The crowd fell away.

Christine almost tripped over her fabulous designer shoes, a fantastic pair of blue Louboutins. She shone in a blue satin dress she wore like skin.

Sabine's eyes flicked from her impressive shoes to ride up the outline of the Australian's athletic legs, which didn't quit until they hit her toned butt. She smiled unashamedly at Chris's stunned face. That one look revealed more than any others they'd shared.

Christine ran her fingers through her smooth, auburn locks and sucked in her bottom lip as she watched Sabine moving towards her. Then she handed her champagne flute to the woman she'd been talking to and moved towards Sabine.

In that moment, it was like Sabine had taken one of her much-loved stilettos, and using it like Cupid's arrow, shot it through Christine's heart, making it impossible for either woman to escape. For Sabine, it was like she was home as her heart filled with all the passion and fire she'd denied herself all these years.

When she was within touching distance, the buzz of people around them dissolved as the magnetic pull between the pair intensified, drowning out all else. Chris started to say, 'I see you've found your balance. Can I—'

Sabine wasn't standing on duty any longer. She slid her slightly shaking hands over Chris's slender hips to take her mouth with nervous ruby-red lips. As the song hit its climax, Sabine pulled back, the lights making her eyes sparkle. 'Will you still have me?' The silken question hung in the fragrant air between them.

Christine's eyes misted as her lips trembled into a glorious smile. Then, looking lost in Sabine's boldness, she dreamily answered, 'Of course … I love you.'

With nothing binding them to an incomplete earth, they embraced and rejoiced in warmth and excitement at the prospect of finding what they'd been chasing.

This was forever. They would take on the world and be happy—together. They had found true love and their everlasting 'more than'.

BECOMING SAOIRSE: LONDON 2009

SAOIRSE GRADUATED with honours and then enrolled in the LSE Master of Finance. Over the last months, life had settled down into another comfortable routine. Callan took Jessie to school on his way to work in the mornings, like he always did, leaving Saoirse to have the house to herself. Hilton dropped by, knocking loudly on her door, as was his wont.

What was different this morning was the toned Scotsman warming the bed she crawled from. The cool satin of her robe flowed over her hot, naked skin far more smoothly than her rough stumbling down the stairs. Still wiping sleep from mascara-fuzzed eyes, she opened the door to an ever-smiling Hilton, who strode in. 'Hi, my Irish cream, how are you today?'

'You sound particularly upbeat, my little dumpling.' She pushed her now-blonde locks with dark undertones off her face. 'Can we just use normal names? I haven't had coffee yet, and the only *too-sweet* I need should be in it. I'm fine, by the way.'

After his trademark who-hoo laugh, his face dropped and his voice went flat. 'Cut the crap, Creamy. You have a man in your bed, don't you? You're wearing a lovely shade of fucked-all-night.' As he spoke, his devilish smile returned. 'So, you should be more than fine. Do tell?'

Saoirse tightened her robe with a disgruntled tug. 'Yes, a Scotsman. Um, Andy. No, Drew. No wait, Alistair.'

'Oooh, we have gotten to know one another, haven't we?'

'Hey, too early for any of that. This is a no-judgement zone until at least nine.'

'Creamy, it's ten o'clock.'

'Day off, and last time I checked, I was an adult.'

'No judgement, just worried.' His brow creased, something he'd been doing too frequently when it came to his friend. Saoirse hadn't seen it as she went to the coffee machine. Hilton sat at the breakfast bar, taking his laptop from the tan messenger bag swinging from his shoulder. 'Creamy, I have something important to discuss. You need to ask Mr Sexy-kilt to go … Oh, hellooo, handsome.'

A dishevelled Alistair chose that moment to come down the stairs. He gave Hilton a grunted, 'Hiya,' while he struggled to straighten his shirt and jeans. Shrugging, Alistair smiled and tried to hold Saoirse's gaze. 'I'll call you. Yeah. I'd really like to take you to din—'

'Bye, Andy.'

'Alistair,' corrected Hilton.

'Yep … Alistair. Bye.' Turning her back on him, she took a long sip of coffee, savouring the jolt that spiked through her over-used body. When the door closed, she turned back and held up her hand. 'Don't say it.'

'What, that you seem to be bonking your way around the United Kingdom? Last night Scotland, the weekend before Northern Ireland. Quite the routine you've got going. When you get to Wales, let me know. I'd like to be part of that. Mmm, a lover with a great set of pipes and pins like Tom Jones. Duffy can take a back seat. I won't be needing any mercy!'

She rolled her eyes.

His shoulders dropped along with his voice. 'Creamy, I get it. I really do. And most nights, I'm right there with you. But lately, well, you need to slow down a little. No matter how many very handsome, very hunky guys you try on for size, they aren't going to fit. Not when you have to fill that gaping hole in your heavily shielded heart.'

'Hilton, it's too early. I know what I'm doing. No relationships, no connections, no strings. I'm fine with it.'

'Lovely, it's me. Come on.'

'Hilton, I tried, okay. It turns out I don't know anything about what size fits me. I've tried some guys on for longer. Let's see: there was the married liar, a violent undergrad, a vengeful date-site reject, and the many who just didn't care enough to stick. All of them let me down or turned on me because I said no. So yes. No connections, no love, just lust. Seems to work best.'

'I'm worried, Saoirse.' His face dropped to a rare seriousness as he used her name.

'I can handle myself. You can stop worrying. Or get in the queue behind my brothers.'

Hilton's eyes widened. 'Saoirse, stop. None of that is on you. It's on them, the bastards that didn't deserve you, couldn't take losing you.'

'No strings, it's best.'

'Saoirse, we both know that's not true. You have these passing-ships-in-the-night hook-ups to prove to yourself—most of all—that it's for the best. Darling, it isn't. Even if these guys wanted to see you again, you're making it very clear you don't want that. You're lying to yourself, pushing every man away, to thicken up those shields.'

'Don't do that, Hilton. Don't Freud me.'

'Someone has to say it. Even Jules is worried, and that's saying something. She thinks you've gone too much for the bite and spice and forgotten the sugar and kisses.' Louder now, he said, 'You will listen to me because I'm your friend and I love you. God, if I was straight, I'd lose thirty pounds and grow a foot taller just to be yours and wrap you up in the love you deserve. Don't you push me away.'

He pounded his fist on the breakfast bar's stone top. 'Don't you dare do it.'

Holding her head in her hands, she said, 'Wow, shit's got real, real quick this morning.'

'Yes, and it's not about to lighten up anytime soon.' He hugged her, gripped her hard, made her see him.

Now she was starting to understand his seriousness, which Hilton seldom showed. 'Hilton. What's happened?'

'There's no other way to say this. Saoirse, you've been hacked again. This time, he tried to go for your bank account and drain it.'

'Fucckk!'

'Don't worry. I'm better than him and stopped him. I was alerted about some suspicious activity with your account and credit cards through my tracking software and your bank's security. Between the two sets of security, we stopped him. If you haven't already, you'll get a call from your bank.'

'I turned my phone off last night.' Now it was Saoirse's turn to hug Hilton. She lay her forehead on his shoulder. 'Thank you. Tell me?'

'The trail led back to Rhett Micard. Mean anything?'

'No.' She pinched the bridge of her nose as her fingers pressed into closed eyes, hoping to still the noise. 'No. Nothing.'

'He didn't figure on the extra layer of security I put on your iden- tity details, bank accounts and cards. He left tracks, like fingerprints, all over the place. He's an arrogant SOB. I'm quite sure it's the same guy. Mitch Trader is Rhett Micard.'

'Oh God. Is it Tyson?'

'I can't prove anything, so don't go near him and ask. It'll only make it worse. Leave it to me.'

'Will this ever stop?' She held Hilton and trembled.

'I think I have an answer to that. We need help, though. The police haven't got the time. They need more evidence than we have.'

'What do you suggest?'

'I've spoken to Sabine and Chris. They're ready and willing and, as it turns out, very able. Christine is back working part-time as an attorney. When I mentioned it, she immediately said we need a private investigator who works for her firm. He does everything, particularly cybercrime.'

'Are you sure? How much will it cost?' Rubbing her eyes, she tried to stop the tears burning her throat.

'Don't worry about that. Christine says he owes her a few favours. He's also done work for Jules, and she's helped him make some good money. We have an appointment this afternoon to meet this PI guy, Blaise Roberts.'

'You're sure about this?'

'Yes, Saoirse. The guy who's fixated on you is escalating. We need more proof than we have at present for the police to act. The laws against cyberstalking are still struggling to catch up. We need to start—I can't believe I'm going to use a sporting analogy—but these are strange times. We need to attack, not just play defence.'

While shocked, Saoirse was somehow reassured because she had friends who were looking out for her. That was far more than any stalker had. She clung to these comforting thoughts, trying to keep the terrible ones from storming her mind. She thanked her lucky stars for Jules, Hilton, Sabine and the lovely Christine.

* * *

He took up his regular position in the park. The bench sat on a small hill and gave him an uninterrupted view of the house. As it was a big park, people didn't particularly notice him. It didn't matter. He used a few different disguises so no nosy whinger would suspect anything.

He'd make sure she didn't get to play happy families for too much longer. He knew which window looked into her bedroom. Maybe he'd break in and leave her a calling card. It was risky with the yappy mongrel dog to contend with. It was always around. Then there was the snivelling brat. She was always around, too. He'd have to fix that.

He'd nearly lost it over the fucking Korean's continual meddling in his business with Saoirse. He hadn't expected the pillow-biter to match him. If he couldn't steal her identity and drain her bank accounts, there were other ways. In the past, he'd given in to his temper, that knee-jerk reaction where he enjoyed the rage pulsing through him. Yet it had cost him. This time, anger wouldn't distract him from his goal.

After the next onslaught, when she was scared shitless, he'd snatch her from right under their noses. He'd enjoy taking her, savouring her, then he'd show her who was the boss. The storage lock-up he was renting nearby was nearly ready. He was just waiting for the arrival of the restraints he'd use on her. The lock-up was his lair. Everything needed to hunt her was stashed there. His apartment, which wasn't far either, was an empty shell. Anyone snooping wouldn't find anything except what you'd expect from a lonely LSE student.

He laughed now—loudly. He'd already turned the Irish skank into everything he'd wanted—a slut. She'd taken to one-night stands to stop the hurt from all the pricks who had rejected her— once he'd intervened, of course. Now she knew how it felt to be well and truly rejected. She didn't get to tell him when she wasn't interested. He did the leaving. He'd noticed she was still weak and needed others, like her brother, to do her fighting.

* * *

They walked into the crowded Soho eatery. Hilton held her hand then jolted it a little too tight, more at what his eyes spied than for support. The two of them came upon Blaise Roberts. He was tall, rugged and hard, so very military tough. His hair was a silvery-streaked, sandy buzz-cut that set off his tanned skin. His body was Saoirse's type: broad shoulders that narrowed to sexy hips and muscular thighs. She and Hilton had to stop themselves from swooning. Hilton whispered, 'A little older than we usually go for, but if you don't want him, I do.'

In a hushed moan, she murmured, 'Back off, Dumpling, we're here on business.'

He had whisky-coloured eyes that made her squirm every time they locked with hers. When he spoke, he had a voice somewhere between rolling gravel and a whip crack. After introductions, he asked questions and took notes when they answered. She found him so easy to talk to, although very businesslike. 'Saoirse, from what Hilton has passed on and the brief history you've given, I can start tracking this guy. I'll need anything else you have.'

'By all means. I'm at your service.' Hilton was as captivated as Saoirse.

'Ah, thanks, Hilton. I meant Saoirse. I have a few friends at the Met. I don't know if Christine mentioned I used to be a detective inspector with the Metropolitan Police before I quit to work as a PI for Chris's firm. Because of my connections, I'll be able to do more wide-ranging digging. Stalking is very personal. I'll need a list of names of your male friends, spurned boyfriends and lovers. I'm not a voyeur. I have to start crossing names off the list to find this guy.'

At this point, Saoirse fell mute. Feeling very self-conscious and very much like the slut her stalker wanted to paint her as. He'd succeeded in minimising her, once again.

Hilton turned to her. 'Are you okay?'

Like a mouse, she replied, 'Yes, I'm fine.' Then she gathered herself, and with the tone of a lion said, 'I won't hide.'

Blaise spoke without emotion. 'None of this is your fault. He wants people, and especially you, to pay attention to him, to be in control. Don't let him win. You and I are going to make a pact.'

She could only nod, and Hilton did the same, such was the PI's magnetism.

'We're not going to let this bastard make you feel like you need to hide or that you should be ashamed of anything. If you only remember one thing I tell you today, let it be this—this guy is the worthless person here, the coward. Not you.'

'Then I have a name for you, Tyson McNamara.'

* * *

Over the next week, Saoirse received a flurry of emails and texts traced to a Marc Herditt, which were as threatening as they were disgusting. Then Jules and Sabine were sent shocking BDSM photos of Saoirse in various poses. Quickly on the heels of these disturbing communications came a series of phone calls, direct messages and emails from multiple men propositioning Saoirse for kinky sex. Some were more explicit, soliciting violent sex and extreme BDSM.

As Saoirse's cyberstalker became more threatening, Blaise began keeping a closer eye on his new client. Saoirse resisted at first, but she begrudgingly agreed to Blaise increasing his surveillance to more than her computers after the phone calls and emails. He tailed her on campus, searching for any strangers that were more regular than random. As the days sped by, he became all too aware of Saoirse's resilience. While shaken, she didn't yield.

Blaise had stopped himself from being fascinated by the silver-grey of Saoirse Mahoney's eyes. Such dazzling and distressed yet determined eyes. He prided himself on being immune to clients. Rules were rules, and that was how it had to be.

It didn't take him long to trace the emails, DMs and unsolicited propositions to a hardcore BDSM site. Along with her contact details, shocking photos of Saoirse in various poses wearing different BDSM paraphernalia were posted. As expected, the images were high-quality photoshopped pictures. Blaise had the site take down the photos. Saoirse's cyberstalker had now committed crimes that the police were interested in and could prosecute. From that moment, things seemed to free up for Saoirse. She thanked Blaise, saying, 'I feel like, for the first time in a long time, I have a chance to beat this bastard.'

His confidence that he would quickly stop her stalker lasted for as long as it took a tearful Jessie to come rushing towards him as he delivered Saoirse home. 'I can't find Waffle. She didn't come running when Daddy and I got home.'

An edgy Callan appeared in the hallway. 'She's not in the backyard or anywhere. Jessie and I were going to look in the park. She must have got out somehow and gone exploring. Do you want to come with?'

They searched for an hour before Saoirse and Blaise found the blood trail. The crumpled body was under a hedge, a couple of houses down the street in the opposite direction to the park. The cute little dog was a bloody mass of tan fur and violence. Saoirse screamed as she sank to her knees and held her head to cry.

They told Jessica that Waffle must have escaped the yard and was hit by a car. Blaise called the police because he found a blood-stained note stuffed into a long wound when he moved the body. It held words familiar to Saoirse. It read, *I told you to pay attention to me. WHORE.* Saoirse disintegrated. Blaise watched Callan hold her, while feeling as comfortable about her distress as an extra finger sliding into a glove.

Saoirse then held Jessie close, and they cried. It seemed as if the hours had forgotten to pass. After putting Jessie to bed, Saoirse sat with Blaise, her mascara smudged in a miserable scrawl of watery black lines marring ice-white cheeks. He spoke to her in quiet words, trying to soothe away the shock of the loss and the fear that partnered it.

His frustration at not being able to stop her stalker lessened slightly when he convinced the police to become more interested. It seemed Saoirse's stalker was likely the same man who'd tried to take Jessica years earlier. He had become more organised and bolder in that time, which had refined his craft. It was then Saoirse admitted to Blaise she'd always been bothered that when she first met Tyson, before she'd told him, he'd said Jessie was her niece rather than her daughter.

The following day they met up at a café. When Blaise motioned for her to sit, he resisted the urge to reach out and touch her, to reassure her. It wasn't his usual way. 'There's good news. He's been creative in the past, careful, patient. Previous emails have bounced around through different IP addresses. Hilton couldn't get close enough to him. With these latest attacks, he got a little sloppy, allowing us to narrow it down to several cyber cafés in the city.

'The dog was a desperate act because he was thwarted at every turn. He's clearly moving up a gear, angry he couldn't mess with your bank account and cause more than a hiccup in your daily life or ruin your reputation with your friends. Especially since the BDSM site took down everything and none of those scumbags who propositioned you hurt you.

'Because you haven't cowered with fear while continuing to live life, we've drawn him out. Give me a couple of days. I've got the dates and time stamps for when the emails were sent. I'll get the CCTV footage from the cafés in question. When that arrives, I'll sift through the footage around those times and narrow down the field. We may soon know what our guy looks like.'

He could see that bothered her as she blanched then struggled to bring herself under control to utter, 'If I see this coward, maybe he won't seem so scary.'

Blaise's eyes connected with hers. 'Have you ever thought of self-defence classes?'

'Once, when I was in Australia.' She shrugged. 'I never could stick to it for any length of time. Never thought I'd need it.' She shook her head. 'That was stupid of me, wasn't it?'

'There's still time. I could give you some tips, some training?'

'I'd like that.'

'I've asked the local police to drive by your house regularly. Because he tried to take her years ago, they've also alerted Jessica's principal. I've got an associate I trust who'll keep an eye on her as a favour. You, I'll be sticking even closer to.' Her bloodshot eyes whipped up to scorch him. He raised his hand to wag a finger at her.

'I won't take no for an answer. This bastard has stepped it up to a whole new level.'

She half-rolled her eyes, then nodded. 'Okay, okay, I understand.' She rubbed her forehead to ask, 'Can I buy you a drink, then? As a thank you and an apology for being difficult.'

Blaise appreciated her showing a little of the confidence he knew she possessed but had been afraid to show because of all the crap that one scumbag had thrown at her. 'It's my job, so no thank you or apology needed. But I'd like a drink. Make mine a lemonade, though.' He smiled sweetly. It was the first time he forgot his rules and showed what he was feeling.

One drink became another with dinner. Before he recognised it, something shifted between them. It was quick and intense. The uncertainty of so many things had him tempering the heat rising between them. 'Saoirse, I have to say I have a rule. I don't get involved with clients.'

He thought he saw a stab of pain roll through her eyes before she nodded. 'Well, we better call it a night, then.'

'There's no rule against me seeing you home safely. In fact, at this time of night, I'd recommend it.'

She snapped, 'Given I lost the argument to have you bloody follow me everywhere, I guess I can't say no.'

The jab of her anger, her fight, pleased him as much as it had him feeling foolish, but rules were rules. Then Blaise led her from the bar to his bike, a Harley-Davidson Fat Boy. When those silver-grey eyes fired at the sight of it, and a soft smile graced her beautiful pink lips, she seemed to shine a light that caught him, and he knew, just like that, it was no longer a job. Saoirse was leaving her handprint on his heart. He *would* stop this guy.

They rode through London, fast, across the lit-up Albert Bridge, a stunning sight as the sparkling London skyline framed it. She clung to him, wrapping her arms around his lithe, leather-clad body. The faster they went, the colder it got and the more she nestled into him. Blaise tried to stem the sensations buzzing through him. He felt her supple body and rounded breasts push against his back, making her grip on his heart intensify. He'd had other women cling to him as they enjoyed the pleasure of his bike, but this was somehow more invigorating.

What was she doing to him? It was more than a damsel in distress thing. Being in his mid-forties, he'd come across his fair share of women in trouble. Saoirse Mahoney was all that, yet it was he who was totally at her mercy.

Somewhere in the wild, carefree moments driven by the big-cat purr of his Harley and the freedom of the crisp, late-night air, they found a shared oneness. It thrilled him as much as it confounded him. He dropped her home and was the perfect gentleman. After she thanked him, he returned quickly to his bike before those pooling silver eyes of hers had him doing something he was fighting hard to resist.

It ended up taking another week before Blaise had the CCTV results. Although he remained close, he and Saoirse came to an unspoken agreement of mutual restraint. However, it was clear they both found it hard not to seek a more tangible connection from the other. In that time, her cyberstalker escalated. He tried to hack her final master's thesis and failed, thanks to Blaise and Hilton.

Following that, he tried to stoke Saoirse's fear through more direct means. She opened the front door one morning to find a doll with blonde hair like hers. It had a carving knife stabbed through its chest and was doused in what turned out to be pig's blood. The horrible effigy was wrapped in a scarf she had lost at LSE. Her cyberstalker was dangerously near a tipping point, which meant coming out from behind his laptop and psychological shadow games to achieve his ultimate goal: to confront Saoirse in person. Blaise kept this thought to himself, although he suspected Saoirse knew it too.

* * *

Finally, Saoirse and Hilton met Blaise to view the CCTV footage. They huddled around a backroom table in one of Sean's Irish pubs in the city. Blaise set up his laptop. 'I want you to watch these clips and tell me if anything or anyone strikes you.'

She expected to see Tyson McNamara appear from the pixels. Then, while watching the third CCTV clip from the café called the Cyberbean, a much older, bony hand of unwelcomed recognition seized Saoirse. Cold dread crushed her spirit as she realised she'd been prey for far longer than she'd ever entertained. Shivers ran up her spine as quickly as the shadowy figure pushed his glasses up his nose. He had a long, dark ponytail looped through the back of a baseball cap. He was thin now, and wore the nondescript ball cap low over a face covered with the sparse scruff of a thin beard. None of it hid his crow's beak of a nose nor softened the angles of his familiar face.

'Can't be. No, *no!* That was years ago.' She felt the colour drain from her face, and her lunch threatened to come back up. Before Hilton could move, Blaise had his tree trunk of an arm around her trembling shoulders, pushing his chair close.

'Take a breath and just talk to me,' Blaise said.

'Replay that bit of the skinny guy with the ponytail, jeans and black hoodie. The guy walking to sit at the back table.' She steeled herself as Blaise replayed the clip. Again, she saw the movement, the crow's beak nose, the sharp features. 'Brisbane 2000, I was a legal secretary. A guy ...' She lifted her head to study her hunter as she ran her fingers over his image. 'Chad something. It's the nervous tick—pushing his glasses up his nose. I thought him just a harmless sleaze.' Her hands and body were shaking more now. 'Um, I'm not sure of the order of things, but ... he lusted after me. It all began when he tried to cop a feel and stick his tongue down my throat. I slapped him.' She began sifting through her memories, recounting them to Blaise and Hilton.

She dragged her emotions back to gain some control to state, 'By far the worst thing he did was to my boss and her daughters.

She had him reprimanded for his treatment of me and for tampering with our PCs. So he hacked her PC and put her daughters' lives in danger, urging men my boss came up against in court to hunt them.' Her voice no longer quaked as she growled, 'I should have thought of him with all this computer hacking going on.'

'How did you deal with him?' Blaise was taking notes now.

'I didn't. A good friend of mine did. She told him to stop or she'd rip his balls off and nail them to his forehead so people could see how puny they were. Might I add she had a firm grip of said balls at the time and was wrenching them, hard.'

'I'm in love.' Hilton held Saoirse's hand. 'Who was this goddess?'

'Daniella Malone, my boss. Senior associate at the firm. Through Daniella's insistence, I started sexual harassment proceedings against him. He was fired from the firm soon after, anyway, and that was that, or so I thought.'

'Can you remember his full name?'

'Blaise, it was so long ago. I've tried very hard to forget him.'

He rubbed her shoulder. 'Anything you can give me, besides the nervous tick.'

She took a gulp of cider. Closing her eyes as it slid down her throat, she tried to make her mind turn a searchlight on a murky part of her past. 'He was a pudgy redhead then, scruffy. He was in the IT department. Chad, Chad ...' She snapped her fingers several times in quick succession. 'Merritt. Chad Merritt!'

'Well done.' Blaise kissed her forehead, and they both shot back in their chairs. He looked embarrassed. She was confused. Smiling, Hilton simply raised an eyebrow.

'Um, right.' Blaise jotted down the name. 'With a name and time of employment, I should be able to track his movements.'

'Hold on, hold on ... Don't you see it? Oh, why didn't I see it earlier?'

They turned and looked at Hilton, who took Blaise's pen and notebook. 'Is that Merritt with a double T?'

'I think so, yes.' Saoirse pushed back her blonde locks to peer at what Hilton was writing.

'Well, knock me down with a pink feather. The guy really is an egotistical simpleton. Don't you see it?'

Both still stunned, they stared blankly at him.

'The names, they're all anagrams of Chad Merritt. I told you I was good at code. Look.' Hilton proceeded to spell out all the names again on the notebook's page, using the letters from her cyberstalker's real name, Chad Merritt. He wrote down Mitch Trader, Rhett Micard and Marc Herditt—they were all a perfect fit. 'See, as I said, arrogant SOB. You, Blaise, you must stop him hurting my darling Irish cream.'

'Absolutely.' Blaise's eyes quizzed Saoirse's. 'Okay ... Irish cream?'

'Long story.' Saoirse felt her cheeks heat.

He snapped right back to PI mode. 'Hilton, you're sharp. It would've taken me much longer to see it. It connects him to everything. He's arrogant, and that'll lead to his downfall.' Turning back to Saoirse, he retrieved his pen and notebook from Hilton. 'Okay, Saoirse, is there anything else that felt off around that time, similar to stuff happening now? This guy isn't too original, but it could help in tracking him.'

'It's so long ago. So much happened, and then again, so little.' An unnerving prickling made itself known as it walked between her shoulder blades.

With a resigned exhalation, she replied, 'Let's see, Cairns, a city north of Brisbane. I was holidaying there and staying at a backpackers.' She told them about the small, creepy things that happened and the venomous brown snake under her bed.

'That's why I was more than happy to leave when a lovely guy, Damian Costa, offered to be my guide on a solo tour. No one knew where we were until we came back to civilisation. I had no problems on his tour. It would've been hard to do anything because there was no way anyone could follow us. Most of the time, we didn't know where we were going to end up each day. The only set date was our return date at our accommodation booked in the small town of Kuranda.'

'Sounds like it was good you followed your intuition and left the backpackers,' Blaise said.

'When we did get back to Kuranda, the very next day we had car problems. Maybe he was waiting for us to re-emerge. It wouldn't have taken much to ask around when we'd be back. The place we stayed that night was managed by the same guy as the place in Cairns.'

'Okay, let me get this all down. Callan told me you went to Sydney after Brisbane. Anything out of the ordinary happen there? The more we have, the stronger the case against him and the more likely we'll see a pattern. Especially if he's used anagrams of his name when he travels.'

Another visible tremor had Blaise moving back to slide his arm around her shoulders. His support made it easier for her to go back to the pain. 'My car tyres were slashed. Then ... Oh God.' She pressed a hand to her mouth as another realisation hit. 'I was seeing this guy. It turned out he was married. I swear I didn't know. I found out one night while he was at my place. Someone smashed a rock into his car windshield and left photos under my car's wiper. They showed him and me, um, kissing. There were others of him and his wife.'

'Anything else?'

She flicked her eyes to his, not shocked that a seasoned detective wouldn't raise an eyebrow at what she was saying. What surprised her was that he held her more firmly, and she felt safe telling him anything, everything. 'There was a note, large red letters, *He's married. Whore!* At the time, I thought his wife had done it, and the tyre slashing, too.' Taking another sip, she opened up as she had never before. 'Finding out he was married cut me so deep, it hurt for some time. I did adore him. I left soon after for London because Callan's wife passed, and he needed help with Jessica. The rest you know.'

'Okay. That's all I need for the moment. Thank you, Saoirse.'

After taking another long swig, she set her jaw and stated with a cold tone, 'I will not run and hide because of a bully. If Daniella taught me anything, it was not to give him that power over my life. Screw him! Let's put some pressure on him and end this.'

'It's good to hear you say that. I'll get him.'

By now, it was dark outside. Hilton had a date to make. He kissed Saoirse's cheek. 'Although it's a little confronting, this is the best news. Alas, my Irish cream, but I must skedaddle.'

'You can't stay?' Saoirse squeezed his hand. 'You've helped me from the start. One drink to say thank you.' She didn't want to be alone with Blaise. He'd all but told her to back off, and then he'd kissed her and held her. The mixed signals were making her head spin and her heart thrum as they layered over the anxiety of discovering Chad Merritt was her stalker.

'Creamy, there'll be plenty of time to celebrate. I hope to have more good news to add to those celebrations. I have a date tonight with my Barbadian coconut, who has finally come out, at least to himself and his family. Apparently, his sister knew all along.'

She sprang up and gave him a hard hug. 'That's fantastic. Finally, both of us get some good news.'

'You know it. Creamy, I'll catch you in the morning. Blaise ... best PI ever.' Hilton winked. 'Besides, I think you two need to be alone. Have fun now.'

Nerves clubbed Saoirse's body as she sat at the table. Blaise pushed his laptop into his backpack and asked apprehensively, 'Another drink, another dinner?'

'I'd love that, I really would, but you said you didn't ... want—'

His lips slid over hers, and everything blurred. 'Oh, I want.' The clubbing dissolved into a resonant tingle that grew to a crescendo of desire.

Still vibrating from his touch, her world came back into focus. 'But you've gotten to know me—warts and all—it's not too flash. My history with guys, I mean, don't feel you have to—'

'You don't have warts, Saoirse. Besides, I like the "and all" *very* much.' He swung her around in her chair so she faced him, reassuring hands on her shoulders once again. 'Let's you and me get something straight. You've done nothing that you should be punished for or ashamed of. This guy is a sicko.' He ran his fingers down her cheek. She was mesmerised, his golden-brown eyes becoming aged cognac to her darkening pewter-grey. He shook his head. 'I've told myself to stop. I'm supposed to be a tough PI, but when it comes to you, I'm like a lovesick adolescent.' He shook his head. 'I guess rules are meant to be broken, and you're making me break mine.'

She chewed on her bottom lip. 'Blaise, you know my history. I find it hard to take a chance on anything other than temporary.'

He gently tugged on her chin, releasing her lip. 'I'm older. I've never been married, don't have a significant other. Not because I'm married to my work, it's that no woman has ever made me feel like I could or should change. Seems we both have reasons not to start anything up.' Her heart thundered at the feel of his hand on her shoulder. The other he curled around the nape of her neck. She let him pull her to him, and when their lips met, she rode the rush of heat. Then, like molten iron hitting air, the surge of heat shattered into a hundred sparks. Her heart skipped when he said, 'I stick. I'm not going to let you down.'

Saoirse swallowed tears as they flooded her. 'They're the words every male before you has *never* said.' She shut her eyes to halt the flow, only to feel her tears roll freely down her cheeks. Blaise brushed them away before she opened her eyes to hold his gaze.

Then she spoke. 'For you to say those things, even when you know my reputation ... it leaves me lost, yet found.'

The motorbike ride to his place was a dream. The first touch of his fingers on Saoirse's naked torso left her quivering. The craving she had for him turned her core to heated satin. When he entered her, he took her slowly, allowing the moment to last, both savouring the exquisite instant when they joined. Sensations swirled and flooded them as he took her under, and she lost her breath along with her sanity. Places she'd shielded from her tempo-rary lovers suddenly needed no defence from the passion Blaise brought.

He was her willing slave as she surrounded his hardness like a rippling fist. They sank further into the depths of their ecstasy. She rolled them and rode him, trying to capture that exquisite need.

At first, her lips toyed with his, then they feasted. When the muscular planes of his magnificent torso bunched and twisted, she held on to be breathless and underneath him once again. She accepted the heaviness, loved the weight of him covering her, driving her into the mattress, their hearts drumming against each other. He kept pumping into her. She whimpered when he took her breast into his mouth, tantalising it with his tongue.

His tongue's mastery—the way it danced over her pink lips, her skin, and the way he tasted when he returned to capture her mouth —all of his skilled worshipping sent them soaring. Yet it was the depths he plundered as he claimed her in every way that shot her to climax, like a star shooting into freedom. It was unlike anything she'd felt. Blaise was right there with her, shouting her name in a whirl of sensation that had him flying into the same freedom. A beautiful place they'd created together.

She could remain tangled up in the sheets forever while he stayed spread over and held within her. Then her sanity returned, driven by the burn in her lungs as she gasped, 'I'll move when I get feeling back in my legs.'

'Oh, wait.' He chuckled. 'I think I may have ...' He rolled his weight off her. 'Stopped ...'

She gulped some deep breaths. 'Yes, that's it.'

They lay there sucking in air, enjoying the heaviness, the pure ease that weaved around them.

Until out of nowhere, a sadness hit her. It was familiar, a habit formed from the ghost of Sydney and a frequent companion ever since. Such completeness couldn't last. She'd long ago stopped believing in the pretence. Saoirse sat up and swung her legs over the edge of the bed, before staring for a few beats, amazed at how scattered her clothes were.

He wrapped his arms around her torso and pulled her back down to his bed. 'Are we okay?'

Turning away so she could escape his all-seeing eyes, she whispered, 'More than okay.' She tried to shut down the emotions that had her wanting to shed tears. 'I just thought you'd want me to go. Now that we've ...'

With a velvet-gravel growl that had her core trembling, he said, 'Saoirse—no.' He took her hand and made her roll back to him. 'I told you. I stick. The last thing, the very last thing I *ever* want you to do is go.'

She closed her eyes. *Too much, too raw*, she thought.

'Stay, Saoirse. I see you. *The real you.*'

'You don't know what that means to me.' Her voice smoothed to a creamy lilt as she regained control. 'How much it means ... it's like you've known me forever.'

'Maybe I have.' He moved over her body like satin and kissed her, but not like before. This time he worshipped her, slow, deep and tender. She willingly surrendered and gave the very core of herself to him as he gave all of himself to her.

* * *

He'd shaved off his beard and cut his long hair to a short back and sides, which was now dyed brown. Chad watched her lithe body shimmer in a figure-hugging floral dress as she slipped her phone into the ex-cop's jacket pocket. 'Thanks, Blaise. You'll only have to hold it until I finish the meet and greet with the department heads.' As they entered the event, Chad went on his way.

He'd seen the way she'd swayed close to the ex-cop and how he'd run his hand across her back. They were moves of two people who'd been intimate. 'It just won't do. She's mine,' Chad muttered. His temper coated his mood as quickly as the sweat slicked over his skin from the six-flight climb. It was a necessary hike because it was easier to avoid CCTV cameras by taking the car park's stairs. Now he clung to the shadows as he skulked over to her car.

Ever since she'd slapped him in Brisbane, something had short-circuited in his mind. His crazed desire to break her and have her had consumed him. Especially after she'd humiliated him with the sexual harassment charge and got him fired, like his mother had done to his father. That's when the burnt-out circuit became hard-wired. The fixation became his manifest destiny.

There'd been prostitutes he'd beaten and maimed, but no one cared what happened to them, and mostly they weren't believed. He'd never been caught. Which proved once again that women were just trash to be thrown away when used. It also showed how smart he was. His Irish bitch would give him his ultimate climax to the punishment he meted out on women. All women must be punished for what they did to men—for what his mother did to his father. His mother was a slut, too, who lured his father into a trap and then wanted the money, not the child.

It was Chad's turn to walk up Saoirse's delightful secret garden path, and there would be nothing delightful or secret about his visit. First, he'd defile her while her silver eyes finally saw him and only him, then her heart would take its final beat.

The ex-cop was clueless. Chad was so far ahead of him. He couldn't even tread on Chad's dust, let alone see it. Chad had worn disguises whenever he ventured into the city to use Cyberbean's free wi-fi. He'd let the PI and the police see him. The memory had his lips jag up in an ugly smirk. That's right, Chad knew they'd check the CCTV footage. He used it to his advantage, sending them in the wrong direction. They'd be looking for a non-existent shadow with long hair and no name. They had no idea about him, didn't know where he lived or where his lock-up was. That's where he planned to party with her. Guests should bring presents to a party to honour the host. She would give him absolution and victory, the only gifts he wanted from her. His smirk widened as he thought about it.

The ceremony for master's students provided the perfect opportunity. He salivated at the thought of having her this night. She'd learned nothing from Brisbane and parked in the same spot, or thereabouts, every day. Chad nudged the creaky CCTV camera off centre. This time there would be no CCTV footage.

He stifled a snigger as he crouched down beside her car with his knife and bag of electronic tricks. He'd disable the car alarm and wait in the back seat. Chad knew she'd be alone as the ex-pig had parked his Harley on the street. She'd finally be his.

* * *

The event was open-air. As the evening wound down, the chilled lips of an evening breeze kissed her. The skin under Blaise's fingertips shivered as goosebumps rose. 'You're cold. Is that our cue to go?'

'I guess it is. Let me see if Hilton's ready. I said I'd give him a ride home.'

Hilton joined them as they walked to where Blaise's bike was parked. 'Surely Hilton can take me from here?'

'Saoirse, we've been through this—'

'Look, he hasn't done anything in a while. I know you're tired and have other case reports to write. Take a break. I just want to feel like we're a normal couple rather than you being on the job, having to watch my every move.'

'I enjoy watching your every move.'

She gave him a look where her silver eyes fired with adoration, and he relented. 'I guess Hilton's got you.'

Hilton saluted. 'At your service. Just call me Oh. Hilton double-Oh-yes-please! I'll make sure Creamy is delivered home safe and sound, not the least bit shaken or stirred.'

It had been such a perfect night that their good moods saw them laughing all the time they were in the elevator. As they walked to her car, Hilton kept her giggling by relaying a story about what he'd found on one of the department laptops he'd brought back to life.

She was just about to step to her car when suddenly the door swung open and a man launched himself at them.

Before she realised what was happening, Hilton seized Saoirse's shoulders and swept her away from the man who'd lunged forward with the knife. Saoirse heard rushing footsteps and turned as a figure bulleted past her. 'Saoirse!' A frantic Blaise shouted as he pushed them both behind him. 'Stop right there, Chad.'

Chad did the opposite. He ran.

Blaise saw Saoirse and Hilton were okay, so he charged out to chase after Chad, but a car sped up onto the same car park level. With the driver focused on finding an empty car spot and his loud *doof-doof* music, he saw Blaise too late, jerking the wheel away from him and into Hilton and Saoirse's path. Blaise turned and dived, pushing them out of the way as the driver slammed on the brakes and swerved again, this time back into a concrete column. Hilton and Saoirse landed hard in a bouncing tangle of limbs while Blaise rolled. They dusted themselves off as Blaise went to give chase once more, but Chad had disappeared into the dark. Given the wails coming from the car, Blaise had no choice but to go back to attend to the driver.

When the PI returned, he grabbed Saoirse in a rib-cracking embrace. 'Good God. Your phone was still in my jacket pocket. I ran up the stairs to give it to you and saw ...' He took Hilton in a one-armed macho hug. 'Oh, Hilton, jeez, man. I saw you put your body between Saoirse and him. Are you alright?'

'Yes. But I think I'll stick to just plain Hilton Oh from now on because I can safely say I'm a little shaken and a lot stirred.'

* * *

The weeks edged past. The police and Blaise's investigation closed in on Chad Merritt, especially after they had footage of him running from the LSE car park and onto a bus. Even though it had been dark, they managed to describe the knife-wielding car park loiterer to the police. The lead gave everyone a boost, as did the knowledge that Chad had been clearly shocked when Blaise used his name to confront him.

Saoirse submitted her final work for her master's, knowing she had a job offer from a New York firm. Having many things to feel thankful for, she celebrated with friends at Callan's house, which had become her home in every sense of the word.

Callan had a quiet moment with his sister. 'I like him. I can see he lights you up, the happiness he brings to you. He's a little older than I'd have thought you'd go for, but it works. I'm so proud of my little sister. And I've never really thanked you for stepping up when I was a mess.'

Over the years, there'd been many unspoken thank yous. There'd been shared cups of coffee before dawn and glasses of sympathy and whisky on heartbreaking, silent nights. Nights when it wasn't night-mares that brought tears, but the dreams of what could have been. Both brother and sister shared those.

'Jessie is the lovely little girl she is because you were there when I couldn't be.'

'Don't sell yourself short, Callan, once you got yourself together …' She cocked her head. 'Let's say, between the two of us and our ups and downs, we've kept her world normal.'

He smiled, but it didn't lighten his eyes. Saoirse knew he wasn't as happy as he'd once been. Lara had brought light to his life and warmth to his heart. Taking a careful breath and even more care with her words, she said, 'When are you going to find someone to bring that light back to you and give you true happiness?'

'Lightning doesn't strike twice. I don't think my frozen heart is up for it.'

She cupped his cheek with a gentle hand. 'It never will be if you don't open yourself up to the possibility. Jess needs to see you whole again. To see you smile with your heart truly in it.'

She saw him soften a little. 'Okay, I'll try. No promises, though.'

'There's hope, at least. So cheers, big brother, to a future shared with someone to fill our hearts with love and light.'

Later that night in bed, when Saoirse and Blaise were still holding each other long after the afterglow had consumed them, he kissed her fingers and his eyes sought hers. 'Saoirse, I see the care you give to others, your bold openheartedness. I want that in my life. My heart is yours. I love you.'

She stiffened and then realised there was no fear as she was taking every breath with him. He saw her, the fire and dark. 'You know, I've been coming to the same conclusion about you.' Her lips moved to kiss him.

'I know it's been so quick,' he whispered against them. 'But I've come to know you, being your quasi-bodyguard these past months and …'

'When you know …'

'You know.' He chuckled as Saoirse stretched her elegant body up over his. Not the curvy half-pint of Guinness she looked like when she left Ireland nearly ten years earlier. Now she was more like a sleek glass of champagne.

Tossing her golden locks back, she announced, 'They also say when you know, you have to let it out, loudly.' She shouted with a silken smile. 'I love you, Blaise Roberts.' As she hugged him, both their hearts struggled to beat, overflowing with their combined love and the light they ignited in each other.

* * *

He'd seen the police hanging around his apartment complex. Then a couple of plain-clothes plods had knocked on his neighbours' doors. *Soliciting donations for Doctors Without Borders, my arse.* He packed meticulously, swept the apartment to ensure he didn't leave anything, grabbed his go bag and laptops and left for his storage locker.

Anger was no longer his banished companion. It was wrapped

around him like a long-lost lover. There'd be no stopping him this time, even though the plan had changed. He'd used body padding, a skirt and frumpy blouse, along with joggers and a long, reddish wig for his latest disguise. Then he'd visited the bank, where he topped up with a little more cash from one of his safe deposit boxes which he had spread all around the city and the world. Good old Dad dropping off the perch was the windfall he'd needed. He'd picked up his new fake ID and passport while dumping a hard drive into the box.

He'd camp out at a dingy hotel until he finished his odyssey. He wouldn't strike now, because they were all on high alert. He'd wait, because he wanted this one to be messy, and he'd take more than her.

For now, Chad smirked, and his eyes rolled up under heavy eyelids. His hand moved faster with thoughts of what he'd do to his prey. As he became frantic, his breathing became choppy. Then his body jerked, and he groaned with pleasure, releasing into a tissue like a feckless schoolboy. Chad would sleep now and wait. She'd pay —they all would.

twelve

ANOTHER PORSCHE AT THE CEMETERY: CALLAN'S STORY

A CEMETERY IS life's great leveller. No matter how impressive or simple the headstone, how wise or witty the epitaph, it doesn't matter: everyone is dead, everyone equal. However, it doesn't mean that life has ceased. Cemeteries have a life all their own. Part of that life is witnessing the array of people who visit the dead and the sentiments they carry.

The cemetery bears witness to those bringing or seeking solace and to those craving meaning from death and the life they have to continue to live. There are the rare and unexplainable happenings, like a connection between the spirit and the living. Then there are the rare but explainable incidents, like seeing two Porsches parked in a cemetery car park early in the morning.

Callan Mahoney visited the cemetery every Friday morning. Initially, when his wife, Lara, had first passed, he'd visited far more often. He'd felt more than empty, a bottomless pit of nothingness. At a loss as to what his role could be in a world that could take his life force away so callously.

Lara's aneurysm went undetected inside her skull for twenty-eight years. When it exploded like an overfilled balloon, it took his beloved as quickly as the snap of death's fingers. That instant left him aimless and struggling to go on. If not for his now six-year-old daughter, he would have gladly forgotten how to eat, how to breathe, and slipped away as quickly as Lara had. Then he'd have shared forever with her.

With a sweet babble of words, Jessica held her daddy's hand as they made their way to the headstone, where she helped him place roses in a vase. Her sing-song words never failed to lift Callan's mood.

As he stood in front of his wife's headstone, he wrestled once more with endless guilt. He'd left Lara at a time when she most needed him, and then she was gone. He both tortured and consoled himself by remembering the curve of Lara's smile, how it crinkled the corners of her eyes, making their brown lighten and his heart lift. He zoned out, caught in the lost feel of her, a touch that used to still his heart and soothe his mind. Then he remembered how she stirred such passion, which would burn so deep that everything within him iced over when he'd lost her.

When he next felt something besides grief, it was Jessica's hand tugging his. 'Daddy, come see this lady. She has a funny light, and she said if I stay really still and quiet, I'll hear Mummy talking to me.' She puffed. 'Please tell me, Daddy, please. Is that why you're so quiet all the time? Because you hear Mummy talking to you when you're quiet and still?' Jessica was excited, hardly taking a breath. 'The old lady said Mummy is proud of me like the old lady is proud every day, every way of her daughter. She says Mummy says I've grown into a pretty girl. She says her daughter's pretty, too, but older than me. She did, Daddy, she did. She said Mummy said,' Jessica's voice dulled, 'that she's sad that you're not happy. But you are happy, mostly, aren't you, Daddy? The lady said to call her Sarah.'

'Hang on, Jessie. Slow down, what, who?' Alarm spiked as stranger-danger warnings flooded his mind. It drove fear into him more than most fathers, ever since Jessie was taken from Saoirse years earlier. 'Where is she?'

'Over there.' Pointing a tiny finger, she pulled him towards a large, tall obelisk.

Now anger pulsed. Who was this woman to fill his daughter's head with such futile hope? 'Can you see her?' he said while thinking, *When I catch up with her, she's getting a piece of my mind—interfering old biddy.*

Callan rushed past the shiny black marble column. Looking through the field of headstones, he saw a bus pull away from the kerb in a whirl of milky-grey exhaust.

'She was just here.' Jessie twirled. 'But isn't it great that Mummy thinks I'm pretty?' With a whole-body wiggle, she smiled with joy. 'We can talk to Mummy.'

His heart was crumbling, his mind burning. He sank to one knee to look into Jessie's mother's eyes. A colour of which his daughter was now the only living custodian—that particular mocha brown. He gently pushed his daughter's auburn hair off her face. 'I think she must have taken the bus home. I can't see her.'

'But she said—'

'Jessie darling, I'm sure she's a nice lady, but what she was saying about talking to Mummy ... Um, you've mixed up what she meant. She probably said it to make you feel better about Mummy not being here. Because you know she's in heaven, she can't talk to us anymore.' Before Jessie could protest, he said, 'She was certainly right about one thing.'

Her bottom lip quivered. 'What?'

'You sure have grown into a very pretty little girl.'

They nearly tumbled over with the force of her jump as she wrapped her arms around his neck, kissing him on the cheek. He stood swinging her around to delighted squeals, feeling his temper melt and his troubled mind cool. As he set her down, Jessie's brow creased. Callan's cooled mind began to stress. He should have expected more questions. She was at the age where she asked them incessantly. He tried to predict which part of the old biddy's interfering he would have to hose down. Then yet again, Jessie surprised him.

'Daddy, why is your skin so smooth in the morning and then prickly at night?'

His mind settled as he gave a relaxed chuckle.

* * *

Anika Carlson eased her Porsche into the cemetery car park. She stepped out into the early morning. With a solitary white rose in hand, she made herself take time to notice a copper-toned sun's rays spear through the scattered morning clouds. It calmed her. After a couple of deep breaths of the crisp morning air, the sweet scent of fresh-cut grass and roses surrounded her.

Anika didn't hear the crunch of another Porsche's tyres on the car park gravel or the honks and rumble of traffic clogging the nearby road. Slipping off her heeled mules near the tall jet-black marble spire, she curled her toes into the lush grass and felt the worry roll off her. It was such a beautiful morning. Maybe this time, her mum would join her, and they'd share memories of her dad and thoughts about work and Anika's latest sketches.

* * *

The following Friday, Anika was early. As she pulled over, she took a deep breath, savouring the smell of the car, not of its newness, but because her mum's perfume still lingered within it. Sarah, her mum, had worked hard, and when her father passed, Anika and her mother had worked harder. Their mother–daughter loving connection had strengthened as they'd tried to fill the void left by her father.

After four years, her mother decided to marry again. Sarah was a vibrant, loving woman, and she deserved happiness. Anika just couldn't see how her new stepfather was going to give Sarah that.

This unresolved argument became the thin edge of an enormous wedge named Brian. He injured their loving connection. He didn't break it, but he forever damaged it. When Anika found it hard to tell dreams and nightmares apart in the dead of night, she'd be swamped with helpless feelings about how she and her mum had left things.

The sun rose above the trees standing at the cemetery's edge, like soldiers forming a guard of honour. Soft rays hit the angular top of the monument, giving the black marble a mirror-like appearance. Moving from the wooden bench near her family's shiny obelisk, Anika kicked off her stiletto pumps to curl her toes into the thick, fresh grass. It was something she'd learned from her mother to help settle her thoughts. She walked barefoot to the tomb and placed a single white rose on the second bottom step. As the sun warmed places left cold from the retreating shadow, Anika remembered how she and her mother loved summer mornings like this. Would this be the morning they'd manage to push all the noise aside and talk to each other?

As she ran her fingers over the gold letters of her father's name carved into the stone, she heard a noise. Turning, she noticed a little girl skipping towards her, vibrant red highlights streaking through her brown hair, which was tied into two lopsided pigtails. She had a smile on her face and laughter in her eyes as she stopped to pick up one of Anika's heels. Slanting her head, she said, 'These are pretty. Can I try them on, please?'

Looking around to see where this sunbeam of happiness had come from, Anika answered, 'Ah, I think they'll be too big, too high.'

'Please, please, I promise not to dirty them.' The girl swung back and forth a little as she twisted up the hem of her pink baby-doll dress.

Taken by her cuteness, Anika answered, 'Um, well, does your mummy let you wear her shoes?'

'No, but my mummy doesn't need shoes. She's in heaven.' The

girl chatted away as little girls tended to do. 'Daddy's sad, he misses Mummy, so we come to visit her grave every Friday morning. But she's not there, in it. It's just a sss-symbol. You know, something to remind us she was here. We go for breakfast at a grown-up place afterwards.'

Not pausing for a breath, she continued, 'An old lady who looks like you told me last week that if I'm still and quiet, I might hear Mummy talk to me. I told Daddy maybe she'd talk to him if he believes. He doesn't think it could happen. I believe it, so it will happen. How can anything happen if you don't believe? But I've been quiet for like forever today, and she hasn't spoken to me ...' She raised a finger to point at the sky. 'Yet.' She pursed her lips before saying, 'Maybe next visit. Can I try on your shoes now, pleeease?'

Anika's heart was twisting so much over the little girl's story that when her barrage paused, Anika nearly missed her chance to talk. 'If you tell me your name, I'll let you wear my shoes for a bit.'

'Jessica Mary Mahoney—Jessie. And for real, I can try on your shoes?'

Anika was closer now. 'Pleased to meet you, Jessie.' She offered the little girl her hand. 'I'm Anika. And yes, go ahead.' After shaking Anika's hand, the child promptly flopped down on the grass.

Jessie slipped off her shoes as she tried out the new name, 'Thank you, Ani. No, An-nik-a ... is that right?'

'Yes, that's it. You're smart. Most grown-ups get it wrong first try.' Looking around, she said, 'I'm sure your dad must be wondering where you've got to.'

Jessie didn't answer, too besotted by Anika's shoes.

Now surrounded by the serenity of the morning's birdsong and with a refreshing breeze serenading her skin, Anika was recapping what Jessie had said. A warm shiver ran up her spine and tingled her shoulders. 'Wait. You spoke to a woman who looked like me.'

'Yes.' Gingerly sliding through the grass in the sapphire pumps, Jessie said, 'She had more wrinkles than you, and her hair was greyer. She was nice, though, like you. Oops.' Jessie caught herself on the bench when her ankle rolled a little as she went to turn in the too-big-but-fabulous shoes.

Anika's heart was now trying to pump out of her chest. Before she could ask any more questions, there came a terse growl.

'Hey, stop! Jessie, get out of those shoes.'

'Aww. Daddy. The nice lady said I could.'

'I told you, no talking to strangers.' He stepped up to his daughter and glared at Anika. 'You've got no right. Were you here last week? I'd appreciate it if you didn't fill my daughter's head with fantasies about her mother talking to her.'

'I didn't—' Anika began but he cut her off.

'Jessie told me a woman visiting this grave talked to her. You have no right to be filling my daughter's head with your fanciful tales.'

'Daddy, please don't get angry. Anyway, it wasn't Ani-Anika! Did I say it right?'

'Yes, Jessie, you did.' Anika was starting to steam.

'It wasn't Anika who told me. Daddy, don't be angry, please, I've taken the shoes off,' Jessie offered, bottom lip quivering.

Her father's temper ebbed. 'Oh.' He picked up Jessie and stroked her hair to comfort her. 'Sorry, honey-bun. Sorry.' His embarrassed eyes finally met Anika's as she fisted her hands on her hips. Her blue eyes, which were so light they were almost platinum, scorched him.

'You need to listen to your daughter.' Anika raised her chin and stood to her full height, carrying herself with elegant strength, a stance her mother said Anika took when she felt she was being attacked. 'We were having a lovely conversation until you came over, hurling your unfounded accusations around.' She took her honey-coloured pony in each hand to tug it tighter and tried not to yell. 'It's no way to act in a place like this. We're all grieving here.' Through her anger, she saw him for the first time. While this impertinent father wore his melancholy like a tailored black business suit, she realised that his actual suit no longer fitted him because he was haggard and thin. It hung and flapped around his body like a listless flag on a pole.

'Ah, you're right. I'm sorry.' His eyes blazed out from hollow sockets while his chopped-at ebony curls fell over his face, making it look long and gaunt. 'It's just Jessie is all I have, and she means the world to me. I go out of my head if she's out of my sight.' He rubbed Jessie's back, kissed her and set her down. 'I'm really sorry, Jessie, Daddy was just worried about you.'

Jessie nodded, suddenly shy, as she burrowed into her father's legs.

Seeing the loving interaction staunched Anika's temper. 'Maybe we should try this again.' Stepping up to him, she offered her hand. 'Anika Carlson, and you are?'

He gripped her hand firmly. 'Callan Mahoney. Nice to meet you, Anita.'

'No, Daddy. Anika. It's Anika.' As she stepped out from behind her dad's legs, Jessie raised her shoulders and rolled her eyes at Anika. 'Grown-ups.'

'That's right, Jessie.' Anika smiled up at Callan, who seemed momentarily lost.

He managed, 'Ah, you've met Jessie.'

Anika's smile widened, and she saw him do a double-take, focusing on her mouth, before darting away. 'Yes, I've met your lovely daughter. She's quite a talker.'

'That she is.' Handing Anika her shoes, he said, 'Sorry if she was a nuisance.'

'Every little girl deserves a chance to walk around in fine shoes. I didn't mind.'

'Thank you. It was very kind of you.' His eyes skimmed up her body, and Anika felt a zing of excitement at his attention, which surprised and confused her.

Jessie tugged at his jacket sleeve. 'Ask, Daddy. Ask.' With a lopsided, embarrassed smile, he knelt as Jessie scrambled to whisper in his ear.

The whole scene, Jessie's cuteness and Callan's embarrassment, had Anika suppressing another smile. While some intense whispering continued, an odd flutter rolled through her.

Callan cleared his throat as he straightened. 'Jessie was wondering if we could buy you breakfast as a way of apologising ... mainly for me?'

For more than a couple of seconds, she became distracted by the dimples that showed up like new moons on either side of his mouth when he beamed at her. 'Um.' She glanced at her watch. 'I guess. I've got time for a coffee before my first meeting.'

* * *

The coffee was rich and robust, just as Callan liked it. The café was a hybrid, child-friendly but sophisticated, also as Callan liked it. Jessie skipped off to the playground. With their conduit to conversation gone, an uncomfortable atmosphere settled between Callan and Anika.

Nerves began rattling through him. She was not an old biddy at all. In fact, she was a young woman in her late twenties—a *beautiful* young woman. When she'd smiled at him at the cemetery, the warmth of it had hit Callan right in the middle of his chest. Then, when her smile had widened, the heat seemed to blow right through him until he reminded himself that he couldn't experience such feelings anymore. Now with her closer, he lost the ability to string together words as her mesmerising scent clouded his senses. He'd always had a weak spot for Marc Jacobs Daisy. 'Anita, ah, Anika, what do you do?'

'I work for, no.' She took a resigned breath. 'Recently, I've become CEO of the Carlson Foundation, here and overseas, at least until I sort out a few more things. You may have seen our community outreach programs. They're all around the country.'

Callan's years as a solitary man not wanting to engage women in any sort of discussion meant his conversation style had become stunted, like that of a failed foreign-language student. 'Huh. That's surprising. Do you do fieldwork? I mean, it must be where the real challenging work is.' He tried to give her a compliment but fumbled. 'Then again, you do look like the type best suited to be behind a desk.' He'd noted she filled out her powder-blue skirt and navy blue blouse to perfection. She was all business, a woman with purpose who didn't look like she sat still for long. Energy seemed to almost visibly radiate off her. When he corralled his mind, she was speaking.

'Oh, I'd much prefer to be in the field. But at the moment the foundation faces a real funding threat, and all my time is tied up keeping everything afloat.'

'It surprises is all.'

Her mug hit the table a little too hard. 'Which part surprises you? That I'd prefer to be out amongst it or that I look like I don't?'

'Working for a charity, that's the surprise given the car you're driving. Trust fund?'

There was a defiant, dry, cutting edge to her voice. 'I save well. Are there any more ways you'd like to insult me today?'

'Whoa! I didn't mean ... Sorry, that came out wrong. I'm very rusty at this.'

'Totally corroded, I'd say. If you ever had it. You're driving the same type of car. Clearly, you must think that only trust-fund babies, or is it wankers, drive Porsches. If I'm the trust-fund baby, what does that make you?'

She was shoving back her chair as he tried to dig himself out of the avalanche of trouble he'd buried himself under. But every time he opened his mouth, he seemed to dig himself in deeper. 'Wait, I'm very sorry. I haven't taken a woman out for coffee or anything in years, and unfortunately, it's obvious I suck at it.'

Jessie came running and unwittingly saved her dad as she

squealed, 'Anika, Anika, Anika! It's your mummy. Your mummy, she's Sarah, isn't she?'

Callan wasn't sure if it was his mea culpa or Jessica's question that stalled Anika. She nodded before huskily answering, 'Oh, um, yes, she is. Why?'

'She told me last week that she's really proud of you.' Jessie was buzzing. 'I remembered, Daddy. I remembered.' She gave a twirl that had her pink dress balloon out like a bell.

'That's so lovely of you to say.' Anika's eyes gleamed before they soured to a harsh pale blue to glare at Callan. 'You must get your good manners from your mother.'

Jessie kept talking, not noticing her father wince. 'She's the one who told me if I was very still and quiet, I might hear Mummy talking to me. Sarah said that she hasn't spoken to you in a little while because you're angry with her. Are you angry at your mummy, Anika?'

'Jessie, that's enough.' Callan tried not to sound too gruff. 'Anika, I apologise for both of us.'

'No, it's okay. No. I'm not angry at my mum,' she said sadly. 'Last time I saw her, the only person I was angry with was my stepfather.'

Jessie was on a mission. 'Sarah said my mummy wouldn't like Daddy being so sad and he shouldn't be, because my mummy loved him very much and she knows he loved her with all his heart. Now he should just get on with it.'

He sniffed, '"Just get on with it", such a Lara thing to say. Jessie must have heard that from me.' Another staggering silence yawned between the adults. Their eyes met, but as quickly as they'd connected, they darted away.

Callan saw that Anika was knocked a little off her stride, but he didn't know if his bumbling or Jessie's comments had caused her to drop her shoulders. He felt useless. Everything he said seemed to come out wrong around this woman. She made him nervous, and now a debilitating disappointment ruled him.

Before he could say anything, she peeked at her watch, picking up her bag. 'Right. Well, I really should be going. This has been lovely, Jessie. You're a real sweetie.' Her chin rose as she muttered, 'Let's not do this again, Colin.' Rolling her eyes, she smiled at Jessie. 'I mean Callan.' Now his shoulders dropped.

* * *

The following Friday morning, Callan was trying to understand why there was a tightness in his chest as Jessie chatted about hoping to see Anika and her mum again. This time, there was only his red Porsche in the cemetery car park. The cemetery was still, and the silence seemed to eat every noise, even the diesel rattle of a bus pulling away from the bus stop. He surfaced from his grief when Jessie came charging towards him with a tan leather-bound note-book in her hand. 'Daddy, Sarah said this is Anika's and that she'd dropped it. We should look after it until we can give it to her.'

He flipped through it, seeing pages filled with beautiful sketches of landscapes, trees, busy city streets and the Columbia Road Flower Markets. Also scattered between the pages were lovely personal thoughts and poetry. Then there were portraits of an attractive older woman. A photo fell from the pages. Running his fingers over its smoothness, he became bewitched by the woman's eyes as he steadily realised he was looking at Sarah. She had given her captivating-coloured eyes to Anika. In return, her daughter had written beautiful words to her mother and sketched her with love.

It made him remember Anika's stunning beauty more vividly, even if it had graced their life too briefly the Friday before. He'd thought about her too regularly in the last week. Her eyes and smile triggered heat to flow within him. A warmth threatened to melt the ice around emotions he thought were frozen forever.

'Daddy, Sarah says she can't give it to Anika because they're not talking. But I'm to look after it until we can return it to her.'

'Were Sarah and Anika here this morning?'

'Only Sarah, but she didn't stay long. She wasn't as bright this morning.'

'I don't know how to contact Anika. Did she say how?'

Jessie took the thick leather-bound book and flipped through the parchment pages. 'The first page, see there's Anika's name and her phone number.'

'Okay. Let's call Anika when we get back to the car.' He couldn't call another woman while he was standing near his wife's grave. Familiar, cold guilt began to claw at him.

Being on the phone meant he was less overwhelmed by the look or scent of her. While he didn't quite hit the heights of charming, he was happy to land on civil.

Anika seemed more receptive to him, almost positively sunny as he heard her relief. 'It must have slipped out of my bag when I was there yesterday. I'm so indebted to you for finding it.'

'Jessie found it.'

'There's nothing for it, then. I need to thank you both. How about you come for dinner tonight when you drop it off? Is six p.m. early enough for Jessie?'

'There's no need for that. We're only returning your notebook.'

'It's very dear to me, that book. You don't know how happy it makes me feel to have it back. It's the least I can do. There are some of my mum's sketches and poems in there, too.'

He smiled at the joy in her voice. 'Alright, but can I bring something?'

'Jessie will be plenty. Anything you or she can't eat?'

'She's a six-year-old. There's a lot. Not that she can't eat, more she won't.'

'I was thinking pizza, gourmet for us, and I'm guessing margherita for Jessie.'

'Perfect.'

At dusk, they wound their way through the streets of the Isle of Dogs, following Anika's directions to her apartment. The tower was closer to ritzy, London Docklands chic than economical, dog-box territory. As he parked in the visitor's car park, Jessie was trying to burst out of her seat. 'It's really nice, don't you think, Daddy, that Anika has invited us over to thank us. And we're having pizza, my favourite. She's such a lovely lady. Like her mum says.'

'Yes, I guess so.' The closer the lift sped them to the penthouse, the more regularly he wiped his clammy palms on his jeans while changing his grip on the bottle of wine. He found this woman a riddle. Was it typical trust-fund-baby sensitivity or actual insult at being anything but? She was far from typical anything, and as he knocked on her door, he hoped that he'd find answers tonight.

Anika greeted them with bare feet and a smile, sans make-up. Her breathtaking natural beauty did just that as he struggled to form words once more. 'Hah ... Hi.' Then the scent of Daisy hit and he was a goner—a grinning fool.

Jessie took the lead, wise beyond her years. 'Hello, Anika, Daddy meant to say thank you for inviting us.' Even so, she still had the honest innocence of a six-year-old. 'He gets all tangled up around you. It's your perfume,' she blurted out. 'I heard him tell my aunty that he's a sucker for Daisy.'

'Is he now?' Anika smirked, which glided into a sympathetic smile at seeing Callan's mortification.

'Ah no, that's, not a, well I ... oh sod it.' He laughed. 'I think I've just removed all doubt about that.' The admission and her disarming gaze extinguished a few of his nerves.

He didn't notice, but Anika sighed and relaxed as well. Jessica was the only one fully at ease.

'Daddy has some wine for you.'

'Yes, it's a nice Chianti. I thought it would go well with the pizza.'

Callan brought the bottle from behind his back at the same time as Jessie shifted the notebook from behind her back. 'I have your notebook.'

Anika swallowed a giggle. 'Thank you both very much. Did you guys practise that move?'

Callan and Jessie looked at each other and then at Anika, causing the three to share a laugh. If he wasn't still unsure of Anika, he might have believed she gave him a second, longer stare. However, Callan did suck in a sharp breath when she bit down on her bottom lip as her gaze landed on the five-o'clock shadow fuzzing along his jaw. He wondered if he should have shaved. Callan knew he was still too thin, but hoped he looked healthier in black jeans and a navy long-sleeved T-shirt than in his suits.

They entered the chic apartment bathed in warm lighting and stylish, cool harmonies. Beautiful music floated out to greet them from a stereo hidden somewhere in the considerable space. Callan never thought he'd be bewitched by bare feet, tattered jeans and a faded Red Hot Chili Peppers T-shirt. Yet as he followed Anika's swaying hips down the polished hall, he was just that. He broke from his trance long enough to murmur, 'A Chili Peppers fan. Finally, common ground.'

She turned and threw him another smile. This one had his heart lift off and then melt as Christina Aguilera kept singing softly about freedom, beauty and self-discovery, concepts he believed lost to him.

Dinner came and went as an unanticipated ease settled over the trio. Lured to the lounge room by *The Princess Diaries* one and two, Jessie settled down, stretching out on the oversized grey couch and leaving the adults to finish their wine on the terrace.

'That's very thoughtful, to have *The Princess Diaries* for Jessie. They're some of her favourite movies. How did you know?'

'Educated guess.'

'So, no nieces or illegitimate but equally stunning daughters you're hiding somewhere that honed your skills as a consummate little-girl whisperer?'

'Wow, Callan, was that an attempt at humour?'

His dimples winked at her from the corners of his lopsided smile. 'I guess. I hope it worked better than my attempts at conversation last time we met.'

'It has, and that would be a no to both the nieces and daughters.' She took a sip of wine. 'I'm an only child, but I have friends who have little girls. Plus, what's not to like: Julie Andrews and Anne Hathaway are both strong women leads. Not forgetting a young Chris Pine, yum.'

'Yes, that about nails the attraction of it.' He stuttered a little. 'I mean the first bit, ah, not the Chris Pine bit.' His dimples twinkled again. 'He's not my type.'

'It's the eyes, right?'

'Exactly! Smouldering eyes might do it for some, but sadly … not me.'

She gave a midnight laugh, and he grew in confidence.

'So, any Chris Pine types throwing smouldering looks your way?'

Anika replied, 'No, I'm a solitary soul. Mum and Dad always said I'm not meant to be alone, that like with them, when it happens it'll be like being struck by—'

'Lightning.' His voice filled with raw hoarseness. 'Like with Lara and me.'

She matched his huskiness as she drifted. 'I haven't been struck … yet.' Time stood still as haunted eyes studied restless ones.

He made himself ignore the quiet spark he recognised as thawing lust and looked away. Anika provided a mundane circuit breaker. 'What does a widower of a six-year-old do?'

'I'm a pharmacist. My business partner and I own several pharmacies around East London. I work in the main one. It allows me to have flexibility with caring for Jessie.'

'You must be good at what you do, given the car you're driving.' She cocked her head. 'I've recently decided you're not a trust-fund wanker.'

'I deserved that.'

'A little.' As they'd drained their glasses, they moved inside to the kitchen.

Anika put her glass down on the kitchen counter and turned to take his. 'You do a wonderful job with Jessica. If you don't mind me asking, how long has it been since your wife passed?'

'It's okay. It'll be five years next month since Lara's aneurysm killed her.' He visibly shuddered. 'In the early days, my parents and Lara's parents helped out. But it was my sister, Saoirse, who was a godsend. She helped care for us and got me back on track. Now she's just finished her master's in finance, and I suspect she'll be moving on soon to live the next chapter of her life. Saoirse's been everything to us.' Not wishing to dwell on his sorrow, he shifted the conversation. 'And you, when did your dad die?'

He saw puzzlement flicker across her face.

'That's who you and your mum visit, right?'

'Kind of. Hunter Carlson died six years ago. My mum doesn't visit.'

'Is that because she finds it too hard?'

'Sarah Carlson was many things, but finding things too hard was not one of the things she indulged. But no, she doesn't visit because she—'

'Oh, wait. Sarah Carlson. You mean, *the* Sarah Carlson, she's your mum? She's like Mother Teresa. How many humanitarian awards has she been given? She's phenomenal. Her charity work is legendary. She was always on the frontline, locally and worldwide—'

'Do you need me here for this conversation?'

'Hang on, hang on, your mum passed away, like ...'

'Six months ago.'

'Wow, that's ... not long.'

'What part of she's dead don't you get?'

By now, he knew her getting angry tone. Especially since he always fired it up. 'No, please, don't take this the wrong way.' He held up his hands. 'Isn't it still so raw and being an only child, it must be so. Sorry, Anika, I didn't mean anything other than you amaze me, you don't show the hurt. I mean, isn't it still so fresh?'

'Well, not all of us wear our grief like a straitjacket for all to see.' Her voice slapped out at him. 'Some of us just try to move on. And grieve in other ways.'

Something was wrenching at him. It may have been the pain rolling across her face like thunder in an angry sky. But no, it was something else. Then it happened—the penny dropped. 'But Jessica? She said your mum spoke to her last ...'

'I don't know what that was about. All I know is it makes me more certain that there is more than only life and death, just like there's more than black and white. Mum, Dad and me always believed in more. That a spirit could linger in this world long after the body ceases to exist. Be good in this life and it won't just end as ashes.' She waved her arms around. 'Whichever it is, I can't explain it.'

He had a dim memory of his mum, Mary, saying she had spoken with spirits of unsettled souls. It was years ago. He and his brothers had laughed, but now their reaction appeared stupid and hurtful. 'Why put yourself through such stuff, stirring everything up, never letting it settle?'

'You mean how you've let losing Lara settle?' She gave a defiant shake of her head.

'It doesn't help. None of it. Talking about it. Making Jessie believe—'

'How is it wrong? Jessie made me feel happy. I don't know why or how ... but somehow, if she did speak to Mum, it was wonderful for me, and for Jessie, too. Don't you dare try to take that away from me. You have no right.'

'It's stupid to think—'

'Who does it hurt?'

'Me, that's who it hurts.' He slapped his chest, eyes glistening. 'Me.'

'Don't be so selfish. Look at the love and happiness in your daughter's face. Think of the joy it brought her and me.'

'It stirs it all up. And I'm the furthest from selfish. I'm thinking of Jessie. I don't want her hurt.'

'That I understand, but you're the adult. You need to deal with your pain and anger so you can help her.'

'Please don't tell me how to parent.'

'I would never do that.' Tears clung to the corners of her eyes now.

'How did Jessica know those things … how?'

'I don't know. What I do know is Mum's spirit is not at rest, and my stepfather is the reason.' She was starting to shake, and Callan could see she was in pain. 'Don't you dare take away that hope.' Then the dam broke and her words and tears flowed. 'I know he did something. He killed her, I just know. The last time I saw her, she was sick, really sick, confused with vomiting and diarrhoea. I had her hospitalised. Brian came and discharged her before they could do any actual tests. He took charge of her and stopped me from seeing her. If she was herself, she would've never allowed that to happen. I went over and banged on the door, but he wouldn't let me in. Into *her home*. He wouldn't let me see my own mother. Said I was trying to turn her against him. He called the police and told them I was trespassing. Brian got a restraining order out on me, saying my mum was scared of me.

'I managed to speak to her on the phone. Mum was always so sharp, yet the last time we spoke, she was having trouble forming words, thoughts. I gathered from what she could say that she was in unbearable pain, the cramping intolerable. We were both in tears. She told me she loved me and to look on the card. It would explain everything. She was very clear about that. I don't know what it means. Then the connection dropped out. He did something. I know he did.' Rubbing her hand over her face, she wiped at the tears. 'She comes to me at night in my dreams, or maybe they're nightmares. After I wake up, I have these terrible feelings of helplessness and dread.'

'Anika, stop it. Can't you see what it's doing to you?'

'Shut up. I have to,' she choked out. 'Well, I *believe*. I have to. I have to find out. Now he wants the money. Brian's hired forensic accountants to go over my and the charity's accounts. I've hired lawyers to fight him. It's all a bloody mess. It's draining my own money, but I don't care. I'm keeping the foundation running, saving it from a greedy man's nastiness,' she sobbed. The words were coming as freely as the tears sliding down her cheeks.

While Callan didn't understand all of it, he knew enough, and for the first time since Lara, he wanted to ease someone else's pain. He wrapped Anika up in his arms and rocked her until she settled. Her body softened against his.

He looked down into her water-filled eyes. 'Sorry, I didn't mean to take advantage ...' He pressed his lips into a grim line. 'I always seem to be apologising to you.'

'Then let me even the score.' She took his lips with hers, releasing a soft heat that ignited feelings in his cold core. Emotions he thought he'd never have for a woman again, let alone want to feel them again. When she pulled back, a sad smile creased her full lips. 'Sorry about that.'

Anika's warmth rolled through him like an unstoppable train. He couldn't explain what it meant to feel again, to have a woman unlock those sensations and to want her to. 'Uh-huh, um, I don't need you to—oh, just shut up.' Losing control, he stormed her mouth. She kept melting long-restrained emotions that, until she kissed him, he'd fought to keep frozen.

He loved her taste, the wonder of having her this close, and the surprise that she'd want to give such tenderness to him. His lack of control caused whiplash anger. There was confusion as a battle raged between wanting to feel the passion this woman was offering and his anger at dishonouring Lara. 'You just don't know, you can't, what this does ...' Taking her by surprise, he angled his body in, trapping her in the corner of the kitchen counter.

She didn't show any fear. Instead, she rose to his advance, welcoming this new sexy danger he wore. 'Come on, Callan, let it all out.'

'I can't do this. I can't.'

'What are you afraid of?'

'Nothing.'

'Liar!' Now they were toe to toe.

His eyes were blazing molten platinum-grey, chest rising and falling, like the ebb and flow of a storming tide. 'Why do you keep pushing?' His warring emotions had him slapping his right hand on the counter.

She juddered at the noise yet kept her voice calm. 'I don't mean to.' She reached out and cupped his cheek with a caring hand, surprising him by not rising to his anger. Her voice a husky whisper, she said, 'I recognise your fight. It's been five years. Pushing that button shouldn't be so raw, cause such pain.' He couldn't escape those penetrating silver-blue eyes, the ones that turned him to glass. His weaknesses visible, she found the question at the centre of the pain. 'Why are you still so sad?'

The intensity of her stare made her words, although delivered softly, arrow straight to his heart and the truth. 'We'd fought, and I stormed out of the house. I wasn't there to help her. She died alone, not knowing how much I loved her. I didn't say it that day.'

She threw her hands in the air. 'That's not the real reason. Come on! I expected better, especially if you're putting your life on hold.' The surge of her temper jolted him like his slap on the counter had her.

'You don't know what it's like.'

'Oh really! You want to go down that path with me?'

'But ...'

'What? You think it doesn't hurt me to know Mum and I hadn't spoken at all those last days, that I didn't get to say goodbye— couldn't get to her to save her. Her legacy, her work, is in jeopardy, and I might not be good enough, smart enough, or have the boundless energy Mum had to keep the foundation going, like she would want it to. It hurts. It scares me, too.'

'Of course it would. But for me, there's also Jessica.'

She cupped his face again, this time with both hands. 'When the sun doesn't shine through a storm, do you expect it never to shine again?' Her voice, with the perfect velvet touch, struck at his heart.

'You know it's there, no matter how savage the cold and the wind, how long the rain and the dark linger. You know it's there.'

'Yes.'

'Why would you believe Lara thought for an instant your love for her had waned just because you hadn't said it that morning?' He felt so off balance until she brushed her lips over his and his world steadied. 'Sorry to tell you this, but you're an easy guy for a woman to read. The love you showed her every day wouldn't be hidden by one dark cloud. It would shine through like a powerful beacon.'

'How do you do that?' he asked with a voice like sandpaper on wood.

'How do I do what?' Her voice was the silk to his raspy tone.

'Take the pain and rawness away?'

'I don't know. Only that I understand pain, sadness and anger. Yes that, the last especially.'

He felt the harsh edge of his words blunted by her caring honesty. The smooth softness of her touch, her tone and the purity of her gaze calmed him like a soothing pain reliever, and he revealed the truth. 'If I'd been there, maybe I could have saved her.'

'Now we're getting somewhere. The real reason for the rawness of your grief is guilt. I know about that all too well—guilt over not being able to save the one you love. I say this with the utmost respect and care. Are you a doctor? Did you have a full intensive care unit hidden somewhere in the house? Because that's what it would've taken to save her. Even then, they may not have had the time or recognised it straightaway as a ruptured aneurysm.'

'Don't mock me.'

'I would never, but stop torturing yourself. I recognise the symptoms because I've been doing the same. We're a pair, aren't we? You know you're an intelligent man, but grief is ...'

'A peculiar disease we can succumb to at the oddest times, even when you feel cured and stable.'

Anika reached across to push his hair back off his brow. 'Yes, and when we least expect it, grief brings back the sadness, anger and worst of all, the guilt.'

He shrugged. 'Definitely two peas in a pod.'

Now she whispered, 'It's okay for you to feel …'

'Guilty …'

'No. You've done enough of that. You're allowed to feel alive, experience happiness, joy. Leave guilt and its cronies to take a back seat.'

'You get to the point, don't you?'

'I haven't got time not to. Callan, for Jessica's sake, you must go on and live. You have to show Jessie there's more to life than her mother's death.'

This time it was his turn to frame her face with his hands and draw her in to take her lips in a long, tender kiss that had them both warming, burning. His tongue fluttered over hers, and she tasted divine. She held on to him as they rose on a heat that blossomed into a craving, a persistent desire for more. She gripped his shoulders then slid her hands over his chest around to his back to press him to her. Soon his arms enveloped her, wrapping her in his heat. 'Live with passion in my life again, you say?'

Her breath came in a dreamy hush. 'Yes.'

'Since meeting you, feelings I thought were dead to me have begun to stir again. I've lost the fight to stop them.' He trailed his lips up her throat. 'Or is that won the battle.' He could hardly hear his words over the thumping of his heart. Blood was pumping hard in his ears. 'I should definitely do this more.'

The next frenzied minutes were like a bliss bomb had exploded. He boosted her up on the counter, heat and hands everywhere. They were under her shirt, skimming over her skin, his fingers rolling over her nipples. His mouth claimed hers as his body pushed in, parting her legs. She tangled her fingers through his ebony curls, tugging and pulling as she feasted on him, nipping, sucking and tasting.

They were lifting off. Before they'd risen too far, Anika rasped, 'Wait. Not like this.' Her hands sliding over his chest slowed. 'Guilt and grief can't be the things that bind us. Our minds have to be free of everything but us. I don't want the two of us to have regrets.'

He froze, wanting to grab and take her, knowing they couldn't. If they did this now, grief and guilt would be the threads that bound their hearts together. Then the two emotions would be their destroyers. The ropes that would hang them. They needed time to be sure the right emotions were driving the passion. 'You're right. Not yet. Sorry, I don't usually lose control.' He stepped back.

'I'm not looking for an apology.'

'Still, I shouldn't have.'

'At least we've proven one thing.'

'Which is?'

She tapped a finger on his lined forehead. 'More than guilt and sadness reside within these handsome, smouldering features.'

He tilted his head while his eyes tracked the graceful movement of her body sliding from the counter to the floor.

'Come to dinner, Callan, just me, no Jessie. A proper date, no expectations other than good food, great wine and even better company. I'll even wear a killer dress. Everyone, even someone as guilty, sad and angry as you, needs to dip their toe back into the fun end of the pool. And for more than a couple of wild, bliss-filled minutes.'

'You don't like to waste time, do you?'

'Why play hard to get? We've proven there's a mutual attraction. Let's see what happens if we nudge this thing a little further along.'

'Alright, then.'

They reached an agreement for a date, time and place. Callan almost floated through her sleek urban apartment to the lounge. Jessie had fallen asleep as *The Princess Diaries 2* rolled on. Callan sighed as he gently brushed a wayward strand of reddish-brown hair off Jessie's face. Bending, he kissed his daughter's cheek. The little girl stirred. 'Jessie, it's time to go, honey-bun.'

With a sleepy stretch, she said, 'Daddy, what's an SD card? Is it like a birthday card?'

'What?' He looked at Jessie and then in astonishment at Anika. 'I swear you have the most amazing mind.' Hugging his little girl, he kneeled next to her. Then he patiently explained as simply as he could what an SD card was and how it was used. Callan promised to show her the one he had at home where he stored photos and videos of her to send to her grandparents.

'That must be what Sarah does. I forgot to say, but she told me this morning that Anika had to look for the SD card in the beast's ashtray.' Jessica rubbed a knuckle into a bleary eye, then looked straight at a now shaking, wide-eyed Anika. 'She said you should look for it. Do you have a beast, Anika? Sarah said it wasn't a scary beast. It was a fun beast.' Then Jessie whimpered, 'Anika, what's wrong!'

Callan ran to the trembling woman who was folding over herself as she slid down the wall she'd been leaning against.

Jessie followed him and said, 'Oh, Anika, I didn't mean to make you sad. Your mummy said it would make you happy and give both of you a piece. No, that's not right. Give both of you peace.'

Callan helped Anika to one of her cosy grey lounge chairs. Tears breached her eyes to spill down her cheeks. He felt like he was in a car without a steering wheel, ill-equipped to steer her to a safe place and quell the shock. 'Anika, let me help.'

'Please don't cry.' A heavy, solitary tear trekked down Jessie's cheek.

Callan kissed Anika's forehead. When he pulled back, he no longer saw vulnerability etched on her face, but determination. While he'd recaptured the capacity to give limitless care.

'You're a good man, a very good man.' Anika leaned forward and hugged Jessie. 'Oh, Jessie darling, please, I'm not sad.' Looking up into Callan's steady gaze, she took his hand, giving it a reassuring squeeze.

His eyes glistened as he handed her a handkerchief, desperately trying not to think the feelings swirling within him had anything to do with attraction. Yet he was certain they didn't have their origins in guilt and grief.

With a soft chuckle, she wiped at her tears. 'Look at you being all gentlemanly.' She seemed to reset. 'Now then, that was a bit of a shock.'

'Can you explain it to us?' Callan tussled Jessie's hair as she burrowed into his legs.

Taking a deep breath, Anika began. 'Some of it, I guess, yes. The beast is Mum's Porsche. She used to call it that because she loved the way the engine growled.' She smiled at Jessica. 'Yes, it is a fun beast. Mum and I both love cars. Mum would say, "Everyone needs one splash of vivid colour in their life". This was ours.' She wiped at new tears. 'She gave it to me in both her wills.'

'Both wills?' Callan asked.

She shook her head. 'Brian, my stepfather, maintains my mother wrote a new will as she became even sicker. Apparently, Mum left all her money to him and next to nothing to the foundation in the second will. She gave me the car in both wills. He doesn't care about the car, so I have it. I'm challenging this second will. The only will I, and the Carlson Foundation lawyers, have, has her leaving most of everything to the foundation.

'The most distressing thing is I'm having to contest my mum's competency at the time of writing this supposed second will. Which she didn't tell me about and didn't use the foundation's regular lawyers to draft. Brian's saying she changed her mind about the foundation, about me—that it was her last wish that Brian should inherit all her money. As you can imagine, it's a substantial amount. Now I'm having to argue she couldn't possibly have understood what she was doing to change her will and to whom she should give her money. It makes me seem like an uncaring, money-grabbing bit —' Looking at Jessica, she stopped. 'It makes me look like a terrible daughter.' She dabbed at her wet cheeks.

'I don't care about the money for me. I care for the foundation. That's what I'm fighting Brian for. The Carlson Foundation must continue. It's a no-brainer. Mum would have always wished that to be the case.'

'At least you have the car to treasure,' said Callan.

'Yes, it's cold comfort. Mum liked putting her earrings or sometimes loose change in the ashtray. I've never looked in it. I thought it was empty.'

Callan's voice was soothing as he said, 'Do you want us to come with you to look?'

She held up her hand. 'Give me a moment.' She flexed her toes into the plush lounge-room rug. It looked like she was trying to centre herself while testing that the floor hadn't fallen out from under her. Her breathing under control, she handed Callan his handkerchief with a sad smile. 'Thanks.'

'How about you keep it.' There was the genuine likelihood she would need it again before the night was through, whether they found an SD card or not.

Callan was having trouble reconciling that Sarah Carlson had been communicating via his six-year-old daughter from beyond the grave. There had to be some other logical explanation. With Anika still pale, he decided he could wait to unravel that conundrum.

* * *

Anika's Porsche was indeed a sight. 'Your mum didn't skimp on bringing the beast.' On seeing it up close for the first time, it stole his breath almost as much as its owner did. He hadn't really taken notice of it when she'd followed him to the café that fateful morning. His mind was preoccupied and anxious over how to talk to a strange woman while having coffee. Then there was the matter of how the hell his six-year-old daughter had talked him into inviting her.

When he returned from his thoughts, Anika was rushing her words, her pitch a little higher than usual. 'This car is one of the best she ever owned. It was delivered to me after she died. Wait until you hear the engine. It's unreal.'

'Of course, it's a 991 Carrera GTS.' Nervous chatter, he realised. She wasn't sure she wanted to face the disappointment of not finding anything, or confront the future if she did. 'It must corner like a housefly.'

Hearing his delight, she gave a grin that blew the beats out of his heart, causing him to lose his hearing and sight for a moment as a sensation he hadn't felt in a long time took hold.

She kept talking as she unlocked the car. 'Of course, Mum wouldn't settle for any colour. It had to be agate grey.' Her eyes went hard. 'She never settled for anything until Brian.' He saw her fight to will the bitterness away. 'I love the low-profile rims with red brake calipers. It's like putting the beast in a bow tie and tux.'

Anika hesitated and fell silent as she reached for the doorhandle, her hand trembling. Callan's mind went blank as he felt the anxiety humming off her. Jessica once again bridged the divide. 'Do you want me to help? I can look for you. But I think Sarah would want you to do it.'

'You're right. How'd you get to be so smart?' With a quick swallow, she gripped the door handle and swung it open. 'Best to just get it on with it.'

Callan's heart stuttered when she used words that triggered so much warmth in him.

Jessie looked at her father. 'Like Mum used to say, right, Dad?' He could only nod dreamily.

Anika flopped into the driver's seat as Callan and Jessica peered in. She pushed the ashtray open. Her shoulders dropped. 'See, empty.'

Jessie leaned across and hugged her. Then she slipped her tiny fingers into the ashtray. That's when they all heard it, a barely there rattle. 'It's loose. Does it come out so you can empty it, like in Dad's car?'

'You *are* smart, *really* smart.' He could almost hear Anika's heart pumping hard, echoing around the garage.

Anika flicked the tray up with her fingernail to search the space below. She released a rush of breath. 'Empty. Shit!' She glanced at Jessica. 'Oh, sorry.'

'It's okay.' Jessie leaned back, giving Callan a knowing look. 'Daddy uses that word a lot.'

Anika dropped her head in dismay and rolled the black plastic ashtray container around in her hands. Then in the dull overhead car light, she saw the bulge. Blending perfectly with the container's flat underside was a strip of black tape. It covered something stuck to the container's bottom surface. She jumped out of the car, pushing past Callan and Jessie. With her hands still shaking, she managed to hold them still long enough to rip off the tape and there, just as Jessie had said, was an SD card.

'Shit a brick!' Echoed around the parking garage.

'See, I told you, Anika, Daddy uses it, too.'

With her eyes blazing, Anika turned to Callan. 'I don't have an SD card reader.'

'Daddy?' Jessica stared at Callan, tilting her head at him and then back to Anika.

'It looks like you're coming home with us.' Suddenly, he felt embarrassed at his leap. 'Or not. I could bring the card reader to you.'

She didn't blink. 'I'll follow you. Let's go.'

* * *

While Callan tucked Jessica into her bed, Anika paced downstairs in his kitchen. *Nervous hands need something to do*, she thought. Coffee, they'd need coffee. As the clock ticked past eleven, she searched cupboards for mugs and sugar, and was ferreting around in the fridge when she heard him come in. 'Um, it's not what it looks like.'

He smiled. 'What, you're looking for something else other than milk in my fridge?'

'I didn't want you to think I was taking over your kitchen, your space.'

They were both anxious again, she noted. Both were jumpy

about what secrets were on a piece of technology and what was going on between them. *Keep busy, yes, that's best.* 'Why don't I organise coffee and you grab your laptop?'

He motioned towards the coffee machine. 'I assume you know how to work it.' She looked at the machine and nodded, prompting him to say, 'Good, I'll have an espresso.'

She caught herself being thankful she was here, in what should've felt like a stranger's kitchen. Instead, it felt safe. Then the main reason for that sensation walked in, offering her—an almost stranger—the use of his laptop, his home, his shoulder. Yes, he was a really good man. Better than that, he was honourable.

They sat down on stools at the kitchen bench, sipping coffee as he turned on his laptop. Anika held the card in her fingers, frozen. Callan's hand came over hers, a simple move that had her heart sighing and her mind believing, *We're in this together.* Sliding the card into the computer port, they held their collective breath. He opened the only file on the card. It was a video of a kitchen.

A thickset man came into view. He had a swagger, wearing very noticeably expensive clothes in a scruffy way. The gold and diamonds of his large, expensive watch and ring glinted as he placed a bottle on the counter. He warmed soup in a microwave and served up two portions in different bowls. In the flower-patterned one, he stirred in a heaped teaspoon of white powder from the bottle. He then poured two cups of coffee. Again, he stirred a heaped teaspoon of white powder into the mug with flowers on it. He jolted when a woman who looked like Anika, although much older and very frail, came into view. Dressed simply, her mother was sliding herself into the kitchen on a walking frame. The man pushed the bottle behind his bulky body, speaking with more mean than caring. 'I told you to stay put. I'll bring the damn soup to you.'

The woman coughed. 'It's okay, Brian. I know you're taking good care of me, especially now I'm sicker. The good news is I feel a little better since coming home from the hospital. Maybe I should've stayed longer? Given you a break.'

'No! You'll stay here under my care. You'll get better on your own. That freeloading daughter of yours won't get her hooks into you to make me look bad. You know she only wants to get at your money. She's a spoilt brat. That's what she is.'

Turning towards the camera, away from Brian, Sarah said, 'Oh, honey, Anika loves me dearly as I love her. She has no ulterior motives.' Her painfully thin mother wiped at a tear. 'Anyway, I thought I'd try to eat a banana before lunch.' As she pushed herself closer to the camera, it became apparent that it was a phone camera, hidden behind a fruit bowl, with its video recording. Over her shoulder, Brian pushed the bottle behind the microwave, out of sight.

Sarah looked fearful and frail as she grabbed a banana, and then the image blurred as she grabbed the phone. She was whispering, 'Don't be scared, be brave. Ani, I love you, baby girl. You're my best gift to the world. Love you so much. He has control of everything. You won't be able to get to me.' The video went black.

'Oh God, oh God.' Anika had held it together, but now she dissolved into helplessness. 'I should have done more. I should have broken the damn door down to get to her. I should have told the police to shove the restraining order and fought harder.'

Grief hadn't crept back in to sadden. Instead, it had rampaged in to destroy. Guilt, her grief's most lethal weapon, was injuring, wounding, hollowing her out. 'He must have taken her phone soon after that.' She pointed at the screen, tears running in rivulets down her cheeks. 'See the date, it's before my last call with her. That's when she said the card would explain everything. He must have found the phone and destroyed it to stop her from calling to get further help. But she was smart enough to hide the SD card. Bastard!'

Callan held her and let her cry, to release her pain. 'You're not alone any longer. I'll help you face this.'

She swiped at her tears and snuffled into his hanky. 'How can you say that? This is more than offering me your hanky. You don't know me.'

'I know you'd let a complete stranger's daughter wear your

designer shoes. I know you loved your mother and father deeply, that you care for those less fortunate than you with a passion beyond your years. I know you're a talented artist, and your poetry shows you have a beautiful soul. My last and best point is I know what you're facing, the guilt and grief at not being there to save the one you loved.'

'I can't ask you to do this.'

'You're not. I'm stepping up to do this because a wise woman once told me there's more to life than the death of a mother.'

Anika gave a teary nod before she let her anger rise. It felt right and just. 'I want Brian to pay. I want him to rot in jail. It's time I did what I always do and get to the point, no time for guilt, anger or grief. How do we find out what the white stuff is?'

Callan met her eyes. 'There's the fiery, never-sit-still, take-no-prisoners woman I first met. So, tell me her symptoms again?'

'Initially, she was tired all the time, which was odd as Mum had boundless energy.'

'Like her daughter.'

That brought a small smile to her face. 'It was like she had a flu she couldn't shake. Then came the headaches and sores that didn't heal. Mum started coming in to work less and less because she started having devastating gastric symptoms and disorientation. It was horrible. She was withering away before my eyes. Her body seemed to be shutting down. That's why I got her to hospital. In the short time she was there they stabilised her, and she seemed to be getting better.'

'Did they take blood tests?'

'Yes, they didn't show anything that could cause what she had. Brian came and discharged her, spinning a story that she was fine. It was only stress because of me trying to control her to get her money. He was her husband, so they released her to his care.'

Callan rubbed his chin. 'What does Brian do for a living?'

'Before his living was bleeding my mum dry, he was in mining. He worked in the processing plant for a gold mine in South Africa.

That's where they met when she was out there on foundation work. He retired after marrying Mum.'

'Now we're getting somewhere. I have an idea what the powder might be because of the gold mining and those symptoms.' He did a quick Google search. As she watched over his shoulder, he said, 'Arsenic, that's what the white stuff probably is.'

'Why?'

'It's used in gold mining. That's how he most likely got access to it, because it's hard to get hold of these days. Being poisoned with it causes those symptoms. It's mostly tasteless and odourless. Your mum wouldn't have tasted anything different if it was put in her food or drinks. In the 1800s, the French called it inheritance powder. I think you can guess why. Lots of elderly parents died a painful, mysterious death.' He ran his fingers through his hair. 'It says here that it can clear rapidly from the blood. Probably why it didn't show up in your mum's blood. Plus, arsenic poisoning is very rare these days in countries like the UK. They wouldn't have tested for it.'

'In that video, he hid the bottle as soon as Mum came in. He'll have got rid of it, all the evidence. He's smart. We have no proof. He'll say it was magnesium powder or some herbal remedy, something to help her get better.'

He interrupted her, 'He may not be as smart as he thinks. There are some things that you can't get rid of, even in death.'

Anika caught on, having watched her fair share of TV crime shows. 'Not this time. There's no body to exhume. Mum was cremated. Her ashes are stored in an urn next to my dad's in the obelisk at the cemetery.' Anika rubbed her eyes. 'There's no hair or tissue to test.'

'It doesn't matter. There are ashes. They can be tested. Arsenic is a heavy metal. Heat doesn't destroy it. You can test the ashes for it. There's no possible reason that any toxic levels of arsenic should be found in your mother's ashes unless she was poisoned.'

'You mean ...'

'Yes, get her ashes tested, and if they turn purple, then arsenic is present. The deeper the purple, the more arsenic.'

Her silver-blue eyes were large and luminescent. She dared not breathe.

'Anika, we have him.'

That's when the lightning bolt hit, leaving a wonderful energy surging through her. 'Thank you. Not only for giving me Mum's peace, but for the beautiful man you are.' Anika dived at him, taking his very breath, planting kisses along his unshaved strong jaw, her words silken at his ear. 'I know you think it's illogical that Mum could've spoken to Jessica from beyond the grave, yet you overlooked that to help me. To care about a stranger's pain when you were still struggling with your own, you are a rare man, indeed.'

She pinned him with a searing gaze. 'Callan, this attraction, it's not driven by shared guilt and grief or even anger. This feeling, the one overwhelming me, it's about hope and a promise of new, exciting beginnings.' She placed her hands on his shoulders. 'Do you want to take this ride with me?'

She'd already struck the match to his slow-burning fuse in her kitchen. Now in his kitchen, a white-hot flame ignited. She could see it unfreeze all his passion. It was his turn to take, to want, and come alive with desires he hadn't set free in a long while. This time, he took her mouth with a ferocity that had her breath hitch in her throat. A thick molasses utterance escaped him. 'Oh God, yes.' Uttering the three words broke and shattered the last chains he'd wrapped around himself. 'Don't go home tonight. Stay.'

* * *

Over the following weeks, the worlds of Anika, Callan and Jessica changed for the better. Callan now believed lightning never struck twice in the same place, until it did. Anika discovered that before she'd even really known, the bolt had struck her. She'd been part way to resisting, with no understanding of the strike's power until it consumed her. Now Anika had no wish to be without it. She only wanted to share it with Callan and Jessie.

As Callan was about to grab a mint-green shirt, Jessica offered her advice. 'No, Daddy, not the green shirt. You need to wear your crisp white shirt with those grey trousers. It'll make your eyes pop. Anika will love it.'

'How do you know such things?'

'Aunt Saoirse teaches me.'

He hadn't spoken to Jessica about her role in helping Anika to find the SD card. Life had been hectic ever since Anika had tried but failed to keep him from the angst of going with her to the police. Callan would have none of it and had been by her side, supporting her fight to have her stepfather charged with murder.

Brian kept lying and Anika kept believing that the proof she had would hold. Then, in taking the higher ground, she was believed by the police and Brian was arrested. Subsequently, his claims about the second will were thrown out of court.

Anika told Callan that since her mother had died, she'd forgotten how comforting it was to have support. She and Callan had spent tumultuous days at court, then shared time with Jessica, and when they could, sizzling nights in each other's beds. The two had discovered that it was quick and complete when lightning struck, like the love growing between them.

They shared as much time as they could with Jessica when she wasn't at school or asleep. When the three visited the cemetery, there seemed to be no surprise visitors. When Brian was finally charged and a date set for his trial, they made time for their planned date. Callan learned that Anika was a woman of her word. As promised, the dress she wore was a killer. When she strode towards him, the red silk of it hugged her curves, moulded her cleavage and highlighted her stunning legs. His jaw dropped. 'That dress is going to do me in!'

Her fingertips curled around his chin and picked up his jaw, while her smiling lips touched his cheek with a throaty, 'Mission accomplished.'

Preparing for another date, Callan slipped on the white shirt Jessie selected. He decided now was as good a time as any to ask, 'Jessica, how did you know those things to help Anika?'

'I told you, Daddy, Sarah, Anika's mummy, told me. I heard her because I believed, and I was quiet and still. Anika wasn't as quiet or still as she needed to be, and you didn't believe.'

'Honey-bun, it doesn't make sense. There are no such things as ghosts.'

'Oh, Daddy, that's your thing. Grandma Mary says I've got the family gift, like she has. Sarah's gone now because she's at peace. She doesn't need to visit me anymore.' She gave him a little squint in an attempt at a wink. 'But Mummy says to say hello. She loves Anika, and she's glad you're finally moving on and just "getting on with it".'

thirteen

SAOIRSE IS SAOIRSE: LONDON 2010

CHAD HAD WATCHED Miss Too-important-to-care double park, leave the keys in her unlocked car and skip into the small, out of the way Tesco to pay for her petrol. It was both pleasing and perplexing. She was the fourth customer to do the same thing in the afternoon rush hour. How stupid were these people? He decided his perfect moment had come. She had parked so poorly that he had more of a blind spot to work with from where the CCTV camera was pointed.

There would be no slip-ups this time. He pulled his floppy hat down over his face and was careful to hike up his long skirt over his dowdy blouse, so his neon-pink joggers showed—conspicuous for a reason. Let them notice his feet. The rest would be a distorted blob.

Chad wanted his Irish bitch scared and broken. She wasn't nearly enough of either, yet. He wore the body padding and curly red wig with his large woman's clothing to be doubly careful. He allowed enough of the red to poke out from under his mum-type sunhat. If any tosser civilians decided to help the police, they'd see what he wanted them to.

Once more, the Irish bitch had slipped back into the complacency of her happy family mode. All the while, the police investigation made his life fucking unbearable. He couldn't eat and was jumping at his own shadow. It was the wrong way around. Didn't she know he was the hunter, not the prey? The rage felt like it was about to rip him apart. It was time to hit those responsible for the crushing, mind-jerking pressure. There were so many targets: her latest fuck, the fag of a computer nerd, the blonde business slut and the dykes, not to mention the brother, his bimbo and the brat. All of them needed to be punished for giving her protection and keeping him from having her sooner. Why didn't they see her for the whore she was? It was like his mother all over again.

Chad wanted to inflict maximum pain on all of them. Then she'd blame herself and be distraught with anguish. He'd leave her in no doubt that she was responsible, and her friends would run from her. Then he'd grab her when she was at her weakest. For now, anger radiated off Chad as he gripped his backpack, kept his head down and slipped into the car.

The CCTV footage would show a blur in a floppy hat stealing the car. Some eyewitnesses would say they saw an odd-shaped redhead with curly hair hanging around the Tesco. Others would say a pregnant woman, the less complimentary would say a fat woman with ugly bright shoes. They'd all agree on the shoes. Initially, when the burnt-out car was found, there would be nothing the police could find to solve a tragic hit-and-run.

* * *

Hilton Oh stepped off the bus at the stop closest to Saoirse and Callan's house. He took his usual route. Striding into the busy intersection, he had to cross before turning down the quiet street to Saoirse's, bouncing along to his music. He was excited that he could finally share his good news about his follow-up dates with his hunky big Barbadian—who was now not so much a coconut but all pure black magic.

He was halfway across the busy intersection when he dropped

his phone. He was all thumbs as he'd tried to find his favourite song to strut to. The Bee Gees' 'Stayin' Alive' was his ultimate strutting song, and he felt like strutting. Hilton was that happy.

* * *

Meanwhile, Saoirse was bouncing around her kitchen, making dinner for Blaise, Hilton, Jules, Sabine and Chris. Callan, Anika and Jessica would join them too. It was about the same time the police were going to drop the hammer on the arsehole that was Chad Merritt. Saoirse would be free to be with Blaise and not have to look over her shoulder. They'd work out what to do about New York.

She added some final thyme and a sprinkling of parsley to her coq au vin, Blaise's favourite. She still had about ten minutes before everyone arrived, so she poured two flutes of champagne. She couldn't believe how happy she was.

* * *

Having heard the police were about to storm his quarry's lock-up, Blaise, with a bounce in his step, swung a leg over his Harley. He started it and headed to Saoirse's for dinner with her friends. He finally had someone in his life that brought excitement and the expectation of a more fulfilling future. While he never thought it was for him, now he made plans for two, which made him smile and his heart thunder.

Spotting a florist on the way, he decided to stop. *Roses*, he thought, then he decided, *No, too run-of-the-mill, expected. Pink lilies, yes, like her lips.* He bought as many as he could fit into his saddlebag. With the large bunch in his arms, he started back across the road to his bike.

Chad Merritt, aka Mitch Trader, aka Rhett Micard, aka Marc Herditt, was driving around the block for the second time, keeping an eye on his prey's house. To make sure his plan would succeed, he'd disengaged the airbags.

As he came around the corner, he couldn't believe his luck—there was one of his targets in front of him. He'd do this, and then she'd be next. She'd be pathetically weakened by grief. Particularly as what he was about to do would send her friends running from her because they'd fear him and the pain he'd wield like a scythe. Chad gunned the Range Rover's engine and aimed for the man in the middle of the road. As he hit a hundred clicks, he laughed maniacally. The next thing to bounce that day was an honourable man's body as a stolen Range Rover hit it.

* * *

Not long after they'd swept up the bruised, bloodied and broken lilies to clear the street, a grief-paralysed Saoirse was by Blaise's side. They'd wheeled him from surgery and into ICU. At around three a.m., Callan and Anika managed to get Saoirse home, where a doctor sedated her so she'd sleep. Hilton and Jordon took over the vigil beside Blaise's bed. When they were exhausted, Sabine and Christine stayed, followed by Jules and Tomas.

These very different people, these different personalities, living all the different types of love, were connected to each other because of one woman's love, and that was a tribute to her. This woman who was striving to find her place in the world. Saoirse had loving friends who were always there for her and a family that never failed her. As Blaise was an only child whose parents had passed away years earlier, he had no family. Now friends and family blended to make a complete supportive family circle around Blaise.

Then Blaise's other family came to offer help and solace. His police force friends checked in. Their mood was a mix of controlled pain and simmering anger. They would catch the coward who had done this. Chad Merritt was their number-one person of interest. He'd slipped through the attempt to arrest him at his lair.

* * *

Saoirse rose in a daze the following afternoon. The pain and emptiness had her struggling to move. It was like she carried a too-heavy yoke around her neck. The coq au vin had long since cooked dry. Her bitterness rose like the bile and tears at seeing the ruined meal. It was meant to be a loving symbol. Now, all it represented was pain. She flung the dish into the kitchen sink and watched it shatter, like her heart.

Her world was in a similar state. It had been ever since she'd answered her phone to the news of Blaise. Right then, she'd collapsed into Hilton's arms. Now she crumpled, curling up on the kitchen floor in tears. Jessica found her and coaxed her to sit as she urged her aunt to drink some water.

There was no keeping Saoirse from Blaise's bedside. She stayed with him day and night, hoping and praying he'd wake. She couldn't eat, couldn't sleep. The only thing she did do was quickly go out of her mind. Every time she looked at his motionless body in the ICU bed, helplessness and hurt crushed her.

Logically, she knew the blame for Blaise's injuries lay totally at Chad Merritt's feet. But guilt-ridden despair was an animal she couldn't tame, and it feasted on her resolve until she blamed herself entirely for Blaise's injuries. Each day he lay unconscious, she became weaker. He was the only one who really knew her. Now there was only emptiness. It filled and suffocated her. Callan, Jules and the rest of Saoirse's friends had no choice but to call in the big gun to drive some sense into her and kill the beast that her misplaced hopelessness had created.

Mary Mahoney arrived from Donegal and went straight to Saoirse's side. Her daughter was in such a dark place it seemed even the light of a mother's love couldn't shine. But if anyone was going to reach her, it was Mary. Their loving connection was so strong.

'My lovely girl, your older brothers never went easy on you because you gave as good as you got. Your strength earned their respect. So why in God's name would you give such a snivelling, weak bastard power over you now? You're not to blame for Blaise's injuries. No, that rests solely on Chad Merritt's shoulders. You're only an excuse, his excuse. Fight, girl! Fight for the man and the life you need and want. Blaise wouldn't want you wasting away and drowning in self-pity. Your man's going to come out of it, and that's when you'll need to dig deep. That can't happen if you worry yourself into sickness now.'

In full Mother Mary mode, she took Saoirse's face tenderly in her hands and said, 'Listen to me. You will eat and rest, my lovely girl, and let me take some of the load. Then we'll talk this out until you see some reason.'

While Saoirse stiffened her resolve, she never wavered, and stayed by Blaise's side. Nonetheless, Mary had her way, and Saoirse did eat a little and slept more. It was against all odds, but he woke. When Blaise's eyes fluttered open, Saoirse's was the first face he saw. She kissed and hugged him. The joy was like a glorious, warm sun shining on them.

When the doctors told him he'd never walk again, that sun fell into a cloud, sending a shadow over them as deep as it was long. Blaise tried to push her away, but Saoirse stayed by his side, ever resolute. She was made of stronger stuff, and that made him stronger.

The New York offer came and went. Saoirse took every breath with him as he persisted with his rehab. She helped, cajoled and, when necessary, scolded, but overall she inspired. They caught a glimpse of the sun again when the Mahoney family and Blaise's friends helped him move into a new apartment specially equipped to deal with his needs.

The shadow engulfed them again when the doctors said he

would never make love to Saoirse as a man should. Blaise became angry and withdrawn. He erupted once they were home and tried everything to force her to go. 'Just get out. I have nothing for you. I don't want you around reminding me of what I can't have, what I can't feel. What I can't give you. You're pitiful for staying.'

Then he called her some more names before he said, 'I don't love you. It's time to move on. Just fucking go.'

She stepped up to him, wouldn't take a step back. 'You know, that's the first time you've lied to me.'

'What, you can read minds now?'

'No, but I know you and the fact that you refuse to look me in the eye says it all.' By this time in their relationship, she knew how her eyes grabbed his attention, affected him, and how his eyes let her see his heart as much as he saw hers. She simply bent to him and took his head in her hands, cutting him off mid-tirade.

With wide, doe-like eyes the colour of storm clouds, she told him, 'Nice try, but if you're going to swear at me and try to kick me out, you're going to have to do better than that.' She held her tears and kissed him. When he started kissing her back, their tongues tangling, she knew she'd broken through his paper-thin charade. Pulling away, she waited for those darkening aged-cognac eyes to see her. 'My brothers would call that attempt to send me packing pretty shite. And you being a big, tough, seasoned detective and all.'

'Saoirse, why would you want to stay?'

'Because you told me once you saw me, the *real* me. I see you, the *real* you, the man I fell in love with. You're still all in here.' She placed her hand on his heart. 'Some parts of you may not work like they used to, but here.' She pressed her hand harder to his chest and with the husky lilt he loved, she said, 'Here is still the same, if not stronger. That's the whole of who I fell in love with. You're right here, far bigger than your parts.'

She lay beside him that night and held him close. No matter what he said, she stayed. Then, in the very early hours of the next day when his tears came, she wiped them away. 'You told me that you stick. You weren't going anywhere. Well, I stick. I'm not going anywhere, either.'

Then even with him broken, she showed him he could feel, have her and above all, give her love. Deep, enduring love, where they kissed and ravished each other's mouths and lips—all her lips. They stroked, plundered each other and drew out their burning desires. She showed him that her words were true. Their hearts still beat for one another, even if the timing was a little different. It didn't matter because their love remained.

Autumn greyed into winter, and they were happy. Then came another offer from New York. This time an investment banking group wanted her. On that same day, the police caught up with Chad Merritt. He was trying to flee the country on a fake passport under heavy disguise as an elderly gentleman. They uncovered two of his safe deposit boxes at two different banks. Inside they discovered a stash of money comprising several foreign currencies, a few false passports and one very incriminating hard drive. They arrested him for attempted murder and various cybercrimes, the burnt-out Range Rover eventually giving up some DNA and linking Chad to it. Ironically, the DNA was found in part of a not-so-burnt-out bright-pink jogger.

Saoirse only told Blaise about Chad.

Some weeks later, Blaise received an offer to work in the Metropolitan Police's growing cybercrimes division. He accepted. It gave him renewed vigour and purpose to his life, widening his vision from only concentrating on Saoirse. It was a healthy change for them both.

Eventually, the scales of justice swung the couple's way, and Chad Merritt was sentenced to ten years, with possible parole after seven for good behaviour. He wouldn't torment Saoirse for some time. She took total satisfaction in knowing that every day a nasty coward like Merritt was in prison, he would have to learn how to live with fear riding him. She doubted he would survive as well as she had.

Another offer came from the same New York firm. This time they sweetened the deal to have her join them. She felt Blaise's eyes track her as she slid into their bed. 'When were you going to tell me? It's been a week since the second offer.'

When she hesitated, he said in that velvet-gravel timbre that made her core tremble, 'For this to work, we have to be honest with each other. It hurts that you felt you couldn't.'

'How did you find out?'

'Jules let it slip.' He held up his hand. 'Before you get angry, it was an honest mistake. She dropped by to say hello. You had left for work, and we got talking.'

'It's not what you think. It's more about me being a coward—'

'Which you've never been.'

'I am this time. You want honesty. I didn't know how to tell you. I knew you'd push me to go. The fact is, I don't know what to do. I'm scared.' She gave him a watery smile. 'My love for you is everything I know. I can't walk away from that.' She didn't bother to stem the flow of her tears. 'I can't uproot you to come with me to start another life.'

When he saw the tears and the rawness of the honesty they carried, he moved, using those tree-trunk arms and his muscular torso to roll over her. He held himself above her so she would see him and the tears in his eyes. 'Saoirse. Look at me. You're the reason I'm alive. You're the only one who's ever known me at all. When I was fighting to stay alive, your presence, your voice and your face were there, believing in me and telling me to fight. I know your love is undeniable and sustaining. Now I have to fight for you.'

He dipped over her to kiss her. His tears mixed with hers as he grabbed her and rolled her over. She straddled him as he clutched her hands. Blaise choked out the words, 'I told you once I never wanted you to go. Now you must. You've given me wings, but you need to fly as well. Otherwise, it feels like I'm trapping you, and sooner or later you'll start to resent me for keeping you here, caging you. You need to go if only to answer one question. Are you staying here because you're a loving person and don't know how to say to me, *I've got to try this?'*

'You know it's not like that. How can I without you?'

'Because you have to. I can't come with you. I won't find work like I have here, or subsidised housing.' Cupping her cheek in his massive hand, he added, 'I don't want you to have regrets because of me.'

'I wouldn't. I just don't know.'

It was his turn to put his hand on her heart like she had done to him not that long ago. 'I'll be right here with you. I won't be able to keep flying if I trap you to the earth. You have to leave me, to fly as high as you can, as you deserve.' His eyes were swimming with love, this tough man who'd survived hell. 'Saoirse, you are an amazing woman to love and an even better one to be loved by. Don't you ever forget that.'

'What do I say to that?' She wiped at tears.

'You say, yes, I am. Thank you.' He gave her the smile she'd always remember.

'God, you are so ...' She was sobbing now.

His whisky-coloured eyes darkened. 'And so are you.'

She collapsed over him, breathing in his familiar manliness and clung to him. She couldn't let go, wouldn't until she had no choice but to. They yielded to the burn of their love, allowing it to consume them.

* * *

Saoirse left London in 2010, a braver woman of the world. Yes, New York was waiting for Saoirse Mahoney, waiting to inspire her with brand new possibilities. A concrete jungle where dreams were made and lost. Given what she'd overcome, there wasn't anything she couldn't do.

After she touched down and found herself walking through the whirl and bustle of Times Square, she felt she should do a Mary Tyler

Moore-type twirl and throw her beret into the air and shout, 'Yeah! This Irish girl—now a woman—was going to make it, after all.'

She'd come a long way from the teenage girl who'd left Ireland full of soft, ambitious energy and hesitancy, where she lingered at the edge of life. She was also far more than the young woman who'd left Sydney for London, drowning in melancholy.

While no longer drowning, there was a thin film of sadness left clinging to her skin. Blaise had given back her wings and pushed her to fly, but her heart was still tethered to his. She cherished and wore his love like a stunning tailored garment.

Having to be separated from this love came with equal amounts of anguish and conflict. Overall, she worried the many challenges that lay ahead in New York would mould her to a different shape. Would the tailored garment of his love eventually annoy and pinch her skin, feeling too constricting like a straitjacket? Would she have to, at some time, take it off to give her the necessary freedom to fly into a new orbit of possibilities, or would their love always fit perfectly? Either way, while the sum of the parts of Saoirse Mahoney was becoming more substantial, the parts were still not greater than the whole, and for that, she'd keep searching and find her place in the world.

acknowledgments

Thank you to Jess Mudditt and all the brilliant people at Hembury Books who have supported and believed in Saoirse and me. It's been one long journey.

To Alex Nahlous, who ploughed through and helped polish the original Saoirse all those years back, you've kept me going when times were a little daunting and a lot frustrating.

And to my husband, Russell, who has supported me through the highs and lows. Who had the patience to read all my books, live with my crazy mind through discussions of plot lines, and characters running off the rails, all the while trying to make sense of it all.

coming soon

Joshua Bodekker was the kid the sun French-kissed every morning. But he died and became a man the day he took a knife to his grandmother and let the darkness overpower him.

Since then, he's been trying to control the beast that resides within to atone for his past. Taking a job in New York, where the light never sleeps, he seeks to build a new life away from the long shadow of his past.

He becomes mesmerised by a silver-eyed sensation of a woman. With each glimpse, this mystery woman weaves her way through his life. Josh's estranged Aunt, Angelica Bodekker, unknowingly introduces him to the woman he's fantasised about, Saoirse Mahoney.

Josh and Saoirse must fight for their futures by confronting the darkness of their pasts. Will that evil rise again to finish what was started years before? Can they save each other, and is there a love worth saving?

Pre-order:

https://www.amjaxon.com/love-connections-joshuas-story

TOO MUCH ROMANCE SERIES

Prequel: BRAVELY: Too Much Too Young

MADLY: Too Much Too Soon

DEEPLY: Too Much Too Late

TRULY: Too Much Is Never Enough.

LOVE CONNECTION SERIES

Saoirse's Story

Joshua's Story *(coming soon)*